ENCRYPTED

ENCRYPTED

By

Carolyn McCray

Text Copyright Carolyn McCray

ISBN-13: 9781482320275
ISBN-10: 1482320274

ACKNOWLEDGMENTS

So many people contribute to any book that it is hard to list them all. However, I intend to try!

This book would never have come into existence without, of course, Jim. Ever cool. Ever there.

Ben, who faithfully edited the manuscript through its many, many, many incarnations.

Dee Dee, who has believed in me for so long it is almost impossible to remember a time without her. #andnothatsnotadissonyourage

PROLOGUE

Fortress of Kaffa
Genoese Outpost
AD 1347

The sentry stood upon the watchtower, although he knew not what good it did. For eight long months this outpost had been under siege. Just outside of arrow range, the Mongols' leather tents stretched across the horizon as far as the eye could see—each with its flaming red flag, fluttering a salute to the great-grandson of Genghis Khan. Savages in fur-lined uniforms patrolled the front lines, making sure that the Italians did not escape their stony prison. As the last rays of daylight struck, the gilded domes topping each tent glowed as if they were bejeweled.

Their captors…The Golden Horde.

Without thought, the sentry reached his hand out to steady himself as a man-sized boulder slammed against the wall not ten feet below his position. The impact jarred his ankles and wrists, but his mind barely registered the attack. Over the past months, the catapult bombardments had become almost commonplace, like the dripping of rain from a thatched roof. Day and night without relief.

Yet from the first day, when the Horde charged over the easterly hills, none thought the Mongols could stomach a long campaign. The Genoese settled in, feeling protected by the mighty stone walls built by Italian craftsmen. Each day, they expected the khan to strike his tent city and move on to easier conquests, but this barbarian was no fool. He must have known, just as the sentry's king did, that this port along the Black Sea was strategic to the flow of riches from the Far East to Europe.

Cut off from their docks and their supply ships for months, the sentry and his once proud countrymen were reduced to hunting rats to feed their families. But even the vermin grew thin and scarce. What would they do when even the mice were gone?

On the other hand, the Horde was blessed with waves upon waves of reinforcements and fresh supplies from the east. The khan must have smelled desperation in the air. The fortress must have reeked of it.

Movement to the south caught the sentry's eye. It was too early for a night raid. He squinted against the glare of the gilded tents. A group of four, and now six, men were striking out from the camp. But for what purpose? And why away from the fortress and their eastern route home?

Seeing them, the sentry felt his first glimmer of hope. The men were dragging litters behind them. Litters filled with the Horde's dead!

There truly was a God in heaven above!

* * *

Travanti dug his heels into the horse. Shouts rose behind him as he galloped through the camp, but he cared not. A flame to the south lit up the night sky. The conflagration meant only one thing. Death. The Black Death. Which made the news he bore even more vital. His horse skidded to a halt outside the khan's tent. Two large guards tried to block him, but his hood fell back to reveal his shorn blond hair. They both backed away.

Though not of Mongol descent, Travanti was the khan's honored messenger who traveled unscathed though the Golden Horde's great realm. The guards backed away from his path, but they held their sword hilts tightly. How they wished to cut him in half. Yet, they did not. Fingering the deep scars on his arm, Travanti felt the source of his influence.

If these dense guards ever doubted the power that he wielded, they just needed to look toward the southern sky. So many warriors brought low—and not by steel. Not by the ax blade of an enemy. No, they died from unseen demons. Demons that took hold of flesh and pulled it apart, as a fat woman would a shank of lamb.

When the guards balked at opening the tent's curtains, Travanti parted them himself. There was no time to stand on formality.

It took a few seconds for his eyes to adjust to the gloom within. Once debauchery of the lowest form happened here. Dancing whores adorned themselves with jewelry that equaled the weight of fattened piglets. But now, only a smoldering fire pit remained. A few of the khan's women clung to blankets at the edge of the tent, coughing and wheezing like sick chickens, plague stricken.

Travanti ignored it all and strode to the khan's gilded throne. But the Mongol lord had lost so much weight that the gold chair seemed to swallow the ill man—as if he were a child trying to be a king.

The boy knelt in a bow, but it was not for the barbarian's honor. No, Travanti supplicated himself to the man who stood behind the throne. Even hooded and hunched, it was clear that the khan's advisor did not suffer the ills of the Horde.

"Sire, I journeyed to Tana, but they were all…" Travanti paused until the khan raised his eyes, "*dead.*"

"My eldest? My wives?" the khan asked, but from his tone, it seemed that he already knew the answer.

"All."

Before Travanti could respond, the Mongol rose from his throne, pulling a gilded dagger from its sheath. The sharp blade found Travanti's neck.

"Then, how is it that you still live?" The khan's hot breath was upon Travanti's face as the Mongol shoved the boy's sleeve back to reveal the elaborately scarred pattern on his arm. "Is this what protects you? The words of your so-called angels?"

Before the khan could slit his throat, a coughing fit took away the Mongol's will to punish. Collapsing onto the cold metal of his throne, the heir to the Horde spit up a handful of blood. Satisfied warmth spread through the boy. Dare to strike a child of God, and this was the ill anyone would suffer.

The Mongol called over an equally plague-stricken guard. "Prepare to retreat."

It was only then that the hooded man stepped into the smoky light. "Is this how the great-grandson of Genghis shows his mettle?"

The words stirred enough anger in the Mongol that he rose to his feet, gilded dagger drawn. "Enough! Or I will show you the steel of a khan."

"Brave words for a man who wishes to slink off in the night."

The khan stumbled back a step. The force bled from his voice. "What would you have me do?" He pointed to his blackened skin, punctuated by oozing pustules. "Or can you conjure a salve for this?"

"I doubt not that you are defeated, but seek you no vengeance?"

"With my last breath," the khan hissed.

For the first time since his second master had taken him in, Travanti saw the hooded man smile. "The Heir to the Horde has spoken."

* * *

The sentry felt ill at ease. It was the damned silence. The Horde had fallen quiet as more and more of their kind burned atop pyres. No more catapults. No more bone-rattling impacts. He should have been happy, jubilant—yet, he was not. Not until he and his countrymen were upon the high seas, sailing for Italia. Sailing for home.

"They cannot last another day," another guard said, breaking the strange, new quiet.

The younger man seemed right. Activity buzzed around the Horde's camp. Hopefully, it signaled panic and disarray. A messy Mongolian retreat would make their escape by sea all the easier. The sentry was so busy imagining sea breezes in his hair that he nearly missed the incoming projectile.

"Down!"

He shoved the other soldier to the stone as the catapult's load sailed overhead and landed with a sickening *thud* in the courtyard.

"Their last gasp," the younger man said as he brushed off his tattered uniform.

Leave it to the Mongols to continue the fight up to their dying breaths.

"No!" A scream arose from the courtyard. "Run!"

The sentry headed down the ladder as he remembered the early days of the siege, when the Horde had catapulted barrels of oil followed by a few volleys of flaming arrows. The fortress was ablaze for days. Even though no more kindling was left, the sentry still feared what the Mongols might be capable of.

Rumors of magic, sorcerers, and witches were rampant.

Ever prepared for the worst, the sentry nearly lost what little was in his stomach when he saw what the barbarians had flung over their wall.

"No!" a woman screamed next to him. "It cannot be!"

The body's foul odor bit his nose. Bloated and rotting, there was no doubt what had killed this Mongol. The plague.

"Quickly!" the sentry said to the nearest guard. "Throw it into the sea!"

"Beware!" a shout come from above, but the sentry was already charging the yard as the loud *thunks* of the catapults carried over the night air.

"Flee!" a woman shouted from somewhere above.

But to where? They were penned in by four stone walls. They had nowhere to go.

He raced across the courtyard without concern, bowling over a mother with a babe in her arms and knocking a boy on his arse. Nothing mattered. Nothing but informing the captain. He took the steps two at a time, bounding up to the war room.

The sentry shoved the door open, not bothering to stand on ceremony. "Sir, the Horde has…"

Was he too out of breath, or could he not bring himself to say the words that would doom the outpost?

"They fling bodies? Is it true?" the lieutenant asked, grabbing him by the collar.

"Aye, it is true."

The lieutenant spun on his heel toward the captain. "We must flee by ship!"

"And spread this darkness to our home?" the older man asked.

"No one has fallen ill yet. We must make haste."

As much as the sentry loved his captain, the lieutenant's words were music to his ears. Home. They could flee by sea. Home.

But the captain slammed his fist onto the table. "Nay. We will dispose of the bodies downstream, and quarantine all who—"

The captain's words were cut off. At first, the sentry did not know the cause, but then blood trickled from the senior officer's lapel. With a wet *thud*, the captain fell facedown onto the table, revealing a hooded man with a still-bloody knife in his hand.

The room filled with the sound of steel being unsheathed. Yet, all were stunned. No one moved forward. No one even breathed.

"Flee this city, or all your lives are forfeited," the man said forcefully.

The sentry stepped forward. Church envoy or no, this man could not butcher their captain before his very eyes, but the lieutenant held him back as he sheathed his blade.

"To the docks," the lieutenant ordered.

It took not a single heartbeat before everyone in the room broke rank. Their captain wasn't even cold, and his officers were scrambling all over themselves to disobey his orders. All made haste to the ships—vessels that could sail far, far from here.

The sentry stood, frozen.

His desire to flee was equal to the other men, but he owed his life thrice over to the captain. How could he betray him so callously? So he stood as the others coursed around him. Except for one. One person *entered* the room. A boy. A young, blond boy. One whom the sentry had never before seen. After such a long siege, how could that be?

* * *

Travanti didn't even glance at the stunned soldier. Why should he? Within a single breath, his second master pulled the blade across the man's throat and pushed his body on top of the captain's. Such power in the thinnest of blades.

"The Hidden Hand must know of our success here," the hooded figure said, indicating for the boy to come closer.

"Of course." Travanti bowed his head as he rolled up his sleeve.

"We must be certain that these ships reach Italy, and then north." The hooded man's dark brown eyes were alive with possibility. "All of Europe must fall."

The boy bit his lip as the blade sliced into his skin. What was a little pain when so much more good remained to be done?

CHAPTER 1

Undisclosed Location
Present Day
9:00 p.m., MST

The archaic symbol glowed red and then flared gold across Ronnie's ultra-high-resolution LCD screen.

"Damn it, people," she muttered. "I'm a little busy here. Could you spam me later?"

Each stroke of the brilliant script was crafted in a masterful flourish. Calligraphy. While the illuminated writing might possibly have been the most beautiful art Ronnie had ever seen, the symbols blocked her from making the third largest unauthorized funds transfer in history.

Others might call her task thievery. Ronnie liked to think of it as "wealth redistribution in action."

With minimal keystrokes, Ronnie wiped the symbols from the screen. The insurance records were back, front and center, and ripe for the picking. Four thousand dollars a year for car insurance? Please. The company might scam their money legally, but she had just found a way to *take* it more creatively.

Crap. The IM window appeared again, flashing those gilded letters. Ronnie closed the pop-up. She blocked the pop-up. She deleted the pop-up. She deleted the program that created the pop-up. But still, the unintelligible lettering scrolled down her screen. Obviously, fatigue was setting in. She had already been at this hack for over three hours. Slowly, and ever so carefully, she had insinuated herself into the insurance company's mainframe. But at this point, how could she truly be "one" with her computer if her joints were complaining?

Ronnie straightened upright until her back rested against her wooden chair. Sometimes pure genius could not be rushed. Raising her hands above her head, she purposefully relaxed her muscles and began a measured set of stretches to loosen the knot in her neck.

Normally, when she hacked, she did it in style. A leather, heated, massage-controlled, ergonomic masterpiece of a chair. But when delivering the deathblow, Ronnie liked to go medieval on their asses. And maybe even a little ninja. Though there was absolutely no reason to, on a monumental night such as tonight, she always dressed in sleek black. Ronnie had pulled her dark blonde hair into a tight bun. The ribbed turtleneck clung to her every curve and rubbed most agreeably against her skin as she worked the kinks out. Two-inch heeled boots added more height to her already tall frame.

Damn, but she looked good tonight. Too bad that nobody was around to see it. But given her vocation, how could there be?

As she flexed her head to the far left, she found only bare wall. To the right, she noticed only torn wallpaper. There wasn't even a light fixture on the ceiling. Absolutely nothing distracted her. What other luxuries did she need when she had a rickety chair and a table for her wireless, Web-enabled, two-TB, and fifty-six-G RAM laptop? She needed nothing else. Except maybe a massage.

Outside the window, fireworks exploded, washing the stark room with yellows, greens, and reds. With each *boom*, the crowds in the streets cheered. Ronnie liked to think that the revelry was for her financial remodeling initiative, but she knew it was May fifth.

Cinco de Mayo. And boy, did these Latinos take their partying seriously.

As seriously as her secret admirer was about IM'ing her. The symbols scrolled and flashed and scrolled some more, obscuring the company's financial slush fund—a healthy two billion dollars. Two billion dollars that *she* wanted—but couldn't get to—because some freaking overexuberant fan was trying to impress her. Ronnie stretched one last time, and then cracked each knuckle.

"Exactly how much did this firewall cost me?" she asked into her subvocal microphone as her fingers flew over the keyboard again.

"Four point seven million," Quirk said. His voice sounded slightly effeminate as it relayed through her intra-molar receiver. Plus, the young hacker sounded distracted. Too distracted, given that his cut was a good 13 percent of their take-home fee of seven million.

Flicking her thumb, she brought up a webcam view of their cold room. Four perfectly white walls, not eggshell white, not Navajo, not light vanilla, but pure, white walls. Not because they *had* to be that color for the computer hubs, but because Quirk insisted that the room contrast with his hair. If he went to the expense of dyeing his hair twice, once with pitch black, then dark-lighted with midnight blue, the young man wanted to stand out. Not that anyone else was ever going to set eyes on him either, but Quirk could really be a queen when he wanted to. So, white the walls were—no big deal.

Ronnie's eyes flickered to the thermometer on the cold room's wall, showing a stable fifty-two degrees. That *was* for the computer hubs. Air-conditioning blew down from four evenly distributed vents, keeping the CPU towers running smoothly. Ronnie readjusted the webcam's angle to see what in the hell was keeping Quirk so distracted. Her assistant was looking at the far wall, with its dozens of computer monitors.

The two center screens showed the activity on Ronnie's computer, but the others were wildly divergent—radar views, real-time satellite images, and websites upon websites. But the screen that held her assistant's attention was a television report.

"Is the plague making a comeback?" The subject was not all that surprising, given her assistant's inclination toward mild-to-moderate hypochondria.

"Quirk," she threatened.

Ronnie watched the über-hacker shrug as he answered, still staring at the news report. "Give or take a couple of hours of overtime."

Symbols suddenly blocked her entire screen.

Ronnie was done.

"Then why in the fu—" She was so busy trying to extinguish the screen overlay that she couldn't even curse properly.

These were the never-ending symbols. "How in the hell is someone hacking *me*?"

Her tone must have clued Quirk in to the fact that a pay cut was on the horizon. He turned off the plague report and typed a few commands into his network of twenty-odd computers.

"They're not hacking you. They're riding a carrier signal from an ISPN that you've given direct, mainline access to."

"No way! I haven't—"

Quirk swung around to stare straight into the webcam. His color contacts-assisted glacial blue eyes sparked with annoyance. "Maybe you shouldn't be banging Napster while going up against a Fortune Ten company."

Ronnie was glad that she didn't have a camera on her. Otherwise, Quirk would have seen her cheeks flush red as she found the offending window. Sure enough, she was trying to download Panic! At The Disco's live bootleg. A track she had been hunting down for over a week. Downloading at 325 bytes/sec, better than CD quality.

"But I'm so close," she whined as she continued to hack into the insurance company's multilayered firewall.

"You've *got* to cut the flow," he directed. Quirk could sound straight and even forceful when he wanted to.

"Do you have any idea how hard it is to find this quality bootleg—?"

Quirk cut her rant short by announcing, "You've just tripped an embedded alarm."

Okay, that wasn't supposed to happen. She held her breath as Quirk ran the cross-checks to see how bad it was. By the furrow of his brow and the bulging vein in his ever-so-pale forehead, she had tripped a doozy of an alarm.

"The FBI has been alerted to your extracurricular activities."

"All right, all right," Ronnie conceded as she aborted the music download. Still, the symbols trickled down the left side of her screen, and then finally stopped. A single, gilded letter hovered in the corner. She was about to swipe it away as well, but she found that her fingers hesitated. Something about the symbol stopped her. It was too pretty to just throw in the virtual trash can. With fingers flying, Ronnie took a screenshot of the symbol and then terminated the IM.

With any hope, permanently.

She had some serious wealth to redistribute.

* * *

Special Agent Zachary Hunt grabbed his coat and holstered his weapon in the same motion. "Come on!" he shouted to the other agents.

This was it. The Robin Hood hacker was online. This was his chance to catch her.

Running through the maze of desks comprising the bull pen of the El Paso FBI field office, Hunt didn't even bother to enter the glassed-in tech support room. He just pointed a finger at their resident geek, Warp.

"You know what to do!"

"We're on it!" the tech replied, even though he was the only person in the room. But Zach didn't have time to worry about Warp's multiple personality disorder. Zach had one thing, and one thing only, on his mind.

Her.

Still on the run, Zach hit the back of his partner's head. "Grant. Now!"

He hit him hard enough to spin Special Agent Fifer around in his chair. The twenty-nine-year-old stood up smoothly, his weapon holstered and his coat already on. Within two steps, Grant was at his shoulder. Too close to Zach's shoulder.

Six months ago, when Zach first met him, the guy was five feet, nine inches. Maybe on a good day, he stood five feet ten. But now? Fifer was somehow almost *six* feet tall? Grant might be young enough to still use the "I trained at Quantico" line to pick up women, but old enough that his growth plates had closed. Clearly, Fifer had to be putting lifts in his shoes. What level of hidden insecurity did that reveal about his partner?

Across the room, two agents laughed, causing Zach to crack the verbal whip.

"Move, people!" he shouted as he made his way to the door.

Ten steps out, and he'd be in the car. In thirteen minutes, he would be in the vicinity of the world's most-wanted hacker. Within the hour, he'd have her bagged.

"Wait!" Special Agent Markum called out.

Zach didn't even break his stride as the salt-and-pepper agent hustled over, handing him a "High Priority Fax." Okay, anything faxed couldn't be all that high priority. As Zach fixed his jacket collar, he scanned the page.

"Outbreak of Bubonic Plague in Europe. Report ASAP any cases in the United States."

"No kidding," Zach said as he tossed the paper onto his desk and exited into the warm evening air. If he saw anyone with black, blotchy blisters in his travels, he'd let them know. Otherwise, his focus was absolute.

Tonight, this yearlong chase would end.

He *would* arrest the Robin Hood hacker.

* * *

Ronnie cursed under her breath, which meant that Quirk heard every expletive, given the subvocal microphones implanted on either side of her voice box.

"Now, now," her assistant chided. Like he didn't cuss a blue streak if a single line of his own code got corrupted.

But even with the colorful language, the bright, gold symbols were back, covering her screen. Covering the back door to the company's financial accounts. Obviously, her assessment of permanently shutting down the IMs had been a bit overoptimistic. But she had to admit that something else distracted her almost as much as the glowing text.

The FBI had been alerted. Which meant that *he* was alerted that she was up to no good. Was he on the job when he heard? Was he at home? Was he on his way?

So many questions. So few answers. How could she concentrate on a bunch of stupid numbers when her instinct was to pace until she knew for sure?

"You planning on breaking into this account sometime tonight?"

Ronnie put on her game face. "I'm getting to it. Patience, goth-boy."

This was crunch time. She had a large fortune to acquire, and no FBI agent, no matter how hot, was going to get in her way.

* * *

"You're going too fast," Grant whined.

Zach's eyes flickered over to him. Special Agent Grant Fifer was holding onto the "granny" handle for dear life. Once his partner realized that he was under scrutiny, he removed his hand, but his left hand remained plastered against the dashboard.

"We've got to slow down to make a right up ahead."

Like Zach hadn't already memorized the route they had to take. It was etched in his mind even deeper than the Miranda rights he recited to anyone he arrested.

"Seriously, it's not that far ahead," Grant persisted.

Overhead, the night sky lit up with silver as fireworks exploded brilliantly. Zach should have known that she was going to strike tonight. She would use the crowds to limit mobility and the loud explosions to cover any noise she might make while accessing electrical panels. The Robin Hood hacker did not make the FBI's Most Wanted List for lack of brains.

Zach prepared for the right turn that Grant was so worried about when red lights flashed and bells went off. A train crossing. A train-barreling-down-the-tracks kind of crossing.

He wasn't going to make it.

Zach slammed on the brakes. Out of the corner of his eye, Zach saw Grant's body fly forward against his seat belt. Even with braking that hard, they still weren't going to make it. Jerking the wheel to the right, Zach pulled the emergency brake until he couldn't pull it up anymore. The smell of rubber filled the car as the tires skidded into a nearly perfect ninety-degree turn. Sure, Grant's door bumped the red and white crossing bar, and they sprayed gravel everywhere, but they were on their way.

Fishtailing through the loose rocks lining the tracks, the tires finally found pavement and accelerated once more. The train laid on its horn as they passed. Given that it was going in the opposite direction, it seemed like they were traveling hundreds of miles an hour. The windows were just a blur, and before they could count the number of cars, they were clear of the train.

"Oh, Gawd…" Grant moaned. He must have realized that the next left turn they needed to take was just up ahead.

The bars rose over the train tracks as Zach repeated his earlier maneuver. Hard braking, wheels spun to the left, emergency brake for a crisp turn, release all of the above, and step on the gas. After nearly flying out of their seats over the tracks, they were zeroing in on their prey again.

"You know," his partner began, and then licked his lips again before finishing, "you *really* need to get laid."

No, Zach needed to catch her.

Warp's excited voice came over their earpieces. "We just ramped up our new twenty-two gig RAM processor and—"

The geek was answering a question from, like, five minutes ago, and not even the right one.

"That's great, Warp," Zach said, trying to remain patient. "But are you integrating with the insurance company's computer?"

"We will be in the loop in…Three. Two. One!"

* * *

A *Star Trek*-like Klaxon sounded from Ronnie's four-way speakers. Red lights flashed from her illuminated keyboard, warning her that the FBI had docked with the company's mainframe.

"Honestly, Quirk, could you be any more of a nerd?"

"I just keep raising the bar," her assistant said with a certain amount of satisfaction. "Warp's begun his countermeasures. Plus, they've got six cars en route." With a playful tone, Quirk finished up. "Check your watch."

She had almost forgotten. Pulling back her tightly knit sleeve, Ronnie found a highly collectible, yet normal-looking, Batgirl watch. The time flashed benignly, but when she hit the Date button, the entire surface of the watch transformed into a mini street map. Her location blinked in green as four red dots sped toward her.

"Is he with them?"

"What do you think?"

Ronnie's heart raced at the thought. Zach not only knew that she was on the job, but he was racing to her location. She imagined his strong hands gripping the steering wheel, and his jaw clenching with tension.

"Which car?"

"Guess," was Quirk's only clue.

Sure enough, the fastest blinking car was a good measure ahead of the other five. As much as Ronnie thrilled at Special Agent Hunt's arrival, she didn't want to actually get caught. So with renewed haste, she packed up her laptop and stowed it in her Hello Kitty backpack. Okay, maybe a pink and white sack with a large silver reflector strip wasn't exactly ninja, but a girl had to be true to herself.

Lastly, Ronnie pulled on a pair of black leather gloves, careful not to disturb the rows of white beads dotting the palms. "Switching to keyless-keyboard mode."

"We have seriously got to think of a better name for those gloves."

Glancing at her watch, she found that Zach had already covered half the distance. Damn, he was a good driver.

"Yeah, I'll work on a cool acronym in my spare time," Ronnie countered as she put on a pair of wraparound sunglasses, waiting until the metal in the frames attached to a thin cable running up through her turtleneck. The liquid LCD lens was now in communication with her laptop and, therefore, Quirk.

"Reroute visuals," she ordered. Instantly, an image of her laptop's screen bloomed onto her lens. Wireless at its coolest. "Infrared ready?"

"Please..."

"Computer-buffered image enhancement online?"

Quirk had possibly even less patience than Ronnie herself. "Just get your butt in gear, and let me worry about the hardware."

More fireworks exploding reminded Ronnie that she only had a narrow window of time before the crowd dispersed. "I'm heading over."

"Just do me a favor and actually lose them before you make the rendezvous."

Ronnie grinned. Quirk hated this part—the moment of truth. Pitting one's skills against another's. His favorite part of any mission was building all these toys.

Hers, though?

Using all these toys.

* * *

Damn it, Zach cursed as the car idled noisily. A knot of drunk and stumbling Cinco de Mayo revelers stood between them and her. He could see the goddamn building she was in. He just couldn't get to it.

He gunned the engine, but no one seemed to notice. All eyes were on the glittering blue and orange sky. Zach didn't give a crap about the fireworks. He honked the horn. At first, people just booed him. Then they noticed the flashing blue and red lights. Finally, it must have penetrated their thick skulls that they were hindering a pursuit, for they cleared a path. Zach roared through it, covering the two blocks in seconds.

Skidding the car to a halt, Zach leapt out. He didn't bother to check to see whether Grant had even survived the journey.

"I think we've got her stumped!" Warp's high-pitched voice was a little too much for Zach's earpiece.

"Whatever. I asked, like three minutes ago, which entrance is closest to her position?"

The techno-geek was a child prodigy, or, given his penchant to argue with himself, *prodigies.* Unfortunately, Warp had the attention span of a gnat.

"Oh, yeah. North by northwest."

Zach turned back to Grant, who was only now extracting himself from the car. "I'll take the front."

"Who named you Agent in Charge?" Grant huffed.

Zach was in no mood to pull rank. "Establish the perimeter, and then take the back."

Without hesitation, Zach charged toward the building. He was so close that he could smell her.

* * *

Ronnie took the stairs two at a time. She had no doubt what the commotion was outside. She was being pursued. And a little too close for her comfort. While she climbed, Ronnie continued typing into what appeared to be thin air, watching the results of her actions unfold on her lens. This time, the money would be hers for sure.

Then her least favorite command flashed before her eyes. "Access Denied."

"No!"

"I told you," Quirk chirped.

"Stay out of it," she mumbled as she continued the hard climb, both up the stairs and through the myriad of cyber defenses.

"You're going to have to stop running, Ronnie." Before she could interrupt, Quirk continued, "The beads are registering each impact of your feet as a keystroke."

"Okay," Ronnie responded, "That's clearly a design flaw."

"Hey! Those are state-of-the-art, pressure and directionally sensitive ceramic fusion—"

Ronnie shook her head vigorously, even though Quirk couldn't see her. Of course, she kept going right on up the steps. "Whatever. They're not working now."

"Because they are *supposed* to be used in a dust-free, static-controlled room cooled to fifty-two degrees."

"Like I said, design flaw."

Before Quirk could retort, another "Access Denied" flashed across her screen.

"Bitch all you want," Quirk added. "But you ain't hacking any deeper until you stop clod-hopping."

As much as it pissed her off, her assistant was right. She stopped, turned to the wall, and used it as if it were a keyboard, making sure each stroke was accurate and precise.

"That's better," Quirk stated.

This time, "Access Granted" bloomed on her screen. Quickly, the two billion dollars began to transfer into her little ol' account.

"No, *that's* better," Ronnie stated as she resumed her ascent.

CHAPTER 2

Quirk pulled on a cashmere sweater, making sure he didn't muss his hair gel as he watched Warp once again try to thwart his boss's attempts to drain the insurance company's account.

"Sorry, Ronnie, but you're going to have to keep up the pressure until the account is drained."

She must be heeding his advice, because suddenly her proficiency rose steeply. Why did she put herself through this? Why wasn't Ronnie content sitting in a cozy room like this? Quirk surveyed the snow-white walls punctuated by plasma screens. Why risk exposure—or worse, capture—when you could snuggle up with *Project Runway*, or...

Quirk sat up straighter and watched the telecast. Sure enough, another plague bulletin. Like he already didn't have enough to worry about with Ebola and the West Nile virus? The plague, too? Did his suffering never cease?

"Is it just me, or are they getting better at this?" Ronnie asked. Was that a hint of desperation he heard?

Quirk focused his attention on her laptop feed. Sure enough, she was smack-dab in the middle of a standoff. The great Robin Hood hacker was stymied. He was actually happy that, every once in a while, Ronnie was reminded of why she needed him and his very specialized expertise.

"Warp may have made some improvements, but no one is as geeky as I," Quirk said. He knew how to drag out a dramatic pause. "We are going cold."

With flamboyance that Liberace would have been proud of, Quirk pressed a button, and a panel under the main computer tower opened up. Even at fifty-two degrees ambient temperature, frost poured out from the chamber of liquid nitrogen. Slowly, the tower lowered into the vat of freezing solution.

He watched as all processes on her laptop sped up exponentially.

"Whoa, there," Ronnie said as her typing accelerated to keep pace with the processor speed. "You *are* lord of the geeks."

He knew that, but it was still nice to hear it every once in a while. Not all was hunky-dory though. "Yeah, the only downside is that we have to finish the transfer before the chips completely freeze."

"And how long is that?"

"Yeah, um. I'd hurry."

Quirk watched the computer's internal temperature plummet as the red dots converged toward Ronnie's glowing green sphere. "And I mean spatially as well as temporally."

"Huh?"

There was no way to say it gently. "They're closing in on your position."

* * *

Zach paused. Were those footsteps in the upper stairwell?

"Is she directly above me?" he asked Warp.

For once, the techie's answer was direct and prompt. "She's two floors up, and thirty feet to the south of you."

"So, let's get moving," Grant urged as he joined Zach.

If the junior agent thought that he had startled him, Fifer was greatly mistaken. Zach had picked up on his entrance a good two stories ago. Those lifts inside Grant's shoes must have given him away.

"Took you long enough," Zach grumbled. "Let's go."

"Aren't you going to bitch me out that I'm not guarding the back?"

Zach rolled his eyes as he continued up the staircase. "If I'd needed you back there, I would have told you to follow me. Now, *move!*"

"But it doesn't make any sense," Grant whined. "Why is she going up?"

"Don't know," Warp said, and then quickly followed up. "But we've got a new problem."

No, Zach thought. There were no other problems. Tonight was a problem-free zone until he caught her.

"Um, yeah, guys, Interpol has requested that we take custody of an arsonist that tried to torch a Picasso at the El Paso Museum of Art."

Was that all? A modern art critic with a Bic lighter? That didn't even register on Zach's problem radar. "Can do, after we wrap up things here."

"More like *now*."

Was that Warp being bossy? "Excuse me?"

"Sorry, Hunt, but Interpol is working on behalf of the Vatican." Zach was about to ask what in the hell that had to do with anything even remotely involving him, when Warp rushed on, "And the deputy said to cut an agent and have him head over to the museum."

"Just one?" he asked.

"Just one."

With a savage grin, Zach turned to Grant. He could kill two birds with one stone. Make the deputy happy and ditch his partner.

"Screw you!" Grant shot back, but his partner must have seen in Zach's eyes that he wasn't in the mood to be screwed with. The younger agent turned to obey, but couldn't keep from mouthing off. "You know, one day they're going to fig-ure out that you're trying to catch her for yourself—and not because of the warrant, asshole."

Not worrying about whether the statement was true, Zach headed up the stairs alone.

* * *

Ronnie hit the roof door at a run. She didn't need to look at her watch to know that they were on her ass. She contin-ued her flight across the dark roof as the fireworks display reached its crescendo. Each explosion was brighter and larger than the last. And each time, as they were designed to do, her infrared glasses adjusted and avoided that completely uncivilized whiting-out normally associated with light bursts. She might even consider a raise for Quirk if he kept developing bleeding-edge technology like this.

"South by southwest, right?" she asked as she geared up for the jump.

"The wind is coming in from the east, so it should be an easy—"

Putting all her concentration into her leap, Ronnie didn't hear Quirk's next words. She was only steps away from the edge. Throwing her weight forward, she planted her lead leg and—

A series of fireworks exploded one after another in blinding succession. A haze of white light obscured her vision. Disoriented, Ronnie tried to abort her jump, but there was no way. She had built up way too much momentum. She tried to correct in midair, but her legs were forward. Waving her arms, desperate to shift her center of gravity, she felt herself start to lose altitude.

In another breath, her lower body slammed into the edge of the other roof. She tried to force her upper half over the ledge, but gravity was a bitch, and she slid down the brick wall. Flailing, somehow one hand caught the ledge. Forcing herself to remain calm, Ronnie grabbed the ledge with her other hand. Under that much pressure, her gloves' beads began snapping and popping.

"What in the hell are you doing out there?"

Quirk's tone was livid. But she was hanging by ten fingers from the side of a freaking five-story building. "You had better hope that I die right this minute!"

The snapping, crackling, and popping continued.

"*You're* upset?" he squealed. "Do you have any idea how hard it is to wire those beads?"

* * *

"I've stopped the bleeding! I've stopped the money transfer!" Warp was nearly beside himself with pride. Problem was, that wasn't what Zach wanted to know.

"That's great, Warp, but I asked whether you had an image yet?" Zach repeated as he carefully checked the fifth-floor landing. There wasn't anywhere else to go. The roof door was right in front of him. He needed to know what was on the other side.

"Sorry. Our satellite feed of the area is fritzed."

Of course it was. Hacking into the NSA-secured satellite computer was child's play to this chick. Zach's jaw clenched and unclenched. This was not how he pictured this bust going down. "So essentially, that means I'm going out there blind?"

"No, no," Warp assured him, adamant. "Another satellite will come into view in three minutes."

Zach looked at his watch. The second hand was going around way too slowly to wait another one hundred and eighty seconds. Not when she could be right beyond this door. He tightened his grip on the gun.

"I'll be on the roof, then."

* * *

Ronnie ever so carefully swung her legs to the side. Her only chance of getting off this damn ledge was to use leverage to counteract the gravity that wanted to plummet her to the pavement five stories down. But she lost another finger's grip and had to abort her attempt. The added weight popped more beads.

"*Now* what are you doing?" her assistant complained as she hung precariously by one hand.

"So help me, Quirk..."

Before she could work up a really good revenge plan, the squeak of hinges stopped her. She knew that sound. She had just made it when she opened the rusted roof door. They couldn't be that close, could they? Could *he*?

Adrenaline fueled her muscles, and in one panic-driven move, she swung her leg over the ledge and wrestled the rest of her body over. But she couldn't stop there. She needed to get away.

* * *

Zach abandoned caution. He heard something. It must be her. "How far?"

"It looks like the south-by-southwest corner." Warp said. "Sixty feet ahead."

He checked his corners at a run—until he realized that wasn't a step up ahead. That was the ledge. "Warp, buddy, twenty feet of that is open air."

"What?" Zach was about to explain, but Warp's excited voice cut him off. "Hey, we just regained the partial satellite feed. Oh, boy..."

"Oh, boy, what, Warp?"

The techno-geek cleared his throat before he answered. "Well, you see..."

"Warp!"

"She's on the other roof."

Turning back to the ledge, Zach looked at the gap between the buildings. There's no way that she jumped it. No way, right? He checked the ledge, no sign of a grappling device or ladder.

She *had* jumped it.

He backed away from the ledge as Warp reported to the rest of the agents, "We have lost the suspect atop the—"

Warp didn't finish his sentence because Zach wasn't backing away in defeat. He was giving himself room to build up speed before he leapt. The distance flew by, and Zach actually thought he had a chance of clearing the ledge, but at the last second, his trajectory flattened. His body made it over, but his shins weren't quite so lucky. He went down, hard. But he was across.

Damn, that hurt! But he rolled up and was on his feet before his body could tell him to stay down. Nothing broken, or least nothing bad enough to stop his pursuit.

"Belay that last," Warp said as Zach brought his gun to bear. "Hunt is still on her tail."

* * *

Ronnie ducked behind another chicken coop. Unlike the last bare rooftop, this one was a maze of shacks, coops, and downright garbage. Good for hiding, but not so good for navigating while still attempting to siphon money protected by triple-encryption layers, and now the FBI. Especially when half her beads were out on her keyless-keyboard-mode gloves.

She also made a note to tell Quirk that he was right about one thing. They did need a cooler name for those.

"Ronnie, *come on*," Quirk begged. "We've got over a billion. Let's cut and run."

"Never," she said as she made her way to the other side of the stinky coop, and then typed frantically, making certain that money still flowed into her account.

Pigeons squawked to the north, irritated by her pursuers.

Quirk must have heard it, too. "Okay, can't you hear the heavy footsteps of fate behind you?"

Damn it, she had to stop again to block an extremely clever move on Warp's part. "Yes, but as you know, we don't get our 'commission' unless we nab the entire amount."

"Which sucks, I might add."

Grinning, Ronnie overrode another line delete, and the money really started pouring in. "It does, and I don't know about you, but I want to buy some more toys."

Shouts carried on the wind took a little bit of the satisfaction away, but she was still the best, and that money was *hers*, damn it!

* * *

Crap. Real crap. Chicken crap. It was slippery. Zach quickly scraped the bottom of his shoe and continued his pursuit. She was so close.

"Well?" he whispered into his headset.

"Yeah, hold on."

Zach's brow furrowed. Warp might give you the wrong answer to your question. He might hyperventilate. But put you on hold? That didn't sound good.

"Hold on?" Zach asked.

"I'm, yeah, okay. *No bueno.*"

Zach paused his steps, but kept his gun at the ready. "To what, Warp?"

"Um, well, you see…we lost not only the satellite feed, but the patch into the corporation's account."

"So we're *all* blind?"

"Yeah, pretty much."

Behind him, Zach could hear the other agents gathering force, weaving through the ramshackle maze. Bolder, he moved forward. Satellite or not. Patch or not. He was going to get his woman tonight.

* * *

Hah! Ronnie had kicked Warp out of the server onto his pasty white ass. The money was pouring into her account like a thunderstorm. Only a few more minutes, and her life would be enriched by another two billion dollars.

Sweet.

"Resting on your laurels?" Quirk asked.

With the FBI out of the cyber picture, she could resume her headlong flight, because two billion dollars didn't do anyone a lot of good in prison. And she could see the stairwell door. Another ten steps and she would be free!

But the muzzle of a gun at her neck brought her to a skidding halt. She was caught. Red-handed.

How?

The gun cocked. It didn't matter how. He was serious.

Slowly, she raised her hands in the air. "All right. All right. I give up." Still, the man pressed the barrel to her flesh. "Just don't shoot."

The man pulled the gun back, then pulled the trigger.

Water shot all over her chest and face. Laughter poured out of the maze as half a dozen kids tumbled out, all firing water guns at her.

"Damn it, remember what I said about expensive electronic equipment and water toys?" Quirk demanded in her ear.

Ronnie couldn't answer, as she was laughing too hard. Even when she "lost" these little simulations, there was fun to be had. She got to hone her skills, keeping her sharp for the day that the FBI was *really* on her ass, and she gave these kids a fun-filled evening of cat and mouse.

Flipping several coins in the air, Ronnie smiled. "*Mucho bueno.*"

The kids scrambled for the American silver dollars as she looked out over the horizon. Mexico City. Alive with Cinco de Mayo festivities. Alive with fireworks. Alive with youth.

A view like this, and, very shortly, two billion dollars richer?

Nights like this didn't come along very often.

* * *

"Oh, God!" Warp wailed as if it were his own money being stolen. "She's got one point six. Point seven."

The geek's distress stripped away any last bit of caution in Zach's search. He rushed through the maze.

"Point eight. Point nine!"

Was that her up ahead? If he was going to stop her, it needed to be now. He burst through the last of the shacks, gun arm out, safety off.

"Freeze!"

No Ronnie. No one at all. Zach stumbled to a stop as Warp finished his countdown.

"An even two billion. She's got it all!"

But he didn't need the geek's announcement. Zach already knew it. Knew it, because a laptop was propped open on a chair. The screen flashed an orange $2,000,000,000.00, along with her lovely catchphrase "Better Luck Next Time!"

Zach charged over to the keyboard. Maybe with Warp's help, he could somehow trace her. Find out where she really was.

But before he could even voice this hope, the number on the screen started going down. Fast. Maybe they were able to get the upper hand on her, for once.

"Warp, were you able to install the reverse worm?"

"Hell, no. She shut that puppy down hard."

Zach stood there, confused. "If we aren't reclaiming the funds, then where is the money going?"

But he didn't need to wait long. Once the new account had drained one hundred million off, it automatically closed and flashed, "Ethiopian WHO Hunger Relief Program." Immediately, another account opened, and twenty five million filled it. The "Ukrainian Alternate Energy Source Program," and then another.

Enraged, Zach knocked the laptop from its perch. "Damn it!"

Other agents rushed to the scene, staring at the spectacle Zach was making, but he didn't care.

How could this have happened?

How?

Behind him, Agent Halbaucher called in the update. "She's left us a decoy. Let's set up a four-mile perimeter and—"

"Don't bother," Zach stated, regaining his composure. "She's nowhere nearby."

He looked up into the night sky. There was a satellite tasked directly above their position in Texas. A satellite specifically located to capture her movements. Instead, Zach was certain that she had used it to track him. She was probably using it to watch him right this very second.

Halbaucher stepped up next to him. "But protocol states that—"

Zach shook his head and looked away from the sky and his fellow agents before anyone could see the hot tears springing to his eyes.

"She's probably not even in the country..."

CHAPTER 3

CDC Animal Research Facility
Plum Island
9:48 p.m., MST

Dr. Amanda Rolph squirmed in her seat. The 1950s-style conference room with its peeling paint and probable asbestos-filled ceiling only exasperated her claustrophobia. Especially as another dozen people entered the cramped room.

Fighting the urge to jump up and run from the room, Amanda looked out the window. Moonlight illuminated acres of green farmland rolling out from the laboratory complex. Sheep lazily grazed, oblivious to the dire threat looming from the east.

Yet even amongst this pastoral scene, signs of this once-proud institution's decline showed in broken fences and rusted machinery left to become part of the scenery. As newer and much more modern level-four disease research facilities sprang up around the world, Plum Island became obsolete.

Their facility was slated for decommission, to be replaced by a brand-spanking-new facility in Kansas—until now.

Now that the plague was making a resurgence? Plum Island was once again the jewel in the CDC's crown. Who else would be researching the bubonic plague but a bunch of silly animal researchers out in that old, decrepit facility? Since the plague had been treatable with a very high success rate with antibiotics for over a half century, the amount of funding that went into bubonic research was 0.0092 percent of the total CDC budget. The Black Death was a thing of the past—accounting for less than a thousand cases and only a handful of deaths per year. Compared to malaria with its 225 million people infected each year? The plague's research had been relegated to this crumbling facility.

Only now it looked as though the Black Death had just been taking a break.

Guess the joke was on the naysayers. Unfortunately, all those naysayers were arriving on Plum Island in droves. It was one of those awkward mountain-coming-to- Mohammed moments. They couldn't move Amanda's zoonotic research to the mainland without a literal act of Congress. The pathogens she studied were some of the most lethal in the world. Therefore, all the CDC brass had to come to the island. And not just the CDC, either. Beyond their normal complement of Homeland Security staff, Plum Island now hosted agents from nearly every US law enforcement agency.

Which was fine and all, but seriously, why did they need ATF agents? This was the *plague*. Nevertheless, that forced a conference room meant to hold thirty to somehow cram in over seventy people.

At least Amanda was already seated next to her assistant, Jennifer Neffer, rather than coming in late, trying to find a place, like the stragglers who entered now. Plus, her grad student was somehow able to transmute her anxiety into a type of excitement. Her hands were shaking, but not from fear, like Amanda's.

This was her very first agency-wide briefing, and the only thing she hoped for was to be passed over. *Just don't call on me*, she chanted in her mind, making sure that the fates had plenty of warning. But how could she *not* be called on? She was the only one in the room whose sole research subject was the plague and since well, the Black Death was making a comeback, she was going to get tapped—no doubt about it.

Before Amanda could formulate a plan to divert any questions, Dr. Art Henderson, the recently appointed head of Plum Island's languishing facility, rushed into the room, with three assistants hot on his heels. What should have been a nice pre-retirement position had become a lightning-rod post.

"Hello, all," the silver-haired Southern gentleman said as he set a stack of papers on the end of the table with a thud.

Was it the sudden noise or his stature that made Amanda cringe? Sure, she had seen her boss around the building over the last few days, but never this close.

Every time she had almost crossed paths with him, she had ducked into someone's office, the bathroom, or even just turned around and gone back the way she came. Amanda knew her intimidation was silly. He wasn't that tall. Maybe six feet three inches, but he towered over her. He wasn't that fat. Well, for a physician, he was way too overweight. It was even rumored that he snuck out onto the roof and smoked a few cigarettes. Quite the scandal.

But it wasn't even that. No, every time she was about to pass him, she knew he'd look down and say, "Who is this uneducated imp? Get her from my sight."

Or something akin to that.

He had the look of a man who could figure out in an instant that Amanda was out of her depth. So what if she carried a 4.25 grade point average throughout college? Who cared that she had gotten into med school at the age of twenty? Who cared that she finished a doctoral program at the same time? Who cared that her doctoral thesis on atypical disease transmission routes had gotten her a keynote speaker position at the AMA pathogens conference?

That was research. That was all accomplished within the incredibly safe confines of college campuses. This was the real world. The big, fat, overwhelming real world.

Amanda took a deep breath. This was all happening too fast. The sudden change of directors. Her promotion to primary researcher. And now the damn plague and all that it implied. Her head swam, and she tried to slow her breathing. Now would not be a good time to have a panic attack. Or an asthma attack. Or faint. No, none of those would be impressive to the audience here today.

Henderson abandoned his attempt to find the report. He looked at the dozen or so doctors sitting around the table, anxiously awaiting his first remarks.

"As you all know, this is only my fourth day on the job, and I'm basically relying on security to make sure you are actually on my staff, so feel free to chime in if I ask a question in your field of expertise."

Somehow, hearing her new boss's own admission that he was overwhelmed helped Amanda get a grip on her own growing anxiety. Maybe he wasn't the ogre that she thought.

The large man dove back into the stack of papers, obviously intent on a certain page, but quickly gave up again. "The nationwide bulletin has been issued?"

"The fax went out to all FBI and Homeland Security offices," the scientist next to Amanda spoke up.

Dr. Henderson searched the room for the person who spoke. "I'm sorry. You are?"

"Dr. Vincent MacVetti..." the scientist paused, apparently waiting for a glimpse of recognition from the director, but when he got none, MacVetti continued. "Besides being head of our domestic branch, I'm also the point person for all upper-echelon law enforcement communications."

"Right," Henderson said, then looked at the rest of the group. "How about everyone just shout out your name if we've never met...Or even if we have?" Henderson turned back to MacVetti. "Emergency rooms?"

A voice came from the other side of the table. "Dr. Evylin Tarmel, head of Medical Coordination." Once Henderson found the tall woman, she continued, "And yes, an alert has been distributed to all emergency rooms with populations above one hundred thousand citizens."

"And no group has taken credit for the outbreak?" Henderson asked of everyone and no one in particular.

"No," came the answer from the one man in the room without a white coat. "Sorry. Andrew Devlin, your CIA liaison."

"So no one is jumping out of their skin to take responsibility for the return of the Black Death?"

The shorter man shrugged. "As a matter of fact, the hot-listed groups are going out of their way to make sure that we know it's not them."

Henderson nodded, obviously processing the information. His eyes scanned the table. "Who's the lead on the *Yersinia pestis* bacterium?"

Amanda paused long enough that everyone turned to look at her. The director followed their gaze. "Cat got your tongue?"

She liked it better when he was bouncing around the room. Why did he need to talk to her? Take MacVetti—he could easily answer any questions. But Henderson fixed her with his gaze and frowned. Her time was up. She cleared her throat, buying her another half a second from doom.

"Dr. Amanda Rolph."

"Any new cases reported in Europe in the last four hours?" Henderson asked.

"No, sir." You know, this might not go too badly if she could keep her answers to two words. But then, Jennifer nudged her. *Damn it, if her assistant wanted to say something, she had a tongue.* She nudged again, but Amanda kept her gaze forward.

Luckily, Henderson didn't seem to notice her assistant's prompting, since he moved on. "And still no cases in the States?"

Everyone in the room shook their heads.

"So this could be a natural anomaly after all," the director said with a significant amount of relief.

Again, the audience seemed to answer as a single being, with a warm murmur of agreement.

Devlin nodded the most vigorously. "We might have dodged a bullet on this one."

"All right, let's keep up the—"

Before Henderson could finish his statement, Jennifer stepped on Amanda's foot. Right on her little toe. Amanda couldn't suppress a yelp.

The director's sharp eyes turned to her. "Dr....?"

"Rolph. Amanda," she quickly added, as if being personable would stop a scolding.

"You wanted to add something?"

Amanda didn't want to say another word—*ever*—in this blasted room, but Jennifer's foot hovered over her own, just waiting to stomp down if she shirked.

Clearing her throat, Amanda plunged in. "Sir, I think we are just experiencing a lull in the spread."

"A 'lull?'"

The sarcastic texture of his question was not lost on Amanda, but the die was cast. She couldn't back down without possibly needing a cast for her foot after Jennifer was done with it. "I believe these documented cases are just the warning shot over the bow."

"That's ridiculous," Devlin spat. "Terrorists go for the big bang. They wouldn't test-drive a bioweapon."

That was just what she needed. Arrogant dismissal. If there was one thing that could get her over her pathological shyness, it was being dissed.

Her tone sharpened. "Nevertheless, this dip in cases is just a delay from the incubation period."

Henderson cut in before Devlin could restate his disbelief. "I'm assuming you have some scientific proof to back up your claim?"

She might have temporarily had the courage to go toe to toe with an arrogant, uninformed, and nonmedical CIA liaison, but Amanda wasn't sure she had the nerve to face off against the whole room, let alone the director. But again, Jennifer was not allowing her to back down. Her assistant brought up a map of Europe on the cramped room's sole plasma screen. Each documented case of the plague was highlighted in red.

"We are aware of the zero patient, Dr. Rolph," Henderson stated, sounding more annoyed than curious.

And Devlin wasn't far behind. "Again, there are no Middle Eastern, Sub-Asian continental groups that have—"

She should keep Devlin around. He bugged her enough to prod her out of her self-imposed introversion. Glaring, Amanda challenged the liaison. "Doesn't this pattern feel vaguely familiar to anyone?"

"The Asian epicenter is not uncommon, with diseases such as influenza and—" MacVetti was on a roll, but Amanda cut him off.

"I mean, regarding the plague in particular."

The audience again formed a beehive mind-set, and their mumbling turned to downright scoffing. But Jennifer came to the rescue again. Her assistant brought up another map next to the current outbreak. They were nearly identical.

"What's this?" Henderson asked.

"The plague," Amanda answered plainly.

Before anyone could show their disgust, the second map sprang new cases, rapidly spreading across the whole of Italy.

"I...I don't understand," the director stated.

"This map is of the first plague. The Black Death."

Luckily, Devlin was the first to find his voice. "You aren't implying..."

Amanda shook her head. "I'm not implying anything. I'm saying that someone is re-creating the original bubonic plague. Down to the epicenter. The spread over the Black Sea. The lag in cases."

Everyone watched thousands upon thousands of red dots spread over the map.

"Everything," Amanda said just before the room erupted into argument.

Neighbor argued with neighbor. Some shouted at Amanda, others just spouted off to no one in particular. This was why she didn't want to say anything—but exactly the reason she had to.

The only one not engaged in various states of disbelief and denial was Dr. Henderson. He was on his feet, but calm, studying both maps. The director turned back to Amanda. "Why couldn't this just be a natural resurgence of the disease?"

Luckily, she had prepared for this question. Amanda had raised it herself several times during her research. "Because the region has changed dramatically since the last outbreak. The migration routes of the nomads have been eliminated—"

"But—" Devlin tried to interrupt. However, Amanda wasn't about to give up the floor until her point was made.

"And unless I missed something on *Nightline*, the Mongols aren't attacking an Italian outpost in Sub-Asia and hurling their plague dead over the walls." She turned back to Henderson and leveled her tone. "The last disease spread was highly dependent upon several circumstances. Circumstances unique to that era. Circumstances that could never be naturally re-created today."

Amanda took a long, hard look at the second map that was now so covered in red dots that no one could distinguish individual specks anymore. The map was splashed with huge red splotches, as if the screen itself had contracted the disease that had killed a quarter of the known world. But Mother Nature wasn't leveling the evolutionary playing field anymore.

"Someone is seeding this disease purposefully."

* * *

Lino allowed the motorized walkway to carry him along to his gate. Others bustled past him, not content with the speed of the conveyor belt underfoot. The young man didn't even look up when they bumped into him, mumbling their apologies— or not, given their level of civility. Why should he bother?

Instead, Lino kept his hand to the rail. When it felt completely dry, he would put it back into his coat pocket, dampen the surface of his palm with the contagion, and then place it on the cool metal again. It slid under his touch, unknowing or uncaring that it carried the single greatest threat to humankind on its smooth surface.

Pulling up his sleeve, he scanned the intricate scars carved into his arm. He was on schedule. He would easily make his flight.

His work here in Venice was almost done. Within the hour, hundreds of unsuspecting citizens from dozens of nations would be contaminated. Within a day, they, and anyone they came in contact with, would be dead.

There was no more rewarding work than this, Lino thought as he stepped off the walkway and headed to gate twenty-two.

CHAPTER 4

Second Undisclosed Location
10:02 p.m., MST

Ronnie wiped sweat from her brow as she stared at the intricate alarm pad. She probably should have taken a taxi to the cold room, as it was a good three miles from the rooftop. But with the streets still full of partiers, she decided to hoof it.

At first, it had been at a nice walk. Her intent had been to soak up the sights and enjoy her victory. But with each passing step, she felt her feet move faster and faster until she covered the last mile at an all-out run. *Had* Zach been after her? How close had he "virtually" come to catching her? She *had* to know.

But this damn door alarm stopped her. What in the hell was this week's code? Why couldn't they just use retinal scans and DNA sniffers like everyone else? But, of course, Quirk disagreed, saying that was way too techno-geek. Which meant that they used elaborate, obscure, and usually extremely pop culture-oriented passcodes. Not geeky at all.

Let's see…

Okay, the first number was the day *Raiders of the Lost Ark* was released. The second was easy. The month of Gene Roddenberry's birthday. The third? Another no-brainer. The year that *The Sonny & Cher Comedy Hour* went on the air.

Yeah, maybe she shouldn't let Quirk pick the codes anymore.

At first, the pad flashed green, but once she put her gloved hand on the door, the screen turned an awful shade of magenta and began beeping loudly. Crap. This was a "hot" day. She had forgotten to key in the secondary code that they used on nights she was breaking about seventy-five international laws. Quirk took their security seriously.

If she let go of the metal, the handle would explode before she could get outside the blast radius. If she didn't key in the correct code within the next thirty seconds, several hidden tranquilizer dart guns would shoot her.

And, typical, she had only listened with half an ear when Quirk was picking the backup code. Was it Aragorn? Spock? Han Solo? No. Ronnie distinctly remembered that Quirk was giving up on fantasy. He wanted a real man. With a real body. With real biceps.

That was it! Biceps. The scene from *Speed* when Keanu Reeves pulled himself up from under the bus. As the beeping accelerated, Ronnie typed in "Jack"…She could hear the mechanism inside the doorframe getting ready to shoot her with enough tranquilizers to knock out a horse.

Her fingers typed "Traven." She didn't want a repeat of the last time she screwed up a secondary passcode. It should have been simple. The original airing date of the best episode of *Enterprise*, but she had typed in the date using the typical format instead of the *Star Trek* standard Stardate format. Lo and behold, she had woken up, flat out, two days later.

Not fun.

Luckily, "Jack Traven" was the correct answer, and the alarm pad chirped the theme to *The X-Files* as the door opened. She rushed into the cold room, just in case those tranquilizer guns were feeling a little twitchy, but two things brought her feet to an absolute stop.

The first was the blast of chilled air. After just running in eighty-degree heat, with 100 percent humidity conditions, the room felt frigid. Nearly freezing the sweat to her face.

The other was the image on the main screen. There, in full Technicolor on the sixty-two-inch main screen, was Zach's picture. He *had* come for her. He was up on a roof, looking skyward. Knowing that she was looking down on him. And by the look on his face, he had just realized her ruse.

Wow, was he was *pissed*. Even though they had never met, Ronnie had enough surveillance footage of him to tell his mood by the throbbing veins on each side of his temples. The slight squint of the right eye. He only did that when he was totally torqued. But could she see a slight upturn at the lips? Was he at all impressed, or even amused? Or did he just want blood?

With great effort, she turned away from the screen to find Quirk meticulously caring for the main computer tower. He had to ever-so-slowly warm the delicate electronics back to room temperature.

"So?" Ronnie asked.

Quirk frowned as he looked back over his shoulder. "You mean, if he had been pursuing you in the same ZIP code, let alone the same area code?"

"Duh."

Her dark-haired assistant snorted. "He totally would have busted your JLO-sized ass." He raised his perfectly waxed eyebrow. "Which, I'm not all that certain you wouldn't have welcomed."

"Ha!" she responded, closing the distance. "Not only would I have escaped, I would have still bagged the two billion bucks."

Quirk turned back to his work. "You just keep telling yourself that."

"Did you see me out there? I rocked!"

The youthful hacker's tone sounded unimpressed. "Did you see the gun barrel pointed at your head? It was there, because I taught the kids to simulate Hunt and the other agents' movements exactly." He pointed to the smaller bank of screens as he typed. "Look at screen three if you don't believe me."

But when Ronnie glanced at the screen, there was a plague report. Great. Quirk would be using a magnifying glass to look for boils on his skin for the next six months.

"Sorry, go to four," Quirk said. "I'm TiVoing three's feed."

Of course he was. Then he would drop the show down to DVD and play the "Six Signs of the Plague" report every morning to add to his daily "health checklist."

"Now watch," he ordered.

Screen four split in two. The left half showed Zach and the FBI's movements, and the right showed the kids. As the chase neared a close, the two screens merged so that a cartoon Zach was the one who captured Ronnie, cuffed her, and then pulled her into a passionate kiss.

"Freak," she said to Quirk as she pulled off her gear, throwing the thoroughly soaked equipment onto a table filled with dozens of beta devices.

"Hey, hey, hey!" Quirk shouted as he ran over, picking the discarded items up as if they were the crown jewels.

"Hey, hey, hey, yourself," she said. "You promised me seamless, real-time infrared-to-normal spectrum integration in case of a bright flash."

Quirk was still busy picking out the equipment, drying each with a dust-free cloth. "And how many times did those fireworks go off right by you, and voilà, no white-out?"

"Hello? Blinding snow as I went to jump."

"The video feed took less than zero point one four seconds to kick in."

"Yeah, well, zero point one four seconds is a long time in *midair*," she answered as she tugged off her damaged gloves.

"Then join a freaking gym rather than leaping from tall buildings."

Ronnie chucked the gloves across the room. Unfortunately, they landed palm-side down, popping a few more beads. Worse, they landed on one of her assistant's proto-types. And, given the fact that Quirk was a huge fan of classic sci-fi, many of the items either looked like something out of *Flash Gordon* or a future issue of *Scientific American*. No matter. These were his babies.

Quirk rushed over to his workbench. "Oh! You are an evil, evil, evil woman."

Ignoring her assistant, Ronnie took one of his precious no-dust rags to wipe the clinging sweat from her face. "Fund redistribution complete?"

"Down to the penny," he said without looking up.

"Our cut?"

"Eleven point six two two percent of the total take."

Ronnie smiled. Even beside himself with grief, Quirk knew his numbers. "For a grand total of?"

"A cool two hundred forty-two million, two hundred thousand dollars," Quirk said as he surveyed all the equipment. "But I'm not even sure that covers the damage here."

Once on a roll, not a lot could divert Quirk, so Ronnie turned her back while he enumerated each and every single, tiny component and what it was going to cost to get it repaired or replaced. Besides, she had a download to finish. Rapidly logging on to one of the auxiliary computers, Ronnie didn't find the Panic! At The Disco bootleg, but the new Band of Horses cut was an adequate substitute.

"Well, for once, you're right," Quirk said from behind her.

Given the unusual admission from her assistant, Ronnie swiveled her seat around. She had to see this to believe it. "About?"

Quirk nodded toward the mega-screen at Zach's image. "He's even hotter when he's pissed."

When her assistant was right, he was right. Even though she had them memorized, Ronnie surveyed the agent's every feature. Brown, close-cut hair. Not that G-man buzz cut, but a little longer on top, which made the bangs fall ever so perfectly over his forehead without a hint of product. If he had any mousse in there at all, he was a master at hiding it. Then that strong forehead, with just enough lines to know that he wasn't a youngster, but not enough to make a woman worry that he might need Viagra. And his eyes. What could she say about those? Green, piercing, perfect. Full cheekbones and a square jaw were a given.

Oh, but those lips. What would they feel like? Or better, what would they taste like? Even though the image was a headshot, Ronnie knew the contours of his body. Broad shoulders, six-pack abs, and thighs that made her blush. Guess that's what two hours a day at the gym brought you. Could she get a more perfect fantasy boyfriend?

Sure, some days she worried that she obsessed about a man she could never meet, but hey, what was the alternative? What real-life man could she have? She lived outside—way, way, outside—the law, living a life on the run. And any other hacker of her stature was either gay, or should have been. That lot was pretty pasty and anemic from years in front of the computer.

No, the Zach fantasy was the far superior option. Otherwise, she would have no love life. And women with no hope and no dreams usually ended up in a smelly house with a bunch of cats while they themselves gave up on personal hygiene. She was not going to become that woman. Not with that hunk's picture to keep her company. That and another two hundred million bucks in the bank made her a pretty happy, well-adjusted chick.

* * *

Life was not good, Zach thought as he parked the car in front of the field office. Another three cars pulled in behind him. Even though he had known it was fruitless, they had still done their due diligence and combed the area for any evidence of the Robin Hood hacker.

Of course, there was none. And the one piece of equipment that might have held any clues he had thrown across the roof in a moment of rage. He was sure there would be a write-up on that incident in his future. And did he mention that his shins still hurt like a "mo" from that high-jump stunt?

Before the other agents cast him a curious eye, he exited the car and walked toward the entrance. Walked. He didn't charge toward it, or even stride in that direction. Nope, walking without a limp was about the best he could muster at this point.

As he opened the door, Zach realized that his night was about to get even worse. Grant sat on top of his desk, grinning from ear to ear. The cat that ate the canary.

"I got *my* man…" Grant said, pointing his thumb toward the sole occupant of the holding cell, an older man with even more haunted eyes than Zach. Only Fifer could be proud of bringing in an obviously demented senior citizen who had chosen to torch a painting while security was in the room.

"And you?" Grant asked with that syrupy-sweet tone of someone who already knew the answer to his question.

Zach didn't indulge his partner. Grant might have been away from the crime scene when everything went down, but, no doubt, his partner was filled in on the drama over the radio.

Biting back the pain from his shins, Zach headed for the coffee machine. He had never needed caffeine so much in his life. As he passed the holding cell, the old man lunged, grabbing Zach by the lapel.

"You must release me!"

Zach struggled, but the geezer had a grip like steel. During the struggle, the old man's sleeves fell back to reveal a mass of old scars. What in the hell was this guy into?

"We must burn the false effigy to find the true symbol!"

There was no breaking the arsonist's hold.

"The Hidden Hand must—"

Pulling back, Zach thought he was almost free, but then the old guy jerked him forward, banging Zach's forehead against the bars. Add that to the list of bruises to both his body and ego that he had to endure today. Zach wasn't surprised when his fist flew back reflexively to punch the perp and end this struggle right here and now, but something in the old man's eyes stopped him.

It wasn't insanity.

It was clarity. A level of clarity that Zach didn't know existed.

"Armageddon comes, child," the man said as he released his coat. "You must prepare."

Like breaking from a trance, the arsonist stumbled backward. Zach lunged to catch him, but the old man crumpled to the floor.

"Dude, I got him into the car without resorting to violence," Grant said, obviously mistaking the action as a punch. "That's going on your record."

Zach ignored his partner and watched as the man rose, mumbled to himself, and then finally slumped on the cot. Before Zach could get out his keys to open the cell and ask the old man what he meant, his boss's door flew open.

"Hunt!"

Everyone else melted away as Zach sighed.

"In my office, *now*!"

This night was never going to end.

* * *

The room's energy had shifted from angry grumbling to frantic confirmation as Amanda sat quietly. What else could she do? The sound of typing filled the room as the only layperson in the room continued to study the map.

"This may not be as bad as it seems," the CIA liaison said.

Henderson cocked an eyebrow. "The first plague ravaged Europe and brought on the Dark Ages."

"Okay, probably that bad for Europe, but the EU has been very cooperative about placing travel restrictions on international flights, even instigating body temperature checks before passengers board." Seeming not quite as self-assured, Devlin scanned the room. "I mean, we might be able to keep this from crossing the pond." He paused and looked at Amanda. "Right?"

Amanda kept her eyes averted as Henderson picked up the argument.

"He is right. If these fanatics are looking to re-create the Black Death, this continent might be spared."

"I doubt it," Amanda said before she thought. The spotlight was away from her. Why did she swing it back on herself?

Henderson was on his feet again. "But we weren't involved in the last epidemic."

His logic might feel sound, but Amanda knew in her gut that it was flawed. "The plague claimed a quarter of the world's known population. I don't think *anywhere* is safe this time." She looked at Devlin. He, of all people, knew the resentment that the rest of the world felt toward America. If someone were willing to throw down the gauntlet of bioweapons onto the world stage, the United States wasn't going to get a free pass.

"Especially not *this* country...not this time."

* * *

Lino stood in line, exhibiting patience far beyond his years. While others grumbled about the long delays created by the new ear-temperature check, he was content to wait. The Hidden Hand had anticipated this precaution. Anticipated it, and used it to their advantage.

Just before it was his turn to have the flight attendant insert the cone into his ear, Lino used a cough to cover spraying his ear lobe with the contagion. Apologizing in Italian for the wait, the weary attendant placed the cone into his ear, and then waited for the beep.

Thirty-two degrees Celsius. Perfectly normal. Lino watched as she pulled off the plastic sleeve from the digital thermometer. His intent was not to contaminate the thermometer. That was impossible, since they were using the sterile technique. But the flight attendant? A small bead of contaminated liquid touched the attendant's gloved finger. That was all it took.

He moved forward to make room for the next passenger, but stayed close enough to quench his curiosity. Perfectly executed, the flight attendant gently pulled down on the man's earlobe before she inserted the thermometer. Once it beeped and the cone was free of his ear, the man rubbed it to shake that strange feeling of being somehow violated, and then walked off.

The contagion should last for at least another hundred passengers. Another hundred who would become ill, spreading it to their families and friends. Then, they would die. Then *all* of them would die.

With a grin on his lips, Lino boarded his plane. The non-stop flight from Venice to New York, New York.

CHAPTER 5

Undisclosed Location
10:48 p.m., MST

Ronnie was well into downloading her fourth bootleg as Quirk finished packing up the damaged equipment.

"You know..." her assistant began in his singsong voice. Ronnie braced herself. She wasn't going to like what came out of his mouth next. "When we experience these technical difficulties during your little 'training' sessions, we could take a higher percentage of the total take to keep our profit margin up."

She gave him a "don't go there" look.

It didn't work. "I mean, what's the difference between eleven point four two two and, let's just go wild and say, sixteen point one?"

She gave him her "don't you *dare* go there" look. This one worked.

"Fine, fine. It's your paradise."

Both looked over at screen eight. An ad for a beautifully tranquil island shimmered back at them. Beneath the picture was the price. 4.5 billion dollars. A small price, really, to pay for your own *country*.

Quirk obviously decided to try a new tack. "You know, someone could swoop in and buy your island out from under you before you fill your coffers."

"With this information coming up on Google?"

Ronnie ran an Internet search on the island and read the results. "The island's limited fresh water is contaminated with arsenic. Malaria infestation wiped out the indigenous population." She turned to Quirk. "And now, with the plague stuff I could put in there? No one is going to buy this tiny municipality."

"How did you…" Quirk looked at the top of the website. "That's France's official…" He got up. "Whatever. I'm out of here.

The twenty-something checked his hair in a mirror. What gay man went outside without checking his appearance first?

Ronnie grinned. "We should probably pack up tomorrow and run silent for a few weeks before we head to Japan."

"You don't have to tell me twice." Satisfied with his level of beauty, Quirk headed for the door. "You're not coming?"

Swinging her chair back toward the computer, Ronnie shrugged. "Nah. I've got to re-download that bootleg."

"You're not going to call him again, are you?"

She tried to sound innocent. Really, really innocent. "Who?"

Quirk spun her chair back around and pointed to the larger-than-life image of Zach.

"Come on! That was a phase I went through," she deflected.

Her assistant seemed thoroughly unconvinced. "If you call him, you could give away that we've finally been able to patch into their internal surveillance."

CAROLYN MCCRAY

"Calling him didn't even cross my mind." Except, like, twelve million times.

"And they've upgraded their server. Warp may be a government worker, but he's not stupid." Quirk searched her face. "Today proved that he's caught on to our tricks. He might just be able to trace us."

Ronnie tilted her head. Trace them? Trace the two greatest cyber minds in the world?

Quirk must have read her mind. "Okay, maybe not track us down to this building, but at least within a hundred miles."

"I know, totally, I know," Ronnie tried to sound extremely convincing, since she had already cued up the speed dial number for the El Paso field office.

Quirk gave her that long, disbelieving look, then sighed. "Maybe even *fifty* miles."

"Got it," Ronnie said, trying to sit perfectly still.

"Okay then, tomorrow," Quirk said as he walked out, shaking his head the whole time.

Thank goodness he was gone! Not a second later, a voice came over the Internet connection. "El Paso's FBI field office switchboard. Who may I connect you with?"

* * *

How many different ways could Zach's supervisor say that he screwed up? Dropped the ball? Came up empty? The Agent in Charge was going to have to pull out a thesaurus soon.

"Are you even paying attention, Hunt?" Danner asked.

"Yes, of course."

Danner scowled, obviously not believing Zach one bit. "At some point, we've got to reassess our strategy."

Zach sat up straighter. He had been waiting for this talk. The warm-up to pulling him as the point man on the Robin Hood hacker case. Trying to keep his breathing steady, he studied Danner's face. Even though his boss was a ball-buster, this wasn't easy for Danner.

"You've had a good four attempts, this last one with a running start, and you still haven't even been able to identify where she was, let alone develop a strategy to catch her."

Before Zach could ramp up his well-rehearsed defense, a knock came at the door.

"Later," Danner said with authority.

But despite the obvious dismissal, Agent Hollinger cracked open the door.

"You deaf?" Danner demanded.

"No, sir…" Hollinger answered. "But…"

Danner didn't have much patience on a good day. "But, what?"

"Well, somebody claiming to be the Robin Hood hacker is on the line for Hunt."

"Yeah, right," Danner replied. "Tell her to throw us a couple mil."

Zach sighed. They got at least a dozen calls like this after one of her escapades. News spread fast over the Internet of her victories, and kooks always wanted to take credit.

"Why are you still standing there?" Danner asked Hollinger.

"Um, Warp was pretty excited. He said something about the way the signal was being rerouted had her signature."

Zach was out of his chair. She *had* called the office before. But it had been months. Could it really be her? He looked at

Danner, who clenched his jaw and then nodded toward the door. "Go."

* * *

Muzak. Who put Muzak on their hold anymore? Obviously, the United States Government. While waiting for ever-so-Special Agent Hunt to come onto the line, Ronnie watched yet another plague report. Something about squirrels being a natural carrier, or something. And of course, the TiVo's light was bright red. Quirk must have put "bubonic" into his wish list. She was so preoccupied with making fun of her assistant that she failed to hear him reenter the cold room.

"Ha! I knew it!" he shouted. "You have hunk-itis."

How could Quirk have known? Not about the hunk-itis, that was pretty darn evident, but that she had called Zach tonight? Then Ronnie spotted another brain child that her assistant had developed—a small, perfectly proportioned helicopter nicknamed, Helo. And the worst thing about Helo? He ran silently. Well that and had enough surveillance equipment on it to make the Pentagon drool. That little punk had used the mini-chopper to spy on *her*.

"Shh…" Ronnie scolded as she put her hand over the phone's receiver.

"Shh, my ass. You've got it bad," Quirk countered as he sat down at a keyboard and started double-checking her scrambling and making sure the signal was ping-ponging off dozens of satellites.

Ronnie was about to scold him, but those damn symbols reappeared. How? She had logged on under a completely different account and accessed a new site. How could her stalker find her again?

Working quickly, she tried to shut them down before Quirk noticed. He was a little bit fussy about the whole unauthorized access into his sacred silicon village.

"Oh, you are so in trouble!" Quirk exclaimed. "I told you, no more Limp Bizkit!"

Obviously, he noticed.

"Don't worry. I've got it."

That declaration might have been a bit premature. The ancient symbols pulsed and swirled across the entire screen. The sight was both beautiful and eerie. An otherworldly effect.

"Are we being possessed?" Quirk asked, seeming to only half kid.

"No," Ronnie answered, still trying to purge the message. "The symbols are a modified form of Hebrew."

"Modified by whom?"

"Angels," she stated. "It's *angelic* script."

Quirk looked at the scrolling letters with new respect. "What mailing list did you get on?"

For just a moment, they both stared at the screen with near reverence. As the lettering sparkled, they could almost truly believe that angels handed down the writing to Isaiah.

That moment of amazement was clearly over, though, as Quirk exclaimed, "That's it!"

Before Ronnie could stop him, her assistant disconnected the call.

* * *

Zach rushed into the tech room, with Danner not far behind.

"Line two," Warp said, pointing to the blinking light.

He picked up the phone. "Hello?"

But there was nothing. Just a dial tone.

"Wrong line?"

Warp frantically checked and double-checked. "No way. She was on line two. I swear."

"Maybe it wasn't even her," Danner postulated to the freaked-out tech.

"It was either her or God..." Warp must have realized that he stepped over the line. Way over the line. "Sir."

Zach paced as Danner hounded the poor techie. "I'm not convinced."

"Look at this," Warp said as he showed the signal bouncing around satellites like a pinball.

"So?" Danner scoffed. "There are several dozen hackers who can hide their carrier signals that well."

"Who else could do this?"

Warp artificially slowed the sequence of the bouncing, so that each leg of the journey became the segment of a line. Then the techie broke it down chronologically. Not even Zach could believe what he saw. Each segment of the signal's travel was part of a letter. Which spelled out the Robin Hood hacker's catchphrase, "Better Luck Next Time."

Danner sighed. "It *was* her."

Zach had known that, but now that they were all on the same page, he finally spoke up. "Why did she hang up? Did she detect your trace?"

"Of course she did," Warp said, and then rushed on. "But she's never given a shit about me tracking her..." He glanced at Danner. "Sorry, sir, but she usually gets off on kicking my ass."

"True," Zach jumped in, maybe a little too quickly. "Then why hang up?"

Warp looked over all his screens again. "I don't know. Maybe something went wrong on her end."

* * *

The symbols now invaded all of their screens. Even the TiVo's light blinked erratically. This was bad.

"Seriously, why in the hell would someone spend this much time and energy sending you angel-speak?" Quirk demanded.

Ronnie didn't want to answer him. She was going to get enough grief over this incident as it was.

"Well?" Quirk pushed.

She shrugged, trying to downplay her words. "It's considered the Holy Grail of code breaking."

"Come again?"

"There is intense debate amongst encryption scholars—"

Quirk glared over his keyboard at her. "That is to say, people with *way* too much time on their hands."

"Cipher *specialists* are still wrangling over how angelic script should be read. Right to left, as Hebrew? Yet there is some indication that diagonal is the true form, and—"

"So this is some stupid-ass prank?" Quirk sounded indignant. "Some guy living at home with his mother, challenging you to a code-cracking contest?"

Her assistant was far too perceptive for Ronnie's own good. She had to fess up. "More than likely."

To make matters worse, the symbols accelerated their pace, far outstripping her and Quirk's efforts.

"That's it! No more chat rooms for you," he said. Quirk paused, and then looked over at her. "For an entire month."

Normally, she would balk at such parental treatment, but the damn symbols just kept coming.

"It's just breached our secondary firewall," Quirk announced, his tone dripping with blame.

Unfortunately, Ronnie could not argue. Someone was seriously kicking them around the yard. But who could it be? No one from the government. This hack was too free-style. Too bold. Too flamboyant for salaried work. Then who? She knew or knew of every hacker of this caliber, and none could even come close to penetrating Quirk's insanely layered defenses.

But that left her with the same question.

Then who?

* * *

After hours at the crime scene, another hour of being raked over the coals, and then another chunk of time brainstorming with Warp about why the Robin Hood hacker had bailed, Danner had finally sent him home to "cool his heels." Zach wasn't even sure what that meant exactly, but he was happy to leave. Get out of the stifling office and clear his thoughts.

Making his way toward the door, Zach gave the holding cell a wide berth. The old man was another unsettling aspect of an extraordinarily unsettled day. But the elderly man was turned with his back to the bars, sitting quietly. Too quietly.

Despite his desire to go home and get out of his G-man suit, Zach drifted toward the holding cell. "Hey." No response. "Turn around."

Still, the old man wouldn't move. And he was mumbling again.

Grant, of course, didn't miss an opportunity to hurl a barb. "Want me to grab the Taser gun?"

Zach ignored the jab. Something was wrong here. "Just watch my back." He put the key in the door. "Mr. Loubom?" Still, no response—just an increase in muttering. "Francois?"

Zach just wanted to go home. But, no. This old guy had to be doing some kind of freaky meditation. Zach placed his hand on the man's shoulder. "Turn around, nice and slow."

Finally, Francois complied, tears in his eyes. Then the old man extended a bloody arm. What in the hell did somebody do to him? Then Zach realized that Loubom had used a pen cap to gouge more symbols into his arm.

"Can't you see?" he asked, obviously feeling that his red-soaked arm held some kind of answer. "I must burn the painting."

But all Zach could see was blood—and more blood. He yelled over his shoulder, "Call an ambulance! Get me the first-aid kit!"

Despite the potential danger, he pulled the man's sleeve back down and clamped his bare hands over the wound to stop the bleeding. For the love of God, what had made the man mutilate himself like that?

"They speak to me, you know," Francois said, sounding the most sane he had yet.

But Zach was still concerned that he had really lost it. "Who?"

The old man locked Zach's gaze with his crystal-blue eyes. "The angels."

* * *

Angels *sucked*, or at least whoever was busy cramming angel-speak down their throats, sucked big time. Quirk was running the defensive, while she was trying to counter-hack and break into the intruder's server. That was the theory, anyway. The reality was that things were not going well. Not at all.

Sweat, actual sweat, poured off Quirk's brow. He was never going to forgive her if his hair gel failed because of perspiration.

"Quirk…" She couldn't believe what she was about to say. "Maybe it's time to admit defeat."

"Never," he hissed though bleach-whitened teeth. "I am lord of the geeks."

Overall, he might be. But right now, someone was seriously out-hacking both of them. Yet, Quirk was taking this much harder. The system defenses were his babies. His domain. Someone, somewhere, was outgunning him. Simply put, their opponents had cooler stuff.

"Look, I promise never to divulge tonight's momentary, freakish coup."

Quirk breathed out sharply through his nose. What she suggested ran counter to his über-computer geek ego, but the reality was that they were beat.

"Or even tease me about it?" he asked.

"Not even a pun."

For a moment she thought her assistant would shake his head "no," but Quirk showed her how much he had grown over the last two years when he gave a sharp nod. "Pull the input cables."

Ronnie abandoned her post and dug around behind the towers.

"Holy Batman!" Quirk said as the symbols accelerated to lightning speeds. "It's a self-propagating program, and it's got a foothold. We can't let it get into the core."

"And you would suggest?" she asked, pulling cords as fast as she could.

He sounded downright panicked. "I don't know, but put the pedal to the metal."

The processor lights blinked faster and faster. They had dozens of interlinking cables—each one screwed in as if its life depended on it. She would never make it in time. There was only one thing left to do. Taking a knife out of her boot, she sliced away. Sparks showered and smoke billowed from the secondary towers, but the main processor went down and stayed down—safe from prying eyes.

Crawling out from under the equipment, Ronnie looked up. All the screens had stopped their incessant scrolling, but each blazed with a single symbol. But how could that be? She had just cut the wiring. The screens should be blank.

Before she could investigate further, Quirk recovered from his shock. "Okay, seriously, I am taking away your hacker's membership card."

"It worked, didn't it?" She nodded toward the angelic symbols. "Get a screenshot of that, would you?"

With great showmanship, Quirk hammered away at his now-defunct keyboard. Oh, yeah. She'd cut those cables as well.

"Maybe we should just pack up for tonight," she conceded.

"Ya think?"

Contrite, Ronnie tugged on the free ends of the cables to see what they attached to, but Quirk slapped her shoulder as hard as a card-carrying member of the Rainbow Alliance could. "Just go home."

"But I—"

"You've done enough damage. Go!" That tone was about as close to blowing his top as Quirk ever came, so Ronnie obeyed, grabbing her Hello Kitty bag and hitting the road.

Time to go home and soak out the intellectual defeat with a nice, long, bubbly, bubbly, bubbly bath. Anything to wash away the sight of all those symbols.

* * *

Francois ignored the medic cleaning his wounds. They fretted and lectured. What would they know of his duty to God? They thought him mad. Most did. Yet, being graced with the language of the angels, Francois did not bother with what others thought.

Each symbol, fresh to his flesh, sang to him. The script burned in his blood reminding him of his duty. A duty to stop the Hidden Hand at any cost. They had already targeted Europe. That continent was more than likely lost. Just like the last time, the Hidden Hand decided to make the world over in their hideous image.

That was why, upon hearing of the first case of the Black Death in Venice, Francois left his homeland and trekked to the Americas. He had failed to predict the Hidden Hand's bold move. Now his last hope was to stop the spread across the Atlantic Ocean.

Which was why he sought the Picasso. Yet, even in that, he was thwarted. How he wished to see the script of the angels. To have them talk to him in their purity. Then, he could mark the occasion upon his flesh. Dug in there to forever be at his avail.

If only the agent had listened to him. If only he could have broken through the man's stubborn denial. He could see the compassion in the man's eyes. He could feel the worry through his grip. How many other agents had passed by the cell, not even giving Francois the least regard?

But now, the agent was gone. Off to live his life, not knowing how incredibly short lived it was going to be.

* * *

Jennifer nudged her again. Amanda had shut out the endless interdepartmental bickering and gone back into the only safe place she knew. Numbers. Facts. Science.

So clean. So neat. So precise. So unlike human nature.

She looked at Jennifer. Why had she disturbed her? Why had her assistant reminded her that she was in a room full of her betters?

Henderson cleared his throat, and then Amanda knew why her assistant had given her a heads-up. The director looked ready to make a call. How to handle the current situation given this new, potentially devastating information?

"Unless we have anything else, I am going to brief the · president."

Attendees answered with a quiet rumbling, signaling that they were unwilling to commit to anything yet. Amanda squirmed in her seat, trying to keep her feet out from under Jennifer's abusive heel.

"Yes, Dr. Rolph?"

She was on the spot. No sense in missing this opportunity. "What is your recommendation going to be, sir?"

Henderson rattled them off. "In addition to the current measures, we should step up surveillance on incoming international flights. We'll do postflight temperature checks, and quarantine all those with elevated temps." Amanda didn't even realize that she was shaking her head until the director responded.

"You disagree?" he asked.

She fidgeted under his cool gaze. He wasn't necessarily challenging. But he wasn't exactly being supportive, either.

Finally, Amanda let out her breath and straightened her shoulders. "Sir, we need to discontinue all incoming European flights and ships."

It was Henderson's turn to shake his head. However, Devlin spoke first. "We don't want to create a panic."

Thank God it was Devlin. She could snap back at him. "Um, with all due respect, *yes*, I think we do."

The director looked at his assistant. "She *is* a member of my staff, right?"

"Sir," Amanda said, beginning to feel her face flush. "The risk is—"

This time, Henderson wasn't joking at all. "As I said, we will quarantine anyone, and I mean *anyone*, with a ninety-eight point nine degree temperature."

"But—"

MacVetti overrode her. "Fever is the first and best indicator for the early contagious phase."

While Amanda appreciated her supervisor trying to protect her, even from herself, in this she could hold her own. Well, at least she hoped so.

"In a sick patient, yes." She paused before she really shook the room. What if she were wrong? But this was too important. More important than even her nearly paralyzing social phobia.

"But in a carrier?" Amanda pressed. "No. In a carrier state, temperature monitoring is useless."

The room held a quizzical breath. What she spoke of was beyond unreasonable. It was unheard of.

Devlin just seemed confused, though. "Um, it was my impression that there was no carrier state with the plague."

"Naturally? There isn't."

It was clear by his tone that MacVetti was tiring of her theories. "Then why—?"

Amanda hurried on. "But someone who is vaccinated and physically carrying the virus on their person? On their clothes? That person will walk right through your screening."

Devlin snorted loudly, seeming to convey the entire room's disdain. Yet, somehow Henderson kept his tone civil.

"That would require someone to actually have a vaccine for the Black Plague."

Amanda shrugged, trying not to reveal her innards quivering. "It's bacterial. It can be done."

MacVetti looked her square in the eye. Each glance told her to sit down and shut up. "Do you have any idea of the resources it would take to develop a human-quality vaccine? And do it under *our* radar?"

Amanda couldn't stand the mix of disappointment and anger brewing in MacVetti's eyes. She looked down at her hands to keep from crying—right there in front of everyone. Why couldn't someone with a backbone think of this? Why did it have to be her?

Henderson stood. "My recommendations stand."

The director was almost out of the room when Amanda finally spoke up. "They already have it."

MacVetti's head snapped around to face her. "What are you talking about?"

"The vaccine…" She gulped not once, but twice. "I think they already have one."

Devlin rolled his eyes. "Okay, now *I'm* ready to check her credentials."

But, yet again, Jennifer rose to the rescue by providing visual aids. This new map showed the original spread of the plague, but it centered on areas untouched by the incredibly high death count.

"It has long been a subject of debate on how these isolated population pockets survived the plague, virtually unscathed."

MacVetti's cheeks billowed. He was beyond pissed. "Not so much debate as a conclusion that they carried a gene that conferred natural resistance."

Jennifer didn't need prompting. Her assistant was already bringing up a second map that showed a slightly different spread of the plague. The isolated pockets weren't as crisp, and there were many more small enclaves of survivors.

Amanda used a laser pointer to highlight the new clusters of survivors. "These other pockets are areas of residence of direct, full-blooded relatives of those who survived." Devlin tried to interrupt, but she talked right over him. "Which was determined through tracking of church records, inheritance documents, and lordship titles."

She nodded to her assistant, who brought up a wholly different map. This one showed a schematic of an area in Southeast Asia. Quickly, an unidentified disease coursed over the continent, leaving behind small pockets of survivors, much like the plague map.

"Out of all the documented epidemics, this cholera outbreak is the only one whose pattern is at all similar to the Black Plague 'islands' of survival."

MacVetti sighed. "Like I said, genetic resistance."

Amanda shook her head with authority. "This isn't the fourteenth-century outbreak of influenza. It's the 1970 pandemic." She zoomed in on the pockets of survival. "These 'islands' represent areas with heavy Western influences—and medical workers who were *vaccinated*."

Now MacVetti's bluster wasn't anger. It was confusion. "But for the plague…There's no way…Vaccination theory didn't even come into play for another…Another…"

"Four hundred years," Henderson finished for him.

Shrugging, Amanda switched to the plague map. "Nevertheless, my theory is that a terrorist organization that far predates the Islamic extremists has vaccinated carriers spreading the disease across the world."

The entire room quieted as a new map showed the potential spread of the disease with the planet's current population. Soon, the screen just glowed a bright red.

* * *

Lino pretended to stumble and right himself on the overhead compartment. The pilot had turned off the "Fasten Seat Belt" sign, and Lino had taken the opportunity to make sure that his mission was successful. Certainly, seeding the railing and passengers behind him in line had gone according to plan, but he had not gotten this assignment at such a young and tender age because he only did an *adequate* job.

His superiors knew that he would go to any lengths to see that this disease spread among the heathens. The unworthy. So he dragged his slightly moist hand along the overhead compartment. Anyone he missed earlier would certainly need to touch the lever to get his or her bags out at the end of the flight. The people would unwittingly contaminate themselves.

That was the simple beauty of their plan. The unenlightened masses were such sheep. They grazed the same pasture. They followed along in a single line. They could so easily be led to the slaughterhouse.

Finally, the earth would be cleansed of the undeserving.

Lino finished his journey to the forward bathroom and entered, being particularly careful to lock the door. No one needed to see what he did next. With skill approaching art, Lino meticulously took a hidden blade from his metal belt buckle and carved into his skin his most recent success. He let the blood drain into the sink, as he made absolutely certain the symbols were perfect in all ways.

That was the way of the Hidden Hand, after all.

CHAPTER 6

Special Agent Zachary Hunt's Home
10:32 p.m., MST

Zach pulled into his driveway, still talking on his cell. He might have left work physically, but mentally? Mentally, he was still all over the case.

"That's what you said last time, Warp."

"But we're super-sure that we can locate her the next time she calls."

Entering the house, Zach turned on the hallway light and started sorting the mail. "We'll see."

"You'll see! We've got taps on your home phone, your cell, and all three phones at the Starbucks…"

While Warp rambled on, Zach carefully removed any item of mail with Julia Levie's name on it and set it inside a box. A box filled with the remains of their relationship. A rose lamp and some designer plates. Oh, sorry, *flatware*. Did he feel a twinge of sadness as he surveyed the small box that contained the fragments of an old life?

Nah.

"All the lines at your gym," Warp babbled on. "The grocery store near work and…"

Only half listening to Warp's mind-numbingly thorough list of possible contact points, Zach climbed down the stairs to the basement. After a night like tonight, he definitely needed to hit the stationary bike. Quickly, he pulled off his work clothes and changed into shorts and running shoes as Warp tried to break the record for the longest sentence uttered without taking a breath.

"Oh, oh, and the Blockbuster around the corner. Even that little video store where you get—"

"I got it," Zach interrupted. Where did Warp find all his information? "You've got all the bases covered."

Warp sounded ever so confident. "She can't get in contact with you without us knowing about it."

Zach climbed onto his exercise bike. "Good to know."

Before Warp could launch into another diatribe about the reams of code he had written to track her down, Zach turned off his cell phone. Not just hung up the call, but physically turned off the phone. He didn't want to think about work anymore. He was home, and months ago, he had taken a vow to lead a more balanced life, which meant leaving work at work—at least while he was down here.

As he warmed up his legs in first gear, Zach put in his iPod earbuds. Van Halen cued up. Perfect.

"Hey, sexy," a voice purred in his earbuds.

"Hey there, yourself," Zach responded.

* * *

Sinking lower in the bubbles, Ronnie leaned against the porcelain tub. Clandestine phone calls with Zach. So secret that not even Quirk knew about them.

"I was afraid you were going to miss our time window," she said to cover her almost teenage awkwardness. They weren't even in the same room, and still she felt so very flustered.

"Yeah, sorry I'm late," Zach said. "I had a tough day at work. But you knew that already, didn't you?"

She chuckled. "Tell me about it."

"So what was with the hang-up? Got tired of waiting for me?"

Even though the iPod was voice only, Ronnie could almost see the corners of his eyes crinkle as he gave a sly grin. Or at least that's what she imagined he was doing, and it worked for her. "Nah. Quirk caught me."

The statement wasn't exactly a lie. Quirk had hung up on her. It just wasn't exactly the truth regarding the near-critical meltdown they'd had. Could he tell the difference yet?

"So, were we as close as Warp thought to shutting you down, or were you just throwing him a bone?"

Guess not. Which gave her leeway to embellish even more. "I'm generous that way."

She took a tip of her merlot. Could the night end any more perfectly?

"You realize, of course, that you can't run forever?" Zach asked.

Oh, how she wished she had a video feed. "It's so cute, the way you try to talk me into turning myself in."

"I'm serious," he said, and he sounded it. "How can you live like this?"

"What?" I'm in a penthouse suite." Another embellishment. Who would pay beaucoup bucks for an overpriced room when you had a country of your very own to buy? Besides, this room wasn't half bad. It was clean and had a standalone bathtub. What more could a girl on a budget ask for?

"Yeah, but you're paying for it with someone else's money," Zach shot back.

"Hey!" That hurt. Who was he to get up into her grill like that? "I didn't spend tens of millions of dollars to develop a point-to-point ultra-low frequency communications device that also serves as a bug detector *and* plays music, to have you proselytize."

"Then maybe you should explain to me why you *did* spend the money."

Hello? This was not how the fantasy was supposed to play out.

"You know, *I've* turned to the dark side. I've embraced the criminal life. I don't need to explain why I'm flaunting regulations and protocol." She was going to stop, but she was on a roll even Quirk would be proud of. "Maybe you should step up to the plate and say why you haven't reported our communications to your superiors." Coming down the mountain even more righteously, she asked, "Why have you continued to engage in illegal correspondence with a wanted felon? And don't give me that bull answer about how you are trying to get me to see the evil of my ways."

Ronnie wasn't sure that she was really done, but she was definitely out of breath. That had been quite the rant. She even felt a little light-headed. What exactly could he say to all of that? What did she want him to say? She waited for his response, and then waited some more.

* * *

Zach's legs quit pedaling. Damn, he wanted to be mad at her. He would have loved to just kick sand right back at the unrepentant felon, but Ronnie had a point. What in the hell *was* he doing? Did he really want her to come in from the cold? Wasn't it pretty apparent after the first month of this off-the-books relationship that she would never give herself up? Then what was he doing, still talking to her? What had he gotten himself into? How could he respond to her questions when he couldn't even answer them himself?

As the moments dragged on, the only thing filling this most uncomfortable silence was the music. Thank God it was still playing, or he might actually have to respond to her unanswerable questions.

"Please tell me that isn't Van Halen playing," she teased.

Zach couldn't help but chuckle. Classic Ronnie. She could ride a five-minute anger tidal wave, then hop off and playfully splash you with water. He took the opposite approach. He liked to chew his cud. Hash something over and over again. That was something else she had taught him. Let it go.

"Van Halen?" Zach replied. "Yeah. Yeah, it is."

While she launched into another rant, Ronnie's voice was more playful. "Okay, I spend hours downloading music and risk incarceration to bring you cutting-edge boot-legs, and you're listening to Van Halen? *Sammy Hagar's* Van Halen?"

"Yep, and proud of it," he confirmed, grinning.

"I didn't even load that song into memory, and I certainly didn't put it into your playlists."

Zach's face relaxed into a true smile. This was why he was still talking to her, and he had to admit that it had nothing to do with convincing her to come clean. "I know you are the über-hacker, but I know my way around a mouse."

"And you choose to display that talent by adding Hagar to the mix?"

He played right along. "Yep, and proud of it."

The sound of her laughter filled his ears. Would it sound as sweet in person? "You really need to get out more. And, hey, are you still going to your cousin's bachelor party in Ciudad Juarez?"

Another classic Ronnie move. Conversation jump. Sometimes he needed a diagram to remind him of the fifteen different threads they were following. He'd given up trying to keep their conversations linear. Where Ronnie led, you just followed. Even if you didn't necessarily want to.

"Yep, and *not* proud of it."

"I thought you didn't want to schlep all the way across the border?" Ronnie asked.

Zach sighed. Not the subject that he wanted to spend their precious minutes on, but he knew that she was like a dog with a bone, so he answered, "I don't, but I missed Skip's last one, so—"

"Last one?" Ronnie interrupted. "He's been married before?"

"Oh, he's been married five times and has seven kids." Then, pausing for the perfect comic moment—something else he had also learned from Ronnie—Zach finished with, "All with different mothers."

"And you think our relationship dynamic is weird?" Ronnie joked.

"Maybe there's hope for us yet," Zach quickly added, regretted it, and then didn't.

Had he really just spoken such a truth so casually? When he started to speak, the words had been a joke. A play on words. The sentiment was anything but a laughing matter. Was there any hope, *any* hope at all, for them? And why wasn't she saying anything? Why was there silence again? God, was one of them going to have the guts to actually speak what had been unspoken for months? Did *he* have the guts to?

"You know, Ronnie," Zach started awkwardly, "I was thinking…"

What *was* he thinking, though? He had decided to go to his cousin's party for another reason. And it had nothing to do with familial obligation, but could he bring himself to tell her?

He started again. "Maybe. Maybe we…Or you could…" Oh, Jesus, this wasn't going well. Another do-over. Stick to the facts, and maybe, just maybe he could get a sentence out. "You know, the bachelor party is outside the US, and I was thinking that maybe we could—"

"Zach, who *are* you talking to?" A voice came from across the room.

No, it couldn't be. It was *Julia*. In the room. With Ronnie on the line.

Oh crap, crap, crap!

As his former fiancée walked toward him, Zach fumbled with the iPod, disconnecting the line. Ronnie did not need to hear this.

* * *

What in the hell was going on? Zach might have thought he turned off the transceiver, but he was horribly mistaken. She could hear each and every painful word.

His words came through crystal clear. "Julia? What? How? Where?"

"I still have keys, Zachary."

Shit. Julia sounded as freaking beautiful as her picture. His ex-fiancée had given up a modeling career to work with the homeless. Bitch.

"But why?" he asked.

"You made it pretty clear that you wanted me to come by tonight to pick up my mail?"

Damn! Why in the hell hadn't she installed video surveillance in Zach's basement? She needed to see his face. She needed to see his reaction. Really, she just needed to be there.

"And back to my question," Julia said. "Who were you talking to? And when did you convert the basement into a gym? I've only been gone a few weeks."

"A few *weeks*?" Ronnie squeaked. What the hell?

"Let's not do this again, okay?" Zach mumbled.

"Who were you talking to, Zach? Or would you rather I tell Grant that you've been secluding yourself in the basement, talking to no one in particular?"

Ronnie could tell that hit a nerve with Zach. His words came out far tighter. "Julia, that threat is beneath you…Come on."

Each of his ex-fiancée's words were punctuated with determination. "Who were you talking to?"

Ronnie strained to hear. Was that silence, or was Zach whispering? Had they moved outside the iPod's range?

Finally, a sigh. "Myself," Zach said. "I was…Working on…"

How was he going to get out of this one? Zach couldn't exactly tell the truth, here or *ever,* about them.

"I was working on…self-affirmations."

"Self-affirmations?" Ronnie's words echoed Julia's.

"Self-affirmations?" Julia demanded.

"Yeah, the ones my therapist gave me."

Even through the tinny connection, Ronnie could hear Julia's anger.

"Therapist? You, all-knowing, emotionally so well equipped that he refused for a year to go see someone even after I begged him, is now going to a *therapist*?"

Ronnie could hear that Zach's back was up. "Yeah, the one you recommended. Dr. Webster."

"Dr. Webster?" Julia sure could sound bitter when she wanted to. "Really? Zach, just admit you aren't—"

"Hey, you can call his office and check. Tuesday afternoons, 3:00 p.m."

Julia sounded as surprised as Ronnie by the news.

"You, you went into therapy?" All the bitterness left Julia's voice. "You went for *us*?"

Leaning forward in the bath, Ronnie held her breath. What was his answer going to be? But instead of Zach's voice, she was greeted by a harsh disconnect sound.

"No!" Ronnie yelled as she desperately tried to reestablish the signal. Well? Did you? Did you go into therapy for Julia?

But, no luck. The line was dead.

* * *

How much had Ronnie heard? Zach's mind desperately tried to backtrack the last few minutes' exchange. His heart sank. What must she be thinking?

"Well?" Julia asked. A mixture of fear, tenderness, and hope on her face. "Did you do it for us?"

Grinding his teeth, Zach realized that he owed his ex-fiancée the truth. Well, at least as much of the truth that didn't land him in a federal penitentiary. "No, I did it for *me*."

But he still saw in her face a glimmer of hope. A hope that, if he looked hard enough inside himself, he had perhaps encouraged. Lord knew that they'd done this song and dance often enough in the early days of their breakup.

Zach leveled his gaze at her. She needed to know that he meant each and every word. She had to hear him this time.

"It's *over*, Julia. I'm sorry, but you know it's been over for a lot longer than a few weeks."

Julia reached out and touched his arm as he moved toward the stairs. "But we could—"

"No," he said as he removed her hand from his skin. "We can't."

Rapidly, he climbed the steps. He needed to get Julia out of here so that he could call Ronnie back. The hacker must be going berserk by now.

As soon as they hit the landing, Julia rushed to his side. "I think—"

"Julia!" That was too harsh, but damn it, how many times had they had this exact same conversation? The woman just wouldn't take "no" for an answer. He tried to drop the harshness in his tone, but retain the unequivocal firmness. "And let's be clear—you haven't lived here for almost nine months."

He picked up the box from the hallway table. "So I think it's about time that you put in an address change."

Julia jerked the box from his grasp. "You know, you really are being a selfish asshole!"

Usually he would have risen to his own defense, but that just led to more arguments. More time together. More time for her to convince him of the error of his ways. Why not just be honest for once?

"Yep. Probably I am."

Julia's lip trembled as tears glistened in her eyes. Was she *finally* getting it?

He tried to be gentler with this request. There was no need to hurt her much more than he already had. "And how about those keys?"

Blinking back tears, Julia slowly took the front door key off the ring. "I don't understand what happened. Last year at this time, we were getting ready to marry. I just…I don't understand."

God, he felt like a jerk—what with her eyes swimming in a pool of pain. A pain he had created. But it was also a pain he couldn't take away. He couldn't turn back the clock, or, more accurately, *wouldn't* turn it back, even if he could.

"I don't understand it, really, either, but it has changed, and we both need to adjust."

As she put the key into his palm, she tried to hold his hand, but he purposefully pulled it out of her grasp. Julia searched his eyes one last time. But he knew the only thing she would find there was an urgency to have her out of the house. Finally, she gulped back a sob and fled out the front door.

A year ago, he would have run after her to comfort her. A month ago, he would have waited a few minutes, and then called her to make sure she was okay. A week ago, he would have called one of her friends to let him or her know that Julia would need some support.

Tonight? Tonight, he just threw the dead bolt and raced back down the stairs to the basement. Another woman needed him tonight.

Within seconds, he fumbled with the iPod, desperate to get Ronnie back on the line. Sammy Hagar sang in his ear as he scrolled through the menu. He hit the "Look Up" option, but a message streamed across the screen.

"Unauthorized contact time. If this is an emergency, enter your override code...And this better be life or death, dude."More classic Ronnie. Well, this *was* life or death, so he rapidly began inputting the code. Or at least *tried* to rapidly put it in. What in the hell was Darth Vader's first name?

"Damn it, Ronnie!" he cursed as he searched his memory.

Skywalker. Now, the last name would have been easy. Anakin! His thumb slid around the circular keypad effortlessly. The next one, he knew. Elvis Presley's birthday. Ronnie knew his love for the King. But what in the hell was Steven Spielberg's first feature film?

* * *

Covered in a thick terry cloth robe, Ronnie watched as the second code was confirmed. Zach called back! He hadn't

ENCRYPTED

tumbled into bed with that over-plucked eyebrow wench. All was not lost. Maybe he could explain why Julia said she was still living there up to two weeks ago rather than the nine months ago Zach had told her. And what was up with the therapist ruse, anyway?

He missed the third code. *Jaws*? Was he crazy? You didn't get the director's gig to *Jaws* your first film out. While he tried again, Ronnie held her iPod in a death grip. For the love of God, the movie starred Goldie Hawn! How could he forget about *The Sugarland Express*?

Ronnie knew she shouldn't care this much. Zach was supposed to be a fantasy. And fantasies shouldn't churn your gut like this. But, damn it! She had to know if he lied to her. Did he have that in him? Was he playing her? Just wait until she got him on the line!

But as he keyed in the correct code, she felt her throat constrict. Choking off with emotion. Was he calling back to give her the boot? Was he calling to apologize? What would she say? Could she even say anything?

Come on, come on, come on!

"Ronnie?" Zach asked as the connection completed.

After all that preparing, all Ronnie could squeak out was a weak, "Yeah?"

Luckily, he didn't wait for her to continue. "Look, I didn't want our conversation to end like…Well, like it did."

Her words came out in a rush, along with all the worry. "You mean with the fiancée you told me had been gone for over nine months who was really living with you up until a few weeks ago—interrupting the very first time that we've ever talked about meeting for a face-to-face conversation?"

"Yeah, the one that ended like that."

Damn it, he still hadn't given her any indication of what had happened. Where was his head? His heart?

"First off, let me be very clear," Zach finally said. "I broke off the engagement nine months ago."

Again, her throat nearly shut itself off. Could it really be true?

"Why?"

"You know *why*."

A sniffle was her only response. Nine months ago was the first time she had ever called him. Had he been telling the truth, or was Julia?

"Then why was she pretty adamant about only being gone for three weeks?"

"Look, having her move her stuff out had been like trying to get ticks off a good hunting dog."

She didn't think she loved him any more than when he brought out those down- home homilies. "You couldn't hide the fact that you are from the Midwest if you tried, dude."

"Then you should know that I'm not lying."

True, but…"You lied to Julia."

"When?"

"Self-affirmations?"

* * *

Zach was really, really, really, hoping that Ronnie wouldn't bring that up, but the woman had a photographic memory that rivaled no other.

"Okay, that was to protect her feelings."

"What if she does call Dr. Webster?" Ronnie asked, then waited for an answer. But what could he say? Damn, but the hacker was quick on the uptake. "No. You're kidding, Zach? You're *really* seeing a shrink?"

"No!" was his first response, but then he had to own up to the truth. "Well, he's not a shrink per se. He's a licensed family counselor."

Ronnie, of course, was all over that splitting of hairs. "Same diff," she snorted, and then her tone transformed into true curiosity. "Why in the world would you go into therapy?"

There were so many answers to the question, but he couldn't bring himself to articulate any of them fully. "You know *why*."

"To figure out why you dumped a beautiful, in-the-flesh woman to carry on with a hoodlum?" Ronnie teased, although he wasn't sure how fun this was anymore—to either of them.

Zach sat down hard on the carpeted floor. This was it. The talk. The talk his therapist said he was supposed to have with her for months. Of course, poor Dr. Webster thought that Ronnie was just a shy, Internet divorcée. The doctor had no idea that they were living a real-life *West Side Story*.

"You know, I've kind of adjusted to the whole hoodlum aspect," Zach said. "It's the lack of the in-the-flesh part that's not so fun anymore."

Mötley Crüe began to play as the silence stretched out, and then Ronnie gave a curt response. "I agree."

He took a deep breath before he cast the die that might change his life forever. "The real reason I agreed to go to Skip's party was that it would give me a good excuse to be off American soil for the weekend."

"Your badge is pretty much *useless* in Mexico."

"Yes, it is."

Zach could almost hear the wheels in Ronnie's head spinning. He had a lot to lose if this meeting didn't go well. But Ronnie? Her life was potentially on the line.

"Just because you don't have official standing in Mexico doesn't mean that you couldn't coordinate with the *Federales* to have me arrested."

"I wouldn't do that," he said, trying to reassure her.

"You job is your life, and your job is to catch me."

A year ago, she would have been ever so right. But now? Tonight, when he ached to see her lips turn up in a smile?

"When I'm on duty, yeah it is. But off duty?" He paused. This was so whacked out. Nothing about this made sense, yet somehow, it was about the only thing that felt right to him. "I think I'm proving right now that I can separate the two."

Another long pause on her end. While the silence grated, there was nothing else for him to say. He had made his case. It was up to her to believe him or not.

Finally, she sighed. "Even if I believe your Kansas-honest face and we meet, what then?" she said.

Zach relaxed against the wall. This might actually work. "We talk."

"Okay, dude, if I'm going to risk getting executed for treason, there had better be more than talking involved in this rendezvous."

He chuckled. If his dream last night was any indication, Ronnie didn't need to worry about the rest. "Trust me, if the talking part goes well, there will be way more going on, but we've got to meet face to face first."

All playfulness vanished from her voice. He'd never heard her tone so uncertain. "I don't know…"

Hearing her sound so vulnerable made him want to be with her even more, but that also made him that much more impatient with this phone-pseudo-romance crap.

"Is this really satisfying anymore?" he asked, then hurried on without waiting for her answer. "At first, this felt exciting and dangerous, but now…" Zach was surprised when the words came out of his mouth. "Now, it just hurts." Was it time to be this honest? "All I want to do every night is curl up in bed with you and kiss the top of your head before we go to sleep."

"Okay, dude, if I'm going to risk getting executed—"

"I meant after we do the other stuff," Zach stated, just a little exasperated. Ronnie could spin a conversation about terminal cancer into a joke if she wanted to. But tonight, they needed to actually make progress.

"So?" he asked.

Again, the quiet, concerned side of Ronnie came out. "What if…Well, what if the talking doesn't go so well?"

The answer to that question was easy. She might not like the answer, though. "Then I'll get shit-faced at the party, sleep off the hangover on Sunday, and start hunting you again on Monday."

Her response was a lighthearted, "Okay."

Ugh. This had to get resolved. Zach pressed, "I mean, we've got to see if this connection we feel is—"

"I said, *okay*."

"Damn it, Ronnie, hear me out. We've got to—"

* * *

"Zach!" Ronnie interrupted. When that boy climbed onto his high horse, he just didn't want to come down. "I said okay, *okay*?" I'll meet you in Ciudad Juarez."

"Oh," he said, and then paused. "Really?"

She couldn't help but laugh. Ronnie was certain that was the last thing he thought she was going to say. "Really."

"Wow."

"With a capital 'W,' " she replied. God, how she wished that she had a video feed. Wait. In a few hours, she wouldn't need one. They would be meeting in Mexico. Her stomach flipped, churning up all those butterflies.

"Okay, then," Zach's drawl coming out. "Well..."

The guy was obviously still reeling. Good. She liked surprising him. "We should both get to bed. We've got a big day tomorrow."

"Yeah, right. Okay."

"Night, Zach," Ronnie said as she turned off the connection. She didn't want his freaking out to douse her buzz. How long had she wanted this? How many times, like a teenage girl swooning over a teacher, did she look at his picture and imagine kissing him? But just like that young girl, Ronnie never thought that she would live the dream.

God, did she even *remember* how to kiss? It had been so very long that she feared she'd screw it up. When did you part your lips? What in the hell did you do with your tongue, anyway? And even though she loved to tease him about his sexual hang-ups, she had a few concerns of her own. Not that long ago, he'd been with Miss-Julia-I've-Won-Every-Beauty-Contest-I've-Entered-And-Even-Some-I-Didn't. How was she going to compare to that?

Why in the hell hadn't she done crunches this morning?

* * *

Amanda walked by Henderson's office yet again. Ever since he finished his teleconference with the president, dozens of doctors had flowed through his door—giving reports and taking orders. Six people were still knotted around his desk.

Even though she hadn't been summoned, Amanda paced the hallways. It went against her introversion to be so bold, but she had no other option. She had to convince the director that she wasn't a crackpot. She was trying to stop the worst epidemic that the world had ever seen. Unfortunately, it was rhetoric like that which made people skeptical.

She hovered near the director's door as the researchers slowly melted away. Once the room cleared, Amanda still didn't enter. Who was she to keep pestering the director? But Amanda had to know what transpired in that meeting. Had Henderson presented even a single one of her theories to the president?

"I can't decide if you are the little chicken who thought the sky was falling or a well-informed stalker," the director said without even looking up from his desk.

Amanda hadn't even thought he knew she was there. "You're not blond," she mumbled as she worked up the courage to step forward.

"I'm sorry?"

Oh, God, had she said that out loud? How was she going to get out of this one?

"You did respond, did you not?" the director asked as he looked up from his paperwork. The crinkle at the edge of his eyes took away any sting in his words.

Cheeks reddening, Amanda cleared her throat. "I'm partial to blonds."

The older man chuckled and nodded, as if she had actually said something funny. "Well, glad to know that I'm safe from your obsession, but I'm afraid that makes you a doomsdayer."

"Or I'm the only correct person on your staff," she said before she could stop herself. Where did she get the boldness today? But while she had it, Amanda challenged, "Did you even bring up the subject of suspending incoming European flights?"

The humor left Henderson's eyes. "Do you know how many of those flights are scheduled in the next twenty-four hours alone?"

Without hesitation, Amanda answered. "One hundred and seventy-nine planes with an average of 212 passengers, each for a grand total of 39,000 chances that the plague is on its way."

"We are doing everything we can," the director stated, sounding as tired as Amanda felt.

Still, she couldn't stop herself. "So, are we turning planes back in the air? Refusing to let them land?"

"Dr. Rolph…"

She'd heard that tone before. From practically every professor she had ever had. So, she was well prepared for it. She brought props. And lots of them. Amanda pulled up map after pandemic map on her iPad, dating to the twelve hundreds.

His lips thinned to a tight line. "I might be shy of a week on this job, but I assure you, I am aware of the eighty-year pandemic cycle that the planet goes through."

"Yes, but have you ever asked yourself why?"

"Why, what?"

Amanda arranged the maps in chronological order. "Why *eighty* years? Why is the influenza virus so adept at changing its genetic code and thereby its protein markers? So adept that last year's vaccine is useless?"

Again, could the director sound any more tired? "Far greater men, and women, have asked that question and settled on the fact that it is natural selection."

"Then where did this plague acquire its resistance to antibiotics? Are you trying to tell me that we were overtreating the squirrel population?"

"Dr. Rolph, what you are suggesting is—"

Amanda knew where he was going and had to cut him off. "Is that this new plague has been genetically engineered, weaponized, and then purposefully released."

"Yes, *that* suggestion," he said, combing his thick fingers through his hair. "In certain circles, such a claim would be considered grounds for dismissal."

Stepping closer, Amanda tried to pour every ounce of confidence into her words. "They have the medical knowledge to do this. They have the dedication—"

"Who are *they*?" he demanded.

"I don't know, but…" That was the one factor missing in her theory. Who would do such a thing? But just because she didn't know the group's name, that didn't mean they didn't exist. "Mark my words. By 0900, we will have our first case in the States. By noon, several clusters. By this time tomorrow? You'll get to see what a real panic looks like."

Henderson searched her face. "How can you be so sure?"

Amanda looked over the dozens of maps representing so many years. So many dead. So many chances to experiment without scrutiny.

"Because they've had centuries to practice."

* * *

The sky was still black as Lino's plane landed at John F. Kennedy International Airport. Even the time difference worked in his favor. Before they could even pull up to the gate, several passengers were unbuckling their seat belts and reaching for the overhead compartment. Lino grinned. These braggarts would receive the highest dose of contagion.

While the rest of the passengers were busy jostling for their luggage, Lino sat quietly. Where could they go? All this rushing and jockeying for position—as if it would get them off the plane any sooner. You could almost hear them bleat as they waited impatiently in the aisle. But soon, very soon, you would hear them moaning, begging for death.

Oh, how Lino wished he could see their overanxious faces then. The young man surveyed the passengers around him, counting them off in his head. *One, two, three, four.* If this contagion did its job, one of those four would be dead. He counted another set and studied their faces. Not one of them thought that they were going to die within the next week. Many of them would spread the Black Death to those closest to them. They would know the horror of watching their families and friends fall sick around them.

Finally, the hatch opened, and the sheep began their exit. Lino waited until the knot had dispersed, and then, making certain his hand was moist, he dragged his palm along the top of the seats. One could never be too thorough. This task was too important to leave anything to chance.

Once inside the terminal, Lino was struck with how quiet and still the huge concourse was in the early-morning hours. Almost churchlike. A cough from one of the exiting passengers echoed off the high ceilings. Lino felt a great sense of satisfaction course through him. It was so rewarding to see your handiwork come to fruition.

He was so preoccupied by his sense of fulfillment that he almost missed the unscheduled contact. Anyone else would have passed by the security guard unaware, but Lino could see in the woman's eyes that she had a soul that could watch millions drop around her, and she would stand unflinching. Here was one of his own.

Diverting his course, he approached her, flavoring his English with more accent than his cultured education usually allowed. "Madame, can you direct me to this gate?" he asked, showing her his ticket to Los Angeles. She took the document and studied it before she answered.

"Of course, sir," she responded and raised her arm to point to the left. The casual action pulled back her sleeve, revealing three short lines of tattooed symbols on her wrist. Tattooed, not carved. She was an acolyte, not yet anointed. Despite his disdain for her rank, the guard still served her purpose. He scanned the message again, but it still did not make sense. He was supposed to fly to the West Coast in order to spread the plague from both shores. His eyes flickered to hers, asking the unspoken question.

"You'd best hurry, sir, or you'll miss your flight."

The guard handed him back his ticket. Only it wasn't his ticket. So there was no mistake. The plan had changed. Another challenge.

"Good luck," she said before she walked away.

Lino straightened his back. He would need no luck. He was anointed in blood. He was chosen. But this was no time to rest on his laurels. He had a connecting flight to El Paso to catch.

CHAPTER 7

Plum Island
9:19 a.m., EST

"Dr. Rolph?" a voice asked.

Amanda started awake, jerking her face off her pile of papers. Unfortunately, one CIA briefing had become glued to her lip by dried saliva. And of course, Dr. Henderson was at her door.

"Yes, sir," she said, not knowing why she nearly saluted. It must have been the nearly seventy-two hours without any real sleep.

"I need you to pack up," he said as he brought his tall, wide frame into her tiny, cramped office.

If his presence had not awakened her, his words certainly did. She scrambled to walk back her previous wild theory. Make that wild *theories*. As much as her new post intimidated her, she did not want to leave so soon.

"Sir, if you will just let me explain—"

He shook his salt-and-pepper head. "Just pack."

How Amanda hated being the damned harbinger of doom. Why had she forced her conjectures on her new boss? *Why?* She glanced out to her assistant's desk to find Jennifer packing as well.

At least they could walk out of the building together.

She opened her mouth to argue, but then shut it again. There was no point. By the set of Henderson's shoulders, she could tell his mind was made up.

Sagging under the weight of exhaustion and humiliation, Amanda bent her head. "And whom should I forward all of my data to?"

"Forward?" Henderson asked.

Oh, God. They didn't even want her data? Great. She would be transferred to Michigan to root out Starry-Eyed Duck Syndrome.

"I'll just gather my stuff," she mumbled, rising as she opened her desk drawer. "Do you want security to escort me out?"

Henderson squinted his bloodshot eyes. "What in damnation are you talking about?"

Amanda's eyes shifted from Henderson to her assistant at the door. Jennifer's arms were overloaded with files as she balanced a three-hole punch and stapler under her chin. If they were being fired, Amanda doubted they were going to let Jennifer take off with the best three-hole punch on the island.

"I'm not fired?"

Breath whistled through Henderson's pinched nose as he shook his head. "Clearly, you haven't heard."

"Heard?" Amanda parroted, not knowing what else to say.

"The first American case of the plague." Henderson grabbed a remote control off her desk and turned on the overhead screen. "Reported at 9:18 this morning."

Amanda gulped as Henderson flipped through several channels, all reporting the same thing. "The plague is here."

She looked back at her boss. "Where?" she asked, not needing to qualify where she meant.

"A passenger off a flight from Venice."

Amanda sat down. Hard.

"We are moving you from these offices to the main conference room, where you'll have another dozen assistants to sift through all of the data," Henderson said, but Amanda barely heard him.

Being a harbinger of doom was bad.

Being right? Even worse.

* * *

Quirk stood on his tippy-toes trying to spot Ronnie. Why did she always do this? Wait until the last conceivable moment to board? After all, she had left the cold room at what, 10:00 last night? While he had been up half the night rooting through the carnage of their near miss. Besides, just assessing the damage done, he had to reassure himself that the components could indeed be fixed. He had the knowledge. He had the technology. Making sure his cyber babies kept a positive mental attitude could be time-consuming.

Quirk had fallen asleep between a CPU and a high-speed router. Then at the crack of dawn, he was up, shipping the myriad of components to the States. Even the ones damaged beyond repair would go home for a proper burial.

He looked down at the tickets. Ten o'clock a.m. He looked at his watch. Nine forty. As he was searching the crowd, a man bumped right into him, and then stayed there. Quirk glared down at the squat Mexican, but he didn't budge.

"Um, el personal-o space-o?" Quirk asked, but the man just stood there. Having no greater depth of the Spanish language, it was he who moved to the left to get some breathing room.

Well, not exactly breathing room. The airport was crammed with under-bathed Latin Americans. The stench was so thick that Quirk remembered why he had started to develop nose plugs that could pass as fashion accessories. And given that body odor was a product of bacterial growth, he didn't like to be uncouth, but *ay, chihuahua!* These people were walking pathogen factories.

Which reminded him…

Despite that he was anxious to find Ronnie, Quirk checked his phone.

It is here was still the last text from his CDC BFF. The plague. It had reached North America. New York, in fact. How long until the Black Death cast its long shadow down Mexico way?

Quirk turned to the television screen. All morning long, they had been running plague reports. Granted, these were in Spanish, but Quirk could spot a boil in any language. This show was obviously going over the early signs of the disease. With practiced routine, he went through the checklist.

Fever. Nope.

Sub-mandibular lymph nodes enlarged? Nope.

Blackened patches of skin? Nope.

The patient on the screen stuck out his tongue. It was covered with the worst yellow film. *Yellow* film? Quirk nearly panicked. Jennifer hadn't informed him that was one of the early signs! He hadn't checked it in the mirror this morning. He would have to give Jennifer, his CDC BFF, a scolding—that is, once he found someone to check his tongue. Quirk glanced left, then right. Where was Ronnie when he needed her? He turned back to the rotund gentleman.

"Excuse me?"

"*No hablo inglés.*"

"No kidding," Quirk said, glancing around the crowd. No one looked especially *inglés* equipped. So he stuck his tongue out at the man, mumbling, "Yellowo filmo?"

"Really, Quirk, you need to work on your pickup lines."

He turned back to find his boss right behind him. Quirk kept his tongue out, slurring his words. "Is it yellow?"

Ronnie just shook her head. "Seriously, Quirk, butch up."

She came *this* late, and then gave him attitude? "Where have you been?" he demanded.

"Buying our tickets."

"Are you sun-addled?" Quirk asked as he pulled the travel documents out of his very stylish leather bag. "I've got them right here. I *always* have them right here."

"Yeah, to Acapulco, but we're going to Ciudad Juarez," Ronnie said as the crowd dispersed and boarding began.

Quirk tilted his head. Geniuses could be so damn exasperating. "Is this a real place, Ronnie, or one you made up in your head?"

"We're going to Ciudad Juarez."

"No. Real or not, we are going to Acapulco," Quirk insisted.

An airline employee nodded toward them. "*Señor. Señorita.* You board?"

Quirk put a finger up to "hold" the employee as he turned to Ronnie. "Ciudad Juarez wouldn't happen to be anywhere near El Paso, Texas, would it?"

Ronnie tried to look innocent, but it didn't come naturally to her. "In the general vicinity."

Oh, he was pissed! After everything that happened last night, Ronnie was just now learning that they had to *think* with their big heads. "This is about *him*, isn't it?"

Ronnie gave up on her attempt at naïveté and threw up her hands. "Fine. Go to Acapulco. I'll catch up with you in Los Angeles."

"Has it even occurred to you that he is setting you up? That he's luring you there?"

Ronnie was right back in his face. "How do you even know that he asked me?"

Quirk pulled out the ultimate gay power move—the hand on the hip. "Because you talked to him last night."

"You hung up on—"

"No," he said firmly. The charade was over. The "don't ask, don't tell" phase of this little flirtation was over. "You talked to him after you got back to the hotel room."

"What?" She actually sounded flustered, but his boss must have seen the truth in his eyes. He wasn't bluffing. "I mean, how would you—"

"Darling, did you really think you could spend forty million dollars to develop a point-to-point communications device without me knowing about it?"

Ronnie started backpedaling. Obviously, this was not how she expected this conversation to go. "I just—"

He showed his palm. "Don't." He lowered his hand. "We'll deal with my hurt feelings over being left out, excluded, dissed, and all the abandonment issues this brings up for me later. Right now, I just need you to get your lack-of-squats ass on that plane."

"I can't." Her eyes pleaded with him to understand. "I'm going to meet him."

Even though the airline employee hovered just out of hearing range, the two stood in strained silence. Ronnie had lied to him. She was jeopardizing both of their lives, and didn't even have the courtesy to inform before the fact. In Buffy's immortal words, "Love, man, it makes you do the wacky." Well, it was Quirk's job to de-whack her.

"You *do* realize that Mexico has a well-enforced extradition treaty with the United States?"

But Ronnie stood her ground. "Yes, I do. But just like you risk the White Party every year, I've got to do this."

"Excuse me, but last call," another gate employee said with a thick accent.

Quirk picked up his bags and looked Ronnie squarely in the eye. "Go to your doom. I'm going to the land of bronzed men."

Ronnie just gazed downward, so he turned away from her. But that wasn't all he had to say. "And, just so you know, had I developed the technology rather than you outsourcing it, the music wouldn't skip every time you made a call."

Seriously, what was she doing trying to have a meaningful relationship with Dudley Do-Right, no matter how hot he was? With a burst of self-righteous anger and great aplomb, Quirk strode onto the plane, heading for anonymous sex.

* * *

Francois pretended to sleep. It was not difficult, since the doctor had heavily sedated him to keep him from injuring himself. But there had been no need. The symbols were etched. His task was documented. Until he could burn that damnable Picasso, there was no need to further cut himself. But the agents could not fathom this fact, so they kept a sharp eye on him. They constantly monitored his every movement.

That is, until now. Now the gaggle of agents was clustered around the television. The broadcast drifted across the room. It seemed that the first case of the bubonic plague had crossed the pond. The bull pen was abuzz with anxiety, fear, and excitement.

Americans. Francois snorted before he could stop himself, and then had to cover his action—as if he were just snoring. But the Americans were just so damned arrogant. So certain that an ocean on either coast would keep all danger away. It hadn't worked in either Great War, and it didn't work this time.

Those who were afraid had every right to be. Most likely, they were men or women with children. The Black Death always took a heavy toll, but its most caustic effects were upon the young. Those who were excited were just blasted fools. There was no fighting this plague. No amount of sharpshooting could stop the bacterium from rolling across the country unchecked.

Francois had a difficult time hearing the entirety of the report, as some agents were busy theorizing out loud, while the rest were shushing them. But truly, the Frenchman didn't need to hear the details. He knew enough.

The first case had been diagnosed in a woman who had just arrived in New York from Venice. It could mean only one thing.

The Hidden Hand was here.

He was here.

Francois did not have much time left.

* * *

Ronnie had to shove hard to get her bag into the overhead compartment. She'd packed her entire wardrobe for this little sojourn. Not that she had any idea what she was going to wear. In her line of work, she didn't have much reason to get all gussied up. She looked over her shoulder down the long aisle. No Quirk. His plane had taken off over three hours ago. He was probably touching down in Acapulco right about now, but damn, she could use the gay gene right about now.

Realizing that she was holding up the final boarding, Ronnie sat down in her seat and pulled out a *Cosmopolitan* she'd bought in the terminal. It was in Spanish, but she got the gist fairly well. To get a man, you had to look like a caffeinated model and be a sex goddess. She did not have either strength going for her. Flipping through the pages, Ronnie became very aware of exactly how little she had going for her. Bulimia was suddenly becoming a lifestyle option.

A commotion toward the front of the plane pulled her attention away from the magazine. *Come on*, she thought. They were already fifteen minutes behind because of mechanical difficulties, which was cutting into her panic time. She wanted to get to the bar early and have a few margaritas before Zach arrived. If you were going to get horribly rejected, it was best to do it slightly toasted.

Then she heard an ever-so-effeminate voice whine, "But this is an emergency!"

It couldn't be! But there was Quirk, hands full of shopping bags trying to squeeze past the flight crew. They were never going to let him on with all those carry-ons, but Quirk leaned into the flight attendant's ear and whispered something to make her blush. Still flustered, the woman let him by. If her assistant ever turned his sights toward conquering the females, he would have it made.

After a dozen "sorrys," Quirk was at her row. She couldn't hide her relief.

"I thought you had your heart set on a cabana boy?"

"Somebody's got to protect you from yourself."

Ronnie laughed for the first time in this nerve-racking day. "Yeah, right. You realized if Zach did show up and didn't arrest me, that he'd be looking mighty fine."

Quirk held up his phone and snapped a picture. "You're going to want to capture the memories." He looked down at the screen, and then at her. "You aren't seriously going to wear *that*, are you?"

Under his critical gaze, Ronnie squirmed, but was luckily rescued by the flight attendant, who urged him to stow his numerous bags in the overhead compartment.

"More phones?" Ronnie teased, but Quirk raised an eyebrow as he opened one of the bags.

Her assistant pulled out the skimpiest of skimpy red dresses, then another in black, and another in dark purple.

"Sweetie, if he is going to risk getting fired or even imprisoned for meeting you, then I am going to make sure that he doesn't regret it."

* * *

Zach pulled out the black turtleneck from his bag. Too pretentious. Too George Clooney. Although…Damn it, but guys on the cover of *GQ* were usually wearing one. He shoved the garment back in the bag. It was always good to keep your options open.

He stared at the box of condoms on the nightstand. The pack was brand spanking new. Its plastic wrap was still intact. Jesus, if he brought them along, would it make him look like a hound dog? Would Ronnie get the mistaken impression that sex was the only reason he had wanted to meet her? But what was the other option? If things did go according to plan, would they find some run-down, all-night pharmacy south of the border?

After only a second of pondering the second option, Zach tossed the prophylactics into his bag. Be prepared. That was his motto, but he doubted it was what his Boy Scout leader had in mind.

The turtleneck came out again. He wasn't posing for the cover of a magazine, after all. But if he didn't bring it, what would he wear Sunday when they went out? Zach snorted. Who was he kidding? Did he have any right to think the cop and robber would ever have a second date?

Oh, how he hated his therapist right about now. This was all Dr. Webster's fault. The guy wouldn't stop harping about fantasy projections and fears of intimacy. Every time Zach would complain about Ronnie, the good doctor would always turn the topic around to focus on him. Why was *he* so afraid to meet? Why was *Zach* reluctant to bring the relationship into the real world?

Well, maybe, just maybe, it was because someday he might be forced to arrest her ass. But, of course, he couldn't say that to Webster. Instead, he'd gone and invited Ronnie to meet him, and it hadn't been until after the high had worn off that he remembered that he was breaking about fifteen federal laws.

Bad FBI agent! Bad!

But what good was he to the Bureau when his heart was divided like this? He couldn't stop thinking about her, and not in a "how do I apprehend a fugitive?" kind of way. More in a "How do your eyelashes glisten in the morning?" kind of way.

Okay, that was it. No more internal arguing. No more doubt. No more inner turmoil. He was going, and that was that. Tucking the turtleneck back in before he zipped his bag closed, Zach checked his watch. Crap. He was running late. Well, not exactly late. Late as in he was tapping into the three-hour lead time he had given himself. On the weekend, traffic across the border could be unpredictable, and he wanted to have plenty of time to find the bar and knock back a few beers to take the edge off before she arrived.

Before he could start doubting himself again, Zach headed for the door. Alarm set and keys in hand, he left the house and strode toward his car. Bag in the trunk, and he was ready to leave. But as he opened the car, he noticed a little "Welcome to Our House" garden sign by the front door. A bunny chewed on a cute little carrot. He'd walked past that thing every day for months, and had forgotten it was even there. The last of Julia's decorating touches.

He knelt, pulled the sign from the ground, and chucked it in the trash can. That phase of his life was over.

Zach settled in behind the wheel and went to start the engine when the passenger side door opened. His hand instinctively flew to his gun, which wasn't there. Luckily, the intruder was just Grant.

"What do you want, Fifer?"

The younger agent hopped into the car and had on his seat belt before answering. "Coming to your cousin's party with you."

"You're not invited. Get out."

"Is that a way to treat a trusted colleague, Hunt?"

"Get out."

Grant looked him up and down. "You know, you actually look somewhat fashionable, for once. And to go to a bawdy bachelor party?"

Zach's teeth ground against one another. "Get out."

"Is that really hair product in your hair?"

"Get out."

"And if I am not mistaken, and I seldom am, you got a manicure this morning."

Unconsciously, Zach pulled his hands back from the wheel. How in the hell could Grant miss a shell casing lying in the middle of the street, but somehow know that Zach's nails *were* buffed?

"Get out."

"Hey, all I'm saying is you are looking to get laid tonight, my friend."

"Get out."

Grant put his head back on the SUV's headrest. "Make me."

Zach was certain that he was grinding the enamel off his teeth. He knew he doth protest too much. Grant pulled this kind of crap all the time, and Zach usually just let it slide. After all, to Fifer it was just a two-hour drive to a bachelor party where they would split up until the drive home. But wait! That was his out.

"I'm planning on staying the weekend."

But Grant's face just lit up as he pulled his bag into the car. "Me, too!"

Zach groaned as Grant flipped through the SUV's music selection. "Hey, you got any Snoop Dogg in here?"

This was going to be a really, really, *really* long drive.

CHAPTER 8

Plum Island
10:44 a.m., EST

Amanda stared at the electron microscope picture of the bacterium, *Yersinia pestis,* extracted from a New York plague victim. The pudgy bacterium looked so innocent. Like any other of the millions of Gram-negative bacteria in the body. But this one packed a punch.

Many of her colleagues in this room would argue with her anthropomorphizing a microscopic organ. Was *Yersinia pestis* any more sinister by nature than *Lactobacillus*, the bacterium that helped humans to digest milk? Did *Yersinia pestis* take pleasure in the havoc it wreaked?

To Amanda, the bacterium certainly seemed to. Was it by intelligent design or selection of the meanest that *Yersinia pestis* found the nearly perfect host in the common flea? The bacterium somehow figured out how to hitch a ride on the bloodsucking parasites. Jumping from infected host to new victim in the flea's saliva. Okay, so *Yersinia pestis* had to count on the fact that fleas regurgitated into their bites, but still it was a pretty slick operation.

Add in the fact that because of superstition, all cats—not just black cats—were killed off by the droves in medieval Europe. Which led to an overpopulation of rats, which led to an overpopulation of fleas, and one could see how *Yersinia pestis* could spread so rampantly through the known world.

And *Yersinia pestis* wasn't just clever, but ambitious as well. The reason the plague took such a heavy toll, becoming the Black Death, was the fact that the bacteria attacked the body's immune system, killing or incapacitating the host's white cells. From there, they hit the bloodstream—spreading to every part of the body, destroying tissue as they went.

Forget about sharks. *Yersinia pestis* was a nearly perfect killing machine.

Jennifer walked in and set another picture beside the current plague bacterium. Amanda scanned the new photo. This sample dated back to the fourteen hundreds. *Yersinia pestis* pulled from the tooth pulp of long-dead Black Death victims. It is how scientists first established that the Gram-negative bacteria had been the culprit during the Middle Ages.

Wow, Jennifer was quick. The World Health Organization had just asked Plum Island to verify that the current *Yersinia pestis* was the same strain as the 1347 pandemic. Jennifer hadn't just looked up the files online, but had gone down into the basement and pulled the original reports.

Amanda scanned the documents quickly. Everything seemed to be lining up perfectly. Both the current bacteria and the 1347 plague carried all the same genetic markers. The same bipolar staining. The same negative uptake of indole. In every way, they seemed to be the same strain—except with one vital difference. This new strain was showing significant antibiotic resistance. Even to third-generation aminoglycoside?

Trying not to jump to conclusions that would get her laughed at, Amanda reread the results. It wasn't uncommon in this age of "give a pill for every sniffle" that bacteria had become more and more resistant to common-use antibiotics. Just look at the distant cousin of *Yersinia pestis*: *Mycobacterium tuberculosis*. That ancient bacterium could become resistant to an antibiotic over just the course of a two-month treatment window.

But how had *Yersinia pestis* developed resistance to an antibiotic it hadn't even seen before?

If this didn't support her theory regarding weaponization, what would?

"Thanks, Jennifer."

Her assistant gave her that look, though. Like, "Is that all you've got?"

Amanda studied the reports again. Except for the antibiotic resistance, they seemed the same. Jennifer pointed to the current strain's electron microscope picture. Then to the 1347's photo. They appeared to be identical, except…Wait.

The protein markers on the current *Yersinia pestis* seemed more prominent. Like way more prominent. Like three times as many markers as the 1347 photo.

Amanda sat up abruptly.

Whoever had done this was absolutely evil, yet outstandingly brilliant.

"Get Dr. Henderson," Amanda directed Jennifer. "He's got to see this."

* * *

Ronnie couldn't believe that she had let Quirk talk her into this. Banging another elbow on the airplane's bathroom stall, she cursed under her breath. Another bruise, and for what? She looked in the mirror. It was hopeless. Yet another low-cut, spaghetti-strapped nightmare. Her body shape wasn't meant for silk and satin. The fabric fell awkwardly off her not-quite-so-feminine broad shoulders. Usually, she liked being tall for a woman, but these dresses were cut for some petite little debutante without any cleavage.

The super-Wonderbra wasn't helping, either. Her breasts were a good two inches north of where they normally hung out. She tried to adjust the straps again, but the apparatus was determined to give her perky nipples.

"Well?" Quirk asked from outside the stall.

"I am *not* coming out in this Britney Spears reject."

Her assistant jiggled the door. He was intent to continue this little in-flight fashion show. "Let the audience decide."

Tentatively, Ronnie opened the lock and stepped out. Well, the men gave the thumbs-up, or more accurately, other anatomical appendages, to the dress. The women however, scowled. Ronnie stepped back into the cramped bathroom and threw the bolt.

"Okay, okay. That one was a little bold," Quirk admitted through the door as she ripped the dress off. "I'm telling you, try the black one."

Ronnie looked down at the forest of bags at her feet. "There are fifteen black ones in here."

"The one with the piping and long sleeves."

Even though she didn't know why she did it, Ronnie dug through the inventory. Luckily, only one dress fit that description. There was something different about this dress.

It felt soft on her skin, not all slippery. And the sleeves gave the garment a classier look, rather than the cocktail-whore look the rest had going for them.

"Well?" Quirk prompted.

Shimmying into the sleek, black dress, Ronnie was surprised at how well it fit. The thing might have sleeves, but they made up for that material by not really giving it a back. She could feel cool air all the way down to the rise of her buttocks. The front didn't waste much fabric, either. The neckline plunged down and ended just a hair's breadth from her bra's scalloped edge.

"I don't know…"

"Get out here!"

She was nervous about exiting. Not because they might like it, but because they might not. Ronnie never pictured herself as the type of woman to fill out a dress like this. Dresses like this were reserved for the über-pretty. The ones who didn't dream of electric sheep.

Opening the door, she was met with a rumbling of "ahs." Even the women nodded approvingly.

"We've got a winner," Quirk said then guided her back to their seats. "Now for some makeup." Before Ronnie could ask exactly what he had in mind, Quirk signaled to the flight attendant. "Yes, *señorita*, could you please have the pilot announce that everyone should close their shades, and have him turn off the cabin lights?"

"Excuse me?" she said.

"Lights-o off. Shades-o down."

Even though her words were accented, she made it very clear that she was fluent in English. "I understood your words, *señor*. I just did not believe you were saying them."

Ronnie tried to quiet him down, but Quirk would have none of it. "How else can I apply makeup worthy of a goddess in this harsh lighting?"

The flight attendant's eyebrow shot up. "Genius is always a burden, *señor*. Make do, like the rest of us."

Quirk seemed ready to go another round, but Ronnie pulled him down into his seat. "I just want some eyeliner and mascara, anyway."

Her assistant gave her one of those looks, then pulled out a case that would put Estée Lauder to shame. "I'm thinking that we should start with the gold."

Ronnie gripped Quirk's wrist. "If I end up looking like a transvestite, so help me…"

* * *

Francois remained with his head against the wall, listening to the room with his eyes blissfully closed. News report after news report covered the growing panic that spread from New York outward. Another dozen victims had been hospitalized, and they were not all from the same flight. The first case was not an anomaly. The Black Death was here. He had failed thrice.

When the front door opened, Francois cracked an eyelid open. But he could not have seen what he thought he had seen. Jerking upright, Francois stared straight ahead. He could not believe his luck. There it was. The painting. He had thought it beyond his reach. Stored in some dim evidence locker in downtown El Paso. How could it be in the same room as he?

Not ten feet from the bars that held him was the scorched canvas, sealed in plastic, and carried in by an older agent. But as much as he wished to rush forward and press his claim, the Frenchman knew he could not. They did not understand why he must have it. They did know what it held.

"Dude, get over it," the younger agent said to the older.

The gray-haired agent shook his head. "I'm telling you. They made me sign my life away."

The sandy-blond man shook his head. "The El Paso Police Department just doesn't want to be responsible if anything happens to it."

"My point, exactly. I was looking forward to my retirement benefits."

Francois couldn't help that his brow furrowed. Why would the local authorities release the painting to the Federal Bureau of Investigation? Why, in fact, was he in the Bureau's custody in the first place?

After the rapture of the fire, all was a blur until this morning. Francois had not questioned in whose custody he was in, only that he had failed. He had known it was a risk to set the painting on fire in the museum, but he sensed that time was constricting. Francois should have been at a local jail.

Why had the federal government taken an interest in a crazed old man?

* * *

Amanda studied the readout until her eyes almost bled. Every bit of data streaming in from New York and a dozen other cities only worsened her initial prognosis.

"Amanda?" a voice, seemingly distant and unimportant, spoke.

Startled back to reality, she found Dr. Henderson standing over her. "You said you had something to report?"

Wiping a tear from the corner of her eye, Amanda nodded, signaling Jennifer to bring up the latest information.

"We've got a problem."

"Just one?" the director said as he sat down.

She grinned at his attempted joke, but the theory Amanda was about to present was absolutely no laughing matter.

"The plague is definitively *not* natural."

Henderson stretched, yawning like a man who hadn't gotten any sleep in a very long time. "That is what you keep insisting."

"Now I have proof."

The director sat up. "You have my attention."

"And mine," Devlin said as he joined them near the monitor.

Good. She might need a little encouragement to get through this presentation.

"As you are aware," Amanda started, "the current theory for the New York flight victims is that they were all exposed in Venice." She waited until they nodded. "The only problem with that is the timeline doesn't add up."

Jennifer called up a listing of all the passengers on the red-eye flight. "You are also aware that quickest incubation period for the bubonic plague is twenty-four hours." Amanda pointed to the map showing where each of the passengers had been twenty-four hours from when the first victim became clinical. The dots were spread all over Europe, Russia, and even Africa. "How did all of these people come into contact with the plague in all of these disparate locations, then somehow all board the same plane?"

Devlin snorted, but Henderson nodded. "It would be statistically impossible."

"But what does that mean?" Devlin asked.

Her assistant fast-forwarded the passengers' trek to Venice until all the dots were clustered at the airport. "It means that someone infected them with a strain of *Yersenia pestis* that is much more virulent, moving through the latency phase faster, attacking the body with more force."

"That would imply a level of bioengineering that we are years away from," Henderson noted.

Normally the director would have been spot on, except for the fact that he wasn't. "Just look at how quickly our first New York victim became stricken and sought medical care." Jennifer brought up the medical record. "I mean, the problem with the plague is the fact that the first wave of symptoms seem to be nothing more than the average flu. It isn't until day two or three, when the lymph nodes in the groin and neck begin to swell, that people head to the hospital."

Henderson stood up and read the report aloud. "Upon admission, patient complained of high fever, 102 Fahrenheit, muscle cramping and flushed skin, especially on the extremities."

"If we agree that the infection must have occurred at the Venice airport, those symptoms occurred within nine hours."

Devlin looked from Amanda to the director, and then back at the screen. "I am no epidemiologist..." That was an understatement. "But if I were going to bioengineer a bug, wouldn't I want people walking around for longer not showing symptoms? Wouldn't it spread wider that way?"

Henderson looked Amanda's way.

"It would if you were relying on natural spread of the disease," Amanda explained.

"And if you weren't waiting for Mother Nature?"

Amanda looked at the new map that Jennifer displayed. Cases were springing up all over the country, Canada, and even Latin America. "Then you would be spreading the disease manually. Getting it onto as many airline passengers as you could and have it come on as quickly as it could…"

She nodded for Jennifer to hit the fast-forward button again. Red shot out across the United States, infecting nearly every corner of it. "So that the plague would spread like wildfire."

"I understand how that would augment the exposure to the plague, but you said the bacterium itself was weaponized? That this plague was creating symptoms and death far quicker?"

Amanda nodded for Jennifer to bring up the 1347 *Yersinia pestis* alongside the current plague. Her assistant had even colorized the protein markers—making the tremendous increase in them all the more stark.

Devlin looked clueless, but by Henderson's frown, he understood the implications all too well.

"The increased protein markers are a huge red flag to the immune system," Henderson said, although it seemed like it was more to himself than to anyone else.

"Um," Devlin said. "Isn't that a good thing? The faster this plague is recognized the faster the body can fight it?"

The director seemed lost in a world of his own, so Amanda answered. "Normally yes, but due to the ability of *Yersenia pestis* to invade and even kill the white cells, these markers are accelerating the plague's ability to destroy the host's immune system."

Everyone turned back to the screen.

"This isn't our ancestors' plague," Amanda stated as her assistant brought up a slide of US patient zero's neck—where a large, dark-stained boil already brewed under the skin. "This is a modern-day apocalypse."

Not even Devlin argued.

CHAPTER 9

US–Mexican Border
7:03 p.m., MST

Zach stepped on the gas. They watched the sun go down as they wasted over an hour at the border. His generous three-hour buffer had been whittled down to barely an hour. And with this traffic? He would be lucky to make it to the rendez-vous on time. Up ahead, a streetlight flashed red as car horns blared in the evening air. Zach felt his hands tighten on the wheel.

Nearly three hours of rap would have tested his patience on a good day. But today? Yet another Nelly song came on. The pulsing rhythm did nothing to soothe his agitation. He was ready to punch Grant in the face and shove his body from the car, but that might give away the fact that he was a bit on edge.

"Is that aftershave you're wearing?"

"Shut up."

"Dude, I am telling you. The chicks at this party won't even require you to bathe."

Zach shook his head. "You are pathetic."

"I am telling you, man, that's why your cousin is having the party on this side of the river. These whores, they'll do anything you ever read in *Hustler* and for dirt cheap."

"I'm so glad you are helping counteract that whole American pig tourist image we have," Again, Zach regretted that tonight, of all nights, Grant had decided to tag along.

Grant punched him in the shoulder. "No, dude. I was telling you this so you will relax. I know you're shit with the ladies, but tonight, tonight, you are guaranteed a score!"

If only Fifer knew what he was talking about.

* * *

"What did I tell you about frowning?" Quirk asked Ronnie as he elbowed a nice, little old Mexican grandmother out of their way, bringing them almost to the front of the plane. How long would it take to taxi and empty out a plane, anyway?

"We're going to be late," Ronnie said, echoing Quirk's internal impatience.

But Quirk couldn't let her know that he was just as worried as she was, so he tugged the edge of her dress to bring the V-neck down so it just kissed the top of her lace bra. "As we should be. Now think only neutral thoughts."

Ronnie didn't quite smile at that, but at least she wasn't frowning as the knot dispersed. Quickly, they made their way down the staircase to the tarmac. His boss was right, of course. They were going to be late, but Carson Kressley himself would pull the fashion laurels from Quirk's head if he did not complete the ensemble.

"Over here," Quirk urged as he pulled away from the crowd rushing toward the gate. Once away from prying eyes and cell-phone cameras, he pulled out a pair of stilettos. "Put these on."

"No! Quirk, damn it, we've got to—"

Before his boss could launch into an Aristotle-length diatribe about how late they were, Quirk pulled out the ultimate couture weapon. A mirror. But this was no ordinary mirror. He had obtained this precious object backstage from Versace himself. He unfolded it once, and then pulled out leaf after leaf until they interlocked into a nearly full-length mirror. The sight of herself dressed for a night out on the town shut Ronnie up in a big hurry. A hand flew to her lips in surprise.

Quirk gently urged the appendage away from her face. "Now, now. We have to watch the lip liner."

* * *

Zach gagged back a retch as they entered the "bar." Brothel, landfill dump, or pig farm would also have been accurate descriptions. He had to avert his eyes more than once as strippers bounced their wares rather enthusiastically.

"Zach! My man!" his cousin Skip slurred, as he stumbled over to him. "You came."

Not for you, Zach wanted to say, but didn't want to ruin the sixth-time-to-the-altar buzz that Skip had going on.

"And you brought an *amigo*!" his cousin shouted, even though he was standing all of two feet away.

"He's not my friend," Zach stated, but the two were already in a BFF hug.

Skip tried to draw them deeper into the debauchery. "Come and meet Consuela. She'll do all three of us for twenty bucks!"

Zach resisted the urge, which turned out not to be that difficult at all.

Instead, he let his cousin relieve him of Grant and searched the bar for Ronnie. Of course, he had absolutely no idea what she looked like, but he didn't think Ronnie was any of these washed up and dragged out "women," though.

Or at least he *hoped* not.

* * *

"*Andale*! Hurry!" Ronnie shouted as she hit the back of the taxi driver's seat. She hated to be *that* American tourist, but exactly how long could it take to get across town?

It must have been nearly eighty degrees, and even with all the windows rolled down, sweat trickled down her back. Horns sounded all around them, making it feel like they were center stage in a circus than the city's main thoroughfare.

"What did I tell you about frowning?" Quirk said as he powdered her forehead once again. "I've put wrinkle-filling foundation on you, but darling, it can't overcome furrows."

Well, then, what did glaring do for her makeup? Ronnie wondered as she shot Quirk a harsh glance. "*Andale!*"

The dress constricted her midriff. She could barely feel her legs anymore. And the shoes? She had walked, like, two steps in them, and she swore that she had the beginnings of

CAROLYN MCCRAY

bunions. Each time she looked up she felt like she had blinders on, but they were just the false eyelashes Quirk had applied.

He, *he* was happy for the delay. All the more time to make her into Frankenstein's monster.

She looked at her watch again. Eight thirty-five. She had kept Zach waiting for over a half an hour. Would he wait for her?

As the taxi finally moved forward another two and a half feet, they could finally see what had caused the traffic jam. An overturned goat cart. Yes, a cart pulled by goats. This wasn't happening. She could not possibly miss her one chance to meet Zach over an accident with goats.

She smacked the driver's seat again.

Please don't let it be over because of goats.

* * *

"Honey, honey," Quirk tried to reassure her. "Girls are allowed. No. Girls are *expected* to be fashionably late." He eased her back into the seat. "Plus, putting on lip liner and shouting orders are mutually exclusive." When she went to argue he cocked his head. "So, stop with the talking!"

He could feel her squirm, though. She was a bundle of nervous energy as the hairs on her forearm stood up, and her jaw moved without her saying anything. Had he known traffic was going to be like this, he would have dropped a Valium, or two, into her drink on the plane. Hell, he would have dropped one himself.

Before he could stop her, Ronnie leaned forward and punished the poor plastic seat again. "*Andale!*"

"Hon, I don't even think that's Mexican." He did his best to quiet her. "Settle down, darling. You are going to mess up your hair."

Did she not understand that perfectly coiffed hair required absolute stillness? In this humidity, they would be lucky to get an hour out of the two bottles of hair spray that he put on that mane of hers.

They rolled, gaining speed until the car in front of them slammed on the brakes. They crashed into its rear bumper. Quirk barely kept the powder from spilling all over Ronnie's smoking-hot black dress. He was not going to let a little traffic accident ruin that couture.

Their driver launched out of the taxi shaking his fist, yelling something about a "*bendajo*."

"That's it!" Ronnie said as she opened the car door.

She was out of the car, wobbling down the street.

"You can't run in stilettos!" Quirk yelled after her as he gathered their thousand bags.

Throwing payment onto the driver's seat, he hightailed it after Ronnie.

Heteros.

* * *

"Look over here!" Grant yelled.

However, it wasn't so much "over here" as it was right in front of Zach on the bar. Grant doing Jell-O shots off of one of the working girl's...Well, "leaving nothing to the imagination" was coined for just such an occasion. Some things you just couldn't *unsee.*

As much as you wanted to.

He checked his watch again. Eight forty-nine. There was late, and then there was "stood up" late. Zach dug his iPod out from his pocket. It still just showed Poison's "Every Rose Has Its Thorn" waiting to be cued up. No message from Ronnie.

Not that he expected there to be. Communications outside their scheduled times was strictly on a 9-1-1 basis. He'd barely avoided having his hand blown off last night just trying to explain to Ronnie about Julia.

Was that why Ronnie wasn't here? Julia? Had Ronnie had second thoughts about meeting a guy who had ditched his fiancée for a voice over the line? A felon's voice, no less?

The guy next to him coughed and coughed until he hacked up something onto the bar. Awesome. And if Zach spent much more time in here with the smoke and grime, he too would be coughing up some asbestos lung cheese. To help Zach make up his mind, someone lit up a stogie. The acrid smoke stung his eyes.

Swigging back the last of his beer, Zach rose from his stool and headed toward the back of the bar. Grant called after him, "Where you going?"

"Outside."

Grant laughed as only a drunk could laugh. "What? To meet your mystery lover-girl?"

"Shut up," Zach snapped more out of embarrassment than anger.

Pushing past Skip and his new foursome, Zach made his way out into the alley. With the foul stench rising from the open sewer, maybe he should have gone out the front door. But with the ladies of the night prowling and cars honking, Zach thought he might find some peace out here.

But just like the rest of the evening, this idea was shit, too.

The door burst open as a young woman staggered out the door, drunk off her ass. Was this chick even eighteen?

She practically fell into the wall, doubling over, retching.

Really? This just topped the night.

He wanted to ignore her, but his mother's frowning face wouldn't leave him alone. What did she always say? "Being a gentleman, especially when you didn't feel like being a gentleman, is the measure of a man." He wasn't quite sure if this was the exact situation she had in mind, but he couldn't just let the girl puke all over herself.

Zach went over and cautiously pulled her hair back. It was the least that he could do. She staggered forward another step, lurching with each hurl. Finally, she stopped, gasping and crying. He tried to urge her back to the bar, when she folded herself in his arms.

Yep, this is what you got when you tried to help out. Puke on your brand new turtleneck. Firmly, he put his hands on her shoulders and backed her away.

"Okay, that is not how a lady behaves toward a gentleman."

Suddenly, she lashed out with her elbow, clocking him on the jaw. Reeling back, Zach felt his chin. That was going to bruise.

"What the…?"

Was she just flailing, or…

The roundhouse kick to his belly pretty much proved that the first blow wasn't an accident. He put an arm up to block the next kick, but she hammered away.

"I don't know what your drama is, lady, daddy issues or whatever, but you had better lay off."

She did anything but that. Instead, she hauled back and punched him square in the mouth, splitting open his lip. He dabbed the blood away. Unfortunately, his mother also taught him never to hit a woman. *Ever.*

"I got a barber shave this morning, just so I wouldn't have any nicks." Zach spun out of the way of a groin kick. "That's it!"

What his mother didn't know wouldn't hurt her.

"On a night like tonight, you do *not* mess with a man's equipment!"

He waited until she opened up her midriff for a kick, and then landed a punch to her belly. She doubled over with a groan, yet still came out swinging. He blocked another blow and landed a right hook to her jaw. As she dropped, Zach caught her before she hit the pavement.

Just because he was protecting himself, didn't mean he had to be rude.

What did she think? That he was her john, and she could just roll him?

No matter why the girl had attacked him, this was not going to look good if Ronnie came around the corner. You know, him dragging a beat-up hooker down an alley and all. However, if there was one woman who might understand, it was Ronnie.

That is, if she ever showed up.

Hooking his arms under the woman's, Zach hefted her down the alley. He couldn't just leave her here, exposed and vulnerable.

He might have heard the squeak of a sole sooner if he hadn't been cursing his luck so loudly. Zach's hand flew to his belt—only it was empty. *Mexican* alley. Right. Therefore, no gun. Once he heard the second footfall, Zach was releasing his grip on the girl and came around swinging.

He clocked one guy unawares, sending the large thug reeling backward. The second wasn't quite so easy, but Zach got a backhanded slap in before following up with a lashing kick to the guy's kneecap.

The first man recovered pretty damn quickly and tackled Zach from the side, but he was able to use the momentum to swing the attacker around, and slam him against the crumbling brick wall. An elbow to the solar plexus doubled the guy over.

Shoving himself off the wall, Zach turned to his other attacker. This time, the guy wasn't quite so eager to rush him. Perfect. Zach did the rushing, but held back his blow until he saw the other guy commit his left fist. Which meant Zach came in with a low swing to the guy's right side.

Knocked off-balance, the attacker stumbled, and Zach kicked the guy's hip, hard, knocking him to his knees.

Now to get the hell out of here and find out what—

The prongs of the Taser bit into his shoulder. Current arced through his body.

Agony ripped through Zach's muscles as his teeth clattered.

Falling to the ground, he couldn't fight fifty thousand volts of electricity.

Boots, scuffed and dirty, stepped in front of Zach.

"Get the van back here," was the last thing Zach heard before darkness overtook him.

* * *

Ronnie tried to hurry down the darkened street, but she tripped on her heels. *Again.* She wanted to pull the damn things off, but then her nylons would get runs, and then she would have to take those off, and pretty soon, before she knew it, she'd be standing there in a tattered dress, hair askew.

That was *not* how she wanted to look when she finally met Zach.

"Ronnie!" a voice called from half a block away. "Wait up!"

She ignored it. Far too high-pitched for Zach's voice, she knew it was Quirk chasing after her. Well, he could chase. She had only one stop in mind. Zach's cousin's bachelor party. And she wasn't going for the party favors.

Ronnie was about to make her last right turn when Quirk caught up with her. He grabbed her by the sleeve, jerking her to a halt.

"Don't you dare go around that corner before I get last looks!" he demanded.

"Quirk!"

Her assistant ignored her, though. He pulled up the hem of her dress, revealing far too much thigh for her taste, and then pulled down the neckline. Quirk then cupped her breasts, shoving them up.

"That's enough!"

To her surprise, instead of arguing, Quirk kissed her on the cheek. "*I* could almost bed you...*Almost.*"

She gave him a peck back. That was high praise in Quirk's world.

Taking in a deep breath, Ronnie stepped forward careful to balance properly on her heels. They clicked along as she approached the flickering lights announcing Corona and Dos Equis in the window.

Before she could make it to the door, a van went speeding by, splashing stagnant water onto the sidewalk. She barely jumped out of the way in time. It would not do for her to reek of dog pee and old cabbage.

Straightening her dress, Ronnie opened the door to the bar. Make that *disaster zone*. Sure, there was a bar. With naked women dancing while men groped at their legs. Mariachi music blared as patrons hooted.

This was Zach's cousin's idea of *fun*? Ronnie certainly hoped it didn't run in the family. Ronnie hadn't been to too many bars, but she was pretty sure that this wasn't the norm. What would Quirk call this party? Besides disgusting?

Off the hook. That's what he would call it.

Ronnie's eyes swept over the crowd. No Zach. She double-checked the fondlers, but Zach was not amongst them. Of course, there was a shadowy back area. Would he be back there? Given how late she was, wouldn't he be at the front of the bar? Looking for her?

Unless he found someone else to satisfy his "in person" needs.

She really should just walk out. Try to contact him though their communications channels, but Ronnie felt a morbid sense of duty to make sure Zach wasn't here. Luckily, the naked women on the bar fascinated the bulk of the men. She guessed that despite Quirk's best efforts, Ronnie had too many clothes on for them.

Keeping to the edge of the room, Ronnie made her way to the back area lined with booths. The first one had a couple, well, fornicating. Yes, full-on fornication. Ronnie averted her eyes. She didn't consider herself a prude, but *come on*. They were doing it in a booth in a bar!

Quickly, she made her way down the line of them, finding much of the same. Except, of course, for the last one, which involved a lizard and a bottle of tequila. She really should have just assumed that Zach was not back here.

But if not here, then where?

Had he even come?

Ronnie grabbed her iPod. There was nothing else to try, except to attempt to communicate with Zach.

She should have told him that she was running late.

But really, what kind of bond did they have if he couldn't even wait an hour for her? How did that compare to the months and months that led up to this night?

Once again, though, Ronnie's imagination had gotten away with her. It was so easy to conjure up all of these romantic notions when you only spoke to a guy three nights a week for exactly sixty-two minutes.

As she walked toward the exit, Ronnie cast her eyes to the floor so that she did not have to see why the men were all chanting, "Lo, lo, lo!"

Besides, Zach had his career to think about. Hell, not just his career, but also his freedom. If he were caught meeting her off the books? Forget parole.

Sure, there were a thousand perfectly sane reasons for Zach standing her up. But not a one of them, not one, took away the soul-wrenching pain of walking out that door all by herself.

CHAPTER 10

Ciudad Juarez
9:26 p.m., MST

Quirk watched as Ronnie stumbled out of the bar. Alone. He used infrared goggles to search up and down the street. Where in the hell was Zach? Perched atop a building across from the bar, Quirk used the high-powered zoom to check the entire area, but still no Hunt.

Heteros. They would never learn. And to waste such an outfit?

Still, this turn of events shocked even this world-weary hacker. It had never, ever occurred to Quirk that the corn-fed Dudley Do-Right wouldn't show. Would he try to arrest Ronnie? Sure, Quirk was prepared for that. It played right into the agent's Midwest morality. But to stand her up? To leave a woman in the lurch? To hurt her feelings like this? Quirk never would have guessed that the hunk had it in him to be this cruel.

Using the scope, he zoomed in on his boss. Ronnie looked like absolute hell. Courtney-Love-after-a-bender kind of hell. It wasn't so much her wet dress or the mussed hair. It was the look on Ronnie's face. Complete and utter devastation. He guessed that Hunt wasn't the stand-up guy that he pretended to be.

But wait! A car pulled up to the curb near Ronnie. Maybe Zach was just being stealthy, after all. Ronnie leaned in to the passenger's window as Quirk tightened his focus on the driver.

Oh, no. That definitely wasn't Hunt. It was a toothless Mexican. Even though Quirk couldn't speak the language, it was clear that the man was looking for something other than directions. And there went Ronnie's middle finger, flipping off the potential john.

Oh, that was it! The last humiliation.

Whipping out his laptop, Quirk first checked the glands under his neck to be sure they weren't enlarged. You never could be too careful with the plague on the loose. Then, he looked up Zach's financial information. No one dissed Ronnie like this without paying, and paying a lot.

"Credit score of eight hundred fifty, huh?" Quirk asked the screen. "Well, not anymore." Hunt's credit plummeted to two hundred and fifty. Some homeless people had better credit now. "And don't bother trying to use your ATM, you prick."

Feeling a certain amount of satisfaction after trashing Zach's finances, Quirk packed up his belongings. Now he could see why Ronnie wanted to buy an island paradise and keep it all to herself.

When even a *Waltons*-style guy like Zach turned out to be a dick, what hope was there?

Quirk hoped that the agent felt even a fraction of the pain Ronnie did.

* * *

Zach forced his body to remain slack as the two thugs lifted him from the van. He wished he could say this level of control was due to his highly honed skills, but with the wallop of the Taser hit, he wasn't sure if he could resist even if he wanted to.

Not too gently, they dragged him across rough terrain. Even though his muscles were slack, Zach's mind spun. They must be outside the city, but they couldn't have traveled more than thirty minutes. Forty-five, tops. He tried to keep time by his heartbeat, but there was no doubt that he had passed out a few times. Still, it couldn't have been that long. His cuts and scrapes from the bitch-slapping session stung rather than ached.

No, not much time had passed at all. Certainly not long enough for Grant to notice that he was gone. Zach had to stifle a snort. Who was he kidding? Fifer wasn't going to miss him until it came time for a ride home. Either his partner was nose-deep in tits or a captive as well.

The thugs stopped and knocked at a door. Then, in hushed tones, they obtained entrance. That made three men with him, and at least another behind the door. Zach's heels bounced over a metal landing. No steps up to the door—which meant that this most likely wasn't a residential dwelling. He tried to re-create a map in his head. Where in the hell had they taken him?

As they dragged him across the room, Zach's fingers ran over the rough cement floor. So he was right. This definitely wasn't a house, and the thugs' footsteps didn't echo, which eliminated a warehouse. Was it a store? A garage?

But what did it matter? If this were the usual type of federal agent snatch, this place would be fortified with a veritable army of drug soldiers. Escape, or even rescue, would be impossible. His only hope was that the State Department would give his kidnappers "consideration" and arrange for his release.

If he weren't lucky? Well, not getting to meet Ronnie would suddenly not be his worst regret in life. Not having any skin would be.

They crossed into another room. This one sounded much smaller, and his captors hauled him into a chair. Zach had no choice but to let himself fall face-first onto the table, landing right on his jaw—where the she-bitch landed a punch. Still, he remained passive. Motionless. He kept his breathing slow and steady.

Would this ruse help him obtain vital information? He doubted it, but letting his mind whirl and his training flow through his veins kept the panic at bay. The more in control he felt, the less likely he was to hurl.

* * *

Ronnie stood under the lamppost, hugging herself. She couldn't think of what else to do. First, a man who she thought loved her had stood her up. Then, she was mistaken for a hooker. Tears stung her eyes. If only she hadn't been late! If only…

She choked, thinking of the thousand what-ifs that sprang to mind. But none of them would miraculously make Zach appear before her. But damn it, she was nearly an hour late. Oh, how she wished she could blame Quirk for this, but she knew better. If Zach had shown up at all, he would have waited. It would have taken the modern equivalent of wild horses to pull him away.

Another car pulled up to the curb. Okay, this was the last time she arranged a blind date in the red-light district. But this car was a cab. A cab with a twenty-something knight in shining armor. Sagging with relief, she got into the vehicle, and they sped away from the site of her humiliation.

"Ronnie," Quirk said with actual concern in his voice. Not the usual "your baggy jeans and ill-fitting sweatshirt is embarrassing me" kind of concern, but she simply couldn't face him.

God, why had she let herself believe that Zach cared for her? Why had she risked her heart like that? She was pretty sure she would have been less disappointed if Zach had actually tried to arrest her. At least then, she could have looked into his eyes and seen how he really felt about her. Now? Oh, God, she had to choke back the tears again.

"Come on, hon," Quirk coaxed, and she finally looked over at him. He patted a towel draped over his shoulder. "I'm completely prepared for the mother of all good cries."

Normally, she would have had a great comeback or at least a scathing look to offer, but tonight she just leaned on her assistant and laid her head upon the terry cloth towel.

"And here you go." Quirk pulled out a pint of Häagen-Dazs ice cream and a spoon. "If it's any consolation, this is how I usually end up after the White Party."

For some strange reason, that did make Ronnie feel better—enough to take the proffered spoonful of ice cream.

* * *

Lino arrived at the small airport, greeted by a foursome in long, black, traditional priestly robes. He did not acknowledge their presence. Why should he? While they wore the same frock, none could walk in his stead.

The group parted to reveal another clothed in black, only his robe needed twice the yardage. Deacon Havar. Forced by protocol to bow to this wide-girthed superior, Lino inclined his head, but no more than four degrees. He would not give one so weak in the flesh more honor than that.

The sly insult did not get past the deacon, though. His chest puffed out as he rolled up his sleeve, revealing an elaborate weaving of symbols. Lino scanned them, taking in the minor accomplishments that elevated this man to deacon. Havar had recruited a few souls into the Hidden Hand. He helped create a small-armed guard, the Hand's Shield, to protect their most precious resource. Yet for all of the symbols dug into his flesh, he had little actual experience fighting out in the world.

Lino again lowered his head in well-schooled deference, and then tugged his sleeve up. As Havar read the symbols streaming down Lino's arm to his elbow and back around, the deacon's eyes widened. He glanced up in Lino's eyes. The question was clear.

Was Lino friend or foe? Lino grinned. If one must ask, the answer usually was foe.

In the end, Havar took a step back, not bothering to finish the tale written deeply in Lino's flesh.

"On the morn, we will collect Brother Loubom and the Picasso."

Inclining his head was Lino's only answer. Why waste the breath of one such as Havar? Tomorrow they would have the traitor and his muse so that Lino could get back to his true task.

That of bringing the world to heel to the Hidden Hand.

* * *

Zach heard the door open. The steps were heavy, measured, and deliberate. By the way the thugs shuffled, the general of their little army had just walked in.

"Jorge, I'll get the smelling salts," one of the underlings said.

"Don't bother," the new man said in a thick Mexican accent. "The *gringo* is awake."

Without warning, Jorge punched Zach in the kidney. He couldn't stifle the moan. Fingers dug into his hair and jerked his head up to meet his captor's scarred face.

"Don't ever try to fool me again, *cabrón,*" Jorge said just before he punched him in the kidney again.

"I don't know who in the fuck you think you kidnapped, but I'm FBI," Zach said through clenched teeth, not wanting the man to hear the pain in his voice.

"Good for you," Jorge said as he punched him again. "I'm C-fucking-IA."

Zach's mind raced. Jorge was lying, obviously. But why? Why not just admit that he was a drug lord?

"Who is the Robin Hood hacker?" Jorge asked.

For a moment, Zach couldn't even process the question, which earned him another punch in the kidney. The pain didn't help him process the request any faster. Why did a cocaine distributor care about Ronnie?

"I asked you a question," Jorge reminded him, the threat clear in his voice.

Until he knew what in the hell was going on, Zach kept his responses to a minimum. "Access the files yourself, prick."

Another punch. "When is the last time that you spoke with her?"

Angered, Zach looked into the cold eyes of his captor. "Again, if you are C-fucking-IA, then check the El Paso field office's phone records."

Another punch, and this time Jorge put his back into it. Zach tried to keep his breathing steady, but the pain took its toll.

"I will ask you one more time, and then I will *really* hurt you." The Mexican leveled his gaze to emphasize each word. "When did you speak with her?"

With equal emphasis, Zach answered. "Bite me."

Jorge obviously didn't like the suggestion, because he wailed on Zach's sides. Still handcuffed, Zach had no recourse but to double over. He wasn't going to give the prick the satisfaction of knowing how badly the beating hurt. Finally, the punches stopped, and the supposed CIA agent tossed something onto the table. Zach kept his eyes closed, forcing Jorge to grab him by the hair again.

Opening his lids, Zach found his iPod staring back at him.

Jorge leaned in close and whispered into his ear. "Just because we've got brown skin doesn't mean we don't know a hidden communications device when we see it." He released Zach's hair and straightened over him. "We know you talked to her last night. We picked up a scrambled signal coming from your home."

Zach spit out blood. "Then why the fuck did you ask me?" "Because we need your help."

"Help?" Zach said, a little too high-pitched for an FBI agent. But the word had startled him. Gaining control of his voice, he continued, "Yeah, right." Zach glanced around the small, interrogation-style room. "This is how I'd go about securing an FBI agent's assistance."

Jorge took this opportunity to use his fists again. Zach squeezed his eyes shut and ground his teeth together during the beating. But he was even more committed to keeping silent. He might have been tortured into giving away state secrets, but to give up Ronnie?

Never.

* * *

Quirk struggled with one hand to put the key, an actual stupid, awkward, metal key, into the hotel room's lock and used his other arm to support Ronnie. If she was going to continue to have these little breakdowns, she needed to cut back on the Krispy Kremes.

Finally the lock gave, and he stumbled into the room under the weight of his boss, five thousand dollars' worth of fashion, and another twenty pounds of electronics. They really needed to hire a Sherpa for trips like this.

"Oh, God..." Ronnie moaned, forcing Quirk to look up.

No! He had forgotten about the arrangements he had made. The entire room was awash in romantic candlelight. Rose petals graced the lace bedspread, a red and black teddy hung from the bathroom door, and a large...Well, let's just say sexual aid, lay on the dresser.

"Oh, dear," he apologized. "I was a tad too optimistic."

Frantically, Quirk tried to put away all the reminders of the night Ronnie should have had. He looked over his shoulder to find his boss still standing, stunned, in the doorway. Sometimes he was just too damn good at his job. Way better a job done than Zach tonight.

"Hon, go take a bath," he encouraged. "It will do you good."

Ronnie shook her head, not moving from the doorway. "I'm fine."

Quirk guided her into the bathroom as he looked her up and down. From the streaked mascara to the rumpled dress, Ronnie looked anything but fine. "Let's just say it will do *me* good. Now go."

Almost like a child too sleepy to fight, his boss started to the tub, but Quirk stopped her. "Hand it over."

Ronnie pulled her purse closer to her chest.

"Give it up, woman. I'm not joking."

Still Ronnie clung to the clutch. He had to pry her fingers from the clasp. "Don't make me beat your ass at designer trivia for it."

Reluctantly, she pulled out her iPod, but still refused to hand it over.

This was going to be a long night if Ronnie couldn't bring herself to accept that Zach was a sorry-assed hetero loser.

"And if Mr. Super-Special Agent called," Quirk asked, "what exactly could he say to make you feel better?"

Ronnie lowered her head. She must have known there was nothing, but maybe she needed to be convinced.

"He wasn't in a horrible car accident." Still, she didn't respond. "His brother didn't need an emergency liver transplant." Quirk tugged the communication device from her stiff fingers. "And he wasn't kidnapped by Mexican nationals, so just take a bath already."

* * *

Jorge kicked the back of Zach's knee. "Just tell me when you'd like me to stop, *puto*."

"*Now* would be great," Zach grunted.

Pointing to the iPod, Jorge leaned in, at eye level with Zach. "Then tell me how to work it."

"Oh," Zach said, "Not if I need to do that."

Jorge gave a one-two punch to Zach's already-brutalized kidney. "You don't get it, do you, *cholio*?" He gave a third blow. "You'll tell me, or you'll die."

Aching, Zach kept his gazed fixed toward the one-way mirror in front of him. They would get nothing. Jorge must have sensed his defiance, because the butt of the gun came down hard into his shoulder. Even though it made no sense, it was becoming more and more likely that Zach's captor was a foreign CIA operative. While Jorge was fast and loose with the punishment, the Mexican kept it away from Zach's face. He hit areas that induced high levels of pain with minimal external damage. Zach's own country was doing this to him.

Wincing, Zach knew that couldn't be true. This prick had to be a rogue agent, looking to cash in on the bounty on Ronnie's head.

"Tell me the code, *puto*, or you *will* die."

Zach held Jorge's gaze. "Then I'll die."

The Mexican raised his hand again, but the door opened.

"Torture wasn't part of our deal, Jorge."

Zach knew that voice. He craned his sore neck to find Grant—with that cheesy smile on his face.

Jorge grew even cockier than before. "He is a boy born to milk and honey. A little pain will go a long way."

As Zach tried to process his shock, Grant walked around the table to face him. "I don't know. He's got a pretty big hard-on for her."

"All the more reason to beat the resistance from him."

Zach finally found his voice. "You fucking bastard…this is going on your record."

Fifer shrugged. "Dude, it already has. I was *ordered* to make sure you went to this damn party." He turned to Jorge. "Which, I might add, had a skank factor of 100 out of 100."

The Mexican shrugged. "We had to be sure he went outside."

The conversation was a blur. "Ordered? Ordered by whom?"

"The director himself. Dawg, I am telling you, this is for real. We need the Robin Hood hacker, like *now*."

Zach shook his head, leaning back from the table. Anything to get away from Grant.

"The director would *never*! The FBI would *never* authorize an agent to be apprehended."

"Not on US soil, they won't. But here? Come on, federal agents get snatched all the time. What's one more?"

Zach straightened. Obviously, Grant was in on this with Jorge. Two lowlife scum trying to score the reward for Ronnie.

Grant put his hands on the rickety table and leaned toward Zach. "Dude, why do you think they left you on her case? Jesus, you haven't caught her for how long? They were about to reassign you when she called the field office. Talk about luck, man. They left you on the hook as bait."

Zach's mind spun. They wanted Ronnie, yet they had snatched him. Why not wait until she showed up? The only conclusion was that they didn't know. They didn't know that she was *in* town. That changed everything. He had a slim advantage, and he planned to use it.

"All this for some fucking reward."

Grant slammed his hand down on the table. "Zach, focus. This is a completely sanctioned mission."

Oh, Zach was focused, all right. "Prove it."

Opening a laptop, Grant brought up a report regarding the plague. "The Black Death is back, man. It is here. And the only clue we have as to why it is written in this…"

Symbols unfamiliar to Zach scrolled down the page. They might have been unknown, but they did help clarify one thing for Zach. The US government hadn't gone to all this trouble just to catch an outside-the-law hacker. They *needed* her hacking skills. Another slim advantage for Zach to use.

"Just make the damn call already," Grant said, pushing the iPod to Zach.

Zach turned his head to stare at the wall. "Figure it out yourself."

"And trigger the self-destruct mechanism?" Grant said in a singsong voice.

He couldn't help but look at his ex-partner.

Grant chuckled. "What? You didn't know that the woman you are so desperate to protect had the case lined in *plastique*. The dogs went nuts over it."

Zach sighed. He made sure it was a big sigh. A defeated sigh. He had to make sure Grant and the others believed that he truly had given up. At some point, he would need to contact Ronnie. He just had to make sure that it looked like he was capitulating—and not part of his plan.

Okay, not so much a plan, but the inkling of a plan.

CHAPTER 11

Plum Island
12:02 a.m., EST

Amanda studied the ancient map, looking at the pockets of plague resistance. The key had to lie in these areas of respite. These areas of vaccinated populations. Whoever created this plague must have taken precautions—just like they did back in 1347. They wouldn't let loose a rampant, weaponized *Yersinia pestis* without some kind of vaccine formulated.

They also had to protect the person wielding the bacterium, spreading it throughout the Venice airport and beyond.

She glanced around the room at the other scientists who were tracking the plague. Amanda was certain that they all thought her insane for poring over the 1347 pandemic. She just had this nagging feeling in her gut that if they could figure out how they had done it last time, she could figure out how they could stop it this time.

Jennifer wasn't back yet, though. She'd tasked her assistant with researching any instance of the subject vaccination in relation to the plague. This research could not have happened in a vacuum. Someone, somewhere must have knowledge of this global plot to wipe out the bulk of mankind.

Noticing her assistant hurrying down the hall, Amanda sat up and stretched. Dear God, how long had it been since she'd slept? Forget about showering. Instead of coming into the conference room, Jennifer stood out in the hall, signaling Amanda over.

Stepping out into the hallway, Amanda took the paper Jennifer offered. Her assistant didn't have to explain its contents as Amanda's eyes scanned the e-mail. Despite the fact that she didn't understand half the symbols on the paper, the Latin—the Latin—she did understand. Vindication and fury duked it out in her veins.

Amanda walked back into the conference room as Devlin popped another cherry throat lozenge into his mouth. She could smell the bitter, medicinal smell from here. His tongue must be a bright red by now. Jennifer pointed to the time stamp on the e-mail. Yesterday morning. Amanda went to confront the CIA liaison, but Jennifer shook her head. Her assistant was right. Here was not the place.

Instead, she walked up to Devlin. "Henderson's office. *Now.*"

"And why in the hell would I ever follow your—"

She held up the paper long enough for his eyes to dilate. Amanda didn't bother telling him to follow her second time. He fell in right behind her on the short walk over to Henderson's office.

Several officials sat in a semicircle around the director's desk.

"Sir, we need to speak," Amanda stated. "Privately."

"Well, we were just going over the best way to quarantine those exposed but not yet symptomatic from—"

"This is more important."

Henderson cocked his head, studying her face. What he really should have been looking at was her fists. Those were shaking in barely contained anger.

"All right, then," the director said, and then turned to the officials crowding his office. "Ladies and gentlemen, take a five-minute break."

Amanda moved out of the doorway as the scientists filed out of the office. She didn't look any of them in the eye because they would all be asking the same question with their looks. "What could be more important than containing the spread of the plague?"

Once everyone was out, Amanda stepped into the office, allowing Devlin to pass by her without giving him a swift kick to the shin. Jennifer shut the door behind them.

"I think I had better sit down before you start," Henderson said, landing hard in his leather chair.

She passed the paper to him. As he scanned it, his frown became deeper and deeper. Finally, he looked up at Devlin. "This is your e-mail?"

"I do not know how she got hold of official, confidential—"

"I asked," Henderson interrupted, "if this truly came from your e-mail account."

The man's toe scuffing the floor like a busted third grader gave them their answer.

Amanda turned on Devlin. "All this time, you hammered me about how preposterous my theories were, and here is the proof of them."

"Hold on, Dr. Rolph," Henderson cautioned. "We have some kind of intercepted communication between individuals of an organization known as the Hidden Hand discussing how to best "protect" themselves from the plague. There is quite a bit of latitude interrupting such—"

"Look at the time stamp of the original correspondence," Amanda urged, waiting for Henderson's pupils to dilate. "It is dated over a week ago. This Hidden Hand was discussing it at least several days *before* the start of the plague."

"Mr. Devlin? How would you like to explain the fact that the CIA had knowledge of a group discussing the Black Death along with a possible prophylaxis, and did not feel the need to share it with the division of the CDC tasked with *fighting* the plague?"

Now it was Devlin's turn to squirm.

"It was on a need-to-know basis. My superiors didn't think you needed to know."

Henderson rose from his desk, his fist slamming against the wood. "How about you assume that we do now?"

The CIA liaison's eyes darted to the door, but Jennifer strategically blocked his exit. "Like you said, especially with those unexplained symbols, there were numerous ways to interpret the communiqué."

Amanda wasn't letting him off the hook so easily.

"Who wrote this?"

"I don't know."

"Who was it meant for?"

Devlin looked away. "I. Don't. Know."

"Then, why do you even have it?"

This time, the CIA liaison locked eyes with her. "Why do you think?" His eyes scanned over to Henderson. "I was sent to see if any of you might be involved in the Hidden Hand." Devlin turned to her. "Especially you."

"Me?" Amanda squeaked.

* * *

Quirk scooped rose petals into a small trash can. His burden never ceased. But before he could get truly riled, he cocked his head. Yep, the bathwater was still flowing. Ronnie could try to hide the sound of her crying, but Niagara Falls couldn't drown out that sorrow.

Moving on to the nightstand, Quirk almost threw out the motorized dildo, and then thought twice about it. It hadn't been used. There was no point in wasting such a useful device. He tossed it into his suitcase, and then Quirk came across the infamous iPod. Such a little toy that had caused so much damage. That definitely could go into the trash, but before he could toss it, the thing chimed.

"Unauthorized contact time. Override code being input."

Oh, no. Zach was definitely not going to get back into Ronnie's life with a belated, lame excuse. Even before the bastard could load in the sequence, Quirk aborted the contact and typed in a little message for Mr. Loverboy.

"Go fuck yourself."

* * *

Zach watched the words roll across the screen. He didn't blame Ronnie. She must be confused and very, very livid.

Grant kept a wide berth from the iPod. "What does it say?"

"Go fuck yourself," Zach replied.

Jorge went to his go-to response. A kidney punch.

Fingers flying, Grant brought up pictures of plague victims. "These aren't from the fourteenth century, Zach. These are victims in Italy. Now. *Today.*"

The bodies were bloated and blotchy. Zach could only imagine how they smelled.

"The US might be lucky and have ten percent of the population survive, but Mexico?" Grant said, his eyes sliding over to Jorge. "His people may speak Spanish, but their blood is that of the indigenous people of the Americas. A population that has never seen this bacteria before. A population that has very limited medical resources."

Jorge spoke through a clenched jaw. "A population that will die out completely unless you make that fucking call."

Zach looked at both men, and then at the screen. They *could* be playing him. But Zach did see that fax just before heading out to chase down Ronnie. And he knew that Europe had already seen hundreds of plague deaths. But were these two just leveraging that tragedy for their own endgame?

"She is a hacker. What good is she against a bacterium?"

Jorge's hand went up to strike.

"And so help me," Zach growled. "If you hit me one more time…"

The Mexican chuckled. "You will do what?"

"Let you kill me," Zach held his voice steady.

Jorge looked like he was ready to do just that when Grant stepped between them.

"This plague isn't natural," Grant explained.

Zach's eyes narrowed. What game was Grant playing?

"Look, Langley can't break this code, or at least not fast enough," his ex-partner said. "We need the Robin Hood hacker to break the code so that we can determine how they are protecting themselves from this weaponized strain."

"Who are 'they'?" Zach asked.

"The Hidden Hand."

* * *

"Any organization like this Hidden Hand that wanted to pull something of this caliber off," Devlin continued, "would need some pretty heavy-duty backup. Scientists willing to do their bidding."

"Wait," Amanda said, as her brain finally caught up with her mouth. "Back to me. Why investigate *me*?"

Devlin frowned. "Isn't it obvious?"

Amanda looked at Henderson, who shrugged. "Why don't you enlighten us, Devlin?"

"Too smart for her own damn good," the CIA liaison began after clearing his throat. "She's got a soft spot for the plague, plus, no family. No husband. No boyfriend. Not even a sexting partner. High student loan debt. I could go on all day. Dr. Rolph is a prime target for foreign agency recruitment."

Blinking back tears, Amanda tried to hold her reaction in. To think that because she had lost her parents early, sucked at dating, and decided to take a low-paying government job instead of a six-figure pharmaceutical deal, she somehow was suspect. She looked at Jennifer, who oozed sympathy. The grad student was in about the same boat as Amanda.

"Well, Dr. Rolph, did you help to create this weaponized form of the plague?" Dr. Henderson asked.

"No," Amanda said through clenched teeth.

"All right, then," the director said, turning back to Devlin. "I take it that you don't have any proof of anyone here being involved, or I can only assume the DHS guards would have swooped down on them."

The CIA liaison looked at the floor. "Not yet."

"So, isn't the more important question," Amanda stated, "what is the CIA doing to find this source of 'protection?'"

"I don't know."

Dr. Henderson glared at Devlin. "We are in the thick of it, son. If you know anything, just tell us."

Amanda watched as the CIA liaison popped another throat lozenge in while he shook his head from side to side. Finally he cleared his throat.

"I really don't know," he said. "How they were going to decode the full message was a 'need to know' that clearly I didn't need to know."

As much as she wanted to believe that Devlin was holding out on them, his hunched, puppy-dog posture indicated that he wasn't. He looked more embarrassed that he wasn't high enough up on the food chain to know the details.

Perhaps they couldn't control things out in the world, but they certainly could control things within the facility.

"We've got to start acting like there is a viable vaccine out there," Amanda said.

Henderson shook his head. "I don't want to start a riot of speculation. We need everyone to stay focused on their tasks."

"Fine then, just the four of us," Amanda countered. "But we've got to trust that the CIA is going to find the vaccine and bring it to us for mass production."

ENCRYPTED

The director sat at his desk.

Jennifer nudged her from behind. Ugh. She'd already gone out so far out on a limb that she feared it would crack under her.

"This is why they accelerated the bacterium's virulence," Amanda explained. "They needed to infect as many people as possible before we could develop any of our own 'protection.' Our only hope is to take a successful vaccine and multiply it."

She took a step closer to the desk. Why she had to be all assertive, Amanda didn't know, but she did know this bacterium. She did know what was going to happen to the world's population if they didn't act decisively.

"We've got to be prepared."

Henderson finally nodded. "Quietly, though. Get the techs down in the wet lab prepping for a modified live vaccine. Let everyone think that we're just gearing up for a run of our own."

Amanda took a deep breath—the first she had really taken since the first confirmed case of bubonic plague came from Europe. At least they had a name for who created the plague—The Hidden Hand. They also knew why and how the Hidden Hand hoped to accomplish the most egregious use of biowarfare that man had ever seen.

Now they only had to somehow stop it—the most virulent, antibiotic-resistant menace to mankind.

Okay, maybe she shouldn't have taken that deep breath just yet.

Especially not as Jennifer and Devlin coughed at the same time. She turned to her grad student, who tried to wave her off, but Amanda persisted. Reaching out, she put the back of her hand to Jennifer's forehead. The skin burned.

Amanda snatched her hand back. "How long?"Jennifer wouldn't meet her gaze.

"What's wrong?" Henderson asked.

She turned to Devlin. "And you?"

"And me, what?" the CIA liaison shot back.

Ignoring his rudeness, she felt his cheek. It was on fire. "How long have you had a fever?"

"I feel kind of crummy," Devlin said, his eyes darting from person to person. "But I'm fine."

"Check your lymph nodes," Amanda instructed. Now that she looked at Jennifer, really *looked* at her, she could see the flushing to her arms, the rosy cheeks that did not indicate health.

Devlin barely touched his neck. "No. No. They *can't* be swollen."

"But they are."

Henderson stepped back. "They have the plague?"

Amanda didn't bother answering. What else could they have, the swine flu?

"We've been under lockdown since the first case landed in New York," Henderson rushed on, seeming to want to reassure himself this wasn't happening. "There's no way we could have been infected by..."

Didn't he get it? Didn't they *all* get it? This was no accident. No natural spread of the disease.

"We've been purposefully infected," Amanda said, finding it silly to have to state something so obvious.

"I...I haven't been feeling well, either," Henderson admitted. Neither had she. Everyone had chalked it up to stress and fatigue, when really, someone had been planting the bacteria right in the heart of the laboratory.

"Dear God," Henderson said, his tone wounded. "They truly are brilliant, aren't they?"

Amanda nodded. Who better to infect than the people charged with stopping the plague?

The plan was so simple, elegant, and ironic that Amanda would have laughed, except for the fact that they would all be dead within twenty-four hours.

CHAPTER 12

Ciudad Juarez Hotel
11:12 p.m., MST

Ronnie wiped her eyes. Her hand came back black. It turned out that five coats of mascara and tears didn't play together so well.

Ugh. And with the hot, steaming water creating a veritable fog around her, the stench of the three cans of hair spray Quirk used nearly gagged her. Not that her stomach felt all that great before. Each time she felt any morsel of numbness setting in, that last image of Zach flashed in her mind. The sound of his voice during their last conversation, worried, yet hopeful, caressed her ears.

Fantasy was *so* much better than reality.

After so long in the bath, her fingers had long ago raisined. Perhaps it was time to wash her hair and get to bed. She leaned over the porcelain tub and fished around in her "go" bag, but couldn't find any shampoo. Really? Quirk put that much product in her hair and didn't give her some way to get it back out again?

Feeling leaden, her legs complained as she rose from the bath. Grabbing a robe off the hook, she pulled it on before stepping out into the bedroom.

"Quirk, did you pack shampoo, or what?"

Her assistant turned around, hand shoved behind his back. Ronnie strode over as Quirk held her iPod above his head.

"Is that him?" she asked, already knowing the answer. Her legs no longer felt heavy.

"Who else?" he said, squirming away. "*Someone* has to be strong for you."

"Is that the 9-1-1 override code?"

Her assistant still wouldn't hand it over. "If he's in physical danger, I will bed a woman!"

He tried to stand on his tippy-toes, but Ronnie was a good two inches taller than he. She snatched the iPod from Quirk's grasp and put the earbuds in.

"Zach?" Ronnie asked, half afraid of the response she was going to get. Was he pissed? Distant? Dismissive?

"Ronnie, I—" Zach said before the line went quiet.

"I, *what*?" she nearly shouted.

A rustling came on the line, and then another voice, heavily Latin influenced, spoke. "We have him, so you'd best listen carefully."

Ronnie's back straightened to a rod.

Quirk cocked his head. "What, is he begging you to meet him again?"

She shook her head and mouthed, "He's been kidnapped."

Her assistant snorted. "Yeah, right." Then he went back to packing.

As the man on the line took a deep breath, Ronnie put a bud in Quirk's ear.

"Unless you agree to surrender yourself at the time and place of our choosing, and then do as you are instructed, Special Agent Zachary Hunt will die."

"Damn it!" Quirk muttered.

No freaking kidding. This was one instance where she did *not* want to tell Quirk that she told him so. But here they were. Ronnie shoved her assistant toward his laptop. Quirk popped the earbud out as he sat on the bed.

"All right, all right. I'll put a trace on it," Quirk conceded.

Ronnie turned her attention back to Zach's captor. "I need to speak with Zach."

"You have little room to demand anything."

"Look," she said. "Clearly, you need something from me, and I am not giving it to you until I am sure that Zach is safe."

"Um, perhaps we shouldn't antagonize the kidnappers quite so much," Quirk piped up.

She mouthed, "Find him," as Zach's captor went into some long, rambling speech about how *he* was in control.

Ronnie cut him off. "Put him on the line or this is going to be an extremely one-sided conversation."

No response. Ronnie held her breath.

Had she pushed too hard?

* * *

Zach watched the veins in Jorge's forehead bulge. Guess the operative wasn't used to having anyone talk to him like that, let alone a woman. Grant shrugged, though.

"Let the lovebirds talk."

Brusquely, Jorge stuffed the buds in Zach's ears.

"Hey, sexy," he said, trying not to sound too tortured.

"Hey there, yourself," Ronnie answered, but he could hear the strain in her voice. They both knew that they were being monitored. She hadn't stayed out of jail for so long by being naïve. Naïve like they could carry on an illicit relationship behind the backs of the FBI and the CIA.

"Have they injured you?" she asked.

"Depends on your definition…"

Jorge leaned in close. "Tell her what we want."

"How many are holding you?" she asked. Unfortunately, her question was piped in to the whole room.

Zach answered as quickly as he could. "Five that I know of, but—"

The buds were ripped out. Jorge put them back into his own ears.

"That will be enough," the CIA agent grunted. "Now you will hear *our* terms."

No matter how politically correct Grant tried to appear, Zach knew that no matter what Jorge promised Ronnie, there was no way that he was leaving this room alive.

* * *

Ronnie only half-listened as the man went on and on about the conditions of this supposed meeting. "You will come alone and unarmed, blah, blah, blah."

Or at least, that was all she heard as Quirk's eyebrows nearly met in the middle of his forehead as he pounded away at the keyboard. Finally, his face tilted up with a smile. Quirk gave a thumbs-up and turned the screen toward her.

A nice, green circle showed where the CIA was keeping Zach.

"Hey," she said, interrupting the operative's diatribe. "Let's not do that and say that we did."

She could hear the man fume on the other side before he spoke. "You do not seem to understand—"

"Let me talk to Zach, or—"

* * *

"Or what?" Jorge chuckled. "You will trigger the self-destruct mechanism?"

The operative shoved the iPod toward Zach, who noticed that Grant, ever so brave, backed away to the farthest corner of the room.

"I would warn against it, since your precious agent is the one holding the device."

Well, not so much holding it, as not being able to get outside of the iPod's blast range. Would Ronnie really detonate it? Would she save her skin and crispy-fry his?

Ronnie's voice echoed in the small room. "Really? On no, whatever will I do?"

Zach knew she was·being sarcastic, but Jorge didn't seem to quite understand the difference. Once Ronnie's tone got serious, maybe he would. "Don't screw with me, spook," she said. "I know that you are company trained. So listen to the stress levels in my voice. I am not bluffing. I am not exaggerating. Let. Me. Talk. To. Zach."

Seriously, were they not listening to her? The woman meant it, yet Jorge and Grant grinned stupidly at one another.

"Or?" Jorge asked.

Ronnie's voice filled the room. "You, my dear sir, die."

"You are a hacker who lives off the grid. So what exactly do you propose to do to me?" Jorge challenged.

Zach was pretty darn sure that Jorge did not want to know.

"Don't say that I didn't warn you."

* * *

Ronnie bit her lip. She *was* serious. But was she committed to this course of action?

"You try anything, and I will kill him without hesitation," the operative stated. "Without regret. Without remorse."

She knew that. She'd heard it in his voice. Even if she did exactly what he wanted, Ronnie knew that Zach would never survive his encounter with the CIA. He could raise way too many questions back home.

And unfortunately, they had given the CIA the perfect cover for Zach's death. He had, after all, come across the border to fraternize with one of the FBI's Most Wanted suspects. Zach getting "accidently" killed as he made his escape would be an easy sell.

Ronnie glanced at Quirk. His lips were set in a firm line. As master-level hackers, they always knew that this day might come. Of course, they assumed that it would be one of them on the other side of this call. They were prepared. She just wasn't sure if she could go through with their contingency plan.

"Just give Zach the earpieces," she said, hoping against hope that the agent would finally become reasonable.

"Over my dead body," Jorge growled.

Gulping, she answered, "Okay."

Ronnie nodded at Quirk. He pulled out a small wireless detonator. He rested his hand on hers as she hit the button.

* * *

Zach watched as the red lights on the iPod flashed faster and faster. He'd always thought the lights were just part of Ronnie's fashion sense, but now he realized that they also served as a countdown.

As they blinked at an accelerated rate, Zach hoped Ronnie would know that he forgave her. He wasn't getting out of here, anyway. She might as well protect herself by destroying the evidence.

Jorge smiled fiercely as the iPod's screen bloomed red and the word "Boom," flared white. Then the tiniest *pop* sounded.

Zach stared at the iPod, but it just sat there with "Every Rose Has Its Thorn" ready to play.

Jorge, however, was not so lucky. His eyes dilated, and his smile faded as blood dripped out of his ears.

He tilted back, then forward, before crashing to the floor—dead.

"Like I said," Ronnie said over the speakers, "release him."

Zach leveled his gaze at Grant. "You heard the woman."

CHAPTER 13

El Paso FBI Field Office
9:15 a.m. MST

"Francois," a voice called.

But who would do so, especially flavored with a perfect French accent?

He opened his eyes to find a black-frocked deacon standing before his cell. Francois' blood ran cold, tingling the marks upon his arms.

"Francois. It is time to come home," Deacon Havar stated as he extended a hand into the cell. His sleeve fell back, revealing marks very similar to Francois's own. Some blanched white with scarring. Others oozing fresh. Just as Francois's. Only the deacon's intent was far different than his.

Francois's were carved for salvation. The deacon's for damnation.

"Hey!" an agent called from behind. "Stay back from the cell. Don't let that guy fool you. He goes from zero to sixty."

The deacon inclined his head and slipped his arm out of the cell, his sleeve once again covering their shared secret. "I would like to speak with your superior."

It wasn't until Havar moved away from the bars that Francois realized that the deacon had not come alone. A cluster of four young priests held onto his hem as if they were chicks following their mother. Only one stood apart from the rest.

Lino.

His eyes pierced the air, skewering Francois where he stood.

Francois' scars flared again.

It was as if his own flesh knew that he did not have long to live.

* * *

Amanda sat beside Jennifer in the infirmary. Even though her assistant was hooked up to two different IV lines, she still typed frantically on her laptop. Not that Amanda was much better. By monitoring temperature spikes, she was about four hours behind Jennifer and Devlin. Those two must have been exposed to an early source of contagion, where Amanda and Henderson were hit in the secondary wave.

The director also typed away at the far side of the beds. Amanda balanced her laptop on her knees, working while the IV antibiotics dripped into her veins.

Most other patients crammed into the tiny medical station were more sensible. They rested or watched the only television. Of course, the sole programming consisted of more and more reports of the Black Death's march across America and the world. The only continent still untouched was Antarctica. Since the very first plague victim, all incoming and outgoing air traffic was shut down—much as Amanda suggested in the plague's dawning hours.

How many lives could have been saved if that Venice flight had been turned around in midair? Amanda felt that she should have done more to convince Henderson. She should have insisted on being on the call with the president.

Back then, though, she was the girl who cried wolf. But now that the wolf was literally at their door? Now, she was the girl who everyone counted on. What if she couldn't find the vaccinated populations? What if she couldn't find a vaccine repository?

Jennifer tapped Amanda's computer. The message was clear. *Work.*

Unfortunately, Jennifer was right. No point in belaboring the past—it was gone. They had to find Hidden Hand safe houses. Before she could get back to combing through hospital intake records, Devlin pointed to the television.

"Turn it up!"

Craning her neck to see what all the fuss was about, Amanda found Anderson Cooper on-screen. So, it was going to be a major announcement. The reporter looked haggard. The usual spark in his eye was dulled. Even makeup couldn't cover the dark circles. She'd seen it before. In herself. Anderson wasn't just whipped—he was stricken.

"Authorities are urging everyone to stay indoors, and I couldn't agree more. People, this isn't the time to panic. This is the time to use common sense. Only venture outside if you must get a loved one to a hospital, and even then, wear a mask, or—"

Anderson stopped as a piece of paper was shoved at him from off camera. His eyes scanned the page once, and then again. He looked up, not toward the camera, but to someone to the left of it.

"Is this for real?" Anderson asked. The muffled voice answered her agreement. The reporter still asked, "*All* of it?"

Again, the muffled voice said, "Yes."

Anderson shuffled in his chair, and then his eyes found the camera. "I am so sorry, New York…"

So sorry about what? Now everyone in the infirmary was glued to the television.

"The governor has…The governor has declared that New York City hospitals are now closed. They are overrun with plague victims and can accept no more."

Amanda looked at Jennifer. Neither was necessarily surprised. It was simply step eighteen in the biowarfare manual. At some point, the health care system would become saturated and completely ineffective, which only accelerated the death count. And not just from plague victims. Now, heart attack victims who could have been saved would die. Even cases of appendicitis or a child's strep throat could result in death. The body count would balloon from here.

The only surprising thing was how horribly quickly all this was happening. This should be day three or four into the disease cycle. Not day one.

Anderson shifted in his seat. "But that doesn't mean you *can't* get treatment. Officials are rolling out a program where antibiotics can be delivered to you. Medics will bring the antibiotics to your door, knock, and you must wait at least a minute before opening your door to accept them."

Amanda didn't see why he was so nervous until he cleared his throat, and then had to cough. It was like watching America's slow decline into the plague.

Finally catching his breath, Anderson continued. "They will identify homes in need of antibiotics…well…they are requesting that you put a red 'X' on your door. Again, I am so very sorry, New York."

Amanda glanced at Jennifer. The "X" was not part of the plan. The plan was a coordinated online request form along with door placards to identify plague victims. However, Amanda could see why the New York authorities had foregone those niceties. Again, they weren't supposed to get to this point until day three or four. That would have given officials two to three days to educate the public. Get the placards out to the neighborhoods before they were needed.

Now, though? A bright red "X" probably was more representative of the dire circumstances.

Jennifer raised her eyebrows. *Now, what are we going to do?* was the clear question.

Which was an extremely good question. Amanda thought that she would have hours and hours more of data streaming in from the hospitals, and then the online data from antibiotic requests. How in the hell was she going to track red "Xs" on the doors?

"I am going to need more bandwidth," Amanda said as Jennifer's eyes slid over to Devlin. "And yes, access to the CIA's database. Can you do it?"

Jennifer gave a sly smile as she typed like a madwoman.

Amanda had no idea how her assistant was going to carry out the task ahead. However, if it got her the data that she needed, she didn't care. Not with the plague on the move.

* * *

Lino ignored Brother Loubom. The man would be dead soon enough. His legacy of betrayal ended. Lino studied the half-burnt Picasso. Such an ugly painting. Why would one take God's most perfect specimen, man, and distort it so?

Man was made in God's image. Such a painting was not just in bad taste; it amounted to heresy. It should be burned. Not to see what lay beneath the oils, but to destroy the thing, so that no man's eyes ever had to look upon it again.

With one ear, he listened to the deacon arguing with the FBI officer. Another sign of Havar's weakness. At the first sign that the FBI was not going to cooperate fully and immediately, Lino would have ordered their destruction. They had already spread God's gift to the four corners of the world. These FBI agents would be stricken within days. Why prolong the time that they breathed?

Lino itched to take action. To purify this office and slit the old man's throat, but for now the deacon outranked him. However, with such a poor showing here, Lino seriously doubted how long even that would last.

* * *

While the argument continued between Deacon Havar and the FBI agent, Francois watched the blond acolyte. To look so very innocent, but to be filled with such hatred. Lino seemed the obedient servant, which he was, only to a most vile master.

Francois knew Lino's callous soul from experience. No wonder the boy had risen through the ranks so quickly. Even as a child, the boy had shown no remorse or regret. He had been raised to be the perfect instrument of the Hidden Hand's grotesque experiment.

Havar's group stood cloaked in priestly black. The crosses hanging from their necks mocked Francois's faith and the very church that they pretended to serve. Certainly, these emissaries loved the Catholic Church. However, they wished it to regress to the time of the Spanish Inquisition.

"Special Agent Danner," the deacon barked loud enough to draw Francois from his musings. Havar must have realized that every head in the office turned his way, for his next words were far more measured. "I believe that Interpol made it clear that we were to be given all due consideration."

Francois watched, spellbound, as the Special Agent in Charge sat on the corner of the desk. He did not seem agitated or overly impressed by the deacon.

"And you have been. We have agreed to hand over the prisoner despite the fact that the State of Texas could detain him on breaking and entering charges, arson, and—"

Deacon Havar shoved his chest forward, glaring—the look of a man seldom thwarted. "All of which dim in comparison to Francois's moral crimes."

"Which is why the Attorney General has expedited your extradition request."

Ah, so that is why the federal government cared for someone as inconsequential as he. Of course, the Hidden Hand moved deep within the shadows, orchestrating the events as they saw fit. However, they did not seem to count on the resolve of Special Agent in Charge Danner.

The deacon gritted his teeth. "But the painting—"Is the property of the El Paso Museum of Art, which has declined to donate the work to the church," Danner said.

"But it is damaged beyond repair," Havar said, unable to contain his exasperation.

Special Agent in Charge Danner cocked his head to the side. "Which does beg the question—why *you* would want it so badly?"

Francois felt a grin form on his otherwise stolid lips. Seldom was the Hidden Hand's desire kept at bay for even a moment. It was clear that the deacon had to take a moment to regroup. Spinning a plausible reason why the church would want the half-burnt work of a communist painter took some time.

In the end, Havar simply changed the subject. "Fine, then. We shall depart with Brother Loubom."

Francois tensed. His luck had run out. He doubted very much if he would live long enough to see even the airport once deposited within the deacon's care.

Danner stood. "As soon as the doctor gets here and gives me a medical release stating that he is healthy enough to travel, he is all yours."

"We have a plane to catch."

"And this guy committed arson, attacked an FBI agent, and then proceeded to cut himself up over the last twenty-four hours," Danner stated, indicating Francois. "He's not going anywhere until I receive third-party verification that he's mentally stable enough to travel."

The deacon's wide face blotched with anger—a blazing shade of magenta. A color Picasso himself would have approved of. "So, this is your country's highest level of consideration?"

"Guess so," Danner said, turning toward his office. "Take it or leave it."

The deacon gathered himself to go. "We shall leave it... for the moment."

Swiftly, Havar turned his bulk toward the door, forcing his entourage to hurry behind him. All, except for Lino. Lino stayed, glaring into the cell.

Francois did not flinch from his gaze. The boy may be anointed in blood, but Francois had seen more death than any man should bear. Try as he might, Lino could not unnerve him.

"Lino!" the deacon barked.

The boy's frown deepened as he finally turned away and strode from the office.

Once the door shut behind them, Francois breathed out. Fortune had granted him a stay of execution. But a stay only. He had no doubt that the Hidden Hand would be back to collect him.

Until then, all Francois could do was pray that God sent him a guardian angel.

CHAPTER 14

Somewhere over Mexico
9:34 a.m., MST

Ronnie strained to see past the dusty helicopter window. The rotors beat overhead, drowning out even her thoughts. But she didn't need to hear her thoughts, for she had only one.

Zach.

What if her stunt hadn't intimidated the CIA? What if they decided to kill Zach, rather than release him? She knew that she shouldn't be thinking about that right now, but what else could she think about?

"Visual confirmation," the burly pilot grunted.

The guy must have topped two hundred and fifty pounds. He smelled as though he had drunk two hundred and fifty gallons of bourbon last night. But his hand was steady on the joystick, and damn, he could see farther than Ronnie could.

She pulled up the binoculars to scan the ramshackle tumble of buildings up ahead. Low and squat, they hugged the desert, and the desert protected them with a heavy covering of sand.

"Fire?" the pilot asked gruffly.

"No!" Ronnie answered. "Jesus, no."

The guy chewed on the butt of a long-dead cigar. "Your dime."

She shot a look at Quirk. The question on her face was clear.

Where in the hell did you get him?

Quirk rolled his eyes as he broke out tech equipment in the back of the helicopter. "You do *not* want to know."

Ronnie tensed her jaw. She loved Quirk beyond all measure, but this was Zach's life they were talking about. Without having to say a word, her assistant got the message loud and clear.

"Look, darlin," he said while stringing Ethernet cabling between two computers. "You didn't give me much time to scrape up a combat-ready helicopter pilot."

"I thought you were getting us some gunmen?" she asked.

Quirk glanced up from what he was doing. "Even in Mexico, it's a little hard at four in the morning to scare up some *discreet* gunmen. *Your* request, not mine."

Chewing her lip, Ronnie wondered if she hadn't been overly cautious. Would the CIA expect her to commission a helicopter? Would they expect her to storm their castle? She was known more for her finesse than her use of firepower.

"You're still pinging them, right?" she asked.

Quirk rolled his eyes again. Even distracted and traveling in a speeding helicopter, Quirk could put on a cyber attack show. They had to keep the CIA believing that they were trying to *hack* their way out of this problem. So far, they made runs at the safe house's firewalls, tried to cut off the power, and scramble their security measures. Of course, none of that had worked, but that was also part of the plan.

Given a few days, she and Quirk could have taken the place down from the inside out. However, Ronnie knew that they did not have a few days. It turned out that "in your face" hacking actually took days, if not months, of careful study. Control attacks to monitor how a system reacted, then perform another calculated breach. The process could be slow and tedious, but that's how she had earned her 100 percent success rate. A lot of good it did her now.

If the CIA really did believe that she held the key to unlocking a code involving the outbreak of the plague, Zach had a few hours—*maximum*. They needed quick, decisive action. Not exactly her strong suit.

Ronnie looked over her shoulder at the array of monitors that Quirk had set up. That CIA safe house may look like a ghetto from the outside, but scans revealed several gun turrets covered by desert camouflage, and even a tank hidden within lead-lined walls. Heat signatures showed five people in there, but that could have been a grossly low value. With the right amount of heat shielding, two dozen men could be in there, all waiting to take them down.

How well prepared were the CIA for an all-out assault?

"We *are* bulletproof, right?" she asked. Her nerves were getting the better of her.

"I refer you to the lack of Helicopters-R-Us in the general vicinity."

Groaning, Ronnie really started to doubt herself. "Picking up any signals?"

They had knocked out all satellite feeds in the area and shut down the site's radar and thermal imaging capabilities, but still...

"Besides a rather loud Mexican radio station giving away what sounds like bull testicles to the sixth caller, no."

"Are you sure? The CIA has been toying with—"

Quirk's deep frown stopped her inquiry. Of course, Quirk was checking all the frequencies and bandwidths.

"Sorry."

Normally, he would have made her pay for her micromanaging with some form of 1980s music trivia, but clearly Quirk was giving her some leeway, given the circumstances. For that, she was grateful. She really was not in the mood to figure out the B-side track from the 1982 single by A Flock of Seagulls, "I Ran (So Far Away)."

"And just as a heads-up, it looks like this plague is on steroids," Quirk reported, texting his contact back.

Like Ronnie needed any more bad news.

"So, check your lymph nodes already," Quirk scolded. She wasn't going to check anything until Zach was safe and sound.

"Is that a friendly?" the pilot asked.

She scanned the area ahead. The dirt road appeared empty. Wait! Was someone leaving the safe house through its dented tin door? More accurately, someone was *stumbling* out the door. Trying to adjust the binoculars, Ronnie knocked them out of focus. Her fingers scrambled to bring them back from blurry-ville.

"Should I fire?" the pilot asked casually.

"For the love of all that is holy, *no*!"

Ronnie fumbled with the dials until the image fuzzed out, and then came back into sharp focus. She would know that chin anywhere.

"It's a friendly," Ronnie said with a smile. It was the friendliest.

* * *

Quirk took the binoculars from Ronnie. How such an incredibly competent hacker could mess up the world's most expensive binoculars was beyond him. Fiddling with the multiple rings, he brought Zach's face into such relief that it looked like the FBI agent stood right in front of him.

Even in pain, those features were chiseled to perfection. Quirk let out a whistle. "Even bruised, he is one fine specimen."

Ronnie did not argue with him as she turned to the pilot. "Set us down."

But the beefcake shook his head. "No can do."

"Um...*yes* can do," his boss countered.

Quirk could have warned the pilot not to bother arguing with Ronnie when she was in this mood. But in truth, Quirk wanted to watch the pilot's jaw tense up and down. Clearly, *his* lymph nodes were not bursting with the Black Death.

"We are in a hostile environment chosen by the enemy," the hunk guffed. "If I land, we lose any slight advantage that we may have."

His boss put two fists on her hips and skewered the pilot with a look that would have melted solid metal.

"Yeah, like you said. It's *my* dime." Even more forcefully, Ronnie commanded, "*Land.*"

The pilot grunted. Not quite accepting, but not arguing either. So maybe the guy was as big a teddy bear as he looked.

While the pilot maneuvered the chopper, preparing for a landing, Quirk's phone vibrated in his pocket. For the tenth time. He loved Jennifer with all his heart, but he just didn't have the time to dish on why Tim Gunn wasn't a part of *Project Runway All Stars.* There it went again. Okay, maybe it was actual plague stuff she was talking about. Quirk pulled the phone out and scanned her texts. Jennifer was asking for CIA clearance? Um, a weird request, but since he was already patched into the agency's mainframe, there was no reason he couldn't accommodate her. The CIA wasn't exactly in Quirk's close friend "circle."

"As you wish," he typed, and then routed the data stream to her IP address. Quirk certainly hoped Jennifer's day was going better than theirs.

Then the helicopter set down on the dusty, dusty ground. Before Quirk could offer even the slightest scolding on how careful she should be, Ronnie was out of the helicopter. As soon as her boots hit the dirt, the chopper lifted off again.

"Um, I think Ronnie meant for us to *stay* on the ground."

The pilot looked over his shoulder. "Sorry. It's *not* your dime," he said.

Even though their gazes met for only a second, Quirk felt his cheeks flush and his heart race.

A teddy bear *and* a top?

This must be Quirk's lucky day.

"So," Quirk said as he sat down in the copilot's seat. "How long have you been an illegal mercenary pilot? Hmmm?"

* * *

Ronnie raced toward Zach as he lurched forward. She caught him just before he went down.

She forced a playful tone. "Hey, sexy."

Zach couldn't pretend that he was in anything but agony. "Hey there, yourself."

Even that seemed to take the last of Zach's energy as he sank to his knees. Ronnie lowered beside him. To her surprise, his lips tugged up in a little grin.

"I don't know what you were expecting," Zach said through pain-clenched teeth, "But this is *not* how I pictured our first date."

She couldn't help but smile back. "Yeah, you missed quite the outfit."

How many times had she dreamed of this moment? Their slow walk across the room. Her hair flowing back. His eyes gazing into hers. The reality? She was too busy choking on dirt to really appreciate the moment.

Besides, they didn't have a moment. They needed to get the hell out of there before the CIA decided to drop a bomb on them. *Literally.* Ronnie rose to her feet, expecting Zach to follow, but he stayed down.

"Um, I'm digging the scenery," Ronnie said as playfully as she could under the circumstances, "but we've got to get back into the air."

Zach tugged up his shirt, exposing his midsection—mottled in blacks, purples, and blues. Ronnie's hand flew to her mouth. She knew he had been tortured, but to actually *see* the damage…

And all for *her*.

He could have just told them where she was. He could have lured her here without her being any the wiser. She would have followed him without question. Yet he hadn't. Zach had taken this beating to protect her. If they weren't under threat of death, she would have laid a lip-lock on him right there.

However, she saw the pain in his eyes. Not from the physical pain, but from shame. That somehow it was his fault that he was injured. Too injured to even rise.

Men.

So she joked, "Okay, this is going a little far to prove that you didn't stand me up."

He chuckled. Even that seemed to hurt, but it softened his features.

"Come on," Ronnie encouraged. "We've got an ultrasound on board. Let's get you up there."

Ronnie watched Zach accustom himself to the pain. He gritted his teeth and took three short breaths before he leaned in to her. It took the strength of both of them to get him on his feet, and even then, Zach pressed against her. Not that she was complaining.

As they hobbled over to the landing helicopter, Zach winced. "An ultrasound machine? On a helicopter?"

"Yeah, and trust me," Ronnie said. "It did *not* come cheap."

* * *

Zach landed hard on the chopper floor as it lifted off before they climbed fully in. Zach would have thought at some point that his pain receptors would give out. However, that was just wishful thinking. The helicopter lurched, and he slammed into a metal bench as his vision blurred.

Ronnie tried to steady him, but the damage was done. As tenderly as she could while riding a bucking, accelerating helicopter, Ronnie helped him into a jump seat. Even with all of that, he couldn't take his eyes away from her. Okay, some of that may have been him trying to keep his head from spinning. The other was for a much less practical reason.

She turned to the pilot, sending her blonde ponytail swishing across his face. Zach wouldn't complain. They were finally in the same ZIP code and on the same chopper. Too bad that he felt halfway to passing out.

"Anything?" she asked the pilot.

"All clear," the big man replied.

"*All*?" Ronnie emphasized.

"Nothing on the deck," the pilot said as he held the cold butt of a cigar between his teeth. Zach knew from experience that old dogs like the pilot didn't like to be questioned.

Ronnie swung back to the young man sitting behind half a dozen monitors. From the dark hair to the well-manicured fingertips, Zach could only assume that it was Quirk. How very jealous Warp would be.

"You are sure that you knocked out the satellite coverage for our entire area?" Ronnie asked.

The young man kept typing. "Even the Chinese."

"Crap," Ronnie said, hitting her palm against the bulkhead.

"That's good, isn't it?" Zach asked, wincing as fire shot along a broken rib.

Neither Quirk nor Ronnie looked in his direction. Instead, their eyes met over the monitors. Their years of working together were so very apparent. They'd clearly reached some mutual decision.

Ronnie frowned, but Quirk was all smiles.

"That can only mean one thing," Quirk stated, and then turned that flirtatious smile in Zach's direction. "We're going to need you to strip."

Zach's eyes shot a look at Ronnie. Her assistant was joking, right? From the sympathetic look on her face, Quirk wasn't. Ronnie knelt beside Zach, placing her hand on his knee.

"If they are staying this clear, then they must have planted a tracking device on you."

Damn it! Of course, Grant had planted something on him. That's what Zach would have done if the roles had been reversed. Zach *would* have thought of it if his head weren't threatening to split in two. He tugged his turtleneck up, but couldn't quite get it over his head. It didn't exactly help that Quirk was licking his lips.

"Turn around," Ronnie instructed her assistant.

"But—"

Ronnie gave Quirk a look that could have—seriously—lifted paint off the wall. Zach had always imagined what Ronnie looked like when silence filled their phone conversations. She didn't disappoint. Too bad he was in hypovolemic shock.

Quirk huffed, grabbed a laptop, and turned to the pilot.

"You have other clothes for me, I assume?" Zach asked.

Ronnie looked at Quirk, who glanced over his shoulder, more than a little contrite. Ronnie cocked her head to the side, ready to scold her assistant.

* * *

"What?" Quirk demanded. "I was already three percent over budget." Ronnie tried to get a word in edgewise, but Quirk overrode her. "*You* are the one who said no more spending, *period!*"

Oh, just try to squirm out of that one, little missy. Quirk knew that Ronnie wanted to look all in-charge for her lover boy, but Quirk wasn't taking the fall for this one.

"Quite the well-prepared jailbreak," Mr. Hunk-o-Matic said, and then gritted his teeth in pain. Was it wrong that Quirk found him even more appetizing when his eyes squinted just so?

"It's our first," Ronnie said to Zach, seeming to accept the fact that Quirk had won their last little exchange until she turned to him. "Give Zach your pants."

"No!" he protested in horror.

"Quirk!"

"I can't," he said, a bit sheepish. "I'm going *commando*," he admitted.

Of all the days...

Seriously, what did Ronnie expect after giving him only three hours to plan, prepare, and execute the most kick-ass rescue in the history of mankind? Some small details may have slipped past. Like underwear.

"Um," Zach said with a frown. "Can't I at least keep my own briefs?"

"No!" both Quirk and Ronnie answered. At least they were on the same page about some things.

Ronnie turned to the very confused-looking FBI agent. "The CIA has been experimenting with fiber-thin passive wire elements that can be activated from up to three miles away. We can't take the risk with any item that they had access to while you were detained."

"So if anyone is going *commando*..." Quirk commented. Of course, Ronnie gave him her finely honed "if looks could kill I'd be serving life imprisonment" look. Quirk was about to preemptively respond when a pair of brown camo pants landed on his head.

Snatching them away from his face, Quirk turned to find the pilot in nothing but his nice, tight, form-fitting long johns.

"My, my," Quirk said, smiling. "This day is looking up."

* * *

Amanda maxed out the additional bandwidth Jennifer had gotten to broaden her search. How her assistant scrounged around for access to the CIA's web search monitoring software so quickly, Amanda didn't know—and quite frankly, didn't want to know. They could be convicted of espionage later. Because they certainly couldn't ask for help from their CIA liaison, could they?

She glanced over at Devlin, who didn't even bother pretending to work. If the CIA liaison wasn't using the bandwidth, why shouldn't they borrow it?

Rapidly, she sorted through the searches for "Black Death," and "bubonic plague." The numbers were staggering. In the hundreds of millions. Really, those were not the ones that she needed. Those represented people infected or worried about infection. Those were definitely not the Hidden Hand.

No, she honed in on keyword searches, such as "spread of the plague," and "real-time death count," words that would be more consistent with an organization monitoring the spread of their weapon. She also looked up "survivor stories," and "instances of resistance." The Hidden Hand would be very interested in such information. And with the plague raging throughout the country, those who did not have any form of natural immunity would be identified much faster than the regular Black Death cycle.

Jennifer nudged Amanda.

She looked up as her assistant indicated the infirmary around them—crammed with beds and patients. In fact, there were so many that the newer victims were being set up in the cafeteria. In the end, Amanda had no doubt that every single one of the seventy-nine inhabitants of Plum Island would end up on an IV drip.

Amanda cocked an eyebrow to her assistant as Jennifer nodded toward the back of the room. The one where the first patients had been admitted.

The beds were filled with scientists and guards. Exactly what one would suspect, given that this was Plum Island, after all. Wait. There wasn't just one guard down here, but *all* of the guards. And they were the sickest. One was even on oxygen already. His bubonic plague had become pneumonic plague—the most deadly of the plague strains.

"They infected the guards first." Jennifer nodded solemnly.

Getting the guards sick first certainly did not seem accidental.

"Special Bulletin" blared from the television just before Anderson Cooper came back on.

"The governors of New York, New Jersey, and Connecticut have agreed that hospitals within the entire tristate area are now at maximum capacity, and all three states have adopted the 'Antibiotic Home Delivery' system." Anderson pierced the camera with those eyes of his. "Please, listen. Medical personnel urge you to stay home if you are not infected yet, and to please place a red 'X' on your door if you are. Medics will begin delivering antibiotics within the hour. Please do *not* panic. Help is on the way."

But help *wasn't* on the way. Not really. Even with the most sophisticated of intravenous antibiotics combinations, Jennifer was no better. And Amanda could feel her own lymph nodes swelling and her fingertips tingling as the plague clogged her capillaries.

And now, knowing that the guards had been incapacitated? The Hidden Hand not only wished to eliminate any threat to finding a cure for the plague—they clearly were planning on taking over Plum Island at some point.

Jennifer slammed her laptop cover closed and motioned for the nurse to come over.

"What are you doing?" Amanda asked.

Her assistant's only response was to slam Amanda's laptop cover closed as well. When the nurse walked over, Jennifer tugged at her IV line.

"Don't," the nurse said. "You could yank it out."

With the fierce look in Jennifer's eyes, that was exactly what her assistant wanted to happen. To get unhooked from the IV, so they could go back upstairs and get to work at full throttle.

Amanda turned to the nurse. "Cap us off."

"These medications are vital to your—"

"I'm lead on the bubonic plague," Amanda explained. "Don't make me contradict you." She indicated the other patients. Amanda lowered her voice. "We're just rearranging chairs on the *Titanic*."

The nurse knew that "the treatments" were simply to make them more comfortable until…well…until the end. Finally, the nurse sighed, and began the process of untethering them.

Amanda grinned at Jennifer. They were getting back to work, all right.

CHAPTER 15

Nearby, somewhere over Mexico
10:19 a.m., MST

Grant hated helicopters. They were noisy, dirty, and usually smelled like ass. And this charming piece of scrap metal the Mexican army called a helicopter? Let's just say that in comparison, the bar last night had a Parisian bouquet.

But the ends would justify the means. They had better.

He had not spent a year of his life wearing cheap suits and pretending to care about law enforcement without an impeccable exit strategy. If he didn't get back into his Armani suit soon, he feared that his skin would simply slough off.

Oh, and when he delivered the Robin Hood hacker to his superiors? And helped stop the single largest threat to national security since the Civil War? Um, yeah, he'd get his Armani suit back, and so much more.

"Well?" he demanded of the mustached pilot. Grant would never understand Latinos' fascination with bushy facial hair.

"We have a lock," the man replied in a thick accent.

Grant looked at the digital screen that had hastily been mounted onto the rusting dashboard. Zach's chopper was tracking northwest, just as he had guessed. Soon, this damned assignment would be over.

Good thing, because Grant had his tailor on standby.

* * *

Ronnie glanced away as Zach finished dressing. Not that she didn't want to look. Um, even bruised, those abs were to die for, but they reminded her of the beating he took. For her. Had it tainted his feelings?

Since meeting on that dusty road outside the CIA safe house things had been, well, strained. Granted, Zach was badly injured, and they were fleeing for their lives on a helicopter, but still. The butterflies just wouldn't go away. Each time she caught a glimpse of that strong jawline or those eyes, Ronnie felt as though, somehow, she had entered her own surveillance footage. *He really couldn't be here, with her, could he?*

"So the metal blocks the signal?" Zach asked Quirk, as her assistant stuffed the FBI agent's clothes into an aluminum tube.

Quirk's well-manscaped eyebrow shot up. "Hardly. We want it amplified."

God, her assistant could be such a queen sometimes. She would have stepped in to spare Zach the drama, but she was having a hard time calibrating the ultrasound machine.

"But um," Zach asked tentatively, "aren't we just dumping the clothes over the side?"

"And have them get a quick visual that we outwitted them?" Quirk snorted as he pulled out a model airplane. Okay, Quirk would kill her if she ever used the term "model" for that piece of high-tech awesomeness. It was more like a souped-up fighter jet, only scaled down to be two feet long. "I am *way* cooler than that."

Quirk turned to the pilot. "Speed?"

"Three hundred and seventy-seven kph," the pilot answered in his usual brusque manner.

Quirk typed the number into the small jet's onboard keyboard, but then paused. "Three hundred and seventy-seven?" Oh, my. That man knows how to handle his stick."

"Quirk..." Ronnie warned as she came to Zach's side. If she had any hope of not chasing the FBI agent away, Quirk was going to have to keep the not-so-subtle innuendos to a minimum.

Of course, her assistant did not oblige. While checking the tube's attachment to the plane's fuselage with one hand, Quirk waved his other hand in the general vicinity of Zach.

* * *

"Oh, sure," Quirk said as he put the finishing touches on his baby. "We can risk our lives to save your squeeze, but I can't take a moment to—"

"Quirk!"

Yes, Ronnie, the truth did hurt. But there was no point in pursuing her unjust behavior, since their chopper was being pursued. By men with guns.

"All right. Here we go." He turned to the pilot, who just needed his beard trimmed a bit to really accentuate his jawline. "Ready?"

"Always," the pilot grunted.

Those slightly yellowed-by-cigar teeth and squinting, flint eyes captured Quirk.

"You *did* say that we were ready, right?" Ronnie interjected before Quirk got weak in the knees.

"On my mark," Quirk announced as the pilot gripped the joystick tightly. "Three...two...one..."

In unison, almost like great sex, Quirk felt the pilot turn the chopper as Quirk opened the side door and released the decoy plane. It flew straight and true, directly on the path they had been heading. The metal of the chopper vibrated, making Quirk's teeth chatter as it laid over, gaining speed, taking them nearly ninety degrees away from the plane's trajectory. The decoy plane carrying Zach's tracked clothes should throw those CIA goons off their track by miles.

Once the chopper leveled out and Quirk shut the door, he made a show of dusting off his hands. "I am *that* good."

"Maybe," Ronnie admitted, "but now, we wait."

Yes, waiting. Quirk's least favorite part.

* * *

"Why don't we have a visual?" Grant demanded. The damned digital readout showed that they should be right on Zach's ass by now, yet he could see nothing but blue skies all around.

The pilot just shrugged. Did the man not know that Grant's career—no, *life*—depended on the next few minutes?

However, the mustached pilot seemed to have little regard for career advancement.

"There," the Federale pilot said, pointing ahead.

Grant had to squint to make out the faintest exhaust trail. "That's no chopper."

Instead, it was a toy plane. A freaking toy plane.

They must have realized that Zach's clothes were traceable. He'd have to yell at the techs back home who swore that the thin metal fiber couldn't be found.

"Fire on it."

The pilot popped the safety off the trigger and locked onto the tiny plane.

A warning flashed in bright red on the screen. "Better Luck Next Time."

The Robin Hood hacker's tagline.

"Fire!" Grant yelled, knowing that destroying the plane would in no way get back at Zach and that binary bitch, but he did take a measure of satisfaction as the small plane blew up, scattering Zach's clothes, and about a hundred thousand dollars in tracking equipment, to the wind.

Oh, they might have thought that they won the day, but clearly the Robin Hood hacker didn't realize that Grant had an unlimited budget for this mission.

Sitting back in the flight seat, Grant gave the order. "Activate the secondary tracking device."

The pilot nodded, punching in the code.

Zach wasn't getting away. The sanctimonious prick wasn't going to live another day.

* * *

"How long until we land?" Ronnie asked the pilot. If they were on schedule, they should be able to pick up their get-away car and cross back into Texas within the hour.

Before the pilot could answer, Quirk shouted, "We've got two fast-moving bogeys approaching from the east!"

Ronnie spun on her heel. That couldn't be. They'd knocked out all eyes in the air and had gotten rid of the tracking device on Zach. But looking down at the radar screen, Quirk was correct. Actually, another two blimps popped up on the readout.

"I am telling you, they've perfected it," Quirk insisted.

The FBI agent raised an eyebrow. "Perfected what?"

Ronnie really didn't want to believe that it could be true. "They are at least five years away from field-testing it."

Quirk shrugged. "Guess we are getting a look into the future, then."

Zach leaned forward, guarding his injured ribs. They had shot him full of antibiotics, steroids, and painkillers—sometimes Quirk's hypochondria and encyclopedic knowledge of remedies did come in handy, but pain still etched the FBI agent's face.

All for her, and here she couldn't even save him. Ronnie sat down next to Zach. Gently, she ran her hands over his arms.

"How long were you unconscious?" Ronnie asked.

"I wasn't," Zach stated, but when Ronnie cocked her head, he cast his eyes down. "No more than a few minutes." He looked back up. "Did they shoot me up with something?"

Quirk snorted. "You could say that."

Ronnie glared at her assistant. As if they didn't have enough to worry about. She resented having to be sarcasm patrol as well.

"They've been experimenting with an ultrathin metal fiber that—"

"I know," Zach interrupted. "The clothes."

"Yes, well, no," Ronnie said as her hands coursed over his wide shoulders and back. Oh, to be in such close physical contact for some other reason than trying to save their lives. "What I am looking for is even more advanced. The metallic ions are inert until they are hit by a burst of microwaves, and then they realign, transforming that microwave energy into a narrow burst of radio signal."

The helicopter jolted, nearly sending Ronnie to the floor. It was only Zach's strong hands that kept her seated. For a moment he held her there, despite the danger of them both falling over. Their body heat mingled. God, how she wanted to taste those cracked and bruised lips. Zach leaned in. Ronnie leaned in.

"Um, yeah," Quirk interjected. Ronnie snapped back and began her gentle probing of Zach's skin, trying to find the insertion point. "Once that burst of energy is released, the ions revert to their inert, impossible-to-detect state."

"*Nearly* impossible," Ronnie corrected him. They *had* to find the thin, metal thread—or they were worse than sitting ducks.

"Well, it might not matter now," Quirk said, not sounding like his usual snarky self. "Looks like four jets and a chase helicopter."

To punctuate her assistant's words, a missile went off to the left, rocking the helicopter.

"I take it that this wasn't just a family misunderstanding," the pilot grumbled.

She didn't blame the guy. They hadn't been exactly forth-coming about why they needed the helicopter when they booked it.

It was Zach's jaw that worked overtime, though. "We've got to talk."

"Sure," Ronnie said frantically searching up his neck for evidence of the fiber. "Let me just pour a glass of wine."

* * *

Zach grabbed Ronnie's hand. He loved her sense of humor, but not with this weight on his conscience. "I'm serious."

Another explosion nearly shattered the window behind them as they lurched to the left.

"Ha! Just try to lock on to us," Quirk shouted, working on five different devices.

Zach tugged Ronnie's chin up to face him. "They don't want to *down* the chopper. They want to force us to *land*."

As another explosion rocked them to the right, Ronnie frowned. "Dude, it doesn't—"

"They want you to decode for them, Ronnie, and…" Zach could hardly believe what he was about to say. "And I think you should."

"After what they did to you?" she hissed, pulling away from him.

"Yes," Zach rushed on. "This *is* about the world being stricken by—"

"I get it," Ronnie interrupted, but then her eyes softened. "You don't think I get it? I am totally on board with helping to save the world—"

"Um, with a little help?" Quirk interjected.

Ronnie didn't even glance in her assistant's direction as she answered. "But not for *them*."

Zach could completely understand her reluctance. After the way Grant had treated him? The way he was treating them now? Then, add in the fact that Ronnie was on the FBI's Ten Most Wanted list for cyber crimes. Still, he needed her to hear him out.

"Ronnie, they need you alive so—"

But she shook her head. "Zach, you know that I love your optimism, but they may leave me alive, but they'll kill you." Ronnie nodded toward Quirk and the pilot. "All of you."

"Yep," the pilot said as he ground his cigar between his teeth, all the while flying them through a war zone.

Despite the pilot's expertise, another explosion hit so closely that the wall of the chopper flared red and the helicopter veered so far over, Zach was pretty damn sure that they were going to crash-land. Finally, the pilot righted the aircraft, but now they only cruised a few yards above the ground.

"I think they've decided that even Ronnie is expendable," Quirk informed them.

And Zach couldn't argue. Out of the front, now cracked, window, the two jets banked sharply, coming back for another pass. His own government was going to shoot down a civilian chopper. Grant was willing to kill the very woman who could help him.

"Yeah, we've got a problem," the pilot announced, clutching the joystick with both hands. "We're leaking fuel. I need a plan 'B,' pronto."

What plan *B*? But then, Zach saw Quirk and Ronnie exchange a look.

"What?" he asked. "You mean you *really* have a plan 'B'?"

* * *

Um, yes they had a plan *B*, but if plan *A* had been poorly planned with questionable execution, then plan *B*, well, plan *B* was suicidal. Ronnie was so loath to broach it that Quirk was the one who had to speak up.

"We *do* have El Blinko."

Zach looked at Quirk, then at her. "What's that?"

"An EM gun," Quirk supplied.

"We *hope*," Ronnie countered. Even hope was a bit of a stretch.

"That thing will take down my bird," the pilot grumbled, grinding down on the cigar. However, Quirk was quite full of himself.

"No, no, no," her assistant said as he rummaged around in their gear. "That's the super-cool thing. It is *uni*directional."

"Sort of," Ronnie added quickly as Zach frowned. "It's a prototype."

Despite the pilot's original qualms as the chopper rocked back and forth—nearly spiraling out of control—he seemed more open to the idea than Ronnie.

"How *proto* is proto?"

Ronnie rushed in before Quirk could add his spin to it. "Pretty proto."

Quirk crossed his arms. "It *worked* in Zurich."

"It took out a *city block* in Zurich." Ronnie answered as the chopper rocked nearly horizontal, forcing her to grip the seat, and then get slammed back against the bulkhead as the pilot righted the craft. Therefore, she did not argue as Quirk kept right on putting the EM gun together as they argued.

"*One*," Quirk emphasized, with a single finger up in the air. "Just *one* block." Ronnie tried to introduce some reality to the situation, but Quirk talked right over her. "I'm telling you, I've made some modifications. It's got a *way* tighter range."

This time, when the helicopter bucked, everyone was thrown to the floor. Not that she didn't mind Zach's legs wrapped around her, but she would prefer it not to be because he was busy trying to keep a large crate from falling on both of them.

"It'll work," Quirk insisted as he rose.

"Or?" Zach asked, holding out a hand to help Ronnie to her feet.

"We go down," the pilot finished in his surly manner.

Ronnie's assistant tried to point out the window, except that the chopper bucked and nearly knocked him on his butt. "Like we aren't already."

Quirk must have realized that he had just insulted the pilot, for he quickly followed up with, "Not that you aren't the *best* pilot, but *come on*! Who can stand up to five-on-one action? It is now or never."

With explosions sounding all around and them leaking fuel, what choice did any of them have? The pilot gave a curt nod.

"Goody!" Quirk exclaimed as he put the finishing touches on the device. "I've been utilizing the spark-gap model of electromagnetic—"

"Okay," Ronnie stated, "even *I* don't care. Just get it out."

Quirk pouted just a bit, and then pulled out his prize. Unfortunately, he had modeled it after the classic Flash Gordon ray gun—something that didn't escape the pilot.

"I changed my mind," he grunted.

But there was no turning back. "We've *got* to try," Ronnie said as she held her hand out for the gun, but Quirk pulled it to his chest.

"It's my design."

"Since when have you *shot* a real gun?"

Wounded but practical, Quirk went to turn the weapon over to her, but Zach intercepted it.

"And since when have *you* shot at real people?" he asked.

"Yeah, but—" Before she could fully respond, Zach unlatched the helicopter door, aimed at the planes and fired. The gun revved, making a wicked science fiction whooshing beep sound, and then shot out glitter along with a light show.

"What the—?" Zach asked himself, in shock.

Ronnie tried to brace Zach's hand, but before she could, the gun actually fired. As in fired big time. As in the recoil threw Zach against the bulkhead—nearly knocking him unconscious.

"Sorry. I should have explained that the gun packs the punch of the equivalent of two hundred and fifty thousand joules of energy."

Zach shook his head, trying to clear his vision. "That would have been good to know."

The chopper swooped and dodged as missiles headed their way.

"Not only didn't your damn gun work—"

"It worked!" Quirk insisted. "Just wait!"

But the missiles kept coming.

"I'm waiting…" the pilot said, not sounding at all patient.

"They must have maximum shielding," Quirk concluded, turning a knob on the gun. "This thing is going to eleven."

Ronnie took up the gun, since, you know, Zach was still tilted at a weird angle. She braced herself against the door and fired at the approaching missiles.

Just feet from hitting their side, the missiles sputtered, losing speed and altitude, then dropped from the sky, crashing to the earth. Ronnie didn't wait. She took aim with the holographic sight and fired at the planes.

The gun revved, and at least she was partially prepared for the kick. Her shoulder, however, might never be the same again. At least she wasn't on her butt. The lead plane's wings tilted precariously as its partner's nose suddenly dipped down. The two nearly collided with one another on their way down. The canopies popped off one jet as the pilot ejected.

His plane crashed in a fiery pyre while the other righted itself, streaking out of range.

"One down. Four to go!" she yelled over the wind as Zach gave her a weak smile while pressing the wound on the back of his head.

For the first time in a while, their helicopter actually flew in a straight line. It was a weird sensation. As the other two planes made their runs, Ronnie took aim. She fired, but the pilots must have caught on to the weapon, as they both backed away, trying to outrace the invisible enemy. One succeeded. The other began circling and circling to the right. The EM burst must have knocked out their left rudder controls.

Ronnie would take it. "Two down. Three to go."

Without missing a beat, she aimed at the plane streaking by, and fired. The thing dropped a good hundred feet in the air before rolling beyond the horizon.

"We've only got one plane and the chase chopper to worry about," Ronnie informed Zach. He did his best to look optimistic. "Yeah, about that," Quirk began. She turned to face her assistant. She did not want to know what was about to come out of his mouth. "You only have one more shot."

"What?" she looked down at the EM gun, wishing she had taken more interest in Quirk's side project.

"Remember?" Quirk asked, and then launched into an imitation of her that even Ronnie had to give him credit for. "Why pay for more than five shots? When are we ever going to need more than *five* EM pulses?"

Damn it! She should have known that once she got mixed up with Zach, they would, at some point, clearly need six EM shots. But alas, she was too busy manufacturing an iPod to communicate with the FBI agent chasing her to think of it.

Ronnie turned to the pilot. "Up to you."

"If you can get the plane, I can take the chopper."

You know, she could see why Quirk was drooling.

"I could take the stick," Ronnie suggested to the pilot.

"*You* can fly a helicopter?" Zach asked as he rose gingerly from the floor.

Quirk snorted. "Sure. If Comanche Chopper Extreme counts."

As the plane made its way around to make another run at them, Ronnie helped Zach to a seat.

"Hey, I'm number five in the world."

The pilot grinned. "I'm number one."

Okay. This is going to be fun.

She aimed and fired the ray gun directly in the path of the oncoming plane. The burst must have caught the navigation system. The plane zigged to the left, and then zagged to the right, and then upward. Ronnie lost sight of the plane as it climbed past their view.

"All right," Ronnie stated as the chase helicopter tilted forward, advancing on their injured chopper. "Let's see what Mr. Comanche-Number-One can do."

CHAPTER 16

Somewhere over Mexico
10:40 a.m., MST

Ah, that pilot and his joystick. Quirk was so very glad that Ronnie was finally beginning to understand his new man. Just the way he gritted that cigar between his teeth sent shivers up Quirk's back. Either that, or the constant vibration of the strained metal had settled into his joints.

The pilot looked at Ronnie, then nodded toward the gun turret. "Even number one could use some help," he said.

Quirk raised an eyebrow. Ronnie? On a machine gun? Sure, the woman slayed at video games, but live ammo? However, poor super-Special Agent Hunter still looked nauseated and perhaps a bit dizzy.

"Keep them busy," Quirk said to Ronnie, who was strapping into the gun seat. He looked down at the ray gun. "I might be able to get another wallop out of this baby."

Quirk sat down next to the FBI agent as the helicopter tilted at a forty-five degree angle. Their thighs brushed one another. Normally, Quirk would have made a great witty comment, but Zach looked ready to hurl. And while Quirk loved witty repartee, he loved cleaning off his shoes less.

"How about a forward, circle, right?" Ronnie asked the pilot.

Quirk had absolutely no idea what his boss meant. He usually kept earbuds in when she played, preferring some Lady Gaga or Lady Antebellum to the screeching sounds of war. Of course, the irony of actually now *being* in the screeching sounds of war did not escape Quirk. Maybe next time, he would pay slightly better attention to Ronnie's hobbies.

The pilot, not surprised in the least, seemed to know exactly what Ronnie was talking about. He reversed course and dropped enough altitude for Quirk's booty to come off the seat. Ronnie took advantage of the situation, shooting at the chase helicopter's belly. But the other pilot must have also been a high-ranking member of the Comanche club, because he slid out of range.

Zach's hands gripped the seat beside Quirk. The guy was green. Literally green. Quirk would normally take the time to comfort such a fine-looking man, but, you know, they were in the middle of a firefight.

"X, square, left, left," the pilot bellowed.

Quirk couldn't take the time, though, to watch the aftermath of his actions. Quirk had an EM-burst ray gun to fix. The energy stores were virtually nonexistent. As close as that other chopper was, Quirk wouldn't need much juice to create a burst to take out their equipment.

As their helicopter swerved and dipped and lunged, Quirk calibrated the gun. The power level inched up from red to orange. If he could scrape up enough to get into the yellow zone…

Glancing out the door, Quirk realized that they would not have the luxury for even yellow as the other chopper barreled toward them.

"Don't worry!" Quirk shouted, jumping up and pointing the gun out the door.

* * *

"No!" Ronnie cried out.

Zach ignored his churning stomach and launched for Quirk. But her assistant aimed and fired. Unfortunately, this was exactly the same moment that their pilot turned the chopper hard…into the pulse.

Even though he couldn't see the beam, Zach felt its effects immediately on their craft. While never a steady ride, the chopper now streaked through the sky completely unhelmed. Zach could feel his stomach crawling into his throat.

And the other chopper was no better. It lay over on its side, careening toward them.

"Damn it!" the pilot cursed as he struggled with the controls, hitting each and every button—none of which responded.

"But we were losing!" Quirk demanded, as the other chopper crossed in front of them, missing a collision by inches.

"Losing?" the pilot demanded as he wrestled with the joystick.

Ronnie climbed out of the gun seat, yanking on equipment. "We weren't losing. We were baiting him for a triangle, circle, right, square maneuver."

Zach was clueless, and Quirk looked even less informed.

She huffed as she lifted a large case out from under the seat. "We were going to take out his rear blade!"

"Oh, crap," Quirk said, and then knelt by the case.

"What are you doing?" Zach asked as the two hackers worked frantically.

"Our equipment was completely shielded, so we are going to interface with the chopper's—"

"We don't have time for this crap!" the pilot growled.

To punctuate his words, the chase chopper plowed into a hillside, flaring brightly—even in full sunlight. Smoke billowed from the crash site. Zach stared into the fire. Was Grant burning right now? And did he care?

It turned out, with pain lancing his side, that Zach distinctly did not.

Quirk dragged cabling to the pilot's seat. "Oh, darling, you haven't seen how fast I can work. Now spread 'em."

Had Quirk said that to him, Zach thought, there would have been no spreading. Either the pilot really was as into Quirk as Quirk thought, or the man knew what Quirk needed, for he did readjust for the skinny assistant to get between his legs to the control panel.

Zach grabbed hold of a metal handle as the chopper lost more and more and more altitude. And that ridge up ahead was getting closer and closer and closer.

"Now!" Quirk yelled.

The pilot grabbed the joystick with both hands and pulled upward. At first, the chopper didn't respond, but as the sparsely vegetated hillside flew at them, the vehicle lurched upward as the rotors suddenly kicked into gear. They skimmed over the ridge close enough to yank out some weeds, but they skimmed over nonetheless.

But once over the hill, the chopper again sputtered. Good thing that they were heading toward a valley, because the blades stopped *thump, thump, thumping* overhead.

"What's wrong?" Ronnie demanded.

"Nothing!" Quirk insisted. "I'm patched in."

The pilot shoved the two toward the back of the chopper. "It's not the electronics."

"Then what—?"

"We're out of gas," the pilot said spitting out that chewed-up wad of cigar.

"Oh, crap," Ronnie said, whirling around. "Everyone get strapped in!"

Zach was already ahead of her, pulling the straps over his head and latching them at his waist. Ronnie bounced off the bulkhead and slid in sideways to her seat. Her eyes spoke the fifteen million apologies that seemed on the tip of her tongue. He wanted to comfort her and reassure her that none of it was her fault, but he didn't have time.

Instead, he smiled. A warm smile. A real smile. If they were going to die, it would be together.

"This really is going down as the lamest rescue attempt in the history of rescue attempts," Zach said.

The guilt that haunted her eyes cleared as she strapped herself in. "But come on, shouldn't we get an 'A' for effort?"

Zach leaned in. Yes, she should get an *A*, and a whole lot more. The space between them closed. He could smell the kiwi in her hair. She had laugh lines at the corners of her eyes that he had always imagined would be right there, crinkling for him.

Her lips parted. Finally, he would get to taste—

"Hang on!" the pilot yelled as the helicopter tilted precariously forward, throwing them all against their restraints.

* * *

Ronnie's hand lashed out, grabbing hold of Zach's. The ground was now like a bull's-eye for the chopper. The only good thing from their staggering, limping, and erratic flight was they didn't have much altitude.

How many tons of metal were about to hit—with how many pounds of pressure? She would have done the calculations in her head except for, you know—they were about to find out.

This was it.

She squeezed Zach's hand. How Ronnie wanted to clench her eyes closed, but the sight before her refused to let them close.

The blades hit first. The metal screeched as they bent askew, which, by some sheer, dumb luck, toppled them over so that the gears and roof took the brunt of the collision. The chopper rolled, and the torque threatened to tear the straps that held them in. But in a burst of shattered glass and twisted steel, it groaned to a halt.

"Get out!" The pilot yelled.

Ronnie fumbled with her latch. Her fingers were numb from gripping Zach so tightly. He helped her with the buckle as the pilot opened the side door.

"Now!"

In a tangle of limbs, they all scrambled out as cut wires sparked and popped. They ran and stumbled as many yards as they could before the chopper blew. The force knocked them all to the ground.

Ronnie lay there for a moment, making sure that she could feel all her limbs. It wasn't just shock telling her that she had survived the crash. But the aches and shooting pains from every quarter of her body confirmed that she was, in fact, alive. Rolling onto her back, she scanned the area. Everyone else looked tattered all to hell, but alive as well.

Zach helped her to sit up. God, he looked like hell. Probably just a good reflection of how well she had fared.

She patted his arm as another fireball roared from the wreckage into the sky.

"Okay, so maybe not an '*A*'…"

* * *

Grant winced against the sun, the throbbing in his shoulder, and their abject failure. Who could have guessed that the bitch had an EM gun? A gun that actually shot directional EM pulses? He was seriously going to have to have a talk with the guys in R&D at Langley.

Luckily, their work with ionic metal components was pretty damned cutting edge. As his pilot smoldered on the ground next to him, Grant bit down hard on his back molar. He cracked the thin porcelain cap, cutting his cheek. He would have to have a good talking-to with the tech boys about that, too.

As moisture washed over the filament in his tooth, it activated the metal, creating an extremely temporary broadcast signal.

"No joy," Grant said to the air, thick with acrid smoke. "The package is loose." Of course, Grant couldn't hear his superiors back in Washington, not with his earpiece dead, but he could certainly imagine the general mood. Pissed off and scared. "I repeat. The fucking package is on the loose."

His tongue played with the edge of the cap. Tiny metal fragments floated up amongst the blood. Who knew if they even got that last bit? Grant surveyed the dry, barren Mexican countryside.

While the Federales would send someone for their downed pilots, Grant doubted very much if they would help him give chase. The CIA had already strained relations with the Mexican government over just the concept of kidnapping Zach to get to the Robin Hood hacker.

Now, to know that she'd pulled out an EM gun? They were not going to have the *cojones* to challenge her. No one did. Except for Grant.

One might think that after losing four jets, a chopper, and a literally half-baked pilot, it would have put a damper on his optimism. But Grant just whistled as he headed north.

Round one seldom went to the ultimate victor.

* * *

Zach ground his teeth, which didn't really do anything to ward off the pain in his side. However, it certainly made him feel like he was doing something. Especially since Ronnie had put him on a "hunk" time-out. Or was that what Quirk called it? Either way, it galled him to have to sit on the sidelines as the other three pulled anything functional from the burned-out husk of the helicopter.

He watched as Ronnie brushed aside a stray lock as she rummaged through the wreckage. One would think, after being tortured and shot down out of the sky, that he might be a wee bit resentful of Ronnie.

Lord knew that if his mother had anything to say about it, she would say, "Once trouble, always trouble," or "A lady who puts her elbows on the dinner table is no lady." And he would be steaming right about now.

Granny, however? God rest her soul, she would be saying something like, "Such a dear to try to rescue you, no?" or "It's the effort that counts."

Yeah, he usually did fall on Granny's side. Because how could he be upset with Ronnie? She'd risked her life, Quirk's, and, as it turned out, the pilot's—to save him. How many times did his therapist insist that Zach needed to find out exactly how committed Ronnie was to the relationship? Zach was pretty sure that taking on the CIA was pretty damn committed. He could hardly wait to tell Dr. Webster. *Not.*

Ronnie lugged a large, charred metallic suitcase over and plopped it down before stretching her back. Under any other circumstances, he would have hopped up to give her a hand.

Unfortunately, these were extremely difficult circumstances, as his right kidney throbbed. Literally, *throbbed.* Instead of rising, he nodded to the pilot, who was still in long johns and walking away from the wreckage. "Where's he going?" Zach asked Ronnie.

Ronnie lifted her hand above her eyes to shield them from the afternoon sun. "Probably to get a sawed-off shotgun."

"Wait!" Quirk shouted unceremoniously dropping his equipment nearly on Zach's feet as he rushed after the pilot. "Wait!"

To Zach's surprise, the pilot did stop as Quirk panted the ten whole steps he had to run. "Where are you going?"

"You destroyed a helicopter I'd assembled by hand. Where do you think I'm going?"

"But, but, but," Quirk protested, "can't you stay for lunch? I think I salvaged some Brie and crackers."

Zach didn't think that the burly pilot looked like a Brie kind of guy. So he wasn't exactly surprised when the pilot turned and continued walking down the dusty valley floor.

"He'll be back," Quirk said as he rejoined them.

Ronnie snorted. "Yeah, with a sawed-off shotgun."

"Whichever," Zach said. "We've *got* to get out of here."

Zach did not like the fact that Grant's helicopter had gone down just over the ridge. While he hoped fervently that his ex-partner had died in that fiery crash, they couldn't be sure. And if Zach had learned something over the past twenty-four hours, it was not to assume anything.

"Already on it," Quirk said with a wave of his hand. He popped the locks on a briefcase, bringing to bear half a dozen computers running half a dozen programs that Zach didn't even know existed. "But I gotta say, even if I get our satcom working, we've got to wait for us to move into a new satellite's coverage range. Then, mounting an evacuation could take—"

"Pay double," Ronnie announced.

Okay, Zach hadn't known her for long, but paying *double*? That seemed far outside Ronnie's comfort zone. The expression on Quirk's face and his inability to respond immediately confirmed Zach's suspicions.

"*Double*?" Quirk stammered. "Did I just hear you correctly?"

"Pay whatever you have to," Ronnie confirmed. "I want out of here by nightfall."

"*Ja, mein Kommandant,*" Quirk replied.

Ronnie frowned, and then turned to Zach. "And now we've got some metallic ions to remove."

Damn it. He'd forgotten about the plant. He still had a tracking device embedded somewhere in his skin. You would think that he could feel a microfilament, but with all of his cuts and bruises? Where *didn't* his body hurt?

Ronnie grinned, though, as she sat down cross-legged next to him. Was it the glow of the fire behind her, or was she just that radiant? Not in the high couture, fake eyelashes kind of way. Hell, she had soot streaks in her hair, and it looked like her left eyebrow was half-singed off. But she glowed in the kind of way that he could imagine waking up to each morning.

If they could make it through this, exactly what other challenge could the world throw at them that they couldn't tackle? Together? She reached out to check his left shoulder, but he caught her hand instead, tenderly pulling it to his cheek.

"Ronnie…"

Instead of easing into him, she stiffened. "Not now."

"Then when?" he asked.

* * *

Ronnie gulped. There was Zach, looking all doe-eyed at her. His voice was thick with passion. Why couldn't she just lean in and quench a thirst that had been parching her for months? Except…

"I've had a picture of this..." Ronnie looked into Zach's eyes. One was bloodshot, while the other was nearly swollen shut. He'd never looked so handsome. "A picture of *us* for so long."

"Then why?" he asked, so close that she could taste his cologne.

She simply glanced over her shoulder. The chopper was still aflame, along with dozens of pieces of wreckage. And now, a goat, of all things, walked across the valley toward them. Seriously—a *goat*.

"And this isn't it," she sighed. "It just isn't."

Zach leaned back, seeming to get it, or he just caught scent of her more-than- aromatic scent. Either way, she went back to checking for the filament. Ronnie fingered her way through his hair. How many times had she dreamed of tugging on these locks?

"Then we need to talk," Zach said.

"Talk?" Ronnie asked. "Again with the talking! We haven't even had a first date yet, dude."

Zach cocked his head. *Why did he have to look so damn cute?* Ronnie thought. It was even harder to resist him in person. At least over the iPod he couldn't chide her with those crackling eyes.

"Fine," she said going back to picking through his hair like a groupie baboon.

"Were you serious about helping to decode the Hidden Hand's cipher?"

Ronnie shifted up onto her knees. Between all of the cuts and scrapes and burns, there were a thousand places where the tiny wound from the filament insertion could hide.

"I may hate the CIA, but I'm not exactly going to let mankind get thrown back into the Dark Ages out of spite."

Granted, she wanted her own island to get far, far, far away from other humans, but that didn't mean she wanted them all gone. Well, at least not the majority of them.

"Then I think—"

"Stop," she ordered.

"But—"

"No, I mean stop moving," she said as she parted his hair at the nape of his neck. "I think I found it."

There it was. The tiny punctate lesion. The only reason she found it, really, was because it was starting to scab over. All the rest of Zach's wounds were still fresh and bleeding. She grabbed a pair of jeweler's tweezers from the case next to her and grabbed the tiny end of the filament. Ever so carefully, she snaked the metal out from under Zach's skin.

She held up the bloody fiber that looked more like a spider's silk than a tracking device. Zach leaned in, tilting his head.

"*That* is what gave us away?"

"Yep," Ronnie replied, putting the thing in a lead-lined tube. Quirk would have a field day with the material once he got it back to his mad-scientist laboratory. She had every confidence that he would not only be able replicate the device, but also find a way to deactivate it without having to go all ape on someone.

Once the cap was screwed on nice and tight, blocking any transmission that might give away their location, Ronnie sat back on her heels.

"Now, you were saying something regarding the salvation of our world from a weaponized strain of the Black Death?"

A smile played at the edge of his lips. Good. He was starting to get her dark humor. "Yes, we were," he replied, and then caught her gaze again. How she wanted to get lost in those brilliant blues, but unfortunately, there really was a weaponized strain of the Black Death on the loose. "I recognized something while I was being interrogated."

By the look of the bruises Zach had *before* her efficiency-challenged rescue, he hadn't been interrogated—he had been *tortured*.

"I realized that I had seen the symbols they needed decoded before," Zach said.

"Where?"

Zach grabbed a stick from the ground and began drawing. "Back in El Paso, a crazed old man had carved them into his skin."

Ronnie frowned. "Carved?"

"Yeah. I mean, I just thought he was clinically insane. He'd just tried to torch a painting—"

"The Picasso?" Ronnie interjected.

"Yes," Zach said, stopping his artistic rendering in the dirt. "How did you know?"

Um, besides tracking everything that happened in the El Paso FBI office? Ronnie felt maybe that was something best held back until the second date. She shrugged, trying to look as casual as she could. "Must have caught it on the news."

Luckily, Zach went back to his drawing. "Anyway, I am pretty damn sure that at least one of those symbols was in the Hidden Hand documents that Grant showed me."

Zach leaned back, revealing the symbol.

Crap. Of all the symbols in the world, it had to be that one. The one that had been burned into their monitors back in the cold room.

She turned to Quirk. "Grab my laptop."

"What? Do I look like your bitch?" Quirk said, hand on hip. "Do I?"

Ronnie cut him some slack. After all, his hair was mussed, and he was working in distinctly non-clean room conditions. As he returned to fixing their communications equipment, Ronnie dug through the various cases and found her laptop. She flipped it open, finding the screenshot that she was looking for.

The angelic script glittered gold.

"You mean like this one?" she asked Zach.

"Exactly."

Ronnie sat down hard. "Guess it wasn't spam."

* * *

"How...how did you get this?" Zach asked. He should have known, though, that Ronnie would not be just a step, but a full block ahead of everyone else. Yet, it still seemed shocking to see the same symbol glow on her screen that had been etched in the old man's flesh, and again in the Hidden Hand's papers.

"Long story," Ronnie said with a sigh. "Just know that angelic script has been considered unbreakable for millennia."

Zach nodded. "Yeah, that's the impression I got. Grant said that the entire team at Langley couldn't crack it."

"Well, why didn't they just say so?" Ronnie said, chuckling. "We could have avoided several helicopter crashes if they'd just appealed to my competitive nature."

"So, what are you going to do?" he asked, although he pretty much knew the answer.

Ronnie settled back into a cross-legged stance, stretching her neck from one side to the other. "Um, crack it?"

He was pretty sure that she meant the code and not her neck. But with Ronnie, you couldn't ever be 100 percent sure.

"Just like that?"

"Well, not exactly," she responded, lacing her fingers together and then extending them. "Let Quirk know that I will be back in three hours."

"Be back?" Zach asked as Ronnie began typing. "Where are you going?"

Ronnie didn't answer. Instead, her eyes tracked back and forth across the screen as her fingers flew along the keyboard.

"Ronnie?" he asked, but again, he got no answer. He put his hand up, waving it. But still nothing.

"Quirk!" he yelled.

The young man straightened from his task. "Oh, my God. You two are *so* needy! A match made in heaven."

"There's something wrong with Ronnie."

"Seriously, what?" Quirk asked, although Zach noticed that the man did hurry over. "I *am* trying to save our lives here. Along with keeping up to date on everything plague."

Quirk stepped in front of Ronnie. "Okay, what seems to be the problem?"

"She isn't responding," Zach pointed out, although that should have been pretty damn clear when she didn't even look up as Quirk approached. He snapped his fingers in front of Ronnie. Nothing.

"Really? I mean it doesn't exactly seem to be a great use of time management, but you called me over for *this*?"

"*Yes.*" Zach wasn't sure if he could really fulfill the promise of his "don't mess with me" stare, but he brought it to bear anyway.

Quirk cocked his head. "You really don't know?"

"*No.*"

"She's looping. Cycling? OCD'ing to the max?" Quirk must have sensed Zach's confusion, because he followed up with actual compassion in his voice. "Ronnie's got obsessive-compulsive disorder. She didn't mention this little mental condition? It's her secret behind the sauce."

Zach watched as Ronnie's eyes flickered, watching the data that flowed so quickly across the screen that it was a blur. How could she be reading that, let alone taking it all in? But her fingers raced nearly as fast as the data, moving symbols from one side of the screen to another, turning them over, flipping them vertically. It was like watching a Rubik's cube on crack.

"Did she say anything before she went into the zone?" Quirk asked.

He had to peel his eyes away from the screen. The colors and movement were hypnotizing even him. However, *he* had no idea whatsoever what it all meant.

"Yeah. Ronnie said she'd be back in three hours."

Quirk rose, dusting off his hands. "Well, then. There you have it."

"Have what?" Zach really did not like the sensation of being behind the curve. And with these two? He had a feeling that he had better get used to it.

"She estimated that it would take her three hours to break the cipher."

"What?" Zach challenged. "I thought it was an unbreakable code that has stood up for thousands of years."

Quirk shrugged. "Only because Ronnie hasn't put her mind to it."

The assistant went back to his task. Zach studied Ronnie. She didn't look at peace. Nor did she seem stressed. She just seemed intent. Zach knew that she was smart. Obviously. And cunning. No one got on the FBI's Ten Most Wanted list by accident. But to see that intellect in action?

It truly was a sight to behold.

CHAPTER 17

Plum Island
1:05 p.m., EST

Amanda turned away from the conference room's television screen. As if she needed to hear Anderson give more bad news. Such as, now every large urban city across America had to shut down their hospitals and go to the "Antibiotic Home Delivery" system.

Antibiotics weren't going to cut it, though. Not with Jennifer sitting next to her hacking away. None of the treatments seemed to slow the course of the plague at all. If anything, they just seemed to piss off *Yersinia pestis*.

No, they needed to concentrate on finding the vaccinated populations.

At this point in the conference room, it was pretty much just Jennifer and Amanda. The last of the scientists had gone down for treatment. It was eerie how still the upper floor was after the hustle, bustle, and coughing from the infirmary.

"Anything yet?" Dr. Henderson asked as he walked in. Guess he followed their lead to get the hell out of the infirmary. The director rolled his sleeve down to cover not only the bandage where the IV catheter was, but several boils that were about to rupture.

Amanda shook her head. "No. it could take days to compile all the information."

The director didn't respond. He didn't need to. They all knew that they didn't have several days. If they didn't find a vaccine within the next twenty-four hours…

"What the hell do you think you are doing?" Devlin said bursting into the room.

Trying to play it cool, Amanda shrugged.

The CIA liaison turned to Dr. Henderson. "I'm sorry, but I have to speak to you regarding Dr. Rolph's conduct."

Henderson slouched into the nearest chair. "It is a free country, Mr. Devlin."

Devlin glared at Amanda. "I would like to know why my broadband width has been hijacked by Dr. Rolph."

"I am not sure if you are aware, Mr. Devlin, but we do have a plague going on."

"Yes," Devlin stated, flinging his hand as if he could just brush that minor inconvenience away. "I mean, why is she tapped into the CIA database?"

Henderson swung his head toward her. "That seems to be a fair question, Dr. Rolph."

Amanda's eyes darted to Jennifer. She'd asked her assistant to get her more bandwidth. Guess she should have asked Jennifer where she planned on getting it.

"I'm drilling down into the data to pick up subtle variations in the spread of the disease to extrapolate the predictive model for vaccinated populations."

Devlin sneered. "Through Yahoo and purchase histories on Amazon?"

"Well, Dr. Rolph?" The director's eyebrow shot up. "That data does seem slightly broader than I gave you permission for."

"Permission?" Devlin spat out. "She's committed felony espionage."

An elbow poked Amanda in the back. Damn Jennifer.

"I...I..." Amanda said, still not sure how she was going to explain it. How far she had come. A day ago she would have stammered for ten minutes. Two days ago, she would have just run from the room. Now? Now she would rather ask forgiveness than permission. "I need the data."

"Jesus, give it up," Devlin snapped. "The CIA is all over this."

Henderson rose. "You mean like the CIA withholding vital information regarding the spread of the plague to America within twelve hours? The theory that if we possibly hadn't ignored, could have saved millions upon millions of lives?" Devlin opened his mouth to argue, but Henderson overrode him. "At this point, Amanda gets to follow just about any hunch she wants."

With that the large man hefted himself from the chair.

"Thank you, sir," Amanda responded.

As he walked past, he nodded. "You are welcome. Although it is I who should be thankful that we have a Chicken Little in-house."

Amanda wasn't quite sure if that was much of a compliment. As soon as Henderson was out of earshot, Devlin turned on her.

"Don't get too comfy in your role of teacher's pet," he hissed. "My director will be weighing in."

Politics. It was like being in grade school all over again. Yet, she liked how brave she felt standing up to Devlin. He truly did inspire her to be a stronger person. "Yes, well, given that we are in the worst pandemic the world has ever known, I'm pretty sure that my director can beat up your director."

Jennifer snorted behind her.

She met Devlin's angry gaze. "Are we done here?"

The man stormed out. Amanda guessed that was his answer. She turned to her assistant, who wore a look about as proud as Amanda felt.

"So now that we don't have to be on the down low, let's really start digging into non-affected population movements."

* * *

Quirk really didn't like working in the field. Like, an actual field. With a herd of goats that had decided to see what all the fuss was about. As if it weren't hard enough to try to throw together a sat phone after three-quarters of your stuff got toasty-fried in a crash, you had to keep the various components away from a nanny goat.

A *ding* brought him back to his phone. The text read, *I wouldn't recommend getting the plague. No fun. Just FYI.*

Quirk texted back, trying to keep anxiety from reaching his words. *"Oh, please. You'll say anything to get out of work."*

The next time I see you, I'll be sure to cough on you.

Oh, Jennifer knew how to get back at him. She knew even the thought of such a travesty would make the hairs on his neck stand on end. Luckily, he knew how to get right back at her. Like he was going to let the fact that she was plague stricken stop him from winning this little exchange.

And I will remind you of your last attempt to get rid of that pesky cellulitis on your thighs.

No response. Had he been too cruel? But come on, trying to smear cottage cheese, real cottage cheese, on your legs to make your own cottage cheese go away? Quirk knew the advice had come from a glossy women's magazine, but *come on.*

He was about to text when Jennifer's response came through. *Don't make me laugh. It hurts.*

Quirk ran his thumb over the screen. To have a friend in such pain...

"Looks like somebody is coming," the FBI agent said, as he gazed through the high- definition binoculars that only had one lens working.

Scanning the horizon, Quirk couldn't see anything. "Perhaps it's a mirage."

Heat drifted up in waves as the late-afternoon sun beat down upon them.

"Nope," Zach answered. "I'm pretty damned sure that is a truck's exhaust."

Quickly Quirk typed, *Get rest. I will teach you to dare to exchange barbs with a gay man later.*

Closing the window, Quirk looked out over the rolling hills and, as Zach indicated, there appeared to be a vehicle approaching. Yet, that couldn't be. Quirk was still waiting for the satellite that they *hadn't* knocked out to come into position. The FBI agent rose and handed him the scope. It was the first time in hours that the man had moved away from Ronnie's side. Quirk could sympathize, though. He too, used to stand vigil over her—until he realized that is was just plain boring to sit around and watch a chick type really fast. Zach would learn.

Quirk took the binoculars and squinted one eye. Sure enough, an old, beat-up pickup hauled ass in their direction. Maybe it was just a farmer looking for his goats.

But wait. Was that a pair of sooty long johns that Quirk spotted?

"He is drawn to me," Quirk said as he handed the binoculars back.

Zach took them back. "Yes, but is that a sawed-off shotgun on the rack?"

Even if it was, Quirk knew that the pilot would never use it. Their bond was far too strong.

Within moments, Quirk didn't need any sight aid. The truck came into clear view. How his heart went aflutter as the burly man barreled toward them. Quirk began shooing away the goats and gathering his equipment. His knight in shining armor had arrived.

Zach, on the other hand, stood in front of Ronnie, scowling at the approaching vehicle as if his searing glare alone could protect her. Guess all those meds had kicked in. The FBI agent only looked beaten up, rather than done for.

The truck bounced and jostled over the rough terrain, yet the pilot sat ever-so-cool in the front seat. Quirk was so ready by the time the truck skidded to a halt in front of them. "Hi, there."

"Get in."

God, how Quirk liked a man of action.

Zach eyed the shotgun. "Look, buddy, we don't want any—"

"I'm taking you as far as an ATM at the border so you can put some kind of down payment on building back my bird," the pilot grumbled in his gravelly voice. "After that, you can worry."

"Told ya!" Quirk said just to rub it in. "Help me load up."

But the FBI agent turned to Ronnie, who still had that "I've left this realm" look about her. But who cared? That meant that Quirk got to jump in and ride next to the pilot.

Like he said. His day was looking up.

* * *

Ronnie could hear sounds, but her brain simply ignored them, shunting those electrical impulses away. They had no place here. The only items her brain chose to let through the filter of her mind's eye were the symbols. They blazed before her, brilliant in their glory, fierce in protecting their secrets. She could swear that they were so deeply etched in the back of her retinas that they felt a part of her.

Each red corpuscle coursing through her veins was afire with the symbols—nearly carrying as much oxygen as her blood. They tumbled and sped, taunting her. Teasing her. Luring her deeper and deeper into their game. They were like putty in her hands—only the putty refused to create the masterpiece she envisioned.

For all their familiarity, they were still an inch out of reach. Kind of like how she would stare so hard at Zach's image, straining to make him come alive in her world.

Zach.

The voice. Was it Zach?

She could feel the tug toward the world she had left behind. Yet how could she leave the swarming symbols without understanding their secrets?

Her body shook, and then shook again, knocking her fingers from the keyboard.

"Ronnie," a voice called. A deep voice. A man's voice. Zach's voice?

Roused by the baritone, she let the symbols slip away. Like bright, beautiful sand through her fingers, the code slid through, leaving no trace that it had been there before.

She blinked several times to clear the screenshot she had in her mind.

Where *was* she? A dry valley lay before her. The sun was about to set, so it must be dusk. Why did her butt hurt so badly? And why, exactly, was a goat nibbling at the hem of her shirt? But the most glorious of all wonders was the fact that Zach knelt in front of her. Not a picture of Zach, but the actual man.

Ronnie smiled. The land of gilded symbols was beautiful, but this was even better.

"Ronnie, we've got to go," Zach said, urging her up.

Then the haze of decrypting evaporated as pain shot up her legs. She really needed to stick to ergonomic chairs with vibro-massage.

Zach helped her to rise, and then scooped up her laptop without her even asking. He guided them to the dustiest pickup in the history of pickups. Quirk was already seated with a smile that outshone the setting sun. Which meant, of course, that just to the left of him sat the pilot.

How he got back to them, Ronnie didn't know, but even she was glad to see that he had a new cigar to chew on.

"Did you break the code?" Quirk asked, scooting over to make room for her.

"As far as I can," Ronnie answered, turning to Zach, who loaded up last. "I need to see those symbols on the arsonist's arm."

"Well, then I guess we need to head to El Paso."

Ronnie nodded, and then regretted it. The post-cyber-vortex headache was settling in. Much more measured, she nodded to the pilot, who was now their driver. "El Paso it is."

* * *

Amanda let the numbers scroll by. On one hand, it was scary to see how much data the CIA collected on American citizens. And since the plague broke out? They were tracking everything that everyone was doing. They had even hacked into the Nielsen ratings, keeping track of what people were watching on television.

On the other hand, Amanda was grateful. It provided her with a wealth of information. Almost too much information. She had zeroed in on any household or complex that was not showing extreme stress regarding the plague. Even better yet, dwellings *without* television. The Hidden Hand seemed like an organization that would be primetime-averse.

Still, she struggled to isolate populations. Nothing she found edged into the statistically relevant category. Amanda looked at Jennifer, but her assistant shook her head. Apparently, she was having no better luck.

So far, their calculations had been based on a stringent theorem. Take, for instance, the fact that they only counted a single occurrence of apparent resistance—even if an entire family seemed immune. The theorem stipulated that if one person in the family had resistance to the plague, the rest of the family was highly likely to as well.

However, didn't that apply to the Hidden Hand as well? Wouldn't they have vaccinated clusters of families, or members of the rank and file?

"What if we counted each resistant case as its own nidus?" Amanda asked Jennifer. Her assistant's eyes widened, and then narrowed. Her fingers rushed over the keyboard.

A new set of parameters came up. With many more islands.

Now to just figure out which was the Hidden Hand.

CHAPTER 18

El Paso FBI Field Office
8:32 p.m., MST

Zach lay belly-down on the roof, peering through a set of binoculars to the building he used to call his work—the El Paso FBI Field Office. Now he was surveilling it for what amounted to a jailbreak. However, Ronnie couldn't get any further with the decoding unless they had Francois, and Zach didn't think that the FBI was just going to hand the old guy over to them.

Still, it gave him pause to think of the number of laws he was about to break. Infinite numbers of laws. His indictment would read like a laundry list of class one felonies, and even treason. The only silver lining in this entire screwed-up scenario was Ronnie lying next to him. Of course, he wished it were under completely different circumstances, but just having her chest rising and falling next to his felt right. As a decorated FBI agent, it shouldn't, but it did.

"Looks like about twelve agents, plus another seven support staff," Ronnie said as she swung the binoculars down. Their eyes met. She studied his features. Her mind seemed to work like a micro-expression computer. "You still okay with this?"

"No," he answered honestly.

It was one thing to get caught up in the moment after a helicopter crash. He was all full of adrenaline and fury. But now? In the cool of the El Paso night? Considering an armed assault on his colleagues?

Again, she seemed to read him perfectly. "Quirk's going to do everything he can to neutralize the people in there. We should be able to get in and grab Francois without a shot being fired."

The "should" in that sentence was the one that worried him. If Ronnie were so damned sure that they wouldn't need to fire a shot, she probably wouldn't have had them haul enough armaments to lay siege to Fort Knox up five flights of stairs. The remains of Ronnie and Quirk's equipment were scavenged from the helicopter. Half of the stuff he didn't even recognize as weapons, like the large metal disc that supposedly could alter a bullet's course—or even pull a gun from an assailant's hand.

However, if Ronnie thought she was going to need all of this, then that told Zach just how deadly these items are. Jorge's expression as those iPod earbuds' directional charge blew his brains out would never fade.

Ronnie laid a hand on his arm. Zach was sure that she meant it to be comforting, but it only reinforced how worried *she* was.

"They've declared you rogue, Zach. They have shoot-on-sight permission."

Ronnie was right, of course. Quirk had intercepted the communiqués from Mexico to Quantico. There was no coming back from this. No matter that it was Grant who kidnapped and tortured *him*. The official story had the facts flipped. The entire twenty-four hours had gone sideways—seriously sideways. Too sideways to ever recover his career.

He was an outlaw. Plain and simple.

His mom was going to be so proud. Like Thanksgiving dinners hadn't been awkward enough. Now he might never get to eat overcooked turkey and barely defrosted green beans. Damn it, but he had to choke back tears.

Unfortunately the well-coiffed hacker sitting next to him had no problems with weeping softly as he typed. Quirk's distress at having to leave "The One," their pilot and grudging chauffeur, at the border was still evident in every sigh and sniffle.

"Um, that would be shoot-on-sight for all three of us," Quirk corrected, wiping a tear from his cheek.

True, but the hackers were used to it. Even a few hours of life on the lam left a sour taste in Zach's mouth. His badge hadn't just been a form of identification. It had been *him*.

"If there was any other way…" Ronnie said as her fingers slid down to his hand and gave it a squeeze before she went back to surveying the area.

But there had to be, didn't there? The answer to their dilemma couldn't be breaking out a known arsonist from his FBI field office. Could it? Yet running through all of the other scenarios, Zach came up with nothing. Even if they went to Washington and tried to get Ronnie directly into Langley, no guarantees existed—for her or their safety.

Still. He had contacts. Contacts whom he trusted. Maybe they should try to work through established channels before taking such rash action.

He went to open his mouth when lights across the street flickered, and then went off.

"Quirk, we are still at T minus five," Ronnie hissed at her assistant.

"Hey, that was *not* me."

Well, clearly the power to the field office and the entire side of the street had been cut off.

"This couldn't just be a coincidence?" Zach asked, pretty much knowing the answer as emergency lighting bloomed to life, then crackled brightly, blowing itself out. In the darkened office, agents scrambled for flashlights. Zach scanned the building, his eyes finding the tech support department. Warp rushed into the room, nearly knocking over his Green Lantern coffee cup. "But if that isn't us, then who?"

Ronnie sucked in a breath. Her eyes widened with surprise. "Um," she said. "I think I just spotted some ninja priests."

"What?" Zach asked as he raised his own binoculars. But sure enough, four men draped in black made their way into the building. Zach would have assumed that they were a mercenary team, except each of the men had a bright, white collar at his neck. A priest's collar. Ronnie's assessment was pretty damn accurate. They did appear to be ninja priests.

Quirk grabbed the binoculars from Zach, and then whistled. "Sometimes I love my job."

Then the flash of a gun muzzle, and then another. Those were shots. Shots fired with a silencer. These assailants didn't give a damn about the agents' welfare. His friends' welfare.

Zach leapt up.

"Wait!" Ronnie called out as he made his way to the fire escape. "We've got to modify our entry plan."

Zach swung his leg over the metal ladder. Whether Ronnie followed was her business. He couldn't let his colleagues get slaughtered. Securing his insteps on either side of the ladder, he loosened his hold and let gravity take him down.

* * *

Ronnie watched Zach slide down the ladder. Her eyes flickered to Quirk, whose jaw had dropped. And to think that she might one day, after they got clear of the CIA and ninja priests, she might actually date the guy who had just performed that feat? She watched as Zach hit the ground, un-holstered his weapon, and crouched in perfect FBI-trained position, running across the street.

Shaking off the awe, Ronnie grabbed as many items as she could carry.

"Figure out how they got in," Ronnie ordered Quirk as she climbed onto the ladder. She tried to replicate Zach's maneuver, but nearly broke a finger and risked plummeting three stories. Reverting to the step-by-step method, Ronnie rushed down the stairs—the metal clanging.

"What did I tell you about clod-hopping?" Quirk complained, not seeming to realize or perhaps care that his voice was equally painful against her eardrums.

Trying to strap the diversion disc onto her back, Ronnie raced across the street. Gone was their meticulous plan to enter through the rooftop and come down the elevator shaft, exiting right next to the locked prisoner's cell where Quirk, in a perfectly timed hack, blew the lock. As she caught up to Zach, it looked as though he planned on walking, or more accurately, barging, in the front door.

He stopped at the entrance, and then held up three fingers. Each one that went down tightened Ronnie's chest. Sure, she was a worldly, elite hacker. Sure, she liked to be out in the field. But she also went up against kids with water guns. As another muzzle flash flared from the interior of the building, Ronnie realized that she wasn't quite so fond of live fire exercises.

Shoving open the glass door, Zach charged in, gun at the ready.

"I can't tell FBI from ninja priests, but we've got three bodies moving together down the corridor to your right," Quirk informed.

"They're off to the right," Ronnie whispered to Zach as they made their way through the lobby.

Zach nodded. "That's the direction of the holding cells."

Behind the desk, they found their first victim. Even Ronnie recognized the man. It was Special Agent Markum. Blood splattered his white shirt, pooling around his head. Zach knelt, tried to find a pulse, and then shook his head.

Oh, God. Zach used to play basketball with him.

Ninja priests were no longer so cute.

* * *

Zach tensed his jaw. Revenge would come later. Now he had to put aside the rage building just beneath his breastbone. Not just his office was under attack. The entire world was.

And this crazy old man was important enough to lay an FBI field office under assault. Important enough for Zach to bottle that pressure in his chest and put it up on a shelf, brewing and growing until he let it out again.

He moved them forward in the near dark. His memory of the office guided them around desks and potted plants. Zach pulled Ronnie behind a hibiscus as two bloodied agents ran past them into the street. He didn't blame them. At least they were alive—unlike Markum. They were up against a callous, callous enemy. As soon as the agents left his line of sight, Zach motioned Ronnie to get them on the go.

Tightening the grip on his gun, they pushed through another set of glass doors into the main bull pen. Even in the low light, blood glistened. Men he'd known and worked with for years lay dead on the ground. Their unseeing eyes stared blankly at him. So many wives, husbands, and children to be notified. But no more. Not if he could help it.

The tiniest *pop* sounded at his left. Jerking Ronnie with him, Zach dove under a desk. So they'd left a sentry. A gunman to secure their exit and provide sniper coverage against reinforcements.

Zach lifted his weapon to return fire, but Ronnie grabbed his arm.

"Wait." Ronnie indicated the screen of the palmtop device she held. Zach assumed that he'd be looking at an infrared screen to track body heat, but instead, the image was the polar opposite. It tracked the least-warm objects in the room. Unfortunately, that meant the rapidly cooling bodies flared a bright blue. "Quirk, do you have control over the power supply yet?"

Zach watched as she cocked her head, listening. Either she had an earbud implanted, or, as Warp had long suspected, Quirk and Ronnie truly did have mind talk. She nodded at the unknown reply. "Copy that. You see that vent behind him?" she asked. "All right. You know what to do."

Zach queried her with a look as shots rang out from the other side of the office. He glanced down to the screen. Their guy held on tight to his position.

"Just be ready," Ronnie whispered.

"For what?"

Ronnie indicated the sniper. "Quirk. *Now*."

Billows of cold air rushed from the vent, startling the gunman. Instinctively, he surged forward, away from the cover of the desk. Zach shot, tagging the guy in the shoulder and spinning him around. Pings sounded above their heads as the guy's shots went far wide of their mark. Zach aimed for the chest and pulled the trigger.

Perhaps revenge wouldn't have to wait. The shot drove the guy back, but not down. He must have been wearing a vest. Well, the vest did not protect one place. Zach popped off a shot, square to the forehead. The assailant wobbled, and then crumpled to the ground as Ronnie gasped behind him.

He turned to find her face blanched, and the usual spark in her eye extinguished.

* * *

Ronnie felt Zach catch hold of her arm as she stared at the gunman. She'd seen death before. But never up close. She'd even killed a man, Jorge, to save Zach. But she had simply had to press a button from far, far away. Even Quirk's simulations of the C4 earbuds had used the Powerpuff Girls as examples. A little hard to get queasy over cartoon blood.

This time, though, she'd actually seen a man die. She had seen the life vanish from his features. Even though he was an enemy, she couldn't shake his desperation in the end.

"Ronnie, get down!" Quirk yelled in her ear.

She shoved Zach down with her as the too-familiar *ping* of a silencer sounded as bullets whizzed past her ear. Well, not past Zach's. The tip of his ear now bore a red line. A bullet track.

Ronnie gulped. She didn't have time for shock, survivor's guilt, or even freaking out as shouts carried from deeper in the building.

"Quirk, get Warp whatever juice he needs," Ronnie ordered as loud FBI fire was returned. "And try to figure out a way to flag us as friendlies."

"Will do, but it looks like the main fight is in front of the holding cell. Might want to take the back route."

She turned to find Zach studying her.

"Good to go?" he asked.

"Yeah." Totally a lie.

Zach looked down at her hand, which clutched his tightly. "Not that I mind, but it's probably best if I aim with both hands…"

"Oh, sorry," she said, dropping her grip, but she didn't feel quite so stable as a moment before. "Quirk thinks that we should take the side hall and double back around through the kitchen."

Ronnie went to point out the route, but found that her finger was shaking too badly.

"Got it," Zach said, but studied her face again. Ronnie put on her best "I'm ready for a good ol' gunfight" face. He must have bought it, for he turned and checked his corners before ducking under an adjacent desk.

She followed close on his heels, relieved that the shouts and mayhem subsided the farther they followed the side hallway. Ronnie knew that at some point they would need to head back toward the action, but for now, she would rest her ears and nerves.

Zach put up a hand. Ronnie stopped as he ducked his head around the corner. "Crap."

"What's wrong?"

"Warp's got all the lights back on. We're never going to be able to sneak past the doorway."

Ronnie pulled up the schematic. "No worries. I can just have Quirk—"

The sound of metal bouncing its way down the hallway diverted her attention. There, spinning end over end, was a grenade. A live grenade. Strangely, all Ronnie could think was…*damn, these ninja priests are well armed.*

"Move!" Zach yelled, grabbing her arm and flinging her around the corner. He was on her tail as the explosion lifted them up and off their feet. Fire hit the end of the hallway, splashing some in their direction. They scrambled back, dancing from the flames.

"In here!" Zach jerked open the door to the tech room.

Warp rose from his chair. "Agent Hunt!"

"Get down!" Zach demanded, shoving both her and Warp to the ground as he spun on his heel, firing behind them. A grunt answered as a dark figure retreated beyond view. "Stay here," Zach whispered as he inched his way to the door.

The FBI tech tried to rise, but Ronnie tugged him back down. "When Zach says to stay, you stay."

For the first time, Warp seemed to register that she was even there. His interest had been so focused on Zach that he seemed shocked that another person was in the room. Ronnie had always suspected that the shaggy-headed Warp had a guy-crush on Zach, and now she was sure of it.

"But, but…" Warp pushed his glasses up on his nose. "They are saying that Agent Hunt is doing this."

"Warp, you don't believe anything the 'man' says," Ronnie scolded. For a government-sanctioned hacker, he had a very trusting view of Big Brother. "I need you to coordinate with Quirk."

He blinked twice. "Quirk?" Pulling away, the geek ran his fingers through his hair. "But that would make you…That means you are…"

"The Robin Hood hacker, yeah," Ronnie acknowledged, really needing to get him back to his keyboard.

"Oh, my God. Oh, my God. Oh, my God," Warp said, wheezing as his hands flew to his chest. "Oh. My. God."

Ronnie was used to tech boys gushing over her…online. To see one do so in person was a bit disconcerting. Plus, the whole "another grenade could fly in at any moment" thing was a problem.

"Breath, dude, breathe," Ronnie encouraged.

"Yeah, have him hang around you for a week and see how he feels," Quirk added in her ear.

The tech's eyes darted from Zach near the door to Ronnie and back. "If you aren't attacking, then why are you here?"

"Okay, so we did *plan* to break in," Ronnie admitted, not having time to develop a plausible lie. "But come on, Warp, is this my style at all?"

The tech shook his head sharply. "No. I told them you would have tried to breach through the elevator shaft after incapacitating all the alarms."

"Not bad," Ronnie said. Actually, he was too freaking close to their original plan. She and Quirk were going to have to get more creative. "So, you have got to know that we wouldn't come in with guns blazing."

"You don't even carry a gun."

Ronnie nodded. Warp wasn't just a fanboy; he was a *huge* fanboy. And because he was tasked with tracking her down, he was king of the Robin Hood hacker fanboys.

"And now, we need your help to stop any more agents getting killed."

"Hey, *you* may need his help, but I don't," Quirk argued in her ear.

Luckily, Warp couldn't hear Quirk's disdain. "Okay, yeah," Warp said. "What do I need to do?"

"I don't like it. It's too quiet." Zach stated from the door. "Where's the guy who threw the grenade?"

"Quirk?"

* * *

Maybe it was best that they brought on Warp, since Ronnie clearly thought that Quirk could somehow counter hack the assault hack, keep track of each and every assailant, *and* grieve the loss of "The One."

Quirk checked the monitor, flipping into infrared mode. "He's backed away and stationed himself toward the lobby. I don't think you're going to be able to exit in that direction."

Some static was on the line as Ronnie moved around. If only she'd let him hire a doctor to surgically implant her mic.

"Zach and I are going to head out," Ronnie said in a rush. "You and Warp work on cutting off the ninja priests' countersurveillance."

Yeah, like he hadn't thought of that. How he hated it when she had to show off in front of strangers. "Wow. What a shockingly brilliant idea."

"Just patch him in."

Quirk hit the keyboard, dialing Warp's number. As he watched the two blips that represented Zach and Ronnie move out of the room, a very nervous voice answered the phone. "Hello?"

Well, at least the civil servant was polite. "Yeah, Warp, get your groove on. There's a van parked a block away from the building. We need to lay down some serious interference."

"Wait. Now that I have a communications channel, let me contact the fire department—"

"Done."

"And the closest field office in Albuquerque—"

"Done."

"Then the local—"

Quirk cut the nerd off. "Look, we're going to have every city department plus a gaggle of news choppers descending on us in five minutes. We need to make sure that everyone survives for the next five minutes."

Something shifted in Warp's tone. His voice sounded stronger. Less wigged-out. "On it."

Well. Okay, then. Maybe Quirk *was* going to like having an assistant of his very own.

* * *

Zach studied the palmtop in Ronnie's hand. Although, he could probably guess what was happening from the gunfire and screams. The assailants had the agents pinned near the holding cell. Given the blitz attack, Zach was surprised that three agents still stood. But soon, the assailants would pull out the grenades, and none would be left.

The Hidden Hand must have wanted Francois alive, or this whole thing would have been over minutes ago. To get to the action, he and Ronnie only needed to pass through the kitchen to get to the bull pen, but there was a gap between the desks. A good ten-foot gap—without cover. And the gunmen had taken up protected positions by the doorway.

"I'm going to need some kind of distraction to get into the room," he told Ronnie.

She bit the edge of her lip. "The boys are still trying to make sure that they can't see you get into the room."

"You got anything in that bag of tricks in your pack?" he asked.

"Well…" Ronnie said, a bit of red coming to her cheeks. "We've got a fibrillator."

"You mean, *defibrillator*?"

She shook her head. "No, I mean *fibrillator*." Ronnie pulled a shoe box-sized device from her pack. "Basically, it creates a sound that is known to put the heart into fibrillation."

"You mean—it kills people with noise?"

"*Temporarily* kills people with a finely tuned pitch that overexcites the electrical node of the heart."

Zach stared at the woman he thought he had come to know over the last nine months. But he didn't have time to explore the choices that Ronnie made with her spare time. There were more pressing matters. "Exactly how *temporarily* are we talking?"

"Um…remember how 'beta' the ray gun was?" From his nod, she continued. "Yeah, that EM pulser was miles down the production road."

Since Zach wasn't going to stop his agents' hearts on the hope that they started again, he nodded toward her pack. "Anything else?"

"It's another of our 'super-beta' items. We like to call them 'blue light' specials," she said, hurrying on. "It's a disc that hyper—"

Light strobed as a blast of noise hit.

Well, Zach had asked for a distraction, and someone setting off a flashbang grenade in the bull pen provided it. Actually, *over*-provided it. Luckily, Zach had been so focused on Ronnie's bizarre assortment of devices that he was turned away from the brunt of the flash. And his ears had been ringing since the crash, so no real loss there.

What the flashbang did mean was that the enemy was on the move. So Zach was on the move.

"Stay here," he ordered as he slid out the doorway and into the bull pen.

"No! Wait!" Ronnie yelled, but it was too late. He was committed.

CHAPTER 19

El Paso Field Office
8:49 p.m., MST

Ronnie fumbled with the disc's controls. Dear God, when they developed the damned thing, why didn't they make the "On" button easier to find? That was it. From now on, every item they developed would have a 9-1-1 emergency easy "On" button that freaking glowed in the dark.

"It's the second-to-right control," Quirk yelled into her ear.

Yes, because a second-to-right control on a *round* object was so easy to find.

"Your *other* right!"

Finally, Ronnie hit the correct control, and the metal discs within metal discs began to spin, clunking and chugging—just like a mini-MRI machine. Only this device wasn't meant for imaging. It was meant for protection. Or at least she hoped it was.

Zach had leapt from hiding, firing toward the two assailants. Unfortunately, what he didn't know was that a flashbang grenade was used to signal the guy at the door to join the party. Now the love of her life was smack-dab in the middle of the kill zone.

Over Zach's shoulder, she watched the third gunman raise his automatic weapon. There was no way that the disc would work from here. If anything, it would accelerate the bullets *through* Zach. Not exactly what she needed.

No, the only way to save Zach was to join Zach…unarmed in the middle of a firefight.

But what was a girl to do?

As the gunman braced the weapon against his hip, Ronnie burst from the kitchen, holding the metal disc in front of her.

"Hold on!"

* * *

Ronnie's instruction made no sense. And what in the hell was she doing out here, anyway? Hadn't he told her to stay in the kitchen? Then, Zach heard the rattle of gunfire at his left. He turned to return fire, but even as he squeezed the trigger, he knew that there was no way he could avoid that hail of bullets.

Zach prepared for the pain. But instead, the bullets slowed in midair. He could actually *see* the bullets coming right for him. Zach couldn't help but stare as the bullets slowed to a stop. They hung there in the air for a surreal moment, and then gained speed. But not toward him—toward Ronnie. Or, more accurately, to the metal disc that Ronnie held.

Seeming to sense the shift in the fight, the other gunmen fired upon him as well, with equally bizarre results.

"Hold on!" she yelled again.

Ronnie still made no sense—until his gun wobbled in his hand. Then, it outright fought his grip. Zach clung as tightly as he could, but the damn thing flew from his hand and sailed across the room, hitting the disc hard enough to knock Ronnie back a foot.

Then, the other guns followed suit. At least the disc disarmed them all. The only problem was that Zach's belt buckle started tugging toward her. He grabbed hold of the nearest desk until he realized that it, too, was making its way to Ronnie.

Now paper clips, pens, staplers, and even thumbtacks hurled her way.

"Turn it off!"

"What do you think I'm trying to do?" Ronnie shouted as she took another step toward the kitchen.

* * *

"The third button to the left!" Quirk yelled in Ronnie's ear.

Again, not freaking helpful, as all the desks in the bull pen clattered their way to her. Luckily, the kitchen doorway was too narrow for them to fit through. They piled up at the door like a strange, tangled football huddle. And she was lucky she wasn't smack-dab in the middle of it. The magnet lashed to her arm wanted very much to go to the metal objects as they came to her. Ronnie had to dig her heels in, fighting the mutual attraction.

As she searched for the elusive "Off" switch, she heard a rattling behind her. The refrigerator lurched forward, rocking from one side to the other.

"Drop it!" Quirk urged.

But how could she, if Zach might still be in trouble?

Then the breakroom table and chairs began their zombie-like march forward. As the microwave zinged its way through the air, Ronnie dropped the disc and fled down the back hallway, vowing to make field tests a more essential step in their production process.

Hopefully, if anything, she narrowed the odds for Zach.

* * *

Zach ducked under a left hook and brought his own fist up into the guy's solar plexus. The man doubled over. Zach grabbed the assailant's lapel and jerked him forward as his knee came up to nail the guy in the stomach.

But this ninja priest was no pushover as he tackled Zach around the waist and shoved them both back. Zach's head slammed against the wall, doubling the number of stars he was already seeing. The assailant punched Zach on the right side. It hurt ten thousand times worse than it should have, but after the beating Jorge gave him? Zach was lucky to still be standing.

Using what little strength he had, Zach pivoted, swinging his opponent around and slamming the guy against the ramshackle pile of desks. His opponent clutched at his midriff. Zach backed away, ready for some kind of fake-out maneuver followed by an attack, but the man gasped twice and then fell still.

Cautious, Zach glanced behind the man to find him impaled on the leg of a desk.

While completely unplanned, Zach would take it. He surveyed the room in a glance, finding the other attackers long gone. On the other side of the room lay two agents. Zach rushed over, checking their vitals. Weak, but there. With sirens in the distance, he knew the backup Quirk had called for was already on its way.

Which was great for the downed men. Not so great for grabbing Francois and getting out of here before the police showed up. Plus, he had one wayward hacker to find.

"Ronnie!" he yelled as he grabbed the keys to the cell from a belt that had belonged to one of the agents. Damn it! Where *was* she?

As the sirens grew louder and louder, he'd have to find her once he secured Francois. Zach found the old man huddled in the corner of his cell. Had he been hit? Shoving the key into the lock, he grabbed the door and opened it with a clang.

"Francois?"

The man's head swiveled around. His gaze seemed far off as he mumbled something in Latin.

"Francois, you need to come with me." *And answer about a thousand questions*, but Zach thought he might wait until a little later for that part.

The arsonist shook his head, trying to tuck his body back into the fetal position.

"You've *got* to come with me," Zach urged, trying to get the man on his feet. "We don't have a lot of time."

"No," the old man said in English. "The time is gone."

This only seemed to deflate the old man even more. Like a blow-up doll with the air leaked out, he slumped into a pile of bones.

"Damn it," Zach said shaking Francois. "These men did not risk their lives for you to give up."

Francois looked up, his eyes brighter. "But I am a dead man."

"Not yet," Zach informed the guy as he hauled him to his feet. "Not freaking yet."

"They will come. They will hunt us," Francois said, still resisting Zach as he urged the man toward the cell door. "The end is nigh."

Zach swung the old man around. "Yes, yes it is," Zach agreed, not knowing the whole story, but after the sophisticated extraction attempt, he didn't need to know much more. Major forces were at work, way over Zach's pay grade. But that's what they had Ronnie and Quirk for. He just needed to get Francois's ass out of here before the cops showed up.

"Which is exactly why you are going to pull it together and *fight* them."

Francois eyes sharpened. "Then you believe?" he said as he rolled up his sleeve to reveal the carved symbols.

"God help me," Zach said, suppressing an urge to form the sign of the cross. "I do."

With renewed vigor, Zach got Francois up, only to find a gun pointed at them.

"I'm sorry, Hunt, but I can't let you walk out of here with him."

Zach found Special Agent in Charge Danner blocking their exit.

"You've got to know I didn't do this," Zach said, indicating the dead and wounded around the bull pen.

"We're going to let Quantico figure that out," Danner responded, holding out a pair of cuffs. "Put them on yourself."

Zach declined. "Danner, you've got to believe that I am not overstating the facts, and that if I don't walk out of here with this man right now, the world could cease to exist as we know it."

"I don't have to believe anything, Hunt. I just have to do my sworn duty."

Weighing his options, none seemed any better. Zach could put the cuffs on, which would lead to their incarceration—which meant they were dead. Whether here, being transferred, or in jail, Francois was right. They would be dead. Option two. Charge Danner with a fully loaded weapon, and more than likely Zach was dead, and Francois was still in custody, which would result in the Frenchman being dead.

So far, all options ended with someone ending up dead.

"Don't *make* me turn this on," Ronnie said, stepping from around the corner, holding up the metal disc. Its lights glowed an ominous red. "Don't make me."

Perhaps never gladder to see someone in his life, Zach flashed her a warm smile.

However, Danner more harshly studied the woman, then the disc, and then the woman. "The Robin Hood hacker, I presume?"

"At your service, but unless you want me to take that gun, your belt, and quite possibly the fillings in your molars, I would lower that weapon."

Zach watched emotions roll over his boss's face. In the end, Danner was a pragmatist. He lowered his weapon.

"Grant was the traitor, Danner, not me. Look into it, and you will see."

"Oh, I will," his boss promised.

Backing away, with Ronnie holding the disc between them and Danner's bullets, Zach urged Francois along, but the old man balked.

"The painting. We must have the painting."

"We don't have time—"

But the Frenchman was far stronger than he looked, and jerked out of Zach's grasp. He headed for Danner's office.

"No, Francois. The painting will be in the evidence—"

Zach didn't bother finishing his sentence as Francois walked out of the office with the crated Picasso. Zach eyed his boss. Could Danner be involved? But if Danner *was* involved, then would they really have needed to assault the place?

Before he could ask, sirens blared, bearing down on the field office. Whatever answers Zach wanted were going to have to wait until later. *Way* later. Taking Ronnie's hand, he led them through the back halls of the office. If they could get out the back exit and hoof it to the rendezvous point, they might just make it.

Bursting out the emergency door and into the side street, Zach stopped short. A large SWAT van raced up, skidding to a stop. It wasn't a SWAT van, though, or at least none like he'd ever seen before. This one was coal black, without a single marking. And the men piling out of the vehicle? Each wore black leather, and each wore a cross around his neck.

"Feel free to fire up the disc," Zach told Ronnie. When she didn't answer, he glanced over at her.

"Yeah, about that…"

* * *

"The refrigerator really messed it up," Ronnie continued.

"But you said—"

Ronnie shrugged, knowing that nothing she could say or do would lessen the blow. "I was bluffing. The disc is shot."

The look of disappointment that crossed Zach's face nearly undid her. After a breath, he was back at it, though. "What about Quirk? Surely he must have—"

Yes, she too was used to him pulling something out of a hat, but…"After the magnet fritzed, I haven't heard from him."

She could only assume that Quirk had followed protocol and had gotten the heck out of the vicinity. Her assistant liked to call it the pirate's code.

Zach's expression looked more pained than it had after he stumbled out of that CIA safe house.

"I'm *so* sorry."

Sorry for everything. Sorry for getting him mixed up in this mess. Sorry for not field- testing the magnetic disc in a kitchen environment.

Zach squeezed her hand. "It's okay."

As the men, armed to the teeth, approached, squealing tires also announced the police on the other side of the building. None of it seemed okay.

"I got to meet you," he said, leaning in.

It was absurd timing. It was crazy to stop and kiss right now, but absurd and crazy were meaningless right now. Time hung, suspended.

Then the wash of chopper rotors buffeted them back. Buffeted everyone back as it streaked in from the sky, then hovered right in front of them. Quirk opened the door.

"Told ya he's into me," the young man announced, as the gruff pilot nodded to Ronnie.

* * *

Oh, if only he could capture the look on his boss's face. Except, of course, for the dozen or so ninja priests and law enforcement personnel bearing down on them.

"You coming aboard, or what?" Quirk asked.

Ronnie was the first to snap out of it and grab hold of Quirk's outstretched hand. Zach bounded in after her, hauling a crate in with him. That left the old man, who seemed equally perplexed that there was a helicopter in front of him, yet oddly at ease with the fact as well. Quirk helped the man to board.

"We are good to go."

Which was a good thing, since the ninja priests had also recovered and had begun shooting. As they gained altitude, the old man glanced around.

"How very strange."

Right. This coming from a guy who tried to torch a Picasso.

Bullets pinged off the undercarriage as the pilot swooped them up and away. Ronnie turned to Quirk.

"When did you throw this together?"

Quirk shook his head. "Not me. You need to thank my sunshine at the controls."

In a very rare occasion, Ronnie stammered to express herself. "I…I'm not sure…How to…Huh?"

"Please," the pilot answered. "Like you people were getting out of this by yourselves."

Quirk urged Ronnie into her seat. "To avoid radar, he's going to have to do some spectacular low-altitude flying, so strap in."

Once Quirk got everyone else settled and himself secured in the copilot seat, he nodded to the pilot. "Let her rip."

Oh, and how did he. The helicopter tilted and swooshed through buildings, threading a needle between two high rises and then ducking under a bridge. If this was any indication of how the man handled himself in bed…

Quirk fanned himself as the chopper laid over. Like he said, the day was definitely looking up.

* * *

Lino stood amongst the clamor of the other men loading into the van as the helicopter veered out of view. To think that one man, Francois Loboum, felt him above God's will and escaped the Almighty's wrath. Perhaps the old, fallen priest did have a guardian angel.

Much as Lucifer had his comrades, so must Francois.

Could Francois not see that a cleansing purge was God's way? Seldom did the Bible talk of conferences and political pacts. No, God spoke of fire and plague. Something the Hidden Hand was adept at unleashing.

Lino gave a deep sigh as he climbed into the all-too-modern van. He never should have allowed Deacon Havar to convince him to leave Francois's extraction to others. Lino would have snuck in like a thief in the night, slit the old man's throat, and then snuck back out again without anyone the wiser. But Havar wanted Francois alive.

Certainly the obese deacon had justified his orders that they would compel vital information out of Francois, but Lino sensed it had more to do with Havar's desire to torture the old man.

Weakness of flesh. Weakness of spirit.

And to think that such weakness had caused the death of Brother Michael. The man had been the one who first taught Lino the symbols of the angels. The symbols that would rule his life. But if poor Michael had been careless enough to be killed, perhaps it would not be worth Lino's time to mourn him.

What of the painting? They had long suspected that the communist Picasso wandered from the fold. But to have so brashly impregnated one of his paintings with heresy? Now, that too was in the hands of the unbelievers.

As the van skidded out, filling the night air with the acrid smell of rubber, the driver called out to Lino. "Deacon Havar wants to know your plan from here."

Oh, now the flabby man wished Lino's counsel.

While he accepted the proffered phone, Lino had absolutely no ambition to impart the truth to the deacon. Francois could seek few harbors during such a storm as this. Lino intended to find him…alone.

* * *

Dr. Henderson walked into the room. "Good. You are both sitting."

More than likely because neither Amanda nor Jennifer had the energy to stand. Neither did Dr. Henderson, for he leaned heavily against the doorframe.

"Dr. MacVetti just died."

That didn't make sense. They'd had two guards die, but those men had been deep into the Black Death's grip, with bloody froth at their lips, struggling to breathe as boils broke out all over their bodies.

"But MacVetti was barely second stage," Amanda commented, refraining from checking her own lymph nodes. However, she glanced at Jennifer, whose already ashen lips had gone white at the news.

"He had mild heart disease, but it was enough to throw a clot to his brain. He stroked out."

That was the problem with the plague. Sometimes it didn't wait to kill you itself. It just added fuel to an already diseased portion of the body. No one was safe.

Sounds came from the hallway as Dr. Henderson frowned.

"What is it?"

Amanda's mind went fairly wild with speculation. She had been studying the Hidden Hand so closely that she felt like they were right beside her at times. Were they now coming down the hallway?

Instead, Henderson moved out of the way for half a dozen scientists. Colleagues—most who had not exactly ever been on Team Amanda.

Each nodded as they passed by, and then lined up across from her desk.

"Well?" Dr. Conek asked.

"Well, what?"

"We are here to do whatever you need us to do."

"But—"

Dr. Conek slowly shook his head. "We discussed it. We aren't going to wait down in the infirmary until it becomes a morgue. MacVetti did everything right. Took his meds, rested, and now look at him."

The new group got into their seats as Conek finished. "So fill us in on your Chicken Little Project, and let's get going."

Amanda gulped back tears. Even Dr. Henderson sat down. Jennifer, on the other hand, had no problem handing out assignments. Maybe, just maybe, with ten brains working on the same project, they would find the elusive Hidden Hand.

CHAPTER 20

Undisclosed Location
11:32 p.m., MST

Francois sat upon the motel's lumpy mattress, allowing the woman to examine his arm. While her gaze was obsessed with the markings dug deep into the flesh, Francois only had eyes for the painting that sat across from them, propped upon the faux wood table.

They had not allowed him to burn it. Not yet. On the other side of the room, the FBI agent who had saved him held a lighter and a hair spray can—a cheap and easily assembled torch. The FBI agent did not seem to trust Francois with the items. Which was probably warranted.

The desire to burn the painting and see the beauty of the angels' gift to man flamed inside Francois. He had come so far and thought himself thwarted. That God might have seen fit to grant him another chance? This he would not waste.

"So you read these diagonally?" the woman asked.

Francois nodded. Normally, he would not so casually reveal such secrets, but the woman had the language of the angels all over her laptop screen. And not just any symbols. But those most precious to their guardians. Secret symbols. Yet there they glistened and shimmered. If the angels so blessed her, he would be of no hindrance.

"I had guessed as much. Is it read right to left, down the center line?"

Again, he nodded. This one truly must have a pure soul if the angels had given her such knowledge.

"What I don't get is, where do I start next?" the woman said, indicating to the most recent symbols cut into his flesh. "Do I move the entire set down, or start from the top to create the new center line?"

Francois could not help but flinch as she touched an especially fresh symbol.

"Sorry," she murmured, taking more care as she leaned over his arm.

"When did they begin speaking to you?" Francois asked.

The woman frowned. "Who?"

"The angels?"

The FBI agent stepped forward. "Okay. I've been more than patient. I have taken a lot...well, not exactly on faith here, but on *necessity*."

The dutiful doubters. Those who balanced on the edge of a sword. Not having enough faith, but neither having too much distrust. Francois knew how this man felt. Francois himself had experienced it decades ago.

Then it had been burned out of him.

Literally.

"Perhaps it is best if I show you," Francois suggested.

* * *

Zach watched the old man's face as Francois tenderly dragged his finger along the frame of the Picasso. Zach wasn't exactly a modern art guy, but even he recognized the cubist painting. Francois held out his hand for the lighter and hair spray. It was pretty low tech; however, the items made a handy flamethrower when you were running from the law.

Usually, Zach thought of himself as a man of action. He liked learning stuff by doing. He'd always hated classrooms, with their chalkboards or whiteboards, and desks. Give him a chance to fieldstrip an AK-47 any day over learning the penal code.

But here he stood, not wanting to take action. Sure, it had sounded all well and good to go ahead and burn the rest of the Picasso. Why not? It was already torched along one side. However, standing here in the broke-down motel with one weird eye staring at him, an eye that the master himself had painted, made Zach a little queasy.

Again, his mother would be so proud.

Zach looked at the door. The pilot was still guarding it, peeking out the curtain at regular intervals to make sure that their location was still secure. Then, of course, Quirk was staring at the pilot, so they were covered there.

He glanced at Ronnie, who shrugged. "He insists that the symbols will only be revealed if we burn the painting at a high-intensity temperature."

Hence, the spray can and the lighter.

Ronnie took a step closer, covering Zach's hand with hers. "Quirk, what's the update?"

Her assistant checked his smartphone. "Another hundred thousand cases reported in the last *hour*. And it's confirmed that the entire staff of Plum Island is infected."

The plague was spreading faster than anyone had guessed, and was far more lethal than anyone had feared. If the CIA believed that this angelic script held the key to stopping the plague—enough to set up and kidnap an FBI agent to coerce an outlaw hacker into helping—then well, there had to be something to it.

Still, what in the hell did Picasso have to do with any of this?

Zach could, of course, ask those questions. But by the set of the old man's jaw, he doubted if he would get many answers.

"*I'll* do it." Zach said. Francois opened his mouth to protest, but Zach rode right over him. "That's a deal breaker."

The old man got that look in his eye, like he had back at the field office—right before he tried to pull Zach through the bars. A hint of madness tinged with desperation. Zach held steady, though. While Francois held a lot of information, the old man also needed to learn how to bottle the crazy up.

"*Deal. Breaker,*" Zach emphasized.

Francois gripped the painting's frame, seemingly unable to let go even as he nodded. Ronnie stepped in, and at first gently, and then with more and more torque, pulled the painting away from Francois. Zach bet the old man had some splinters under his nails.

Taking in a deep breath, not believing, out of a day of completely unbelievable events, that he was about to set fire to a Picasso, Zach glanced overhead. The fire alarm had been disabled—not that it had batteries in the first place.

Zach flicked the lighter, watching the tiny flame dance above the metal. He shook the hair spray, more to give himself time to work up the nerve than the bottle needed shaking.

Ronnie gave a tight, not-quite-reassuring smile. Zach hit the nozzle, spraying fire before him. He took a step closer to the painting, watching the heat beat from the flame toward the canvas. He took another step. Now the flames licked the paint, melting it. Zach took care to only torch the portion of the painting already singed, trying to build up the nerve to put flame to the remaining masterpiece. Then the rest of the canvas caught fire, curling and crackling.

In for a penny, in for a pound, right? Zach stepped even closer, bringing the full flame to the painting. An already oddly placed eye melted into an elbow, blurring the image. Then the entire picture caught fire, consuming itself within moments. Only at the end, as the flames converged on the center of the painting, did something gold flicker.

As the canvas went up in smoke, the gilded symbol grew brighter and brighter, pulsing of its own accord, floating before them, flaring a warning across the ages. Zach's thumb stung from the heat of the lighter, but he kept the torch to bear.

If angels did exist and they wanted to speak, this was definitely how they would.

Then the symbol burned nearly white as it exploded in ash.

No one moved. No one even breathed.

"Holy Batman's undergarments," Quirk finally commented.

Snapping back, Zach released the nozzle and the lighter. The room felt too still without the *whoosh* of the fire. He sought Ronnie's gaze, except she seemed to be having a religious experience herself. Zach felt moved, and he didn't even understand what in the hell the symbol even meant.

Ronnie met his gaze. Her eyes were half-closed, as if she'd just been roused from slumber but was not yet awake. He'd never thought that any woman could look so beautiful. Then, she blurted out, "Crap!"

* * *

Ronnie looked through her phone. *Please, please, please let me have snapped a picture,* she thought. Maybe somewhere in that trancelike state, she had actually captured the symbols that they were so desperate to find. But the last photo that showed up was the screenshot of Zach. Um, maybe since he was standing right next to her, she might want to delete that one.

"I didn't get a picture of it," she moaned. She could see it in her mind's eye, but it wasn't one she recognized. Could she remember all of the details for proper analysis?

"Oh, please," Quirk said, turning his smartphone toward her. Footage of the entire event replayed. "And, as a bonus, I now have *on film* that you can't survive in the wild without me."

Ronnie could totally kiss her completely arrogant, gay assistant right on the mouth. Fortunately, he didn't expect that of her. She turned to Francois. At first she didn't understand what he was doing. Then as realization hit, she rushed over, grabbing his hand.

"Francois! Don't."

But it was too late. He had already carved the symbol into his arm.

"You don't have to do that anymore," she chided, taking the edge of her shirt and blotting the blood.

"There is no 'have,'" he commented. "I *need* to."

Ronnie didn't get it, but she did. In her mind's eye, the symbol glittered, sending off rays to the depths of her... well...soul.

"Um," a baritone voice came from the other side of the room. "For the new guy, what in the hell just happened?"

Ronnie turned to find Quirk trying to shush the pilot, but Zach plopped down on the edge of the bed. "Yeah, for a guy who's been on the inside of this...What in the hell just happened?"

She glanced at Francois, but he had retreated once again into his Latin mumblings. Looked like she was going to have to wing it alone on this one. Ronnie turned the desk's rickety chair around and sat facing the men. Crossing her arms over the back of the chair, she gave it her best effort, even though her own mind was still reeling.

"The symbol flaring out is probably the easiest to explain." From Zach's raised eyebrow, she hurried on. "Clearly, they must have impregnated the symbol into the canvas with a magnesium substrate. That's what caused the brilliant light show."

And what a light show it had been. She glanced at Francois, who either nodded or was simply rocking back and forth.

"But why?" Zach asked. "Why, with premeditation, hide a piece of angelic script in a painting?"

Excellent question. How could a modern art painting be connected to a reemergence of the Black Death? She needed to work all this out as much for herself as for the men seeking to understand.

"Everyone wants to keep secrets," Ronnie explained. "From the Templars with their advanced symbology, to the US using the Navajo language during World War II, we want our secrets kept secret."

It was her lifeblood, actually. Revealing secrets, burrowing into others' deepest, most tightly held vaults. Usually, she was after cash. In this case, though, they had created an elaborate encryption to hold something so much more valuable. Information.

Quirk frowned, even though Ronnie knew how much he hated to encourage wrinkles. "But then why put such an important piece of secret script in such a prominent public image?"

Ronnie chuckled. "Have you ever lost your keys?"

"Excuse me?" Quirk countered, now arching his eyebrow.

"Not just you, but everyone. We forget things. We *lose* things. Now imagine an ancient organization trying to operate through the ages. Sure, they could hide their secrets, but then they risked losing them forever."

"And we are talking about the Hidden Hand, then?" Zach asked.

Ronnie glanced at Francois, who shook his head absently. "No. I think the Hidden Hand uses angelic script, but the clues we are tracking down are from a resistance group within the Hidden Hand. Those who don't agree with their goal."

"The Hand within the Hand," Francois whispered.

"Yes," Ronnie agreed. "And I think they prepared for this day. When the Hidden Hand came out from the shadows. The resistance used the paintings as a fail-safe mechanism. So if the worst happened, someone like Francois could piece the puzzle back together."

"In paintings, though?" Quirk pressed, although Ronnie didn't blame him. If she hadn't seen the symbol flare in all of its golden glory, Ronnie wouldn't have believed it either. "Seriously, people, let's at least get them onto floppy drives."

"Francois?" she asked gently, as the man mumbled in Latin. "Why did the Hand within the Hand choose *paintings*?

"It is the angels who chose it," Francois said. Clearly looking confused, he asked Ronnie, "Did they not tell you?"

Ronnie shook her head, "No."

The guy really did believe that angels were talking to him. Which created a minor reality problem. Sure, the symbols were angelic script, but a group of *men* decided on using the paintings for their safekeeping.

"Could it be the theory of hiding in plain sight?" Zach proposed.

"No," Quirk answered flatly.

Uh-oh. Her assistant wasn't used to anyone but Ronnie disagreeing with him—not even a smoking-hot FBI agent. However, Zach had no problem coming right back at Quirk.

"But I might suggest that the paintings, and therefore the symbols, have been doing just fine. That they are still available to us kind of proves my point."

Good one. Not that she would admit that in front of Quirk. It would only rev the hacker up and make him start criticizing Zach's choice of hair-care products.

"Maybe the Hidden Hand chose paintings because the arts are many times protected, even in times of upheaval?" Ronnie suggested, trying to weave between Zach and Quirk. "Considered national treasures? That they, out of any other vehicle, might survive through the ages?"

"Of course," Francois answered. "As I said, the *angels* know best."

Ronnie wanted to press him for a clearer answer, but the old man went back to rocking back and forth mumbling scripture and reading the symbols carved into his arm. Clearly, he had kept meticulous records—a process that seemed to take as heavy a toll on his mind as well as his flesh.

"Okay, I am going to take that as a 'yes.'" Zach said as he leaned in. "Now, the question is, do we have any idea what you are decoding? What this information is?"

Ronnie bit her lip. She hated to speculate. She liked nice, long equations that took as much of the risk out of an endeavor as possible. "My best guess is that they are locations. What we will find in those locations, I'm not sure."

"Well, luckily, you've got my speedy texting fingers, and me," Quirk announced. However, Ronnie was pretty sure the second half was for the pilot.

"What do you mean?"

Apparently just to show off, Quirk texted and explained at the same. "I've got a BFF at the CDC…"

Of course he did. A hypochondriac at Quirk's level? The man probably had a BFF at the Surgeon General's office, the World Health Organization, and probably the American Cancer Society just to be sure to cover all his bases.

"And she says the CIA is looking for Hidden Hand vaccine vaults," Quirk said, then jerked his head upright. "I like the sound of that."

As did Ronnie. Now, some of the text was beginning to make sense. Talk of the nectar given by God and a prick to spare the ferryman.

"Great," Zach said. "Let's go crash their party and get the vaccine."

Ronnie shook her head, though. "It isn't that simple. This is a cipher built with code and layered over code. I need way more information before I can pinpoint any one location." The room seemed to sag as she continued. "I am going to have to correlate this new symbol with all of the other symbols, then extrapolate where the next—"

"That will not be necessary," Francois stated as he rose from the bed. "I know exactly where we must go."

Ronnie waited for the elderly man to elaborate, but he just picked up his jacket and strode to the door. Zach blocked his path.

"Mind filling us in?"

Francois seemed truly perplexed as he looked at each of them.

"Why, Graceland, of course."

* * *

Amanda coughed into the crook of her elbow. Not that she couldn't just walk up to any of the remaining scientists and cough directly in their faces. They were all infected. Each was flushed with fever. Their fingernails were blackening as their lungs filled with fluid.

She didn't blame two who had gone back downstairs. Nor the two who had laid their heads down for a quick rest and were now still slumbering away. Absently, Amanda scratched her arm—only to feel wet, thick liquid under her fingernails.

The boils were rupturing, which meant that her lymph nodes were rupturing. Which meant her immune system's last resorts were giving out. Amanda turned to Jennifer. Her assistant's lymph nodes had been gone for over four hours. Now her arms were a wreck of pustules and open sores. Yet still she typed. Slower than even an hour before, with breaks to catch her breath.

"I want to grow up to be just like you," Amanda said, placing her hand over Jennifer's. Her assistant gave it a weak squeeze, and then went back to calculating the average mean derivation of plague resistance in the tristate area.

"Amanda, you had better listen to this," Henderson said as he turned up the television. Anderson Cooper was back on, and looking a hell of a lot like Jennifer. They weren't even bothering with makeup anymore. How could any makeup cover bloodshot eyes?

"All US air travel has been suspended. I repeat, even small, private aircraft have been grounded. The only aircraft allowed in the sky is Air Force One. Please be advised that if you attempt to fly and ignore demands to land, you will be shot down." Anderson stopped and wiped his face with his hand. "This is what it has come to, my fellow citizens. Anybody that is considering fleeing, please think it through…Where are you going to go?"

Devlin, who must have snuck in during the broadcast, turned the volume back down. "I've got equally bad news."

Seriously, how much worse could any news get?

"Our CIA operative, the one tasked with finding the code breaker, has gone silent. We don't know if he is dead or gone underground because he was hunted, but we're pretty sure the hacker has escaped."

Amanda felt the air rush from her lungs. The entire point of doing all of this was to be ready when the Hidden Hand's code was broken. What were they doing, then? What hope did they have left?

Devlin, though, gave a tight grin. "So, I'd like to offer my assistance in any way I can." He looked at Henderson. "Better late than never, right?"

The CIA liaison then turned his gaze on Amanda. "May I?"

Why the hell not? Amanda thought as she scooted her chair over.

If they were on a fool's errand, they might as well all be fools together.

CHAPTER 21

Memphis, Tennessee
2:57 a.m., CST

Graceland. Graceland. Graceland. Quirk repeated the name over and over again in his head. Graceland. It couldn't be true, could it? He would pinch himself, except, you know, he didn't want to bruise his well-moisturized, delicate skin.

He was so excited that he didn't even complain that the small aircraft they "borrowed" didn't have sparkling water, nor did he even utter a peep when he was crammed in the back of this "borrowed" SUV with the stinky Frenchman and Ronnie. They were in Memphis on their way to Graceland. How could he complain?

Graceland.

Ah, to visit where Elvis had lived and died. To breathe the air that the King breathed.

The only downside to being a world-renowned hacker was that you seldom went sightseeing. You lived your life in safe houses and lead-lined rooms. Which worked out nicely with his desire to avoid all form of germ contact, but oh, Graceland was so worth the risk—of even the plague.

Which reminded him. Quirk checked his phone—no messages from Jennifer. But from the newscasts it looked like Tennessee hadn't been hit hard yet by the Black Death because, well, it was Tennessee. Probably not a lot of travelers from Venice booked their next flight to Memphis. But the rest of the country? Especially New York?

He didn't even try to suppress the shudder. All those infected—breathing, hacking, and coughing. Again, the shudder. Quirk turned to Ronnie to give her a well-deserved "I told you so," to find her laptop open and fingers on the keyboard, but her head was propped up against the window. Given that the French guy was unabashedly snoring, Quirk assumed that Ronnie was asleep as well.

Quirk looked ahead at the passenger's seat to find Zach in nearly the same position. Oh, the nerve! He'd gone all special agent to secure the shotgun position, and then fell asleep? That just wouldn't do.

As he opened his mouth to let the entire car know his disdain, Quirk caught the pilot's eyes watching him in the rearview mirror. Those liquid brown orbs, so like molten chocolate, silenced Quirk. *Fine.* Maybe he didn't have to awaken everyone. He could let them know his disappointment upon their arrival.

Quirk gave a little shrug. Of course, he rolled his eyes so that the pilot knew exactly the toll keeping silent was taking.

Then the pilot winked.

Okay, there were definite perks to being on the road.

* * *

Zach opened the car door and was met with warm, heavy air. It was just early May, and already the South was ready to drown visitors with humidity. He glanced across the street to the wrought iron gates that guarded the mansion. They were aptly decorated with musical notes and Elvis's iconic figure. They were the perfect protectors of the white columns of Graceland, even this late at night, illuminated against the dark sky.

Funny, Zach had been here...how many times? Yet, never at night. During his childhood, they'd come to Elvis's mansion, but always during the day with the mobs and mobs of tours. Which was kind of ironic, since Elvis had moved out here to the "country" to get away from the maddening crowds. In the end, the maddening crowds had followed him to Graceland.

Weird to be here again, especially under these circumstances.

Although Quirk didn't seem to share his unease. Even though they were across the street from the mansion, the kid was snapping picture after picture, making the pilot move this way or that to get the best shot. Of course, he'd said they needed surveillance pictures, but come on, he knew a fan photo shoot when he saw one.

It was odd to think that such everyday, ordinary, sub-urban items such as a strip mall surrounded a prominent landmark like Graceland. The mansion, in some small way, reminded Zach of the White House. How surprised he'd been to find the nation's seat of power surrounded on every side by...well, everything and anything. The White House was an oasis in a sea of city buildings. Much like Graceland.

Next to him, Ronnie began to get out of the car, stretching as she straightened.

"So that's the King's crib, eh?"

"Yep."

"Well, security is so bad that 2005 is calling and wants it back," Ronnie said as she yawned, pulling out her palmtop. "I broke through its firewall in, like, twenty-two seconds flat. After we neutralize the two security guards, we should be able to slide in and get whatever painting we need—"

"Of Elvis," Zach added. "The painting we need is of Elvis. It was his father's last gift before Elvis died.""Okay..." Ronnie said, tilting her head.

Zach tried to shrug it off. "Dad was a pretty big fan. We came here on summer breaks."

It wasn't until that moment that Zach realized that Graceland was the last family vacation before his dad...He shook off the memory. What in the hell was he doing dwelling on crap like that, when the world was under siege by the Hidden Hand?

"Anyway, I know exactly where the painting is hung."

Ronnie went to say something, but Quirk burst into their conversation. "So, are we ready?"

"We?" Ronnie answered. "Since when do 'we' do the actual recon work?"

"Um, since it's *Graceland*," Quirk rambled on, pulling out his tablet. "I say we go in the back here..."

Zach looked at the schematic and shook his head. "Nice try."

"What?" Quirk said apparently trying to look innocent.

Ronnie glanced at Zach. "Yes, I'd love to hear what Quirk is up to."

"That," Zach said pointing to the map, "is the window to the jungle room."

The young assistant took in a sharp breath. He was busted, and he seemed to know it.

"Quirk?" Ronnie pressed.

"Well, yes, it is the jungle room, but that doesn't mean that it isn't the most strategic location for insertion."

Again, nice try. Zach pointed to the room on the map that had served as Elvis's living room. "The painting is just to the right of the front door. *I* go in there, grab the painting, and then come back out again." He nodded toward the pilot. "Our driver will have the SUV revved and ready for the road. I should be in and out within a minute."

Zach thought that pretty much settled things, when Francois stepped off the curb and headed for the mansion.

* * *

Ronnie rushed along with the others to corral Francois back to the car, but the Frenchman was on a mission. Actually, he seemed more like a moth to a flame. He had a singular purpose, and that was to get into Graceland.

"Yeah," the pilot sighed as he stopped giving chase. "I'll get the car."

As Zach tried to wrangle Francois, Ronnie turned to Quirk. "I'll take the property, you take the periphery."

The younger man frowned, clearly wanting to be at "one" with Graceland, but even Quirk must have realized that now was not the time to argue. Her assistant brought up the energy grid that serviced the area with two swipes of his finger across his palmtop.

"Bring down a whole city block so they don't zero in on Graceland as the target," Ronnie added as she set off a perimeter breach at the back of the property. All 13.8 acres to the back of the property. With only two guards, one of them was going to have to hop in that golf cart and ride out to check on the alarm. That would leave only one guard at the gate. Which wouldn't have been a problem, had Francois not decided to go on his walkabout.

The entire block plunged into darkness. Streetlights went out. The mansion's façade darkened. Hopefully, security would chalk it all up to a power surge or downed power line.

Zach was clearly trying not to make a scene. However, no amount of coaxing stopped the old man's march to the gates of Graceland. Even now, the gate's guard exited the little shack behind the fence and stood watching the very awkward group.

"Down all video feeds," Ronnie whispered. Many of these buildings might have backup generators.

"Look," Quirk retorted, "you worry about those gorgeous gates, hon. I've got the rest."

They had to trot to keep up as Francois and Zach reached the wrought iron gates. Francois stopped, swaying from side to side, his eyes intent on the mansion behind them.

"I am really sorry," Zach said to the uniformed guard. "We were just trying to show Grandpa Graceland, and he kind of…"

Zach indicated the clearly altered Francois.

"I understand," the guard said, although he didn't exactly look all that understanding. "But you are all going to have to back up. This is private property."

"You heard the man, Francois," Zach said, trying to urge the Frenchman back. "We've got to go."

Francois refused to budge. Zach spoke to the old man as his eyes darted to Ronnie. "The nice guard can't open the gates for us."

Ronnie knew a cue when she heard one. Tapping into Graceland's security matrix, she hit the controls for the gate. A loud *clunk* sounded and the metal lurched; however, the sides did not swing open.

"What the hell?" the guard drawled, backing up.

She hit the command again. Again, the gate clunked, but did not open. Damn it! There must have been a physical lock that wasn't controlled electronically. The guard went to pull his gun. Zach reached for his, but it was long gone back in El Paso, and since they didn't have a safe house in Tennessee… Imagine that—he was unarmed.

Zach was FBI through and through. He charged the gate, hitting it squarely with his shoulder. The gate groaned but didn't give way.

"Get back!" the guard yelled, pulling his weapon out with a shaky hand.

"The latch," Ronnie urged.

Zach slipped his hand between the ironwork and popped the metal latch holding the gate shut. Freed of its restraint, the gate swung open as the guard stumbled. His hand flew to the radio on his shoulder.

"We've got intruders!"

But Zach was there, knocking the radio from his hand, getting the guard in a chokehold before the man could even raise a finger. "Just relax," Zach said, closing off the man's windpipe. "I swear—it's just like taking a nap."

The guard did anything but relax, flailing and clutching at Zach's hands, and then he slowed, closing his eyes. Zach let up as the guard went slack. He bent down to check the guy's pulse, however. Francois didn't miss a beat as he headed straight toward the mansion's front door. Ronnie checked the security feed. The offsite monitors were only getting static. Unfortunately, the damned the golf cart was making a quick U-turn, making a beeline for the mansion. The other guard must have heard at least some of the guard's transmission.

"Damn it, Quirk," she hissed. "You've got to throw up enough interference to block communications."

"Um, I'm doing my part," he replied. "Yell at Mr. Hellfire in a Hurry up there."

As Zach dragged the unconscious guard to the small shack, Ronnie hurried after Francois. Her assistant didn't keep up the pace. "Quirk!"

"What?" he protested. "I can't hack and run at the same time."

Ronnie had perhaps never felt so vindicated. "Which is why I insist on training under *all* conditions."

"Oh, forgive me. I'm not all Lara Croft."

She ignored his barb, which really wasn't that much of a barb, all things considered. Instead, she concentrated on getting that front door unlocked. Zach caught up with them just as they passed the large stone lions that stood sentry at the entrance to the mansion.

"Are we good to go?" Zach asked on the run.

Ahead of them, Francois climbed the four steps up to the front door and opened it.

Since no blaring alarm went off to wake the neighbors, Ronnie answered, "Guess so."

With the sound of the golf cart's whine coming around the corner, they rushed into the mansion.

* * *

The door nearly hit Quirk as Zach slammed it shut, but still Quirk did not move an inch. Why would he? Here he stood in Elvis Presley's mansion. White, pure white, washed over him—only punctuated by bright blues and reds. Graceland's classic revival style was everything Quirk could have ever imagined, and more.

Sure, it was small by today's standards of McMansions, but Quirk could imagine how Elvis must have felt when he first walked into the house. Coming from such humble roots, this two-story mansion must have seemed like a palace. And the fact that the King decorated Graceland like a palace? Ah, that just captured Quirk's affection all the more.

As an orphan bounced from foster home to foster home, Quirk had clung to an old cassette that some random social worker had given to him, *Elvis: 50 Greatest Hits*. She'd said that if Presley could rise from nothing to be the King of Rock 'n' Roll, Quirk could do anything he set his mind to do.

And being the single greatest hacker was what he set his mind upon. Ronnie didn't count, of course. She was some kind of OCD-fueled cyborg who had code running through her veins.

No, Quirk had risen to his position on some good ol' hard work and lots of panache. And here he stood in the King's presence. Straight ahead, the tiled foyer opened into an elegant hallway. A marble staircase, roped off to visitors, led to the second floor—the floor with Elvis's bedroom, and even the bathroom…where he finally succumbed. Quirk might have raced up those stairs, except his feet were rooted in place. He couldn't move an inch until he soaked up every last glorious moment of what lay before him.

Even the emergency lighting did nothing but enhance the magical surroundings.

To his left was the dining room. How many legends sat at that table and broke bread with Elvis? To the right lay the living room, where the rest of the team was gathered. They were all obsessed with the painting and hadn't stopped to appreciate the low, white couch or the mirror-topped fireplace. And the peacock stained-glass windows that separated the living room from the music room?

Beyond the doorway sat a grand piano. How often had Elvis tickled those ivories? A chill started at the base of Quirk's skull and ran straight down his spine. Quirk was all shook up.

"Quirk," Ronnie whispered, but he ignored her until she grabbed his wrist and jerked him down.

Flashlight beams cut through the windows, sending streaks of light across the room. Light bounced off the mirrors above the fireplace, illuminating the room to nearly daylight.

That was when he saw the painting in question. It was of Elvis. Not the young, brash Elvis or the older jumpsuit Elvis, but the Elvis who had just realized exactly how heavy the burden of fame could become. It was eloquent, yet haunting.

And they were going to burn it.

* * *

Ronnie kept Quirk down, and Zach did the same with Francois. Each seemed in a trance of his own.

Footsteps rang out on the stone steps outside. The guard was coming to check on the front door.

"It's locked, right?" Zach whispered.

Oh. Crap. She'd been a little preoccupied.

As the doorknob turned, Ronnie pulled out her palm-top and keyed in the codes. The knob made it around three-quarters of the way, then caught. The guard jiggled it again, but it held.

Rapid footsteps announced the guard leaving. Luckily, the Presleys didn't trust their security staff all that much, and didn't give them keys to the mansion. They would probably have another good ten minutes before someone higher up the food chain came to check the house.

"We need to get moving."

Zach helped Francois to his feet. "I'll grab the painting."

"No!" Quirk announced—far too loudly, given the situation. In a manner far quieter than his "oh, snap" persona, Quirk continued, "No, I've got it."

Her normally exercise-averse assistant reverently lifted the Elvis painting from the wall and hugged it to his body. "This way."

Quirk headed down the hallway, away from the front door. Zach raised an eyebrow. This wasn't the plan. However, Quirk was right. They couldn't go out the front. They were going to have to make for the back of the property and meet up with the SUV on the other side of the fence.

They followed Quirk down the hallway and past the stairs where he dodged to the left, opening a door as if he had lived here his whole life. They passed through a small hallway and then headed left.

Where they all stumbled to a stop.

"Quirk…" Ronnie threatened.

Thick, green shag carpet stretched out before them, ending at the edge of a pool fed by a waterfall cascading down a faux stone wall. Ferns hung from the rafters, and even the ceiling was lined in green shag.

So this was the infamous jungle room.

When Quirk didn't answer, apparently so enthralled with the carved wooden furniture and strangely, a teddy bear in the far corner, Ronnie elbowed him.

"Quirk!"

The young man had to shake his head several times before being able to focus on her annoyance.

"What the hell are we doing here?" she pressed.

"Um," Quirk said, regaining his composure. "We needed to get to the back of the house. We are at the back of the house."

Several sets of squealing tires announced the arrival of the main security service.

"We must burn it. Now," Francois said. "If we are to be captured, we must all know the symbol, quadrupling our chances of spreading our knowledge."

For an old guy who spent half his time mumbling in Latin, he did have a point. Guess he had been at this hidden angelic script thing the longest.

Ronnie nodded to Zach, but Quirk stepped between them. "Please. Let me."

Normally, Ronnie would have shut her assistant down. However, she heard something in his tone. Not pleading or desperate, not how Francois had been, but reverential. Even Zach must have sensed the change, because he simply handed over the can of Aqua Net and the lighter.

Ronnie whipped out her phone, hitting the video record button. Who knew what Elvis was going to reveal?

* * *

Quirk gently leaned the painting up against the jungle pool. Elvis must have known it would come to this. Or at the least, his father, Vernon, who gave him the painting. They meant for Elvis to be a part of this angelic legacy.

Picasso had already burnt, but you know, it was Picasso. Who but a bunch of chai- loving intelligentsia would care? But Elvis?

Quirk had to be strong, though. For the King, and for the world.

He struck up the lighter. He squeezed the spray nozzle. Fire shot out in front of him. As the flame licked the saintly image, he began to hum, and then sing, "Love Me Tender."

The canvas caught fire, crackling before them. Only Elvis's visage didn't melt or distort. He stayed ever the King as the fire consumed the painting.

To Quirk's surprise, another voice took up the song at "Take me to your heart…"

He turned to find Zach's tenor added to the melody. Soon, Francois and even Ronnie were singing along as the last of the painting flared before the symbol sparked to life. Only this time, it wasn't just a single angelic script in the center. A host of musical notes surrounded the symbol.

So fitting for the King.

Then it was all gone. Vanishing with a final spark that floated down, extinguished only when it hit the pool of water.

A car screeching to a halt just outside the window shattered the eloquent moment.

Was Quirk surprised that their pilot drove the SUV? Not in the least.

"Need a ride?" he shouted.

Zach nodded as he picked up a chair to break the elaborate leaded-glass window.

"Guess he really does know you," Ronnie admitted as the pane shattered.

Yes, Quirk thought, *yes, the pilot did.*

* * *

Ronnie caught hold of her laptop as the SUV bounced over the back acreage of Graceland, and then smashed through a wooden fence. They raced onto other property, angling toward a side street exit from the neighborhood.

At this point, she trusted the pilot to get them out of here. Her focus had to be on this latest symbol. She had seen it before. Or at least the three angelic script runes that made up this altered symbol. Rapidly, she scrolled through her burgeoning inventory of angelic script.

There the three symbols were. Each was the head of a major line of script. Ronnie followed a hunch and took those three lines and overlapped them. Nothing—just garbage. The sequence made no sense. Even with the information Francois had contributed on how to decipher the mess, this newest symbol still made no sense.

Finally, the tires hit asphalt, and they fishtailed onto a two-lane road. Ronnie's elbow knocked into Zach's side. Flinching, he angled his body away from her.

"So sorry," she mumbled feeling like all she had in her for Zach were apologies.

"It's okay," he said, but his clenched jaw said otherwise. "Find anything?"

"I'm not sure…"

Ronnie tried to concentrate on the screen, but that would be a heck of a lot easier if Zach weren't sitting right next to her. Things had been simpler when he was in the front seat. However, when they were all piling into the car after the jungle room, no one had challenged Quirk's claim to the passenger's seat.

Now she was either worried about accidently ramming some part of her body into his black and blue rib cage, or missing him being closer, with their body heat mingling.

Ugh. See? It was thoughts like that which kept her from solving the puzzle.

And quite a puzzle it was. This latest set of symbols definitely wasn't fitting into her very limited view of angelic script. She looked to Francois, but his eyes were already closed, despite the sharp right and left turns the SUV was making.

"Junk DNA," a voice from the front seat said. Quirk poked his head between the seats, showing her his screen. Of course, he had hacked into her feed, reading her work. "Doesn't it look like junk DNA?"

In too much of a hurry to care about Quirk's lack of boundaries and scold him for it, Ronnie studied the garbled text with a new eye. Could her assistant be right? Was this sequence intentionally left undecipherable?

Zach shifted next to her, reading over her shoulder. "I thought DNA was pretty damned important?"

"It is," she answered as she brought up an image of the double helix. "Only scientists have found large chunks of it that didn't make any sense. It is considered 'non-coding' DNA, since it doesn't make any proteins."

Quirk chimed in, "Hence the 'junk' part."

"Only now, they don't believe it is 'junk' at all," Ronnie said as she searched the definition of the term. There it was. "Many believe that it has a *translational* role."

Translation: Yes. That pile of "junk" script was really a placeholder. It told her that something needed to go there. And she knew just the something. Rapidly, Ronnie brought up a sequence she had built back in Mexico. While she couldn't break the entire set of symbols, there were a few that at least made a little sense. She plugged this set into the gap of the "junk" script?

As her mind sought to decipher this new line, Ronnie sensed people talking around her. She could feel Zach move toward and away from her, but her mind whirled with possibilities. Her fingers tapped at the keyboard, dragging this symbol into place, and then rejecting it for another, and then bringing it back, only to reverse the order.

The gilded symbols became like water, malleable and fluid under her touch. They swam across her screen, diving and gliding into place. They pulsed in beat with Elvis's tune, seeming to want to assemble themselves in the right position.

Then, there it was. A list. An indisputable list glistened back at her.

She looked at Zach, or where Zach should be. She looked on the other side. No Francois. Both driver and passenger seats were empty.

What the…?

"Hey!" Quirk called out. "I think she's rejoined us mere humans."

Ronnie blinked, trying to make sense of Quirk's words as Zach leaned back into the car.

"Hey there, sexy."

His playful tone drained her anxiety. "Hey there, your-self." She looked out the door to find they were at a small airstrip. "How long was I out?"

Zach looked at his watch. "A little over an hour and fif-teen minutes. The pilot's got the plane ready. We just need a destination."

She frowned. While she had cracked a large part of the code, it had only given her an extensive list of painters' names. No locations. Just names.

"Monet, Renoir," Quirk read from his screen. "And Charles Schulz?"

Yes, strangely, the *Peanuts* creator was on the angels' list, but after the Elvis painting, nothing would really surprise her. Quirk went on reciting a veritable Who's Who of famous painters. Which was great, but that didn't exactly give the pilot a direction to head in, or a new destination.

"Well, over seventy percent of these artists are repre-sented at the Met," Quirk turned his computer screen, show-ing them the Metropolitan Museum of Art in New York. "I mean, it's not one hundred percent, but…"

Ronnie turned to Zach. "I don't think we can expect one hundred percent assurance for any of this. But based on the amount of 'junk' code I've got, we are going to have to find a whole lot of paintings very quickly."

"Then the Metropolitan Museum of Art it is."

"Of course," Francois stated matter-of-factly, walking past them toward the plane. "Isn't that where you thought we were heading?"

Seriously?

After all that time, effort, and code breaking?

Ronnie glared at the old man's back as he made his way to the twin-engine plane, never wanting to throttle one of her elders so badly in her life. Zach squeezed her shoulder, somehow diluting her anger.

"If Francois knew it all, he wouldn't need us, right?"

Damn right, Ronnie thought as they headed to the plane. She felt like shaking the old man back to his senses until she saw the drops of blood following behind him, like an injured puppy dog.

Ronnie sighed. Francois was giving as much as he could. After carrying this burden for so long, it was pretty surprising that he could give anything at all.

* * *

"There has been a break in at Graceland," an acolyte announced as he rushed into the room.

Very slowly, rising from his meditation, Lino opened his eyes to receive the agitated messenger.

"A man fitting Brother Loboum's description set afire a portrait."

Of course, Francois had. The man was cagey and sloppy all at once. He was privy to some of the Hidden Hand's most sacred truths, yet still could not find his way through a straight-lined maze. For every painting that Francois torched, he lit a beacon in the night for Lino to follow.

And the Presley painting...

Vernon, Vernon, Vernon. Such a dark chapter in the Hand's history. Their core had wavered. Disheartened by modern medicine's ability to prevent or cure the cleansing scourge, they had sought to infiltrate modern culture. Curry favor amongst the elite. What had that Presley boy done besides learn how to oscillate his iliosacral junction?

Those responsible for such a lowering of the Hand's sights were feeble, weak, and ultimately ineffectual. Ones even as easy to manipulate as Vernon had turned on the Hand. Betraying the order and their purpose. Shortly after, there had been a cleansing purge within the Hand.

A purge that rid them of any not strong enough to conceive and execute a worldwide plague of biblical proportions. Lino had been born to this task, and he would not falter.

Brother Loboum would find more than paintings burning at his next destination.

Francois had tipped his hand greatly.

Lino turned to the messenger. "Have the jet prepared. We go back to New York."

CHAPTER 22

Plum Island
4:16 a.m., EST

Amanda jerked upright, blinking, keeping herself from falling asleep. The data was finally starting to make sense. She had identified over ten thousand possible loci. Now the only job left was to hone that down to a Hidden Hand safe house on the Eastern Seaboard.

Yeah, no matter how you sliced it, nothing about it qualified as "only."

A noise near the door attracted her attention. Although a part of her didn't want to expend the energy to even turn her head, she did—but wished she hadn't. Not with Henderson and Devlin dragging a co-worker out.

The director caught her gaze. "We've taken all the food out of the refrigerator units…"

She sighed. He didn't have to tell her what they were using the industrial-sized refrigerators for. Clearly, the death count had risen to a point where they now needed to be concerned about contamination from the corpses. Normally, Black Death victims were burned, but with the rainy weather outside, there would be no pyres.

"How many?" Amanda felt she needed to ask.

Henderson glanced around the room. Half the scientists remained, and most of them listed on their seats looking not long for this world. As the director and Devlin continued their grim task, Amanda glanced at Jennifer.

Her assistant lay over the desk, resting her head on her crossed arms. She was just resting, right? Amanda watched her assistant's chest. It was rising and falling, right? She put her hand near Jennifer's nose, but couldn't feel any breath.

Amanda snatched her hand away. Her assistant was barely recognizable—with her puffy face from lack of lymph drainage to her skin—mottled with oozing boils. Then, those dark blue lips.

Carefully, she reached out and shook her assistant's shoulder. "Jennifer?"

No response. Amanda refused to believe that her best friend was dead.

"Jennifer?" She shook harder.

Then, with a raspy cough, her assistant opened her blood-shot eyes and gave a weak grin. Amanda nearly burst into tears. Instead, she put on a brave face and smiled back, rubbing Jennifer's back. The woman tried to sit up, but Amanda urged her to lie down.

"Get some rest."

Jennifer's forefinger and thumb made the sign for "little."

"Yes, Jen, just a little more rest."

As her friend let gravity close her eyelids, Amanda let the tears flow. She might as well cry while she still could.

* * *

Zach watched through the plane window as terrain streaked by, but not nearly fast enough. The pilot had to keep them under the radar, and therefore couldn't gain the altitude needed to really increase speed. What should have been a five-hour flight was now a grueling six-hour plus roller-coaster ride. To stay out of any major airport or military base's flight zone, they had to zigzag their way up the Eastern Seaboard.

He had to give credit to the pilot. By faking a blown transponder and sketchy radio, the guy had threaded this difficult needle all the way to New York. But the way the pilot kept glancing down at the fuel gauge, Zach had a feeling they were going to make it into the Essex County Regional Airport on fumes.

Even if they had to make an emergency landing, Zach could never blame the guy. If it hadn't been for the pilot, they'd probably still be in Mexico under the Federales' custody, or worse, turned back over to the CIA.

Zach glanced at Quirk, who slept with his mouth open just slightly. Between checks of the fuel gauge, the pilot would glance at Quirk. Who knew how much of the pilot's cooperation was due to financial gain, and how much was because of this somewhat odd attraction? They said opposites attracted, but this was a pretty extreme case. Seriously, who knew how the heart worked?

Zach turned his attention to Ronnie, who was hunched over her computer as Francois leaned on her shoulder, snoring blissfully away. By the way Ronnie fidgeted in her seat and bit her lip, she wasn't in "the zone." He'd already learned that if she were, she wouldn't move a muscle, except for those in her fingers as they flew over the keyboard. Zach wasn't sure if it was a good thing or not that she was only using her normal brain RAM speed.

The Metropolitan Museum of Art boasted some of the most sophisticated antitheft systems in the world. To think that Ronnie could stage a break-in, orchestrated in under eight hours, seemed ludicrous. But ludicrous was the norm these past twenty-four hours.

Every joint ached from the abuse of the last day, but whatever mixture of meds Quirk kept coming up with certainly took the edge off. At some point, though, the injuries were going to catch up with him. And when they did? He wanted a morphine drip, please.

"TXM918, we are still not picking up your transponder," air traffic control stated in Zach's headset.

The pilot rubbed the radio handpiece on his jeans, crackling the connection. "Be advised, Essex, that we are low on fuel and coming in with minimal altitude."

"TXM918, be advised that you *cannot* land here. We are inside the red zone. Please divert to Logan Airport."

"Tell that to my fuel gauge," the pilot said, and then snapped off the radio.

The red zone. As they had flown through the night, they'd heard snippets of local radio stations announcing at first mass evacuations, and then orders of quarantine. They had traveled from the green zone of Tennessee, to the yellow zone of Charleston, to the orange zone of Washington D.C., and now the red zone of New York. They truly were flying into the thick of the storm.

All to burn a bunch of paintings, hoping that it led them to the organization that had started all of this. To find a supposed vaccine. There were way too many "hopes" and "supposes" in that equation for Zach. He preferred a little door-breaking and hot-car pursuit. The closest they were coming to his FBI wheelhouse was to steal a car, stay under the speed limit, and make their way into the Metropolitan Museum of Art.

"This is going to get bumpy," the pilot warned as they dropped what little altitude they had.

Soon, those little specks in the early morning light became cars. Lines and lines of cars. Zach surveyed the freeway as they flew parallel to it. The road was nothing more than a parking lot, though. All eight lanes were at a standstill. Then he spotted the roadblock. They were turning back all traffic exiting the city and putting those cars on the freeway going eastbound.

A car tried to break past the roadblock and strike west over the uneven ground. They didn't get far, though, as the National Guard fired, blowing out their tires. Jesus. What the hell had happened overnight?

Then Zach saw what had happened.

A line of bodies, covered in bright red tarps, stretched for as far as the eye could see. No, not just a line of bodies, but *lines* of bodies. As they flew further, they found bodies not covered by tarps. The corpses' blue lips stood out against their stark, pale faces. Some were already bloating. Others looked like heat-baked dolls.

The plague. Not the theoretical plague or the video footage of the plague, but the *actual* plague played out beneath them. The entire field surrounding the airport was a vast, grotesque morgue.

They were barely over the last body when the wheels touched down on the tarmac. The plane bounced once, and then settled on the ground as wind screeched in the downed flaps.

Zach looked back at Ronnie, her eyes wide and glistening with tears. Their quest was no longer intellectual.

As they rolled down the landing strip and turned toward the hangar, Quirk roused.

"So, what did I miss?"

No one had the heart to answer him.

Pulling the plane to a stop, the pilot unstrapped himself. "I'll go steal a helicopter."

* * *

"Quirk. Stop looking down," Ronnie reminded Quirk, but how could she expect him to *not* look out the helicopter window?

New York, a city they had visited a million times over. A city they both loved, had turned into what looked like the set from a zombie apocalypse movie. Only the dead that littered the streets weren't getting up again. They were dead. *Gone*. Dead because Ronnie wasn't smart enough to figure all this out. A vaccine was out there, but she couldn't find it.

How many other cities would suffer the same fate? How many would die because she couldn't crack the angels' code? Not that she believed the angels had actually sent the code. Because if they were really angels, why wouldn't they just tell her where in the hell the vaccine was located?

"Is it yellow?" Quirk slurred as he opened his mouth wide, sticking out his tongue.

"For the tenth time, no, it looks fine."

Still, the young man went back to his compulsive checking of his lymph nodes. He grabbed her hand off her laptop and placed it against his forehead. "Do I feel warm? I think I feel warm."

Ronnie jerked her hand back. "Quirk, you are *fine*. We've barely been in contact with anyone."

Still, she wiped her palm onto her jeans. It was hard to delete from memory the sight of those bright red tarps and those blue, black lips of the dead. At least now they flew high above downtown Manhattan, so that the carnage below was only offered in fleeting glimpses of disarray.

"Do we have an entrance strategy to the museum?" Zach asked.

Right. They had to get his and everyone's mind back to the task at hand rather than the grisly sight down below.

Ronnie elbowed Quirk. "We are going in by the back loading dock."

Which sounded so confident, only it wasn't. Sure, she'd figured out the guard's inspection schedule based on key carding information, and Quirk had taped a loop of video feed for each of the rooms they were going to hit. He's uploaded the footage to a backup drive inside the security hub.

But the rest? The electronic, all-seeing, all-knowing, and ever-present security measures? Those were going to be a bitch to get around. Oh, how she wished they could do a smash and grab, like Graceland. Here, if they knocked out the building's electricity, iron gates would lower at all the major junctures within the museum and would mechanically lock until an override was entered from inside the security office. Given that they needed to hit over eight of the nineteen departments, that just wasn't going to work.

If she had three weeks, Ronnie could breeze them in and out of there. But in these short hours? With these kinds of security measures? Not that Ronnie would have minded a few weeks with Zach, a la *Entrapment*-style practice, the Met was possibly the most secure building in the world beyond the Pentagon. With art theft being a four-billion dollar a year business and the Met containing, what, forty billion dollars' worth of art, the museum had every reason to be über-cautious.

Which meant they had the most advanced technology installed. Motion sensors, optical lasers, vibration detectors, high-grade steel anchors for paintings, and a host of other preventive measures. The worst of it, though? The Met had adopted the *Catch Me If You Can* rotation of their security. Meaning a room that used to be equipped with lasers might now have vibration detectors. It forced any potential thief to worry about all security measures all the time.

Since she was that potential thief, it was up to her to countermand every conceivable antitheft method known to mankind.

And Quirk wondered why she had so many wrinkles.

"Are you sure about the loading docks?" Zach asked as they flew over Central Park, which was eerily empty. Normally at this time of day there would be early-morning yoga classes and Tai Chi groups scattered across the greens. Instead, the entire park had been cordoned off. But as the plague grew and the panic around it, how long would that last?

Zach indicated across the street from the park to the large Greco-Roman building that housed the Met. The building dominated perhaps Ronnie's favorite stretch of road in the world, the "Museum Mile."

"Shouldn't we go in through the roof, or something?" Zach asked.

Ronnie shook her head. She didn't have time to explain the concept of a security "shell"—the tough outer coating of protection that museums used to keep thieves out. Well over 70 percent of museum break-ins were attempted from the roof or the floor just below the roof. Clearly, way too many people had watched way too many Tom Cruise movies. Therefore, a museum's thickest "shell" was protecting the roof or the floor just below the roof. The second area they secured the most tightly was the front entrance, since another good 15 percent of break-ins were smash and grabs like they'd done at Graceland. While the loading docks did account for over 5 percent of all break-ins, the museum relied on a heavy guard presence during transfers, but otherwise relied on fortified steel doors with elaborate, electronic-locking mechanisms.

Basically, putty in her hands.

Getting in the loading-dock doors never concerned Ronnie. Penetrating the shell was relatively simple. Once they got inside the museum? That's when things got complicated and dicey. While the NYPD was extremely busy taking care of looters and rioters on the eastside, an alarm tripped at the Met would still be responded to in force.

"All right. The loading dock it is," Zach answered, seeming to understand her vigorous head shake.

The helicopter barely bobbled as it landed on a flat patch of the park. The museum was directly across the street. Zach hopped out first, helping her, and then Quirk, of course now decked out in a makeshift surgical mask and gloves, and Francois out of the chopper. The pilot lifted off immediately, streaking away toward the East Thirty-Fourth Street Helipad.

Why did it feel like all hope left with him?

* * *

Zach stopped the foursome at the entrance to the alley. He looked down at Ronnie's palmtop. Half of the screen showed what the cameras were picking up. The footage showed the four approaching from the north side. The other half of the screen showed what Ronnie was transmitting to the security hub—a perfectly empty street.

"They're only seeing what we want them to see. We're good." Quirk reassured them, although it rang a little false, since he was saying it from behind a medical mask.

The other problem was the sunrise. Very soon, their footage loop of early-morning glow wasn't going to cut it.

Francois went to step into the alleyway, but Zach had a tight grip on the edge of his sleeve. The guy was not going to rush them into *anything* this time. "Hold up. Let Ronnie do her stuff."

A smile swept over her lips. Then it was quickly replaced by the grimace that had sat there since landing. She was worried. Really worried, which made Zach *extremely* worried. The woman was usually all bluster and confidence, scoffing at any challenge to her skills with a keyboard.

"Here goes," Ronnie said as she entered in the last command.

The tiniest *click* answered her maneuver. The small side doors to the museum popped open an inch. They all held their breath. Zach's eyes scanned the half dozen screens that Quirk had open on his palmtop, showing each of the security boards. Not a single red light flashed.

Step one, complete.

He went to step out, but Ronnie hissed, "Wait."

"What is that security panel monitoring?" she asked her assistant.

Quirk zoomed in on the set of controls which read "External laser scan."

So much for Step one.

Quirk frowned. "They don't have that one up on a scope. The computer must be scanning the laser feed continuously and only alerting them if there is some derivation in the mean movement."

Zach didn't understand half of that. He just knew it was bad for them.

"I am going to have to ping back the differential as we move forward to keep the mean above the white line."

Again, Zach didn't know what she meant. However, Quirk nodded.

"What do I have to do?" Zach asked.

"Move very, very slowly, and in a straight line. We have got to follow within inches of each other. Otherwise, I won't be able to keep up with the algorithm."

Zach turned to Francois. "Did you hear Ronnie?"

"I might be borderline psychotic, my dear man, but I can hear."

Somehow, that didn't comfort Zach in the least.

* * *

Quirk didn't want to be within inches of anyone, even Ronnie. Yet here they were, shuffling down the street like some kind of time-delayed conga line. Zach had taken Ronnie seriously about the very, very, very slowly part. If it took them much longer, they might as well head to Ronnie's island and wait out the plague.

Balancing his palmtop on one hand, Quirk checked the glands in his throat with the other. Was that left one just a bit larger? Were his cuticles turning darker—foreshadowing the black nails that spelled a quick death?

He tapped his palmtop, bringing up his text program. Nothing new from his BFF. Usually, she was updating him every ten minutes with what an ass their CIA liaison was or how handsome their new director was in a Sean Connery or Clint Eastwood kind of way. Now silence. That couldn't be good.

"Stop," Ronnie whispered.

The group ground to a halt. What now?

"I think I have built an evolving algorithm," Ronnie said, not that anyone but Quirk would understand her. "Zach, take a step forward."

Quirk winced as the FBI agent lifted his foot. Ronnie took no countermeasures. Would her program really work, or was this one of those instances where her ego had slightly outgrown her skills?

As the FBI agent moved forward, the bundle of data that streamed from the sensors to the security computers showed only a steady state.

"Take another."

The program held, delivering the nice, boring data that they wanted it to deliver. Thank God. If Quirk had to smell the Frenchman's odd aroma of stale smoke and pomegranates one more time…. They moved forward more quickly, loosening their formation until they made it to the opened door of the Met.

Zach took their handy can of hair spray and shot it into the doorway this time—sans fire. Laser beams crisscrossed the inner doorway."Ugh," Ronnie groaned. "They must have upgraded."

"Oh, please," Quirk said. What they had done was old school. These museum security companies loved to roll out the bright, shiny red laser beam grid. "Look how pretty they are." When in reality, well, over 90 percent of all museum heists were inside jobs. Quirk just needed to re-create the effect.

Watching his palmtop that gave real-time footage of the door from *inside* the loading bay, Quirk stuck his hand through a gap in the laser sights, keyed in the correct code, and voilà, the lasers went to sleep. Ronnie, of course, compensated by sending packets of data that made it look like the lasers were still up and running.

"Beauty before age," Quirk said to Zach, happy to finally be out of the alley and into the interior of the Met, which had microfine, particle-filtered, and self-contained air flow. Pulling down his mask, Quirk took a nice, big gulp of sanitized air.

* * *

Ronnie set up shop just outside the European Paintings gallery. The large, vaulted room held the bulk of the paintings they needed. The rest were scattered throughout the museum. Some were in the Islamic Art Wing, the Medieval Wing, and lastly, the new American Wing on the second floor. Those could wait until she "picked" the European Paintings lock.

Sitting cross-legged on the cool cream tile, Ronnie cracked her knuckles. She'd picked this hallway since the security measures were minimal because of the guards' hourly physical inspections. Those guards walked by at staggered intervals, supposedly random, but humans were human and built for routine. And the one gallery they *always* passed by was the European Paintings. Therefore, the defenses couldn't be too complicated, since they needed to be reset hourly.

However, any money the museum saved on protective measures in the hallway, they more than spent on the gallery's interior defenses. First, Ronnie had to raise the large titanium lattice gate that blocked the entrance to the gallery. Actually opening the lattice would require only a few commands. Convincing the computer system that the gate was actually still down was quite another thing.

The damn gate had something like fifteen sensors hooked to it. Even the air movement created by the gate rising was monitored by micro-barometers. If she didn't disable or trick each and every one of them, each and every inch that they opened the gate…well…they definitely would not have time to grab the entire set of paintings they needed.

And given the amount of "junk" code left, they needed as many symbols as possible. Whoever had created this cipher knew what they were doing. Because of the sophistication of the code, Ronnie knew that there were linchpins embedded. Symbols that linked to other symbols. Symbols that made sense of the cluster. The Elvis symbol represented one. There had to be more, though. This European gallery represented their best chance to find those invaluable linchpins.

Ronnie was also beginning to formulate an idea that there might be a cipher within a cipher. That the date of the painting might be nearly as important as the symbol itself. If they burned them in chronological sequence, would that reveal a deeper layer to the code?

Could she gain some insight into which of the locations held the best chance at harboring some of this elusive vaccine? Could it help her find a stash on *this* continent? Ronnie refused to think otherwise. There *had* to be a supply here.

True, the Hidden Hand was maniacal and believed in a horrific vision of the world that rattled her marrow, but they were by no means stupid. Like all secret organizations, they had to by their nature be small, compact, and cloistered. If they truly wished to bring about a new world order, they were going to have to deputize a bunch of collaborators. Such as Hitler did in France during the Second World War.

To remain the Hidden Hand, they had to stay small. Which meant that they simply didn't have the manpower to take over the world, even if its population had been decimated by three-quarters. Therefore, they *must* have a stash of vaccines in America. They would *have* to inoculate these collaborators, and most importantly, their families, to have any leverage at all. At least that was what Ronnie chose to believe.

With renewed vigor, Ronnie pinged the gate's defenses, calibrating her attack so that once it launched, it would be flawless.

* * *

Zach studied Ronnie as she typed and typed and typed. Her posture rigid, she was in "the zone," that was for sure. Unlike other times, though, Quirk paced back and forth.

"What's wrong?"

Quirk scowled. "She's obsessing."

"Um," Zach commented as he checked on Francois, making sure that the old man stayed on *this* side of the gate's defenses. "I thought that's what she did."

"Yes, when there are a large number of factors to consider and correlate. But *this*? This is pure nerves."

"How can you tell?"

Quirk showed him a screen, not that Zach could make heads or tails of it. "She isn't calculating *how* to get in, she is calculating the *risk* to get in."

"I don't understand." Actually, that was an understatement, but it did give Quirk pause.

More slowly, Quirk explained. "She keeps cycling scenarios over and over again, trying to get the risk of entry to zero. Which, of course..."

Yeah, Zach knew what little chance any of them had to achieve zero risk.

"But why?" Zach asked. "She's used to this kind of pressure."

Quirk scoffed. "You are freaking kidding me, right?"

"What am I missing?"

"Um, the entire world depending on her?" Quirk explained. "I mean, if we try to hit a bank and we fail, the worst that happens is that other hackers make fun of us. But here?"

Zach got it. *Here* was a completely different ball game.

"Then what do we do?" he asked.

"*We?*" Quirk said backing up. "*We* don't do anything. This is all you, in all your hotness glory."

Zach frowned. His hotness or lack thereof had very little to do with convincing Ronnie to commit to an acknowledged less-than-perfect entry.

He crouched beside her, putting his hand on her knee.

"Hey." Who knew if she couldn't hear him, or just chose not to? "Ronnie, darlin', we've got to get this party started."

The slight shake of the head she gave him was better than nothing.

"Ronnie. Look at me."

She just shook her head again. Gently, he reached out and tilted her chin up.

"Babe, you've got to pull the trigger."

Her eyes refocused from the cyber world to this one. "But if I make the breach, and—"

"We," Zach corrected. "When *we* make the breach, *we* could set off the alarms."

Worry seemed to weigh down her eyelids. "If we set off an alarm. Now? We'll never have enough time."

"No. No we won't," Zach agreed.

Ronnie scanned his face, seeming to wait for him to reassure her. But how could he? Zach was used to holding people's lives in his hand. Perhaps not all of them all at once, but he knew the indecision that could tear at you. Do you shoot now, or wait? Will your inaction or action cause another's death? There was no getting around it. Only getting through it.

"If we delay much longer, though, we will definitely be found."

He cupped her cheek as she slowly nodded. Zach leaned in. Her courage and vulnerability were an intoxicating mixture. Before he could close the distance, a smile tugged on her lips.

"Not here, either," she whispered.

Sure, disappointment stung, but at least Ronnie was back to herself.

* * *

Francois stood at the cold, steel gate. Just beyond the mesh were some of the world's greatest works of art. Pristine. Provocative. Protected. But no more. Now many of them would enter into the realm of the hallowed.

The paintings glistened in the low light. Francois could almost imagine them whispering to each other the secrets of the past.

What had it felt like to take brush to canvas knowing your work would not just be displayed for generations, but physically *secure* for generations to come? Francois paused. Perhaps he did. know The wounds on his arms throbbed, reminding him of his duty.

So many years he thought himself mad. To be trapped with the knowledge of the apocalypse looming. To know that angels existed, but unable to prove their form. Now he was blessed; his doubt had evaporated. This was a time when good and evil stalked the earth, playing out their war through men such as he and Lino.

Francois glanced at the trio behind him. Good souls. Confused, and many times resistant souls, but good, nonetheless. For all their help, though, they still did not believe. They attempted to explain away the miracles dancing before their eyes with scientific this or mathematical that. Could they truly see this through to the end without faith? Without the faith that burned in his chest?

For little did they know, the worst was yet to come.

CHAPTER 23

Metropolitan Museum of Art
7:10 a.m., EST

Quirk watched the security screen as the gallery's gate rattled up along its tracks. So far, so good. Next to him, Ronnie fidgeted with a dozen different values. He wanted to tell her, *honey, it is going to blow the alarm or not*, but he kept silent. She looked to be in a punch-now, ask-questions-later mood.

For once, the dice rolled in their favor, and the gate went up without a hitch, a red flashing light, or people shooting at them.

He picked up the satchel with what remained of their bag of tricks when Ronnie's hand flew up.

"Get back!" she yelled.

No one questioned her odd order. They all scrambled back from the open door.

Quirk scanned all the security feeds. Damn, but one of the graphs was fluctuating from green up into the yellowish orange range. A guard noticed, and began studying the variable.

Temperature.

"Hold your breath," Ronnie whispered, sucking in one of her own. Quirk gulped down some air and waited.

Ever so slowly, the colorful graph flickered into the orange, then back down to a canary yellow, then finally settled in a lovely, light forest green.

"Let it out slowly," she instructed.

Quirk kept his nose pinched as he exhaled air milliliter by milliliter. The gauge went into a concerning chartreuse then morphed back to that refreshing mint color. The guard got bored and went back to watching "Lost" reruns.

Zach scowled. "I didn't think this room had temperature sensors."

"Yeah," Ronnie answered, "Neither did we."

Those dumb rotating defenses, Quirk thought. Okay, they weren't dumb, they were entirely too sophisticated for their own good. They forced the group to drop their core body temperature to seventy-two degrees, be able to move without causing the air to stir, and create no pressure on the floor.

Or, at least that is what an average art thief would need to do. You know, ones without the mad hacking skills. Ronnie was already working on a compensating algorithm. She was feeding data back to the system that compensated for their added heat.

"Francois, take a step forward," Ronnie asked.

"Hold on," Quirk interrupted. "Shouldn't Zach go first? He is the hottest."

His boss frowned, "Quirk, enough."

"No," Quirk hurried on. "I mean, literally, he is the hottest."

He showed Ronnie the heat scan. Zach registered nine eight point *nine*. A good three tenths of a degree warmer than any of them.

"See?" Quirk challenged. "Scientific proof that he's smoking hot."

Ronnie's lips drew down, but she nodded to the FBI agent. "He's right. Your heat signature will challenge my counter-programming the most."

They hung back as Zach inched forward. "Am I supposed to do anything?" the FBI agent asked.

"Nope," Quirk answered. "Just work your natural hottie-self."

* * *

Zach became acutely aware that all eyes were on him. He was pretty damn sure that his temperature was going up under the scrutiny.

"We've got a cool lime going on," Quirk stated, looking relieved.

He guessed that was a good thing as Ronnie instructed Francois to join him, but after a few feet, Ronnie pulled them back.

"You are just too hot, dude," Quirk stated.

That had definitely never been a problem before now.

Ronnie agreed, "Not only are you warmer, but you radiate your heat further, comingling with anyone else."

Before the world's future hung in the balance, Zach had some distinct ideas about how to comingle heat, but now it just presented a roadblock.

"We've got to go with 'plan D,'" Ronnie stated.

"I didn't even know we had a 'plan C,'" Zach admitted.

Ronnie's cheeks flushed a bit. "Yeah, that was kind of 'we hope our luck doesn't run out.'"

Clearly, that had been a pipe dream.

"So, what next?" he asked.

"We don't have time to run a full hack on the temperature sensors. Those are spanking brand new, with all the latest anti-tampering software. The best I can do is run interference."

"But *I* can't go in," Zach clarified.

"Correct." Ronnie said, looking up. "It also means that we can't use the torches to cut down the paintings."

Crap. He hadn't even thought of that. Ronnie truly was running circles around him. "Then, how are we going to get them down?"

"I've got a few ideas, but they are going to take some time," Ronnie explained. "Which means that we won't have time to get the paintings from the other collections. Unless…"

"Unless?" he asked. Not liking the sound of it.

"You and Francois go to the other exhibits."

"No," Zach stated flatly. "We are not splitting up."

"As we know, not all exhibits have the same defenses. The chances that the other, more minor exhibits have all these bells and whistles is slim," Ronnie hurried on, "so you and Francois could gather the other paintings while we figure out how to deal with the bulk of these."

"No," Zach emphasized.

"Zach," Ronnie sighed. "I get it. Trust me. I do not want you out of my sight, either, but there's just no other way to get all this done in the time we have. You've *got* to go."

"*No*," Zach repeated. He did not go through all of this hell to lose her. Even for half a second.

* * *

Ronnie grabbed Zach's hand. God, how she loved his determination and fierce desire to be at her side. Unfortunately, it forced her to speak some harsh truths. Truths she knew might hurt his feelings, but these truths needed to be spoken.

Ugh. How she hated being a grown-up!

"Zach, if you stay, what are you going to do?" His eyes scanned her features. Begging her not to go where she needed to go. "You can't go in the room. So, what are you going to do while our time whittles down?"

"I don't like it."

That was an improvement over the curt "nos" he had been giving her.

"Like Quirk would say, you've got to get your full FBI on."

Zach's eyes followed her gaze as her assistant nodded vigorously in agreement.

He looked back at her. "I am hotfooting it back here if there is even a whiff of trouble."

Ronnie squeezed his hand. "I wouldn't have it any other way."

His features softened as he entwined his fingers in hers.

"Um?" Quirk stated. "Are we going to rob this museum, or not?"

And just like that, Zach was back to being a Special Agent demigod. He dropped her hand and picked up both acetylene torches. "Since you can't use yours?"

"Go for it. We've got to play it cool. *Literally*." Ronnie turned to Francois. "We just need you to tell us which paintings we need to grab."

The old man looked startled, as if he didn't understand why in the world she would ask him such a question.

She coaxed Francois along. "We have the list of painters. Now we need to know which of the paintings we need to burn."

"How would I know such a thing?"

Dear God. Now was not the time for the Frenchman's mind to go offline. "But your carvings, and your time within the Hidden Hand…"

Francois' eyes looked crystal clear as he spoke. "My dear, the angels have not yet told me."

Ronnie blinked. Now they not only needed to get one painting from each artist, but all the paintings from that artist. How long would that take? And could they even be sure to find the right painting with the right symbol?

"So we grab all the paintings from the artist on the list?" Zach asked.

"I guess," Ronnie said, glancing over her shoulder at the room full of the masterworks. That just quadrupled the number of paintings they had to secure.

Zach seemed unshaken by the news. "We're off then."

With that said, he guided Francois around the corner, angling toward the African artwork exhibit. Would he look back? Would she break and ask him to stay?

"Again," Quirk nagged. "The whole world depends on our expediency thing."

Ronnie turned back to the European gallery. "Kind of like how we might have known about the heat sensors if you hadn't been making gooey eyes at the pilot?"

"Touché."

She might have taken more satisfaction in besting Quirk at his own game if she had any clear idea of how they were going to get all the paintings that they needed off the wall without increasing the heat in the room. With about five hours lead time, she could have found the source code for the heat sensors, but they were down to about fifteen minutes before her loop would start to fray.

Quirk must have come to the same conclusion. "We've got a few toys," he said, indicating the duffel bag filled with their beta projects. However, none seemed suited for the task.

"I am thinking that we flash-freeze the metal?" she offered. "Making it more brittle and easier to break?"

"Great idea," Quirk said, and then chuckled. "Of course, that would require being *able* to flash-freeze the metal. And of course, that would lower the temperature of the room, throwing us into the blue on their sensors."

Damn it, her assistant was right. Every scenario she posed in her head was equally improbable. She took a moment to settle her mind, glancing around the room at the masterpieces. Ronnie had been so stressed out she didn't even realize that one of her favorite Monet works was right in front of her—*Water Lilies*. A painting she not only loved but desperately needed to burn if they were going to save the world.

It turned out that stealing some of the most famous paintings in the world was *hard*. Who knew?

* * *

Lino strode through the door. How convenient that the heretics and betrayers had broken into the Metropolitan Museum of Art. One of his men held a computing device, tracing the illustrious hackers' cyber footsteps. This man was, of course, no match for the whore's skills, but they needed to only get so far upon her work. From there, Lino had other plans.

He liked the large echoing chamber they entered. It smelled of musk and pine. To think, once the plague ran its course all places such as this would be the Hidden Hand's. This indulgent notion that the great masters should be availed to the public would cease. Great beauty would be reserved for great men.

His team of four quickly crossed through the docking bay and headed down a side hallway. Lino had limited his team to be numbered four, slipping in under the hacker's shadow.

Rapidly, they made their way to the security station. A large, numeric keypad blocked their entry. No matter. God's grace once again shined down upon them. Long entrenched in the world of art and commerce, the Hidden Hand had many fingers.

One of his men typed in the current access code. Once the door opened, Lino's team burst into the room, swiftly dispatching the guards. Even the one who had offered up the security code. He choked and gagged at Lino's feet. Clutching at Lino's pant leg, asking with his eyes, *Why?*

The answer was simple. Lino tired of betrayers. If this man could so easily be coerced to betray his employer, what did that say for his devotion to the Hidden Hand? One of Lino's men moved to snap the man's neck, but that would not do. No, this man must suffer in equal measure to his fickle morals.

Lino leaned in and whispered, "It may hearken you to know that your family will soon join you."

The guard's eyes dilated and his fingers clawed at Lino's clothes, but nothing would shake his decision.

The long season of betrayal was coming to a swift end.

* * *

Amanda hit the "Refresh" key. Again. Nothing happened. Why wasn't the CIA data updating? She looked over to Devlin, who seemed to be having the same problem.

"What did you do?" he asked.

"I think the better question is, "What did *you* do?"Henderson glanced over. "What's wrong?"

She took a deep breath. Well, as deep a breath as she could with pneumonia rattling around in her lungs. Amanda could feel herself becoming shrill. It was one thing to be called a Chicken Little. It was quite another to act like one.

"The CIA data stream seems to have been cut off."

"Or someone is hogging it again," Devlin countered.

Before she could retort, Henderson put up a blotchy hand. "Or what if it wasn't someone *here* doing the cutting off?"

To think that the CIA had a Hidden Hand mole? Exactly how organized *were* these people? Had they infected Langley as efficiently as they had infected Plum Island?

"I'm going to contact my superiors," Devlin said as he rose creakily.

"You do that," Henderson said, getting back to work.

Amanda stared at the frozen screen. She had been gutting it out. Working on faith that somehow her work could change the course of the disease. That somehow she could isolate vaccinated populations in order to find the cure. But if the CIA was compromised, even if she did somehow pull the rabbit out of the hat, who in the world could actually retrieve the vaccine?

She looked up to find Henderson watching her. He had never seemed quite so grandfatherly as he did right now.

"You can't stop being Chicken Little now, Rolph," the director said, and then went back to work.

It wasn't exactly the most rousing pep talk in history. However, it was exactly what she needed to hear.

Closing out the frozen screen, Amanda focused on the data they had already collected. There had to be enough information there. There just *had* to be.

CHAPTER 24

Metropolitan Museum of Art
7:35 a.m., EST

Quirk groaned as his box cutter snapped off. Again. The stupid painting, a Degas, if he wasn't mistaking his ballerina painters, refused to be freed from its frame. Museums had taken to attaching the canvas to thick metal plates, thereby preventing someone like Quirk from cutting the painting out of the frame. Like he said. Stupid.

Unlike Zach and Francois. They hit the old painting lottery. The other display halls were rotating through much lighter defenses. A little goading from Ronnie's algorithm added to having two acetylene torches and the boys were literally cutting through their grocery list. But he and Ronnie?

They had tried everything to lift the paintings from their moorings—to no avail.

"Be careful not to work up a sweat," Ronnie said from the other side of the room as she worked to free a Giorgione.

"Har, har," Quirk laughed sarcastically, not needing her to start in on his lack of an exercise regime. Was it so wrong that he liked his arms lanky and not muscle-bound?

"No, seriously," she said, blotting her own forehead. "They've got humidity sensors, and while not linked to an alarm, if a guard notices the temp spike and humidity…"

It might have them looking in the wrong direction. *Their* direction.

"Fine, but—"

His palmtop rattled along the wooden floor.

"Quirk!"

"On it!" He dove for the device, snapping it up. That had to be some mondo alert to have kicked off the vibration setting.

Quirk flipped through the screens. Everything seemed fine. They hadn't trigged anything here or in the Pacific Islands exhibit where Zach and Francois were collecting the last of their set.

Wait. What was that? A silent alarm had been tripped. But none of the museum exhibits were armed with silent alarms. Those alarms were about as loud as they could get.

"Quirk?"

"Tasking." He followed the thread of the alarm back to its source. "It looks like it is coming from the core computer."

Ronnie was on it. "Zach, are you anywhere near the security office?"

The FBI agent's voice came over Quirk's earpiece. "No. Is there a problem?"

"Maybe."

Well, not maybe, there was definitely a problem, just whether it was catastrophic or not was the question. Quirk studied all the feeds coming in from the security room. Had two of the guards gone out on patrol? That was off schedule. Had they changed their routine because of the temperature change? But then, where was the third guard? They always left a guard to attend the monitors.

But what was on the security screen? Quirk zoomed in. They had to be kidding! Someone spilled ketchup on the keyboard.

Wait. Ketchup didn't glisten. He risked tilting the camera to the floor.

"Oh, my God," he breathed out.

* * *

"Come again? I didn't get that," Zach stated, finishing burning through the Asian masterpiece, *The Wave,* cabling. The damn thing had to weigh a hundred pounds. How could a canvas and wooden frame weigh a hundred pounds?

"Zach," Ronnie said, then gulped. His ears perked up. It was never good news when Ronnie gulped before speaking. "Someone has killed the guards and set off a silent alarm."

He didn't bother to ask who it was. The Hidden Hand had obviously followed them. He didn't even bother to ask how. They were ninja priests.

"I am on my way back to you," Zach said, but then pulled to a halt as a shadow passed by the hallway. He grabbed Francois and shoved the Frenchman against the wall. Zach watched the bronze mirror as the reflection of four men cloaked in black passed by, then paused.

Ronnie was speaking in his ear, but he turned the earpiece off. The last thing he needed was for his position to be given away by a malfunctioning audio piece. He stood there waiting, hoping the men would move off, but they clearly were having a confab. Trying to decide in which direction to head.

"Lino," Francois hissed, trying to take a step forward. Zach held him in place, but studied the golden-haired man. Actually, this Lino looked like a teenage boy. Yet the others clearly deferred to him.

Luckily, the boy leader was as decisive as he was tall. With a snap of his head, he got the others moving down the hallway. But not all of them. Two were left behind. At exactly the junction Zach needed to pass to get back to Ronnie.

Zach didn't want to admit it, but given the automatic weapons of those two, he and Francois were trapped.

* * *

Ronnie tried not to freak out, she really did, but how could she not? In crisp HD video, she watched Zach retreat into the exhibit.

"Honey, we've got bigger fish to fry," Quirk stated.

She tried to ignore her assistant, but he shoved his palm-top over hers. "Zach is at least *safe*. Those other two are making a beeline for this exhibit." He indicated around them. "And if you hadn't noticed, we are a little shy on defenses."

Quirk was right. That didn't make her heart hurt any less to watch Zach have to slink into the shadows.

"Girlfriend. Now!"

Ronnie tore her eyes from the Asian exhibit feed and refocused on the approaching blips on the grid. Quirk brought up another screen showing the actual men. "It looks like that one thinks he's grade 'A' hacker."

That the man did. From the keystrokes, the hacker was trying to find their heat signature. Which could work to their advantage. Ronnie had to be subtle. She couldn't just give away their position. She had to make the guy believe that he really had broken into one of the world's most sophisticated security systems.

Thank goodness these guys were just that arrogant.

Carefully, Ronnie brought up just the wisp of a reading, and then brought it back down. That got the guy to stop. From his excited hand gestures, he thought he was on to something. Another deft flash of a signal caught his attention. He pointed to a room.

The Medieval Gallery. The gallery where she had planted their false heat signature.

The younger man clearly seemed more skeptical of this "find." But in the end, he trusted the technology rather than his gut. Thank God.

The two turned to the right and headed down a hallway, angling away, a full city block away from them.

"Phew," Quirk exhaled. "Next time, we bring more deodorant."

He was kidding. Ronnie wiped her forehead with the back of her hand.

Now to get Zach the hell out of there.

* * *

Zach wished he could create a weapon out of thin air. A Glock in his hand would sure feel nice.

He made sure Francois followed close behind as they made their way through the Asian Art Wing. Lots of pottery, but no weapons. Why the hell couldn't they have gotten trapped in the armament gallery? He'd take a broadsword right about now. And a suit of armor? Priceless.

"Here," Francois whispered, leading them into the Australian Aboriginal Art exhibit.

Zach tried to resist; however, the old man could be strong when he wanted to be. In the wan light, Zach could make out dozens of the prerequisite pots and clay shards. Nothing that could help their cause, though.

Until Francois pointed out a case. A case filled with aboriginal weapons. Many knives and even a few spears, but those required them to get far too close to the enemy. They needed long-range weapons. A boomerang caught Zach's eye. Not exactly what he would have put on his wish list, but if they were deadly enough to bring down large game, they could work here.

Zach switched on his earpiece. "Ronnie. I need the—"

Before he even asked, the case's latch sprung open. She must have been watching.

"Service with a smile," she replied, only her tone seemed about half as lighthearted as her words.

"Give me five, and we will be on our way."

Turning off the communications device, he turned to find Francois picking up a didgeridoo. The long, hollow stick was decorated with elaborate dots and aboriginal artwork.

"You do realize that is a musical instrument," Zach explained as he picked up a few stone knives just in case.

Francois swung the wooden staff up and over his head, then around his side finally coming to rest in an attack angle.

Okay. Good to remember. Francois did descend from a line of ninja priests.

Cautiously, they made their way back to the fork in the hallways. The paintings they needed were stacked to the side.

Zach indicated to the framed canvases. "If this goes sideways…"

Francois nodded toward the acetylene torches. If they couldn't get the pictures to Ronnie, they could at least burn them, and she could record the symbols. But Zach didn't want to walk too far down that path. If Ronnie wanted to burn them in a specific order, that was what he was going to make sure happened.

He felt the heft of the weight of the boomerang in his hand. The carved wood shaped in a lazy "V" didn't seem nearly heavy enough to do the job. It was either the boomerang or start chucking statues at the armed men. How many years had it been since he'd thrown a boomerang, though? College? Childhood? Would he have the speed or even accuracy to take down one, let alone two, men?

Francois crouched next to him ready to unfurl his attack.

Thankfully, like all sentries, the two men had let down their guard just a hair. One faced toward them, but the other had his back to them. All the better. It would give Zach time to get off at least one good shot if not two before they started firing. When it came down to it, they were bringing a boomerang and a didgeridoo to a gunfight.

Zach gripped the smooth end of the boomerang in his right hand and kept the other ready in this left. Turning sideways, he cocked his arm back. It was a lot like shooting a baseball from first base to catch a guy stealing second base. Using every ounce of strength he could muster from his sore muscles, Zach flung the boomerang at the man facing in their direction.

The weapon whistled through the air, spinning sideways. Not waiting for that one to connect, Zach tossed the second boomerang into his right hand, reeled back, and let it fly.

The first hit the assailant in the left shoulder. Luckily, it was the guy's gun arm that got knocked back. The other boomerang hit the gunman right at the base of the skull. He stumbled forward before catching himself on the wall.

Francois got that dappled didgeridoo whipping as he charged, cracking one assailant in the back of the knee. The first boomerang whisked its way back. Zach caught it in mid-air, turned it over, and flung it again, hitting the man in the chest and knocking him back as Francois brought his staff squarely to his belly.

As the second boomerang came back, Zach caught it. Instead of letting it fly, he raised it. The first gunman recovered, bringing his semiautomatic rifle up, but Zach was there first, using the crook of the boomerang to hook the gun, jerking it from the man's hands. The metal clanged on the floor and skidded out of sight.

Zach pulled the stone knife from his belt.

This was more like it.

* * *

Francois shifted his weight to his back foot, bunching the muscle there, preparing for the explosive movement forward, cracking the staff across the gunman's temple. The skin split, sending the man staggering back. Blood gushed down the assailant's forehead. Still, his lips curled in a snarl dating back to a Neanderthal challenge.

Despite his aching flesh and weary joints, Francois was more than happy to oblige. He arched the didgeridoo back around, slamming into the man's shoulder. They had to keep the men from firing. The sound of a gun's discharge would surely bring Lino back.

For the briefest moment, Francois's arms locked as he remembered the cruelty in the young man's eyes. Lino fed on destruction and mayhem as others ate a meal. His assailant seized the distraction and lashed out with a kick, nearly dislocating Francois's leg from his hip. He truly was getting too old for this. In his young days? Fresh from his years of training, this man would not have stood for three seconds.

Now though, it took every bit of grace and training for Francois to prevent himself from falling to the floor. He tried to bring the staff up, but the gunman's hand darted out, hitting Francois in the throat. Choking, dizzy, and disabled, Francois stumbled away—watching the gun rise, aiming straight for his heart.

* * *

Ronnie's hands flew up to her mouth as the muscles in the gunman's arm tensed, ready to fire. Then Zach was there. The flash of a stone blade as the assailant doubled over, clutching the bone hilt sticking out from his chest.

"Dang," Quirk said from beside her. "They are going primeval on their asses."

She couldn't disagree. The FBI agent blocked a blow from the first man with his boomerang, and then followed up with a right hook. Francois seemed recovered as he brought the staff around and smacked the guy in the jaw.

With that the two assailants were down.

Ronnie watched Zach bring his hand up to his ear, opening their line. "On our way."

"Oh, crap," Quirk said next to her.

"What?"

Her assistant pointed to the screen that had been following Lino and the other assailant. They had left a breadcrumb trail leading away from the European Masters toward the emergency exit. Quirk had even created the scenario that one of them was injured and the other was going back to help them make it out. Her assistant had woven a story of triumph and tragedy for this little mockingbird scenario.

And it had worked perfectly...until now. Lino seemed to sniff a rat as he paused next to the door. He argued with his tech guy. Ronnie chewed her lip. They really, really, really needed him to buy it and leave.

In the end, though, Lino backhanded his assistant, then turned directly to the camera. Ronnie cringed as the man walked up until his face filled the frame and then smiled.

"Zach," Ronnie said as Lino sprinted down the hall, coming right for them. "You've got to haul some ass."

"Working on it," Zach replied. "We're carrying about a billion dollars worth of art."

Ronnie glanced at the screen. They weren't making good enough time. Lino would get there first. "Dump it."

"No way."

On-screen, they watched Zach grab one of the paintings from Francois, freeing up the older man. But now it was Zach lagging behind.

"Get the gate ready," Ronnie instructed Quirk.

"Aren't we leaving?"

She shook her head. Zach was right. The whole point of this endeavor was to gather the paintings. And since they couldn't get a single one off the walls of this gallery, they needed to come up with a plan...what were they up to? Plan G?

"We've got to take our stand here."

Quirk glanced around. This gallery was clearly a dead end. "Then how are we getting out?"

"I have no freaking idea."

CHAPTER 25

Metropolitan Museum of Art
10:55 a.m., EST

"What the hell?" Zach asked, running as fast as he could while carrying what felt like a ton of bricks. "Are these paintings made of lead?"

"Um," Ronnie answered in his ear, "Yes. Some of the frames have lead weights to discourage snatch and grabs."

Okay. Good to know. At least he felt less the weakling. Francois rounded the corner ahead of him at just about the same time a bullet hit a statue and ricocheted right past Zach's nose.

Francois must have been hit as he careened to the right. An arm lashed out and grabbed the older man, dragging him into the European Masters room. Coming right for Zach were Lino and another man, firing away.

Zach swung *The Wave* in front of him, praying that Ronnie was right about that lead thing. Sure enough, the bullets pinged off the lead backing and deflected harmlessly. But that wouldn't last forever.

As the metal gate rattled, closing off the room, Zach chucked the paintings, sliding them across the floor and into the gallery. With one last heave, he dove forward, hitting his shoulder hard, and then rolling into the room.

The metal gate clanged shut.

Alarms went off—ringing, blaring, flashing lights. So much for their stealth entry and exit. Of course, the blond guy shooting at them wasn't helping much, either.

He came up, pulling the gun he'd nabbed from the other gunmen.

"No!" Ronnie yelled, but he'd already squeezed off half a dozen rounds. All of which bounced off the mesh, zipping around the room. "That's titanium-hardened steel."

The good news, though, was that if Zach couldn't shoot out, Lino couldn't shoot in.

Although the young, blond man didn't seem at all discouraged by that fact. He walked up to the metal gate, surveyed its periphery, and then sneered.

* * *

Francois limped forward amongst the cacophony of alarms. "Leave, Lino!"

The acolyte did not seem inclined to obey. His words were flavored by a thick Slavic influence. "Trapping yourself. How insightful of you."

Lino was like a cub prancing about as a full-maned lion. How sure of the world Francois had been at that age. Still righteous in his belief that the Hidden Hand fulfilled God's work rather than made a blasphemy of it.

"You must know, somewhere in your heart, Lino, that your path is corrupt. That God would not want such destruction brought in his name."

The young man's cruel smile only spread. "We are here to finish the work He started. We are *His* Hand."

Perhaps Francois could reach Lino the way another brother so long ago had reached Francois. "Why not allow God to move in his own time? If he wished this destruction, could he not so easily do it himself?"

"Ah," Lino sighed. "Why then, did God give me the means to bring the world so low, Brother Loboum? Why indeed?"

Sirens sounded in the distance, rising above even the clamor around them. Francois had to admit that Lino was not like him. Not in full. For even in his youthful arrogance, somewhere within Francois's heart doubt brewed. The man who stood before him had no such reservations. He had been forged as steel to carry out the Hand's macabre mission.

There was no reasoning with the man. Francois slid the knife through the thin slit of the metal mesh into Lino's side. Was it wrong to take pleasure in the look of surprise on the whelp's face? It was not a fatal blow, but to Lino's ego? Yes, a fine blow indeed.

As the young man pulled his hand away from the bloody wound in his side, Francois found that glimmer of doubt he had been looking for.

"You may be vaccinated, Lino, but you are not immortal."

Fury twisted Lino's face. "Cut through it," the young man barked at his assistant.

"But the police—"

"*Now.*"

* * *

Probably best not to piss off the crazed religious lunatic, Quirk thought but didn't bother to voice, because, well, the crazed religious lunatic was already pissed off.

The metal shone blue under the assailant's torch. They didn't even have to make a very big hole. Just enough for a gun barrel, and then it would be like shooting…well, shooting four idiots in a gallery. Zach had tipped over the benches to act as a cover, but really, how long was that going to hold off the semiautomatic weapons?

Ronnie suddenly turned to Zach. "Burn them."What?"

But, Ronnie being Ronnie, she picked up the acetylene torch and set fire to *The Wave.* The beautifully stylized crest of a foamy ocean wave warped and bubbled.

Quirk grabbed her wrist. "You are going to set off the fire alarms!"

Ronnie glanced at Lino's man who had nearly made a muzzle-sized hole in the mesh gate. "Exactly."

Quirk followed her gaze to the ceiling. "Got it!"

Zach still looked confused, so Quirk shoved the burning painting at him while Ronnie moved onto the next. "Use this to light the others on fire."

Quirk had to give it to the FBI agent. He looked completely perplexed, but did exactly what was asked of him, setting a Manet aflame. What was once a delicate reverential moment was now a fire frenzy. Francois used the other torch to light even more masterpieces. Quirk got his camera out, recording the swirling symbols. So many and who knew in what order, but at the least they were capturing them.

Then, as the flames licked up the wall, the automated fire suppression system kicked in. The first step, the glorious first step, was for a heavy, bulletproof acrylic shield to lower in front of the metal mesh. The plastic guard was necessary to block the doorway so when sprinklers overhead shot out their FE-13 mist, the fire suppression gas would be contained to this room—and only this room.

Lino shoved his gun through the hole in the mesh and fired, point-blank, yet the shield held. A white, heavy mist filled the room. Zach gulped in a big breath and hunkered to the ground. Quirk snickered.

"Dude, that's so 1996."

Quirk took in a deep breath. Modern halogenated compounds were perfectly safe to inhale. Zach looked only moderately embarrassed as he continued setting paintings on fire.

The symbols glittered, dancing amongst the fog like characters in a fairy tale. So many. Maybe too many for his boss to interpret in real time. The mist loved these crackling symbols, though, as the white particles were drawn to the magnesium fire.

The scene would all have been so very beautiful if it wasn't for the little facts that Lino was trying to shoot his way in, the police were about to descend on the building, and the Black Death was on a rampage.

* * *

Zach set the last painting on fire. The mist made the act seem almost magical—as if they hadn't just destroyed a huge swath of the world's greatest paintings. What would his mother call it? Wanton destruction? His only small comfort was that the painters, the originators of these exquisite works of art, had always intended, when the worst came, for them to be set alight. But it felt a small comfort that the only remains left of over a dozen masterpieces were scorched frames.

Suddenly, the gunfire stopped. Zach turned to see Lino step back from the mesh. Was he backing away in defeat? He should have been walking away in defeat. After all, the police and fire sirens were right outside the front door. Instead, the cocky bastard just smiled that cool, insidious smile.

"As I stated," Lino said. "Trapped."

With that, the prick nodded to his man. An explosion rocked the building, sending soot and ash into the air as the lights cut out. Just as the emergency lighting bloomed to life, a second explosion sounded from downstairs, plunging the room into complete darkness. The only illumination in the gallery was from Ronnie's screens.

In the eerie, wan light, Lino's teeth glistened in a fierce smile before he turned and charged down the hallway to the exit.

Ronnie was already at work trying to get the gates to lift, but Zach could tell by the set of her jaw that it wasn't going well.

"Talk to me."

"We've lost the hydraulic lifts to get the gates up."

Zach raced to the front of the room and put his shoulder into it. With a grunt, he pushed up on the acrylic shield. It rose a quarter of an inch, and then slammed back down. Even with all four of them, he doubted that they could raise it the foot they needed to crawl out.

"Tell me you've got a 'Plan H.'"

* * *

Okay, it was more like Plan *L*, for ludicrous. She hoped that everyone in the room remembered that when they packed to break Zach out of the CIA safe house that they had not expected to assault the Metropolitan Museum of Art, let along escape an airtight room, with the police breathing down their necks to boot.

"Helo," Ronnie said. Zach looked confused, but Quirk brightened.

"Oh, my God!" Quirk exclaimed. "Brilliant!"

He immediately swiped his screen, dismissing the security feed, which was now nothing more than a blank blue screen, and booted up Helo's command sequence.

"Do I even want to know what he's doing?" Zach asked.

"Probably *not*."

From the other side of the gate, one of their equipment bags shook and lifted a few inches from the ground. Then the bag burst open, and their small, perfectly-to-model helicopter hovered above the ground.

"Meet Helo."

Quirk's smile could not be contained. "I always knew I liked aviation."

With a few deft moves of his wrist, her assistant got Helo up and zipping down the hallway, when the craft suddenly lost altitude and circled lazily to the left.

"Quirk?"

"I don't know," he said, rapidly trying to compensate. Then his palmtop sparked. Quirk's pupils dilated as he turned to her. "Oh, no. The FE-13."

She was way ahead of him, wiping off her screen, shaking off any remnants of the substance. While it was safe to inhale, if not a little stinky, the one major drawback of the fire retardant was its penchant to fritz electronic devices. Especially high-end electronic devices. Which of course, all of theirs were.

"Pass the controls to me," Ronnie ordered, but Quirk stalled.

"No, it's okay. I've got—"

Then his entire screen went blue, then fuchsia, and then a glaring yellow.

Poor Helo ducked and swerved without guidance. Ronnie keyed in the code, taking control, steadying out the mini-helicopter's flight.

"I'll take it from here," Quirk said, reaching for her palmtop.

"Hey, you might have built it, but who tested out the controls?"

Before Quirk could argue, Zach stepped between them. Physically. "No matter who is driving, I don't get how this toy—" Even Zach stopped at Quirk's sharp glare. "I mean, incredible feat of engineering, is going to get us out of this room, especially since it is flying away from us."

She loved how cute Zach looked when he was trying to go all logical on her. His was a linear mind. God love it, so linear. She and Quirk didn't just think outside the box—they lived *outside* it.

Many people would ask why you would need a perfectly functioning mini-helicopter rigged with a directional blast payload. Those people were not Ronnie and Quirk. Of course, they thought they were going to use Helo during the break-in of the vault at Lloyd's of London, but hey, they at least knew that they might need it for something important.

"Just watch and learn," she teased.

* * *

Lino squinted. Was that a sliver of light up ahead? The emergency exit could not be far. Which was a most fortunate thing, since the yells of the police were in the building. They had enough firepower to subdue any attempt to contain them, but Lino would rather that they make their escape without notice. So, fewer witnesses to dispose of.

"What's that?" the brother next to him asked.

Slowing, Lino cocked his head. A tinny, oscillating buzz filled the air. He raised his gun. What could still be functioning after the complete blackout?

A spotlight came around the corner, blinding him for an instant. He shot reflexively, knowing that he missed the mark. Once his eyes adjusted, a strangely small helicopter flew directly for them. Ducking, the vehicle streaked over their heads, and then made the turn to go up the steps.

They fired, rocking the helicopter to and fro, but the damnable thing disappeared out of sight.

That witch and her mechanical familiars.

They did not have the time to dispose of the witch and her companions. At the eleventh hour, did it really matter? He'd seen enough of the angelic script to know where they headed next.

To the heart of the Hidden Hand.

There, they would meet God's final fury.

* * *

Zach watched the screen as the helicopter bobbed and weaved. It had taken several hits during its encounter with Lino. Would it make it to wherever Ronnie needed it to go? He'd guessed somewhere above them, but since he'd never been to the Met, one of those things that his mother kept bugging him about, he wasn't sure where.

"No, you've got stabilize its flight path by compensating to the right," Quirk whined over Ronnie's shoulder. Backseat drivers were bad enough. Mini-helicopter backseat drivers, Zach imagined, were the worst.

"I've got it," Ronnie emphasized although the chopper did seem to be veering to the left a lot.

Finally, the craft burst from the staircase and coursed into the second level, shining its bright light on the American Wing. Instead of the typical blocked, square galleries on this floor and just about every other museum in the world this new wing was built in what Zach could only describe as "fish eye" bubbles. Each room's front came out in a circular manner, resembling that a fish eye.

This concentric pattern was reflected everywhere in the architecture of the wing. The burnished hardwood floors must have been meticulously cut and shaped into sweeping half circles. Even the glass roof above was held together by curved metal.

No wonder his mom had been pestering him to take her.

"You're losing too much, well, not altitude, but height!"

Quirk was right. The helicopter listed to the left until it finally hit a curved wall, bounced and landed on its rotors, which ground against the beautiful hardwood floor.

"I take it that wasn't supposed to happen?" Zach asked.

Ronnie looked away, frowning. Clearly not.

Zach cocked an ear. He could hear Helo's motor whine. It must have "landed" somewhere above them. He was about to ask why they couldn't just blow the thing then remembered the whole directional thing. They needed the blast directed down, not up.

"Give it to me!" Quirk implored. "We have a connection."

Ronnie didn't seem too convinced.

"Fine, then you try to crab-walk Helo over."

Despite her lack of conviction that Quirk could accomplish the task, clearly Ronnie didn't want to try. She handed Quirk the controls. With the tip of his tongue sticking out, Quirk rocked the palmtop back and forth, his own body swaying almost like he was soothing a baby.

"Come on," Quirk whispered to the screen. "You can do it," He urged as the view tipped this way then that. "You don't want the other über-blinged-out mini-helicopters to call you turtle, do you?"

Whether it was Quirk's finesse with the controls or the coaching, the chopper tilted over, skittered on its side, and then righted itself. A bit of wobbling, but it hovered over the floor.

"That's my boy!" Quirk announced as he guided Helo to land. He indicated the stone benches. "I'd suggest we take cover..."

Zach pretty much knew why, but felt forced to ask. "Because we aren't sure how big the blast is going to be?" Ronnie looking down at her toes confirmed the fact. "Because you guys haven't beta-tested it yet?"

Quirk waved him off. "Tomatoes. Toe-mah-toes."

No matter, they had to get to cover. Zach urged Ronnie down as Quirk scrambled under the other bench with Francois.

"Five. Four. Three," Quirk counted down. "Three and a half."

"Quirk…"

"Fine. Two. One."

The ceiling shook as the overhead explosion shook the infrastructure. It, however, did not collapse. Ronnie went to crawl out from the bench, but Zach noted the hairline fractures running through the paint directly above them. Cracks that converged on the base of the chandelier. Cracks that were growing wider by the moment.

He put his hand on the back of her head and pulled her close just before the crystals in the chandelier tinkled and then came crashing toward them. Glass shattered everywhere as huge chunks of the ceiling slammed down, hitting the bench and bouncing off.

Zach tucked Ronnie's head under his shoulder, using his back to deflect any debris. Finally, the avalanche of ceiling stopped, leaving a strange calm in the air. He looked out from the bench, the air choked with dust.

Ronnie untucked her head. Little specks of plaster coated her eyelashes. Zach brushed them gently with his fingertips, and then dusted off her nose. Their eyes locked. Even before he could lean in, Ronnie put her finger on his lips.

He got it.

Not here.

* * *

"I think I've—" Amanda started but then stopped when she realized that she was the only one awake. Jennifer was conked out beside her. Henderson had fallen asleep leaning back in his chair, and the rest of the scientists were well…gone.

Amanda hated to use that euphemism, but she honestly couldn't even think of the harsh truth.

And where was Devlin, still contacting his superiors? Like she really cared.

Despite the fact that the numbers were becoming a blur, Amanda had narrowed over twenty thousand possible loci down to only a few hundred. Which still sucked. But what was a Chicken Little to do but forge on, believing there could be a way to hold the sky up?

A cough sounded behind her. She turned to find Anderson Cooper on the television screen. His presence had become almost natural. As if the reporter was in the room with them, living, and dying, through the plague with them.

Once his coughing fit was over, he looked back at the camera. "I don't know how much longer I can stay on…" Another cough interrupted him. He must have the pneumatic strain of the plague. So he was right. Probably not much longer.

"I just wanted to tell you personally that it has been a privilege to be with you here, at the end. They didn't want me to report this, but I feel like we have been through so much together, that I must be honest…"

His body wracked with a pneumatic cough, Anderson had to grip the chair to keep from falling over. After a few heaving breaths, he continued. "We have run out of antibiotics. Not just New York or the tristate area, but across the country. Across the world."

He gulped hard, and then chuckled. "To be honest, they weren't doing a whole hell of a lot of good anyway." But then he sobered. "So please, be with the ones you love…and pray. That is all that is left to us."

The screen went static as tears streamed down Amanda's cheeks. She leaned over Jennifer and wrapped her arms around her friend. The woman wasn't even coughing now. A sure sign that the body was giving in to the plague. It didn't even have the energy to repulse the bacterium.

Amanda sent a swift prayer to the heavens, but then went back to her computer. She was possibly the only person in the world who had something other than prayer to offer. She had the cure.

If she could just find the damn thing.

CHAPTER 26

Metropolitan Museum of Art
11:18 a.m., EST

Quirk watched Francois's feet disappear through the hole in the ceiling. They had left Quirk for last, since he was the slightest. See? Not going to the gym could be a positive thing.

He teetered on the edge of the bench that was turned on its end. Zach's hand emerged from the hole.

"Grab hold."

Then an exactly opposite order came from the other side of the gates. "Freeze!"

Three cops. No, four. Make it five—were at the gate. "Police! Get down!"

Get down? Did they not realize everything they had just done was to get *up*?

Quirk grabbed hold of Zach's hand. Thank goodness the FBI agent did go to the gym, as he lifted him through the breach in the ceiling. The poor, late-to-the-party police fired and fired away, but the acrylic guard held.

Once on the second floor, Quirk gained his feet.

"This way!" Ronnie yelled, running toward the stairs that led to the roof garden café.

As he hurried to catch up, Quirk noticed a painting. Sargent's infamous *Madame X*. The subject's porcelain skin nearly glowed against the warm brown backdrop. Her hand pressed against the mahogany table.

"Give me that," he urged Zach. The FBI agent raised an eyebrow, but he must have learned not to bother questioning Quirk's evil genius. Zach handed over the torch, and then headed after Ronnie.

Quirk turned the torch on the ever-elegant *Madame X*. She always seemed to hold a secret, but now she revealed it in the form of a glittering, gold symbol.

Francois was already carving it into his arm when the shouts carried from the stairwell. Time to haul ass. Putting the injured Frenchman's arm around his neck, Quirk urged Francois up the stairs.

They hit the door at a run and stumbled out onto the roof garden. From the darkened museum, the morning sun seemed surreal. Everything seemed so pristine up here. The striking sculptures. The lovely garden. The refined café. Almost as if the brutality of the world had not yet made its presence known up here.

"We've got to contact the pilot," Ronnie said.

Quirk rolled his eyes as their chopper floated up between the buildings and flew straight toward them.

* * *

Zach would never again doubt the pilot's devotion to Quirk. They seemed to have a connection that did, in fact, defy the time and space continuum. Zach wedged a chair under the roof's doorknob, knowing it would not hold long, but perhaps long enough for all of them to get on the chopper.

The pilot expertly hovered the helicopter only inches off the roof as Ronnie helped Francois into the chopper. Quirk was next, and Zach joined them. Ronnie was only halfway in when the roof door burst open.

"Stop!"

So that's what it sounded like to be on the other end of a law enforcement proclamation. Zach hoped he didn't sound quite so nervous. As shots whizzed by, Zach pulled his weapon. Even shooting cover fire could accidently injure a poor cop who was just trying to do his job. Who had risked his life just by stepping out onto the plague- filled streets. Zach couldn't risk one of these bullets hitting the chopper, though.

As chairs blew across the open-air café in the wake of the chopper's rotors, Zach had a way better idea. "Land the chopper!"

The pilot shook his head. "No can do."

"The roof can't support the weight," Ronnie added.

"Exactly."

Ronnie must have caught on to Zach's plan O as she turned to the pilot. "Put her down!"

"Your dime," the pilot grumbled as he lowered the chopper onto the roof.

Within moments, telltale cracks formed under the helicopter's struts. With a tight grin, the pilot tilted the chopper just a bit forward, forcing their weight onto the tip of the struts. Cracks became crevices, which became full-on fracture lines. The cement broke apart as the underlying wooden beams cracked under the weight. Soon, the entire roof listed, forcing the cops to flock back to the stairwell.

Zach hopped in the chopper as it took off, just as the roof collapsed inward. Below them, Zach could see the interior to the previously resplendent American Wing. Now it looked like a bombed-out shelter.

Yeah. He was never getting invited to Thanksgiving ever again.

CHAPTER 27

Skies over New York
11:56 a.m., EST

Ronnie studied the new symbols. They had gathered so much information at the Met that it actually caused her to have a headache. Were there too many symbols, or too few? With each new symbol came a hundred variables. Where each one fit in the intricate sequence that was angelic script, was still a mystery.

However, it was becoming clearer and clearer that these most recent symbols were actual longitudes and latitudes.

The problem? Too damn many of them. Even if she ignored the sites outside the United States, there had to be at least a dozen scattered across North America. And just because there was a dot on a map, that did not mean that a facility was there that stored vaccine.

Would the Hidden Hand have antiserum at each location, or would they control access to their greatest asset and hide it at just one of them?

CAROLYN MCCRAY

With half an ear, Ronnie heard the pilot ask where they should head.

"I think we just need to get out of the city," Zach replied.

Ronnie could already feel the tug of the symbols. Her inner world wanted to consume her entire attention. But not yet. Her fingers flew across her keyboard, and a new set of coordinates appeared on the pilot's dashboard.

"If that's where the lady wants to go…"

The helicopter leaned left as it banked northeast. Zach raised an eyebrow.

"You'll see," she smiled. Ronnie waited for her assistant to pounce on that statement, fracturing the little moment between she and Zach. Wait. What was Quirk doing?

She looked at the back of the chopper. The *back,* mind you. Not the copilot's seat. Not in the jump seat that had an excellent view of the pilot's profile. For goodness's sake, Francois was sitting closer to the pilot than her assistant. Instead, Quirk sat on the floor of the helicopter—turned away from the rest of them.

Even though the symbols called to her like sirens of gold, Ronnie rose and made her way to the back of the chopper.

"Quirk, what's up?"

He looked up, tears glistening in his eyes. And not his usual self-pity tears, but real tears.

"What's wrong?"

He tried to shake it off. "Nothing."

Ronnie sat next to him. Quirk tilted his phone to her. "Jennifer…"

"Your contact at the CDC?"

Quirk sniffled once. "Yeah. She's in the late stages of the plague."

Ronnie squinted to read the texts upside down. That made no sense. The plague normally took four days to reach fatality.

"But isn't that way early?"

He nodded. "That's part of the weaponization. The Hidden Hand found a way to accelerate the plague's course."

Ronnie felt first her throat, then her chest, and then her heart tighten. She thought they had at least another day to find the vaccine. Now they had mere hours?

Quirk looked up, eyes rimmed in red. "Can I tell her anything? Give her any hope?"

Hope? Ronnie just about choked. Since when was she the font of hope? How could she disappoint Quirk, who looked like a puppy that had been kicked and then told Santa didn't exist?

"I'm sure the symbols will help us pinpoint a vaccine repository on the Eastern Seaboard."

Okay, maybe *sure* wasn't the exact word she would use or even *pinpoint* or precisely on the Eastern Seaboard, but Quirk's fingers flew across the tiny keyboard.

Now Ronnie just had to figure out how to fulfill her words.

* * *

Amanda glanced up from her computer to the abnormally still conference room. Without Anderson's voice in the background, the place felt like a morgue.

Devlin was still missing, and even Henderson had left to find some potable water. Amanda turned to Jennifer—only the woman was *gone*. How in the hell had Jennifer gone anywhere? Her assistant was too sick to get very far at all. Amanda's head ached as she rose too quickly. Steadying herself on the table, she let the dizziness and nausea wash over her. The pressure on her neck from her lymph nodes forced her to swallow hard to get her saliva down her throat. Those poor lymph nodes had tried so hard in vain to stop the bacteria's spread to her bloodstream.

However, the beds of her nails had a distinct blue tint to them. None too soon, they would blacken as the bacteria destroyed her blood vessels. Sometimes it really was better to be naïve. Every hour, she could feel the plague advancing in her body. She knew each insidious step the bacteria would take to overwhelm her immune system—and ultimately choke the life from her.

A faint clicking caught her attention. She followed the sound to find Jennifer curled under a desk. A sweatshirt was rolled up under her head as a pillow.

"Jennifer?" Amanda asked as she dropped to her knees. "What are you doing?"

As the woman typed on a tiny keyboard, it became obvious. She was texting.

"We've got to find you a bed," Amanda said, taking the phone from Jennifer's swollen hand.

Her assistant's chest heaved up and down, trying to breathe against the fluid building up in her lungs. Still, Jennifer used up some of her precious strength to press the phone into Amanda's hand.

What could be so important in a text?

Amanda scanned the messages, mainly to keep Jennifer calm, but then stopped when she saw the word "vaccine." Scrolling back, Amanda realized that her assistant had been in communication from someone other than the CDC. That wasn't just against protocol or espionage. It was downright treason.

Then she realized that it hadn't been Jennifer talking about the vaccine, but the other person stating they were en route to *retrieve* the vaccine.

"Who is this?" Amanda typed.

The response on the screen, "Um. Who are you to ask *me* who *I* am?"

Now was not the time to play semantics. "What do you know of the vaccine?"

There was a delay, so Amanda typed, "Jennifer is too ill to text. This is her boss, Dr. Amanda Rolph."

Still, no response.

Who knew who was on the other end of this connection? Was it the people who had spread the plague, or could there really be another faction out there fighting the Black Death as hard as she was?

In the end, Amanda realized that if Jennifer trusted them, then she needed to as well.

"I might be able to help you find the vaccine."

* * *

Quirk straightened up. "Ronnie, look at this!"

As she scanned the text, his boss' eyes narrowed. "How well do you know Jennifer?"

"She's my CDC BFF. If there's an outbreak, she lets me know." Ronnie didn't seem to understand quite how close that made them. "Remember how we avoided that cholera outbreak in Micronesia last year?"

"Vaguely."

"It was Jen who alerted me, way before the official alert went out. She's solid."

Still, Ronnie frowned. "But her boss? Can we be sure she isn't Hidden Hand?"

Quirk typed rapidly. "Are you part of the Hidden Hand?"

"Not exactly what I meant," Ronnie scolded.

Quirk arched his eyebrow, all the way. "Tell me that you have pinpointed the vaccine cache, and I'll put this Dr. Rolph through a full-on Rorschach test." Apparently, Ronnie could not oblige. "Jennifer trusts her, and I trust Jennifer."

He didn't bother to add that Jennifer was also his beauty BFF. How many nights had they plucked their eyebrows together, even if on separate continents? Lord knew that he needed someone girly, since Ronnie thought towel-drying your hair added as much body as blow-drying it.

Ronnie held out her hand and took the phone. She rapidly typed, "How?"

Yep, that was his boss. Miss Chatty.

* * *

Amanda rocked back onto her heels, staring at the text. Such a simple question that begged a thousand others. Not the least of which—Was she really going to go through with handing perhaps the most sensitive wartime information in the history of wartime information over to a stranger?

A stranger who seemed in the position to actually act on her information?

"I have data that isolates areas of probable vaccinated populations."

Amanda wasn't sure what to expect, but the word, "Stateside?" popped up.

"Yes," Amanda answered. "Several."

Another long pause, then, "Here is a secure link. Send me everything you have. Hopefully, we can compare the data and pinpoint a nearby location."

"What's your data's source?"

This time, the response from the other end was nearly instantaneous. "Trust me. You don't want to know."

Amanda was about to ask for a slightly more scientific explanation when the door opened.

"Dr. Rolph?"

Tucking the phone into her pocket, Amanda rose, albeit stiffly. "Yes?"

She found Devlin standing in the doorway. He looked like hell. Dark circles overtook his eyes, and his shirt was streaked with blood.

Amanda glanced down at Jennifer. If this was where she chose to stay, so be it. Amanda reached down to the tattered towel that Jennifer had fashioned as a blanket and pulled it up over her shoulder, tucking the woman in.

"Oh, God," Devlin said. "How long as she been like this?"

Devlin's hand flew to his own lymph nodes. "Jesus. We started showing symptoms at the same time."

That they did. Amanda was about to walk past him when she realized that yes, in fact Devlin and Jennifer had come down with their primary symptoms at approximately the same time. Even spiking fevers within an hour of each other. Yet here Devlin stood, looking like hell but with no boils or blisters, and his fingernails looked pinker than even Amanda's.

She was about to open her mouth, and then slammed it shut again.

Who had been her most outspoken critic during the early outbreak? Who had Hidden Hand materials in his possession? Who refused to send her theories up his chain of command?

Sure, Devlin looked rough, but no rougher than any guy without a shower for two days who had a mild flu. Where was the waxy cast to his skin? The reddened pustules along his arms? Amanda's had ruptured hours ago.

Instinctively, she took a step away. Not because she feared he was infected, but because she feared that he *wasn't*.

Unfortunately, her move allowed Devlin to see her computer screen, which was still uploading the data to Jennifer's contact. His eyes darted, taking in the information. Devlin's fingers gripped the edge of the table, his face flashing fury.

"Dr. Rolph, what have you done?"

He rushed her. Amanda grabbed the only thing nearby—a phone—and defended herself, knocking Devlin across the head. Her antigen-antibody inflamed joints flared as he slumped to the floor.

Of course, that was the moment when Dr. Henderson decided to walk through the door.

"Amanda, what have you done?"

* * *

Ronnie watched as the data scrolled in from the CDC. Most of it she didn't understand. Something about the plague's fomite vectors and intracellular disruption. No, what she needed was deeper. Ronnie opened the file labeled "Vaccine Loci."

She skimmed through the documentation. Clearly, Dr. Rolph had been tracking at first hospital intake data, and then when the hospitals closed, home identifiers who were having antibiotics delivered to their doors, and then finally, the death count.

The numbers were staggering. So staggering that Ronnie didn't even log them in her brain. She just kept skimming until she got to the conclusion, where Dr. Rolph identified small areas around the world that defied a pattern of increased resistance to the plague. Areas where there was a not-exactly-conspicuous lack of plague victims, but a statistical dip in cases. Most would probably chalk those differences up to an anomaly, within the margin of error. As a matter of fact, Dr. Rolph was splitting some pretty fine hairs. Finer than even Ronnie would.

Could these impossibly crunched numbers help identify the Hidden Hand's stronghold? Did they really indicate vaccinated populations, or were they just figments of Dr. Rolph's imagination?

Ronnie hit the icon to bring up the world map. Tiny pockets of statistically lower plague victims sprang up across the globe. While small, these areas numbered in the hundreds.

Gulping, Ronnie leaned back. Long ago, she had accepted the fact that the Hidden Hand had bioengineered the plague, and, being evil geniuses, had manufactured both an antiserum to treat acute cases and a vaccine to protect their own and those that swore allegiance to them.

"What's wrong?" Zach asked. "Is the information bogus?"

No. That was the problem. The information seemed eerily correct. If Ronnie had any doubt about the Hidden Hand's fortitude or ability to carry out a mass extinction, this data shattered it. Each of the tiny dots represented a Hidden Hand presence. Each was either within or near a major population center. They had established their presence exactly where it would be needed once those cities fell to the plague. Nation capitals. State capitals. Seats of power. Places where survivors would look for guidance. The Hidden Hand would be there to pick up the pieces and rebuild the world in their image.

"Ronnie?"

She still couldn't answer him. Not with the ruin of the world staring back at her. To see the scope and breadth of the Hidden Hand's campaign sucked the words right out of her mouth. If their enemy was this well organized, its network sprawled across the world, how well fortified would one of their vaccine repositories be? If the Hidden Hand had these kinds of unlimited resources, how could they overcome them with just a few hours of preparation?

Look at how well the Met had gone. And the museum only wanted to deter robberies. They were not prepared to shoot on sight. She wanted to voice this all to Zach, but she simply couldn't.

Quirk was at her shoulder though, seldom at a loss for words. "What are those?"

Her assistant pointed to the scattered dots located in out-lying locations. While far fewer in number, they still added up to dozens. These were barely blips. When she didn't immediately answer him, he reached over and keyed in a few commands.

Dr. Rolph's map overlapped the map that Ronnie had been working on. Her heart sank even further when the vast majority of the locales did not match. How could that be? Ronnie supposedly had a list of Hidden Hand safe houses, and Dr. Rolph had a list of vaccinated populations. Wouldn't they be the same?

Something was off. It was like looking at a constellation sideways. They were at the edge of a pattern. So close that Ronnie could taste it in the back of her mouth. She turned the maps upside down, inverted them, and even stretched them, but she could *not* get them to line up.

"How did the musical symbols from Elvis factor in?" Quirk asked.

The musical symbols? Ronnie had chalked them up to an homage. What if they weren't?

"Francois, are the members of the Hand within the Hand only painters?" she asked.

The old man opened his eyes. "Of course not."

Ronnie smiled as she scrolled to the Graceland burning. She incorporated the musical notes, translated them into Hebrew, and then modified it all into angelic script. She plugged the numbers in. The map warped and dilated, and then came to rest.

"Dang," Quirk said, pointing to Europe. "Venice is like a red-light district."

The neighborhood of Santa Croce in Venice, Italy, did flare brightly. It took a moment for it to sink in. Santa Croce was a junction of lower plague victims and an area designated by angelic script. Others appeared as well. One in Siberia, and another at the horn in Africa.

"Told you the King was the key," Quirk announced. Perhaps he was right.

She scrolled the new map over. There were several locales scattered in Latin America. Quickly, she scrolled up, pulling the United States into view.

Sure enough, several other junctions glowed red. One in San Simeon, another in South Dakota, with another in New Orleans.

But one? One shone right out at her.

Cutler, Maine.

One of the most northern points along Maine's rugged, rocky, isolated coast, Cutler was exactly the kind of place Ronnie would have chosen if she needed to hide the cure for the Black Death.

CHAPTER 28

Undisclosed Location
12:37 p.m., EST

Zach stood in the center of a perfectly white room. It was almost hard to look at the walls. They shimmered so brightly. Was this what heaven would feel like? Probably for Ronnie and Quirk, since the only things that punctuated those pristine walls were plasma screens, computer bays, and tech equipment he'd never seen before.

"So this is what your cold room looks like," Zach commented, knowing that Warp would give his left nut to even have a picture of it, let alone stand amongst the Robin Hood hacker's infinite greatness.

"Oh, please," Quirk said, rolling his eyes. "This is only a minor backup station."

Ronnie grinned as she loaded up equipment bags. "You should see the one in Tokyo."

Yes, Zach would have to see the one in Japan, because he could not imagine how anything could outdo this one located in the rolling countryside of upstate New York. On the far wall were two magnetic discs very similar to the one Ronnie used in El Paso, only these were about five times the size. A bank of computer drives, three deep, rose up to the ceiling. And the feeds they were monitoring? Zach couldn't identify half of them.

"This truly is…" Zach didn't have the words to complete the thought.

Ronnie's lips bloomed into a full-on smile. "Well, then, maybe I shouldn't show you the armory."

"*Armory*?"

The Robin Hood hacker was known for her ability to run her operations miles—if not continents—away from her target. Besides stealing well over a hundred billion dollars, she had yet to be charged with even breaking and entering. And she had an armory?

"Duh," she said, as she hit a few commands, and the wall with the computer banks slid open to reveal a room not nearly as neat and tidy. Weapons lay at odd angles. Pistols, assault rifles, and even RPG launchers. "A girl has got to be prepared."

There was prepared, and then there was *this*. Not that Zach was complaining, mind you.

"Ever since the Zetas cartel targeted the hacker group, Anonymous, and brutally kidnapped one of them," Ronnie said, her voice not quite as chipper. "We've had to stock up."

Quirk chimed in as he joined them. "I tell her to put her toys away, but does she?" He waved his hand dismissively. "And the pilot is getting antsy. We promised to be in and out in three minutes. You know how Francois likes to touch equipment he shouldn't."

"Take your pick," Ronnie said to Zach, indicating the stockpile of weapons.

Um. Did Zach mention how much he loved her?

* * *

Amanda's hand shook, finding it hard to grip the syringe as she pulled a vial of Devlin's blood out of his arm. The CIA liaison was tied to a chair in her office, his mouth bound by a gag. While shocked, Dr. Henderson had heard her out and decided that they needed proof that Devlin was faking his condition before condemning her.

Someone had contaminated the facility with the plague. Was that person sitting in front of her?

As she pulled the needle from his arm, Devlin roused. He glanced down at the needle poke. Eyes dilating, his head snapped up as Dr. Henderson used the last of the phone cord to bind Devlin's feet to the chair. They'd had to use what they had available. Completely jury-rigging the entire hostage-taking system.

Devlin tried to shout something, but the gag muffled his attempt. But it probably went something like: "Dr. Rolph just sent highly classified information to the enemy." Luckily, Dr. Henderson had agreed with the wisdom of gagging the CIA liaison to keep from bothering Jennifer.

Even though Devlin was bound and gagged, he gave escape a run for its money. He banged the chair back and forth, to and fro.

"Are you sure the agglutination test will be definitive?" Dr. Henderson asked.

"Definitive?" Amanda queried. "No. But highly suspect? Yes."

Trying to ignore the spectacle that Devlin was putting on, Amanda moved to her makeshift laboratory. It wasn't much, but it was enough to perform this basic field test.

Amanda mixed a drop of Devlin's blood with a drop of serum filled with fragments of the bacteria's cell wall onto a microscope slide. If Devlin had antibodies preexisting in his system, they would clump together, forming ringlets. If he didn't, the two fluids would simply mix together, a smooth combination of the two.

"*Umph. Trllmk,*" Devlin tried to say, fighting against the gag.

"Well?" Dr. Henderson asked as his eyes flickered over to the CIA liaison. "If this doesn't clump, we have broken about half a dozen laws for nothing."

"It isn't instantaneous," Amanda answered, well aware that simply drawing Devlin's blood without his permission was considered assault. "It can take a few minutes."

She got discouraged, though, as the fluids just swirled together going from clear on one side and red to the other, to a pinkish fluid in the middle. Absolutely no sign that antibodies were in Devlin's blood.

"Maybe I should check under the microscope." It had been years, probably back in Microbiology 101, since she'd performed such a crude test. "I might be able to identify micro-agglutination."

Dr. Henderson nodded as Devlin nearly tipped his chair over backwards. So much for staying quiet.

When Amanda picked up the slide, tilting it accidentally, a clump settled on the edge of the fluid pool. She had forgotten step three. Rock the slide to isolate the clumping on the periphery.

Gently, she tilted the slide back and forth as more and more—and more—clumps appeared.

Amanda and Dr. Henderson looked from the slide, to each other, and to Devlin.

The CIA liaison was suddenly perfectly still.

* * *

Ronnie shifted on the chopper's seat. Not because of rough flying, although the storm brewing was knocking them around far more on this leg of the trip than it had heading out of Manhattan, but because there was literally no room for her legs. The helicopter's interior was crammed full of computing equipment and weapons.

Zach sat on the floor of the chopper like a little boy next to a Christmas tree. He felt the heft of each gun, turning it over in his hands and checking the sights. Then, if the weapon passed muster, he would try to find somewhere to pack it. He already had, like, four guns on his hip with extra clips, plus a smaller pistol on each ankle. The guy was going to be walking bowlegged soon. "Seriously, Ronnie, there are, like, three other satellites closer than the one you are trying to re-task," Quirk whined, despite the fact he had enough toys littered around him to make him a very happy boy as well.

"I need *this* one."

Quirk snorted. "Ronnie, you've got to get over your superstitions. Just because a satellite's call sign shares your birthday, does not make it your 'lucky' satellite."

Ronnie just shrugged, letting him think that was her reason for wanting this particular satellite. Far better than arguing over the real one. She did, however, have to shut him up before he sniffed out her real ploy.

"There!" she said as she brought up the satellite image of the coordinates off of Maine's northern coast. "Satisfied?"

Hitting the zoom key, Ronnie punched in deeper and deeper to the structure that sat upon that rocky cliff. It was some kind of building. No, more like a mansion. No, the closer they got, the more it looked like the Hidden Hand had built themselves a castle.

A full-on medieval castle.

Although in New England, just being a castle wasn't that big a deal. There were probably a dozen of the structures within a hundred miles. But a castle *this* big? With turrets and ramparts and a central courtyard? *That* was a big deal.

Even Francois, who had gone back to his mumbling meditation, came over for a look. Was it a bad sign that the Frenchman's pupils spread wide at the sight?

"What is it made of?" Zach asked as he rose from the floor and made room on the seat next to her.

She switched modes, finding one of the satellite's opticals that registered density. "Looks like stone, but this portion…" Ronnie indicated the centermost section of the castle, right at the heart of the compound. "Everything is pinging back. It must be some high-density metal. Titanium or tungsten."

"Which is also going to shield the interior to any EM pulse we might use," Quirk added.

Ronnie felt that weight on her breastbone again. Even though she knew the Hidden Hand would have some gnarly defenses, it was still a blow to see them in action.

"Do we have anything to penetrate the metal shielding?" Zach asked.

She looked at Quirk, even though she knew the answer. Even if they had a hundred acetylene torches, it would take them a week to cut through metal that thick. Zach glanced at both of them, but didn't even bother to ask for clarification.

"I'm assuming that this is where they would be hiding any vaccine—if they do have any?"

Ronnie nodded, letting him figure out that despite all the high-tech equipment and firepower they had, they didn't have enough to get to the vaccine.

"What's that flare there on the edge of the image?" Quirk asked.

"I'm not sure," Ronnie answered as she zoomed in to the base of the castle.

"Switch to ground-penetrating radar," Zach suggested. Then, when she raised an eyebrow at him, he finished. "I mean, you have *got* to have some ground-penetrating radar, right?"

Of course her satellite had ground-penetrating radar. She was just glad Zach could appreciate that fact.

A few keystrokes later, the image shifted from opaque angles to a jumble of lines and squiggles.

"Here," Quirk said trying to take her laptop. "Put it through the 3-D imaging software."

Ronnie held tight to her computer. "I've got it."

Okay, after about ten attempts to bring the image into focus, maybe she didn't.

"Don't be hogging the hologram if you can't use it properly."

But Ronnie finally figured it out, projecting the image in 3-D before them.

"Holy mother of…" Quirk breathed out.

"Damn," Zach added.

Even Francois contributed, "*Baise.*"

The castle was massive, with machine guns instead of archers for long-range defense and a metal-encased core, and the grounds had a sprawling underground complex.

"Check out the heat signature," Ronnie said, pointing to the lower chambers. "Or should I say, lack of heat signature?"

One room in the underground complex was showing a stable fifty-three degrees. The perfect temperature to store vials upon vials of vaccines.

"At least we know for sure that they are there," Zach offered, clearly trying to cheer her up.

Which was great—except that they had a major problem. How in the hell were they going to break into the grounds, penetrate that metal shielding, and fight their way through the castle to the staircase that led them down into the completely rock-walled subterranean chamber?

Ronnie looked at the others. No one exactly seemed brimming with ideas either.

* * *

Francois sat back as the rest bandied about ideas for breaching the castle. Did they not know the Hidden Hand would have thought of each of these earthbound ploys? They'd had centuries to perfect their stronghold. Centuries of war and famine and strife to challenge their defenses and shore them up.

No.

The answer would come from the heavens, as it was wont to do. He gazed upon his arm. So many new symbols outlined in dried blood. The angels were talkative of late. Almighty God in his wisdom had retreated from man's daily life. In infinite understanding, God had left man to develop his own free will.

But the angels? Ah, the angels who loved man could not allow such evil as the Hidden Hand to flourish. They had walked amongst man, teaching those who would resist the Hand's quest for dominion over the earth.

Many spoke of the end of days—shouting it from street corners and pulpits. But Francois did not, or more likely, refused to believe, that the true apocalypse was upon them. That this could not be God's will for mankind.

Perhaps it was man who had gotten himself into this position, but it would be grace from on high that would deliver them from it.

Francois felt certain of such. So again, he studied the symbols on his arm, hoping to divine what the angels needed of him.

* * *

Quirk typed. That's what he did best. Coding. Surveillance. Hacking. Ronnie and Zach were busy talking insertion points and tensile strength. While he loved building prototypes, the entire Mexico debacle had taught him one thing…do not try to fire those prototypes.

No, he was much happier with the current plan. Have him run all the cyber interference and leave the Captain America stuff to Ozzie and Harriet over there. Even now, he had found miles upon miles worth of cabling hidden underground servicing buried gun turrets. They hadn't even landed at the castle, and Quirk had saved Ronnie's little hiney yet again.

He glanced over his computer monitor, mainly to check if the pilot was busy flexing those biceps of his, and found Francois, his hands pressed together in prayer. Yep, probably if there ever were a time for full-on begging of the heavens for a boon, it was now.

Quirk sent his own little request up to the big guy when he heard his name mentioned. Not in that good way, where Ronnie was reassuring Zach that Quirk was, in fact, the fastest coder in the world.

No. From the way she said his name, Quirk could tell that Ronnie wanted something from him. A large something. A *mega-sized* something. His eyes narrowed as he looked up to find her standing in front of him, a sickly sweet smile on her face.

Ugh! Perhaps there wasn't a God after all.

* * *

Lino stood, patient and tall. Others scurried about the castle's war room, worried for the fly who thought to spoil God's picnic. The door behind him burst open, and by the insufferable grunting the man made as he crossed the room, it could be only Deacon Havar. Lino did not turn or slide his eyes away from the long-range radar.

"I demand that you step aside, Lino."

The man spoke as if he held God's authority. Seldom did God allow a man such as Havar, filled with consistent failings, to hold *anything* of His—let alone authority.

"Had you allowed me to kill Francois at the field office, we would not be here," Lino remarked. "At this tentative juncture."

From the corner of his eye, Lino saw the deacon scowl. "We would have had to kill the entire office."

"Yes, and how more efficient that would have been, no?"

Havar's cheeks billowed in and out. His fleshy nostrils constricted, making every breath a wheeze. "It was not my failing during the assault on El Paso or the Met. That falls on your narrow shoulders."

A grin flickered on Lino's lips. So many had tried to intimidate him because of his lean stature. So many had failed.

"Again, fruit from the poisoned tree. Indecisive action requires so much tidying afterward."

Now each breath of the deacon's rang in Lino's ear. He tired of this man's pomp and dyspnea. In addition, the fly grew so much closer. Nearly within range of their missiles.

"Go back to your chambers, Havar. Enjoy your last moments indulging yourself."

The man took in a sharp breath. "You have so little faith in our defenses?"

Lino finally turned to the deacon who thought himself the better. "God is our defense. It is only that you should not see our ultimate victory. Regrettably, you shall be in stage four of the plague by the time it is accomplished."

"I am anointed," the deacon hissed.

"El Paso was your true baptism, Father. Had you succeeded, you would have been vaccinated at a ceremony in Venice. Again, *regrettably*, you failed..."

Deacon Havar shook his head side to side, yet Lino could see the man's mind begin to grasp his new reality. A hand flew to his neck, where the glands were already swelling.

"You said it was a side effect of the vaccination."

"I *lied*."

With as much satisfaction as a man of God could enjoy, Lino watched as the deacon realized he would be no better than the paupers who died spitting up blood in the street.

"Sir, they have passed the outer marker."

He urged the deacon to the door. "Enjoy the next few hours…before your lungs fill with blood."

Havar defeated, sagging, shuffling, left the room.

Lino turned back to the radar.

Finally. Time to end this stalemate.

CHAPTER 29

Skies over Maine
2:03 p.m., EST

The helicopter skimmed over the roiling sea. The threatening storm was now in full rage. Rain hit the windshield in sheets, clattering like gunfire. Ronnie steeled herself. Soon, that would be real gunfire.

She glanced over to find Quirk typing rapidly. "Is there a problem with the countermeasures?"

"Did you know that there have been seven shark attacks in the region?" Quirk informed the entire aircraft. "That basically, we are flying over the same waters that *Jaws* swam in?"

"First off, that was Martha's Vineyard. And secondly, it was a *film*." She turned to Zach. "Which was *not* Steven Spielberg's first."

He put his hands up in mock defeat. "I got it."

Quirk returned to finding YouTube footage of local shark attacks as Zach nodded toward the distant speck on the cliff.

The castle. Although, with the weather and distance, the structure looked more like a hobbit house.

"Are you worried?" Zach asked her.

"That they haven't thrown anything at us, despite the fact that we've been in range for two minutes?" Ronnie said with a sigh. "Yes, but this could be an instance of 'they know that we know that they know' kind of thing."

Zach didn't seem entirely satisfied by that answer, but let it go as the helicopter swooped left—taking them overland. This close to the castle, the Hidden Hand's underwater defenses were nearly as good as its ground defenses. Ronnie checked the screen monitoring the various mines and water-to-air missiles. All were quiet.

This assault was like a hack—only they weren't dealing with code, but with actual lives. And like a hack, this attack was as much a mind game as anything. The targets knew that they were vulnerable to attack. They planned for it. The hackers knew that the targets planned for the attack, so they always had to find chinks in their cyber armor. Back doors. Side entrances. Weak firewalls.

It basically came down to who knew what in which order, and whether they had time to adapt. Lino must have known what went down in Mexico. He also knew that he had been outflanked at the Met. Ronnie had a pretty deep bag of tricks, but even she was running out of them. What if she'd shown Lino enough to anticipate her next move?

While the Hidden Hand was filled with soulless bastards, it did not make them stupid. If anything, it made them all the more dangerous. Lines that Ronnie would not cross, the Hidden Hand would leap over with joy.

And clearly Lino was holding back, waiting until he saw the whites of their proverbial eyes. But waiting for what?

"Did you know that shark attacks rise steeply during a storm? The agitation of the water—"

"Quirk." She waited until he looked up at her. "Did you get my laptop in the box?"

He rolled his eyes and went back to his shark research. Yes, Quirk's quirks even got on her nerves at times. But Ronnie knew that when her assistant was on a roll, she couldn't stop him. Or at least not without wild horses. Instead, she simply double-checked herself as they sped over the thick forest surrounding the castle.

The clear box seemed so benign. Yet in the end, it could save all their lives.

"I take it that isn't just plastic," Zach said, leaning over to study the construction of the clear box.

"Not exactly. It is lead-impregnated, airtight, watertight, and maximum EM-shielded."

Zach's eyebrow lifted. "That's been field-tested?"

Ronnie felt her cheeks flush. "Okay, so maybe I should have said, 'in theory' to start off with."

"Okay, but if your computer is in that impenetrable box, then…"

She pulled out an older version of the keyless-keyboard gloves. These ceramic tiles on her fingertips were much larger, heavier, and quite frankly, a fashion eyesore. But at least they had all their keys.

"These are—"

"KeKe-G's," Quirk interrupted.

Okay. That *was* a cooler name. Ronnie went to explain to Zach what her assistant was talking about when alarms blared.

Guess it was time to find out who was faster on the draw.

* * *

Zach steadied the launcher against the floor of the helicopter, which was easier said than done. Between the bucking winds and the pilot's maneuvers to evade the six missiles flying toward them, the best Zach could do was not fall out the open door.

"Fire!" Ronnie yelled from the other side of the chopper, where she manned her own launcher.

He hit the lever, and three countermeasures flew out from the launcher, spraying out in a fan pattern. The missiles took the bait, sharply banking to hone in on the new heat signature. Explosions rang out as the missiles detonated far away from them.

Pretty slick.

"Oh, crap!" Ronnie blurted out. She turned to see that one of her missiles not only did not detonate, but also had banked around, heading straight for them. "It must be backtracking the countermeasure's path."

That smart missile was hauling ass in their direction.

"Zach, fire another countermeasure!"

He wanted to argue that he was on the other side of the helicopter from the missile, but why bother? Ronnie was giving the orders. He hit the lever, and the countermeasure shot out of the launcher.

"Keep us parallel!" Ronnie shouted to the pilot.

The missile came straight for them through the downpour. It felt impossibly wrong that the helicopter stopped its forward momentum and hovered in the battering winds, awaiting its doom.

"Get down!"

Zach threw himself to the floor as the missile flew in Ronnie's door. It scorched them as it exited his door, streaking after the countermeasure. It exploded just above the forest, setting treetops ablaze despite the soaking rain.

Ronnie had one of those smiles people get when they know that they just cheated death. He rose to join her when Francois exclaimed, "Dear God!"

If something caused Francois to take the Lord's name in vain...

The sight through the chopper's window should have been something out of the Dark Ages. The castle before them loomed on the horizon, every bit the symbol of power and domination that the builders had intended. The 3-D holographic image did not do the enormous structure justice.

Red flags emblazed with gilded angelic script whipped in the fierce wind atop stone turrets. Dotted all along the towers were narrow archers' windows—the ancient equivalent for modern-day snipers. And the Hidden Hand had shown itself more than willing to adopt technology. How many gunmen were hidden in the shadow of the stone?

Long, wide ramparts, equally well guarded, connected each tower.

Talk about a tough, protective outer shell.

A huge, elaborately carved wooden gate stood closed. And, Zach guessed, locked pretty damned tight. The empty moat encircled the castle. Were they expecting the storm to fill it?

What did the Hidden Hand know that Ronnie didn't?

* * *

Amanda chewed on the edge of her thumbnail. Not very sanitary in the middle of a plague, but what the heck? She already had it, right? Dr. Henderson sat on the edge of her desk. His shoulders were slumped. A tall, proud man—nearly broken in half.

He absently scratched his itching arm. Probably a boil. Amanda physically had to stop herself from taking her nails to her skin. The burning sensation was nearly undeniable. Her own throat, choked by her lymph nodes, expanded to the size of small lemons.

"We should hear what he has to say," Henderson declared.

She shook her head. "How exactly is he going to explain *that*?

Amanda indicated the five—count them, *five*—slides where they had reproduced the same effect. Each one came back positive. Devlin had preexposure antibodies. Not a whole lot of ways you could get those besides a vaccination.

"Still," Henderson said frowning before he paused. It seemed to take a moment to gather his strength back again. "He would know if he was vaccinated intentionally."

Amanda made sure to keep her face placid. This was one of those times that Jennifer would have stomped on her foot to speak up. Instead her assistant was in a near coma under the table. Amanda wanted to tell Henderson everything, but she feared how he would take it.

She wasn't sure how he would take her little texting adventure, and Amanda didn't want to end up tied to a chair next to Devlin.

"We've got to try," Henderson stated as he stood up. The director leaned over Devlin. "If you scream…"

Honestly, at this point, who would hear the CIA liaison, or more importantly, who would care? With everyone in various stages of the Black Death, a mouthy operative was the least of their concerns.

The CIA liaison nodded, so Henderson removed the gag.

"I'm not the traitor; she is," Devlin said, indicating Amanda.

"See?" she said hoping she didn't sound too guilty.

Dr. Henderson eyed her then focused on Devlin. "How do you explain having active, IgM-type antibodies in your blood stream? Antibodies that take weeks to form?"

"I have no idea," Devlin asserted. "But I *do* know that she sent state secrets to an unknown party!"

Amanda shrugged as Devlin went on to give the entire incriminating evidence. The guy did have a good memory—she had to give him that.

Henderson turned to her. "Well?"

She stuck to the facts as best she could. "When I realized that Jennifer and Devlin had been infected within the same time frame, and that *his* lymph nodes weren't even enlarged, he attacked me. So, I defended myself."

Amanda hoped that was close enough to the story she had given Henderson when he walked in on her. By the cloud over his features he still wasn't convinced, so she motioned toward the computer. "Check it yourself."

A little too quickly, he took her up on her offer.

"Check for an upload link," Devlin offered.

Behind Henderson's back, Amanda frowned at Devlin, which only fueled him more. "Plus, her phone. Check her phone for unauthorized numbers."

Her boss finished with the computer. "Nothing there. He's right, though. I should check your phone as well."

Amanda had done an excellent job covering her tracks on the computer, but Jennifer's phone? She'd been lucky to clear the call log.

She handed over her phone, and then made a show of pulling out Jennifer's as well. "Here are *both* of our phones."

Henderson sat down, squinting at the tiny screen. Finally he set both phones down. "They look clean."

"No. No. No. No." The CIA liaison said thumping his chair forward then back. "You've got the wrong—"

Her boss stuffed the gag back into Devlin's mouth. With a deep sigh, Henderson slumped into a chair. "Now, what do we do with him?"Amanda felt her stomach drop. She had no idea what to do with Devlin, but she had assumed that Henderson would. "Tell someone at the CIA?"

"Who, though?" Her boss postulated as he rubbed his temples. "How do we know they didn't vaccinate Devlin and send him in?"

"There's got to be someone you trust, right?"

Henderson was the director of Plum Island. He had to have connections. He had to know someone who could get the information to someone who could act on it. Amanda didn't want to think that she had to rely solely on the person on the other side of a text to save the known world.

* * *

The time for gawking was over. Ronnie handed Zach a vest.

"What's this?" he asked.

"Your bulletproof vest," Ronnie answered, then turned to the pilot. "Bring us into the landing coordinates."

Zach held up what on the surface might look like a sweater vest. "This? This is bulletproof."

"Yep," she said, pulling on hers, tucking it under her weighed down equipment belt. "Think of Kevlar, only we've added some metal ions to the mix."

"I still don't get the 'bulletproof' part."

Ronnie kind of loved it when he got all Doubting Thomas on her. "Put it on."

After he donned the garment, she flicked a finger at his chest. Which she should have known better than to do as her nail hit solid metal. "Ouch," she said sucking on her stinging finger.

Zach thumped his chest as well, then shaking out his hand. "How the hell…"

"Just like the metal ions in the CIA's device aligned under a microwave burst," Ronnie explained, "these align under pressure. The more pressure, the more the ions bond."

"Creating a thicker and thicker shield?" Zach postulated.

"Bingo," she said as the pilot swooped down into a clearing near the castle and hovered over the landing spot. Ronnie turned to Francois. "You aren't going to stay in the chopper like you promised are you?"

The Frenchman cocked his head slightly. She tossed Francois a vest. Of course because she'd had to give her nice sleek black one to Zach, Ronnie was wearing Quirk's, which, of course, had a prominent Hello Kitty on the front, which meant that Francois got the backup vest with Chococat. She and Francois were just going to have to deal with it.

"We're ready," Ronnie informed the pilot.

"I'm just going to touch down," he answered. "Let you off-load the equipment, then dust off."

Yes, she had gotten used to his aversion of actually landing the chopper. Heaven forbid.

* * *

Francois helped lift a large disc from the helicopter as the helicopter's rotors spun dizzyingly overhead, adding even more force to the storm's pounding rain. Ronnie tossed a metal case over his head. It landed on the soaked grass and bounced. Yet other items Ronnie handed Francois with the reverence of a saintly relic.

Next to him, Zach hauled a crate off the deck, and then stumbled back. Francois caught him by the elbow. Then he, too, felt a shifting underfoot. It could not be an earthquake— not this far north and not this close to stripping the Hidden Hand of all they held dear.

Underfoot, large metal hooks ripped through the meadow waving in the air like so many heads of a snake.

"Liftoff!" Zach yelled above the wash of the rotors.

Ronnie responded, but the wind snatched away her words. Either the pilot heard, or he attempted to get the helicopter in the air of his own accord, but the hooks latched onto the struts of the craft, jerking the craft back toward the ground.

Zach pushed Francois to the ground as the helicopter tipped nearly on its side, bringing its swirling blades just inches from their heads. Crates, bundles, and computers tumbled from the open bay door. Above them, Ronnie clung to a cable. Then, she lost her grip and crashed beside them.

"We've got to stay clear of the rotors," she groaned, nursing the shoulder that she fell on.

Francois could not agree more. Then, the helicopter tipped upright, as hooks from the other side brought it level. Trapped, but level. The pilot fought fiercely, testing the restraints on one side, and then the other.

Zach tugged on one of the hooks. "They must be magnetized."

A strong, unseen force might have held them on. But one of the hooks broke, sending the helicopter tilting wildly to the side. At the least, the rotors were away from them as they scrambled to safety.

But was it truly safe? Quirk cried out from the helicopter, "Incoming!"

Through heavy raindrops, even Francois's old eyes could make out at least six missiles heading their way. And with the helicopter flailing violently, they had a clear target.

"The countermeasures!" Zach yelled, but Ronnie tugged them toward the tumble of equipment.

"Find the EM rifle!"

Zach complied, but Francois stared out across the soaked field, past the moat to the topmost turret. Lino would be watching from there—regardless of a veering helicopter or inbound missiles.

Francois would not flinch.

CHAPTER 30

Cutler, Maine
4:12 p.m., EST

Zach ripped a crate open, revealing a bunch of what looked like ninja stars—but no rifles.

"Here!" Ronnie yelled as she tossed him what seemed like a typical pump-action rifle. "You've got to aim pretty damn close for the EM pulse to work."

Her words sounded impossible. But which of her words had sounded reasonable? Trusting Ronnie, Zach wiped the rain from his eyes and swung the rifle up, targeting the nearest missile. He braced his back leg, ready for the recoil. Yet when he pulled the trigger, there was no more kick than a regular weapon. Did it work? Did the rifle actually shoot something?

Then the missile pitched and wavered, sailing over the helicopter and crashing into the field, exploding in a brilliant red flash. Zach couldn't waste any time staring at the sight. He had five other missiles to take down. Pumping the rifle with one hand, he caught it with the other and aimed.

Keeping both eyes open, he tracked the second missile and fired. It spun on its axis, narrowly missing the chopper before disappearing over the edge of the cliff. After pumping another shot, he turned to the third streaking toward them. Only this one came from the *other* side of the chopper.

"Ronnie!"

She looked up from her task to see the problem. If he shot, the chopper would be caught in the EM pulse. And as the helicopter bucked up and down and sideways, how could he get to the other side?

"Hit the deck!" she yelled back.

Zach didn't understand what she meant until he did as requested. Once on the ground, he realized what she meant. He might not be able to shoot over or around the helicopter, but under? Under, he could do. Zach fired a third time, sending the missile off into the woods to unleash its destruction.

Not having time to rise, Zach rolled to his left, targeting another incoming missile.

Four down. Two to go.

* * *

Ronnie tilted the gopher, trying to get the damned thing to work. Their hybrid, ground-penetrating radar and electronic disrupter was not faring well in its first field test. She could see the hook's controlling mechanism beneath about three feet of dirt. Could she disrupt it? *No.*

She tried everything. Using energy bursts. Low-frequency modulation. Even a high pitched sound blast, yet those damn hooks still held the helicopter in thrall. Inside the craft, she could see the pilot struggling and Quirk hanging on for dear life in the co-pilot's seat.

Nothing was happening as it was supposed to. And it was all her fault. *Again.*

She'd underestimated Lino. She should have known that he would know the best place to land for a frontal assault. Okay, so maybe the whole magnetized hooks thing she shouldn't feel bad about missing, but *still*. If she didn't get ahead of the curve...

Zach dashed past her, setting up for his next shot. As she jangled the gopher's controls, trying to wake it up, Ronnie watched the FBI agent aim. His posture was filled with intent. Muscles tightened. Eyes squinted, he was a chiseled hero through and through. No wonder his body temperature ran at 98.9 degrees.

He fired and hit his mark true. The fifth missile lurched once, and then fell out of the sky, exploding "harmlessly" on the grass.

The joystick jiggled under her touch. The gopher had caught onto one of the hook's controls. Almost wishing the damn thing were a real gopher that could chew through the damn wiring, Ronnie urged the machine to sever the line's connection.

"Ronnie!" She turned to find Zach flexing his bicep, pumping the rifle, and then firing—to no avail. "It stopped working."

No, it didn't stop working. They just ran into the "when will we ever need more than five EM pulses?" phenomenon. Which meant that the helicopter was a sitting duck.

Unless she could get the gopher to do its job, the pilot and Quirk were dead.

* * *

Quirk clung to the seat as the bravest man in the world tried to save their lives. Damn Ronnie and her cost-cutting "Rule of 5" EM pulses. In the real world it turned out the enemy had no such limitation.

He could see the strength in the pilot's arms as he tried to physically wrestle the helicopter from the clutches of the steel hooks. The missile bore down on them. Not that Quirk hadn't felt like he had a bull's-eye on him for the past twenty-four hours; now, he felt as though he had one painted on his chest.

The red-tipped bomb on wings headed right for them, dead on. There would be no riding parallel or countermeasures or—

Suddenly, the helicopter careened sideways as a hook sheared off. Then, another let loose. The pilot hit the stick, shooting the chopper straight into the air. The missile cruised right beneath them, but did not seem fooled as it turned, arcing back around, honing in on them.

Quirk grabbed hold of the seat as the chopper nearly dropped from the sky, recovering just inches from the ground—where, by the way, those stupid hooks were still fishing around for some railings.

"Um. Up and at 'em?" Quirk suggested, never wanting his pilot to feel pressured or anything.

The chopper swooped sideways and then back again, like some four-square dancer. Then back again. Then, it finally angled forward, racing barely above the grassy meadow.

"Did we get hit by an EM blast?" Quirk asked, pulling out his equipment. "I can—"

"No," the pilot grunted as he jerked the helicopter to the right, compensating for a gust of gale-force wind.

"Then what?"

The pilot looked over at him with a tight frown. "We're out of gas."

* * *

Ronnie watched as the helicopter seemed to hiccup, gaining altitude just before it dropped past the cliff. The missile had no such hesitation as it followed. The sound of the blast rose above the wind, and the horizon glowed red.

"Quirk!" Ronnie yelled as Zach grabbed her arm, pulling her back. She hit her earpiece, cycling through the frequencies. "Quirk. Pilot. Anyone?"

"You thought to challenge God's will?" a cool, serpentine voice answered.

As tears mixed with rain, Ronnie steadied her voice before she answered Lino. "You betcha."

"Don't let him get in your head," Zach whispered.

What Zach didn't know was that Lino *couldn't* get in her head. She had to believe Quirk was alive. He was not just vital to the mission, but vital to *her*. She had to believe the pilot was every bit as good as Quirk thought he was.

And she hadn't heard a death cry. What she thought she had heard was a squealed, "I love you." Which she doubted very much was directed at her.

How much had they already accomplished on pretty much faith alone? Ronnie glanced to Francois, who nodded solemnly.

"Game on," she hissed into the microphone. "Game *freaking* on."

Sure, Quirk would have probably quoted *Braveheart* or something, but she thought she'd done Quirk proud. Cutting the connection to Lino, Ronnie headed over to the large metal discs.

"Let's get these set up."

* * *

Zach helped Ronnie use air-compressed pistons to secure the second magnetic disc into position. "Are you sure you don't want to talk about—"

"Nope," Ronnie said then looked at the wreckage of their equipment. "We've got to find the RPG launcher before they get their snipers involved."

He wanted to reach out to her, except that there *really* were snipers probably setting their range. Only the sheets of rain and wind shear had saved them so far.

"Here we go," Ronnie said, pulling a bent and misshapen rocket-propelled grenade launcher from the rubble of their equipment. At one time, the thing probably had been a sight to behold. It should have fit three RPGs in a revolver-style set of chambers. The only problem was two of them were trashed beyond use.

Ronnie shrugged. "I think we only had time to off-load one RPG, anyway."

So much for their grand plan. Two minutes into the mission, and they were down by half the equipment and…well, he didn't want to think about personnel. Maybe Ronnie's "let's embrace denial" technique had some validity to it.

As the storm soaked through to his skin, Zach helped her load the launcher. Then, she backed away. "All yours."

Zach eyed the gate far across the field. It was a little like hitting the strike zone, pitching from center field. And only one chance to make it count. He seldom got performance anxiety, but come on.

Then, Ronnie winked at him and wiggled her fingers. "Don't worry," she said. He had no idea what she meant as she put on a pair of cracked glasses. "I've got your back."

* * *

Okay, that would have sounded a lot more reassuring if her glasses didn't spark and fritz half of her display. However, if her laptop was still working, then she had to believe that the helicopter wasn't at the bottom of the ocean. Right?

Zach set the launcher on his shoulder and leveled the sight. This time he *did* need to brace himself, because the rocket's force nearly knocked him over. She couldn't worry about him, though. She had a missile to keep on track.

How she adored Zach, but his aim was off. Statistics ran down the good side of her holographic glasses showing he was about ten degrees off, and the wind was blowing in from the west, multiplying his error.

Typing into the air as big fat raindrops splattered on her glasses, Ronnie compensated for the angle. The RPG smoothly corrected course, angling straight for the gate. With just a few more adjustments, the RPG hit the castle's entrance, shattering the thick wood, opening up the path into the compound.

For once, things went as planned. Now they only needed to—

"Francois!" Zach yelled as the Frenchman headed across the soggy grass. "Wait!"

But when did the old man wait on anything? "Seriously, we need to put a bell on him," Ronnie commented as she hurried over to the first hyper-magnets. "Zach, set the other one."

Rapidly, she got hers spinning, generating the magnetic field they would need.

"How do I turn it on?" he asked.

"Hit the button to the left…Never mind," she said racing over and turning his on as well.

"Ready" she queried, knowing what she asked.

"Can I say 'no?'"

"If we're going to catch up with him," Ronnie said taking Zach's hand. "Probably not."

* * *

Francois strode across the increasingly muddy field. The rain poured down like a cleansing baptism. Lightning danced in the sky as thunder boomed. Was that God's anger or encouragement?

It wasn't that he didn't hear the shouts behind him, Francois instead chose to listen to the angels. They sang in his mind. He need only look to his carved flesh to know the melody.

He was close enough now to be able to see the gunmen positioned on the other side of the gate, defending the courtyard. He could sense the other men along the high stone ramparts and even those positioned within the towers. He mostly sensed Lino.

Was the acolyte furious that his missiles did not strike true, or did he welcome them to storm the castle? Was the boy arrogant enough to think he could hide behind an army when he had so much to account for?

The sound of gunfire, so much gunfire, filled the air, squeezing in between the raindrops. The metal should be tearing through his flesh, searing his heart, yet it did not. Instead the small lead bullets, so very lethal if they hit their mark, were tugged to the right or to the left. They whizzed past leaving his flesh unmarred.

"Dude," Ronnie said as she trotted to catch up, "you have seriously got to wait for the signal."

"I second that," Zach concurred.

Francois ignored the two who had come to this struggle only so recently and charged ahead.

* * *

Forget a bell, Francois needed a freaking leash, Zach thought. The nearer they came to the castle, the less time the magnets had to deflect the bullets' path. Ronnie fell in behind him as the path carved ahead narrowed to single file only.

Francois hit the bridge at a run, crossing over the strangely empty moat.

Zach's shoulder twinged. Did a bullet hit him? Then, he felt a zap to his belly. What the…?

Below them, the moat glowed blue, and then crackled as bolts of electricity arced and jumped beneath their feet. Which would have been fine—except for the fact that tendrils of current were finding those microscopic metal ions Ronnie was talking about.

"The vests!" he yelled as he ripped his off.

Ronnie looked like she wanted to argue, but then she was zapped in the chest. The girl couldn't pull the vest off fast enough. "Fine. *Kevlar* next time."

The only one who didn't seem to mind—or even notice the problem—was Francois. Which was probably best, since the magnets seemed to be running out of juice, and those bullets were getting closer and closer.

Zach turned to Ronnie. "I don't think we can get much farther."

From her nod, Zach grabbed Francois by the collar and hauled him back. The guards at the gates grew bolder, stepping out from under the stone arch, shooting faster and faster. This had better work, or…Well, jumping into the moat was *not* an option.

Ronnie handed Zach what looked like a heavy pistol. He passed it to the Frenchman. "On my mark," Zach stated as Ronnie gave him his pistol. "And I mean, *on my mark*, Francois, shoot up."

The Frenchman seemed intent on charging straight into the castle, but even Francois must have sensed the firepower blocking his way.

"Three. Two. *One*."

Zach fired, grappling with the gun. A large spike shot out, and then broke apart, expanding into a three-point grappling hook. Next to him, Francois and Ronnie followed suit. They each hooked the zip line to their reinforced belts. Before the Hidden Hand could regroup, the zip line sped them up the wall. Rain, already wind-whipped, lashed into his eyes.

"Keep running!" Zach yelled as the magnets' pull suddenly increased. Ronnie was pushing them to the limit. His guns, and anything metal he carried, tugged him backward. Which meant his quads were doing overtime to keep up with the zip line.

The benefit, though, was not just bullets, but the Hidden Hand's guns were snatched from the men. The weapons flew across the field.

Finally the trio reached the top and flung themselves over the wall. But the magnetic pull was just as strong on the other side of the rampart. They were pinned by the very magnets they needed to use to keep bullets away. Men converged on their position, sans their guns. That didn't mean that the trio couldn't be physically overrun.

"Turn off!" Ronnie urged the device in her hand. "Come on, come on, come on!"

One of those "come ons" must have worked, because suddenly Zach could raise his gun. Ronnie pushed it down, though.

"No. Use these."

She tossed him a set of what looked like ninja stars. Trusting that they were so much more than just steel stars, Zach tossed them toward the rapidly approaching men.

Zach was worried his aim would be off. He shouldn't have been. The damn things must have been heat seeking as they changed directory on the fly, striking each of the men in the chest. Their adversaries stumbled to a stop in unison, clearly expecting to fall over dead.

Unfortunately, they did not.

Instead they regrouped, shouting their rage.

"Ronnie?"

"Wait for it…" she coaxed.

He brought his gun up, shoving Francois behind him, just in case. But Zach never should've doubted Ronnie. The men didn't charge three steps when the stars glowed a bright electric blue, and then Tasered the hell out of them. They dropped like spastic flies to the stone.

Ronnie pulled handful after handful of the stars from her bag and flung them down into the courtyard brimming with the enemy. "They've got biometric sensors," Ronnie explained as she threw more to the men below. "No sense in wasting the charge if they strike wood or metal."

No. No sense in that at *all*. Zach shook his head. He couldn't even imagine the R&D discussions she and Quirk had.

As the last of the men went down, Ronnie repositioned her grappling hook and placed it over the interior lip of the rampart.

"What are you doing?" he asked.

"Getting down?" Ronnie said with that cock of her head that made you feel like a little bit of an idiot.

Zach threw a thumb at Francois. "I don't know how much repelling experience Mr. Loubom has—"

Ronnie hit the switch on her zip line. "They are reversible." She went over the side and slowly walked down the wall. "See?"

Reversible zip lines. Damn if that woman didn't keep on surprising him.

* * *

Lino watched the security monitor as Francois's boots hit the courtyard's stone. Fury swirled over and around Lino, like one of the storm's waves. Had the castle's defenses been left to him, they would have not been so easily overcome. Lino's efforts to spread the plague had gone off with expert precision. He infected the entire world with the Black Death.

How little the commander of this garrison had to accomplish. Repulse three attackers. Deacon Havar had all of the funds, resources, and power to make that happen, yet here they stood, their inner wall breached.

Perhaps it would be too kind to allow Havar to die so swiftly. Perhaps they should give him antiserum, just enough to delay the bacteria's rampage and prolong the agonizing symptoms. God's wrath was a mighty one.

Lino felt a little more at peace with that thought.

"There's another one," a subordinate announced as a monitor blinked out then turned to a haze of static.

Down to only three working monitors, which Lino had no doubt would go down within minutes, Lino turned to leave. Granted, the woman was resourceful—but oh so brash. She might have found the outer defenses, clearly too reliant upon modern technology, easy to scale. However, the inner defenses? Those designed to keep any and all from the serum that could grant life or death? Those she would find not so easy to breach.

"Sir," the subordinate asked. "Where are you going?"

Lino did not bother to answer. If the man could not see God's vengeance reflected in Lino's posture, no words could ever make him understand.

CHAPTER 31

Plum Island
4:41 p.m., EST

"You know that I'm not the traitor," Devlin hissed as soon as Henderson walked out of the conference room.

Amanda cocked her head. "You're the one with the antibodies."

That shut the CIA liaison up.

She went back to correlating the data. With no new information from the CIA databank, Amanda wasn't quite sure what she could accomplish. However, it felt wrong to sit there doing nothing. What could she do besides just sit and watch a staticky television?

"I am telling you—I am *not* Hidden Hand." When Amanda ignored him, Devlin continued. "Since I was *not* vaccinated, there has got to be another scientific possibility for the antibodies. Damn it, Amanda, *think*."

She turned away from him. "So I suppose you were in Sri Lanka in 1996?"

"No," Devlin said, hanging his head. "I was in China at the time."

Amanda's head snapped around. "Where? *Exactly*?"

"Inner Manchuria," Devlin said narrowing his eyes. "Why?"

Crap. Amanda delved back into the CDC archives. "Did you get sick?"

"Sure. I mean, it's Asia. There's a bird, goat, pig flu going around twenty-four seven."

Yes, yes there was. However, in 1996, Amanda confirmed that there had been a minor outbreak of pneumonic plague.

"What?" Devlin pushed. "Why?"

Amanda turned back to him. "It took nearly three years to get the confirmation from the Chinese, but you were most likely exposed to the plague during your visit."

"Great!" Devlin said then frowned. "Then why didn't I get sick and die? Why didn't everyone there get sick and die?"

"Because," Amanda explained, "*Yersinia pestis* is nearly endemic there, infecting upwards of a thousand known cases per year. Occasionally it gets a head of steam and causes an outbreak, but it is a fairly attenuated strain."

Devlin shook his head. "You lost me, doc."

"The more a bacterium or virus goes through a host, it tends to become less and less virulent. Also, the population has more and more antibodies, and so becomes more and more resistant."

"That's where I got my antibodies, then? China?"

"Yes," Amanda admitted. "More than likely."

Devlin sighed heavily, dropping his chin to his chest. Amanda had truly believed the CIA liaison to be the Hidden Hand's mole. It had all fallen into place. No one else in the facility was healthy. Everyone was either dead or was staring down death on the near horizon.

"How about you untie me, then?" Devlin asked.

"Yeah, sorry about that," Amanda said as she knelt down, starting with his feet.

To her surprise, Devlin chuckled. "Just glad to know you aren't a traitor, either."

"So you aren't going to hit me over the head with a phone once I untie you?"

"No," Devlin said. "Definitely not."

"Amanda," Dr. Henderson said as he entered the conference room. "What are you doing?"

She stood, feeling silly, guilty, and downright stupid. "Devlin gained his immunity naturally. He wasn't vaccinated."

"I know," Henderson replied as he pulled a gun on them. "Because *I* am."

* * *

Ronnie paused as Zach opened the door to the Hidden Hand's dining hall. They had made it across the courtyard without incident. As she had hoped, Lino had put the bulk of his men on the wall and the courtyard. A show of force. A force that was now unconscious.

The three rushed inside as Zach closed and barred the door behind them. Ronnie wished she could make the sound of her footfalls disappear. In the cavernous hall, each step echoed off the high, stone walls. Even after seeing the massive dining hall on the 3-D image, nothing could prepare her for the actual room. It truly did seem right out of the fourteen hundreds.

Row after row of thick, wooden tables and benches stretched on for what seemed forever. Thick, woven tapestries covered the walls. Each one depicted a scene from the Bible. Clearly not the part of the Bible that talked about turning the other cheek. No, these wall hangings were the hellfire-and-brimstone kind. Demons ate the hearts out of nonbelievers, and God was portrayed as, um, kind of a jerk.

Above their heads flew banners with angelic coats of arms for each table.

Ronnie drew in a slow breath, trying not to let the stillness overwhelm her. She'd almost rather be fighting off an army rather than walking through this dining hall, seeing the hard-core preparations the Hidden Hand had made. This wasn't just some "hey, let's destroy the world" plot. These people had thought this through. They had seating arrangements already figured out for their new world order.

She typed a command into the air, switching her focus back to her cracked lens. The screen was fuzzy and fritzed every two seconds, but gave her enough information to know that the entire castle's surveillance was down. Which on one hand was great. The enemy couldn't see them. On the other hand, they couldn't see what in the hell Lino was up to.

Sure, they had knocked out over thirty men in the courtyard. That still left well over two dozen guards who could be lurking around every corner. Ronnie didn't realize how nervous she was until Zach's hand found hers. He gave it a squeeze. Which was helpful, since they just walked past a full suit of armor. Each time they passed one of them, Ronnie held her breath, half expecting it to jump out at her.

Quirk, on the other hand, would have been admiring the *Game of Thrones* vibe of the dining hall. More than likely, he would have talked the pilot into trying on one of the suits of armor. But Quirk wasn't here. And who knew what happened to the pilot? They had planned on radio silence until the vaccine chamber was breached. So as long as her KeKe-G glasses were interfaced with her laptop, she held onto hope. It could be a false hope, but it was a hope, nonetheless.

"Isn't it strange that we have gotten this far unmolested?" Francois asked.

Zach looked at her as well.

Ugh. Didn't they know you didn't jinx something like this? There were times during a cyber breach that you just strolled along. Of course, that usually meant that they had something nasty waiting for you on the other side.

"My guess?" she said. "They never expected their shell to be penetrated. Which is why I angled us toward the more social areas of the castle. Away from their security hub."

Zach frowned. "Really? That's what you are going with? That the Hidden Hand didn't want to get the dining hall messy with our blood?"

Damn Zach and his intuition.

"Or..." Ronnie said as they neared the large, thick, wooden door that led out of the dining hall.

"Or?"

Even Francois seemed interested in her answer. Great time for him to tune in.

"Well...or there are twenty men on the other side of that door armed with automatic machine guns?"

Cocking his head to the side, Zach asked, "And which one do you think is more likely?"

"Oh, the twenty armed gunmen. Totally," Ronnie replied.

* * *

Zach gripped his weapon. One gun against twenty? Francois *had* picked up a spear and still had on Ronnie's super special bulletproof vest, but still. Neither of them would last ten seconds once the door was opened.

Ronnie had to have a plan, didn't she?

"Hon?" he asked as she slid her gloved fingers over a statue set in an alcove. It was hard to pay attention to what she was doing, given the fact that Zach could practically see the gunmen on the other side of the stout door. Waiting for him to throw the crossbar up and step into the kill zone that was the hallway. He had a few flashbang grenades. However, he was hoping to keep hold of those for an emergency.

It truly was sad when twenty armed gunmen just didn't quite seem like the emergency it used to. That was, of course, until the door opened.

"Babe?"

"Got it," Ronnie said pulling the statue of a monk off its pedestal. Beneath the wood carving sat a very sophisticated-looking keypad.

That was the Hidden Hand. All medieval on the outside, and all techie on the inside.

"And that opens...?"

"Give me a second, and I'll show you," she said as she typed into thin air. Zach knew that the keys were motion activated, and she could see the results of her efforts in her glasses, but it was still a little freaky to watch.

Francois went to open his mouth, then closed it again, eyeing beneath the door, where shadows definitely moved. It seemed the natives were getting restless. He glanced to

Ronnie who was busy biting her lip. Zach didn't bother to ask the ETA on her project. She would be done when she was done.

He backed up, putting the automatic weapon to his shoulder. The Frenchman too retreated from the door. Soon, the option to toss a flashbang would be gone.

Lightning flashed, illuminating the grand dining hall as if a thousand candles blazed. Thunder rumbled, shaking the stained glass windows in their frame. Even the weather seemed impatient with their progress.

Zach flexed and unflexed his fingers. A loud *clunk* sounded. Zach braced, ready for the horde to come through that door.

"Well?" Ronnie asked. "Did you want to get out of here or what?"

He checked over his shoulder. Sure enough, a passage had opened *behind* them. "How?"

Ronnie shrugged. "They tried to hide it, but you know, I'm *me*."

From anyone else, that would have been pure arrogance. From Ronnie? Just the facts, ma'am.

"They're opening it," Francois said, pointing to the metal spike peeking through the crack in the dining hall door, lifting the crossbar.

"Then let's not be here," Zach suggested.

Zach made sure that Francois and Ronnie were through the door before he entered the narrow passageway. The hidden door smoothly and silently closed behind them.

"Could you smash that?" Ronnie asked as she pointed to the control panel.

Zach was more than happy to use the butt of his assault rifle to demolish the circuitry. A loud crash came from the dining hall, and then the unmistakable clatter of gunfire.

"This way," Ronnie urged him to the staircase…leading up.

"But I thought we needed to get *down* to the vault."

Ronnie indicated the door. "Be my guest to try and get down that extremely well- protected stairwell. For me, though, I'm going to go up to see what the hell they spent so much tech to hide, then follow the secret passage up and over the dining hall and come down behind all those armed men."

Good thing he knew that she'd say no to a kiss right about now; otherwise, he would have planted one on her right this second.

* * *

Amanda felt her strength seep away as she stared at Dr. Henderson, the director of the Plum Island zoonotic disease research facility. Make that the Hidden Hand's mole.

"How?" she choked out.

The elderly man smiled like the gentleman he was not, as he picked at one of his boils. Only it wasn't a boil—it was a fake. He lifted up the boil, revealing perfectly normal skin beneath it. Henderson took in a deep breath with a single rattle.

"That is how you fake the plague," he remarked, seeming surprisingly chipper. Why shouldn't he, though? He'd just won. "And I already warned our Northernmost Province of your friends' arrival. They were more than ready for them."

Amanda's heart rate accelerated. As much of a lying bastard as Henderson was, he still gave away some truth. So Quirk and Ronnie had made it to a vaccine stronghold. And since Henderson only implied that they were dead, Amanda believed very much that they were still alive.

Which meant there was hope. Which meant she needed to find a way to stay out of that gun's way.

Unfortunately, Henderson leveled the weapon at her. "It truly was amazing watching you work, Amanda. I should have shut you down long ago, but you were just so brilliant. I suppose you won't join us?"

As much as she wanted to lie, Amanda knew he would never believe her. Better to go out with her conscious intact.

"No," she answered.

"Too bad," Henderson said as he cocked the gun.

Amanda flinched, waiting for the shot, when Devlin hurled himself over in his chair, knocking into Henderson.

"Run!" the CIA liaison screamed.

She bolted to the side, angling for the door. Henderson righted himself and shot at Devlin. Blood gushed from the side of his head.

Without prompting, her feet got moving, streaking past the director and out into the hall. Shots zinged past her as she made for the stairs. Head pounding, lungs burning, and her muscles complaining, Amanda ran for her life.

* * *

As the trio went up the staircase, the noise of the calamity below subsided. The gunmen in the dining hall must not have known about the passage they now fled. Which only inflamed

Francois's curiosity. What could the Hidden Hand hold so dear they did not tell their own men about it?

Francois's foot stumbled on one of the steps. The near dark conditions were not very helpful to aged eyes. The FBI agent grabbed his elbow, steadying him.

"Just a few more."

Ahead of them, Ronnie opened a door, but did not go through it. "Oh my…"

Zach rushed forward with his gun up, yet even he stumbled to a stop. "What the…?"

Francois cautiously took the next three steps to join his companions. Now he could understand their shock. He might have been equally stuporous had he not had this scene drilled into his head since childhood.

Before them lay what seemed to be the perfect recreation of the khan's great tent. Silk lined the walls and ceiling, making it seem as if they were out upon the Steppes. Rugs covered the stone floor, so thick they made you believe that there was grass beneath the wool. The attention to detail, though, was not why the others had faltered.

It was the mummified bodies positioned around the tent. On the throne sat the great- grandson of Genghis Khan. His serving women huddled in the corner. The only two bodies standing were the Hidden Hand's master, and, standing before the khan's throne was, of course, the boy who killed the world, Travanti. Even now, in death, his pale, pale blond hair shone against his withered features.

The Hidden Hand sanctified this moment—when they sealed their first victory by convincing the khan to throw his infected dead over the fort's walls. An act that set human civilization back centuries, if not millennia. But their plan had worked—perhaps better than even they had imagined. The devastation that the Black Death wrought took its toll on even the Hidden Hand.

They did not seem to notice the irony that the boy-man Travanti actually died of the plague. Their medieval attempts at vaccination were somewhat rudimentary at best.

Francois was ashamed to say he did not denounce and reject the Hidden Hand when he learned of their plan to scourge the earth with the Black Death. Or when he learned they would take the coward's way out and receive the inoculation themselves. No, it had been when he discovered that Travanti had died only a few weeks later of the plague. As a matter of fact, much of the Hidden Hand leadership fell.

The news had struck Francois like a bolt from the sky. As if God himself had shaken Francois to bring sense into him. The Hidden Hand had unleashed hell on earth, yet it had consumed nearly all of them. Their attempt to create a new world order was shattered by the very plague they let loose to destroy the *old* world order.

Suddenly, in that moment of realization, the Hidden Hand's power seemed so very petty. Children playing at a game best left to God. The width and breadth of the Hidden Hand's cruelty and delusion became crystalline. From that spark of clarity, Francois had spent every waking second, and many in his dreams, working to undo the Hidden Hand's scheme.

And here he was—standing within the recreation of the cult's most sacred moment.

Francois took his spear and slashed viciously at the silk.

"How could I guess you would come to defile the womb?"

The sinister sweetness told Francois who spoke the words long before the curtain parted to reveal the latest golden-haired child of the Hidden Hand.

Lino.

* * *

Zach's gun went up, but Ronnie knocked it back down. "No."

Lino cocked his head. "How did you know?"

Ronnie had absolutely no idea what the guy was talking about, but every minute they were debating, they were alive. Normally she would have had faith that Quirk was listening and researching what in the hell Lino was talking about, but now, she was on her own.

"You wouldn't have walked in here if you didn't have countermeasures," she answered, trying to exude a confidence she did not have. Not while her mind whirred. Out of all the places in this damned castle, how did he find them?

The man who wanted to kill off three-quarters of the world's population smiled that really obnoxious smile of his. "The lightest element, yet so very effective."

Zach clutched his gun. "What *is* he talking about?"

"Hydrogen," Ronnie answered at least reasoning through one of the variables. "Hydrogen gas, to be specific."

"Wouldn't we smell it?" Zach pressed, clearly itching to shoot the man who stood before them.

Ronnie shook her head. The Hidden Hand were deranged, but had some serious scientists on their side. "No. It is an odorless, colorless gas that is possibly the most explosive in the world."

Lino, almost graciously, nodded. "It started leaking into the room when you overrode the lock."

Damn it. Of course the freaking Hidden Hand would have physical countermeasures. This was, after all, their freaky, secret shrine featuring mummies.

"One shot," Lino stated. "Actually, one little spark will set off an explosion even greater than a grenade."

He wasn't exaggerating. Not in the least. Even at 4 percent concentration of hydrogen in the air...

"Who does that?" Zach asked.

Well, um, Ronnie didn't bother to voice that Quirk had installed such a system into their latest safe house in Micronesia. Of course, theirs would only have incapacitated the intruder.

"If it's odorless and colorless," Zach said slowly through his clenched teeth. Not shooting Lino seemed to be taking its toll. "How in the hell do we know that he isn't bluffing?"

Lino, however, did not seem to be bluffing at all. "Look at your fingernails." Since Zach wasn't about drop his stare from Lino, Ronnie glanced down at his hand.

Sure enough, the tips of his fingers were blue. There was adequate hydrogen in the room's air to start dislodging oxygen from their red cells. Forget about not being able to fire a gun—or even risk metal hitting stone that would throw off a spark that would ignite the room. Soon, they would get dizzy and disoriented, and then suffocate. Hydrogen caused death about ten times faster than carbon monoxide.

Zach, though, had a distinctly different take on their predicament. "Then the prick can't come after us, either. A kind of hydrogen stalemate."

"Ah, but I have a way out," Lino grinned as the door behind them latched closed. "I wanted to stay to watch you slowly suffocate. To watch God take from you his gift and sanctify our mission."

Ronnie's head was spinning, but she didn't think it was from the hydrogen.

"I say we take the chance," Zach suggested, finger on the trigger.

"Um, remember the Hindenburg?" The FBI agent's eyes flicked over to her as she continued. "Now imagine that explosion contained by stone."

Zach was a bright enough guy to realize that wouldn't be good. At least not yet.

The entire surface of her glasses, even the cracked parts, displayed every fact regarding hydrogen. She'd never missed Quirk more. He would have had this data down cold. Come on, the gas that exploded on the Hindenburg? That was Quirk's wheelhouse.

* * *

Zach noticed Ronnie's fingers stop their frantic air-typing as her face clouded over. Then, like a binary switch, those digits flew again.

"Francois?" she asked.

"Yes?" the Frenchman responded glaring the whole while at Lino.

"How about you turn that spear around and go at him with the wooden end?"

The older man looked at Ronnie as though he was surprised that he'd been the one tapped. She nodded. Francois then fixed Lino with a vicious smile. The Hidden Hand's golden-haired boy didn't seem any too pleased, but equally seemed determined to not be intimidated.

"A single spark," Lino said, low and slow.

Guess Lino wasn't quite as ready to go up in flames as one might assume a hard-core "bring on the Apocalypse" kind of guy would be. Was Ronnie trying to leverage this fact? Or did she have something else in mind?

Francois didn't seem to be thinking past "go at him," though. However, the Frenchman did have enough presence of mind to turn the spear around as he charged Lino. Grabbing a piece of firewood from the cold brazier, Lino defended himself, clearly trying to angle back to the door from which he arrived.

The two men struck and parried, dancing cautiously on the other side of the room.

"What's the exit strategy?" Zach asked as Francois was knocked back. The guy had the heart of a lion, only he didn't quite understand that he wasn't exactly in full-maned form anymore.

Ronnie got that look in her eye. "We are going to make some rain."

As per usual, Zach had absolutely no idea what she meant, and as per usual, he was just going to ride it out with her.

"Open my pack and grab the largest piece of equipment in there."

Keeping his gun aimed at the fighting men, Zach knelt, and, one-handed, opened the bag. "What does it look like?"

"Doesn't matter. It just matters that it is big," Ronnie said as she typed.

Um, that made no sense whatsoever. What did, though, anymore? Zach fished around and came up with an octagonal-shaped doohickey device. He couldn't even guess at its use.

"Got it."

"Great," Ronnie said glancing over. "Open the plastic latch, but don't open it, okay?"

Zach wasn't so sure it was okay. Following Ronnie's instruction meant holstering his gun. And with the crack of wood and groan of impact, he wasn't so sure how much longer Francois could keep Lino at bay.

"Kind of time sensitive here," Ronnie reminded him.

He had trusted her so far. If she wanted a plastic box opened, he might as well open it. "You going to tell me what we are doing?"

"Toss it up there," Ronnie responded. "Have it smash against the stone as high up against the wall as possible."

"But—"

"On my count. Five…"

* * *

Francois doubled over as Lino brought to bear his wooden log. Francois's reflexes were not what they once were, and this young man before him was fresh to his strength. Which is why Francois allowed himself to stay doubled over longer than need be. There was prowess and then there was wisdom. Let the young whelp bask in his power. Let him overreach.

"You know what they knew?" Lino said, circling Francois. "They knew you to be a Judas. They followed you to find the other betrayers."

Francois set his jaw against such petty manipulations.

"Four!" Ronnie shouted.

He did not know what the woman spoke of. It did not matter. Ending Lino's life was his only concern.

"Batisk. Rommey. Floret," Lino went on to list Francois's contacts. "Dead because you were too much of a simpleton to know the Hand allowed you to live only so that you might lead us to them all."

Blinking, Francois tried to deny the truth in the young man's words. It could not be. They had been so very careful. And after Francois had left the Hidden Hand, he had been so bent on finding all the paintings that he hadn't given it a second thought to the others. Francois had just assumed that they disapproved of his seeking the angels' paintings on his own. To know that they all died because of him?

"Three!"

The woman's countdown mattered not to Francois. The time to feign weakness was over. Francois cut up with his staff. The wood shaft should have connected with Lino's chin, but the young man sprang backward, bringing his own heavy log down upon Francois's shoulder.

Ten years ago Francois would have not have fallen to his knees. Twenty years ago Francois could have dodged the blow. Thirty years ago Lino would not still have been able to strike the blow.

As it was, Francois slammed into the floor. Only the thick carpet beneath his knees broke his fall. His mangled arm let loose of the spear as it tumbled beside him.

"Two!"

Francois looked up into Lino's hard, dispassionate eyes. Even with all his errors and the blood upon his hands,

Francois realized that he would have done it all over again, without hesitation.

* * *

"One!" Ronnie yelled to Zach, and then turned to Francois. "Get down!"

Zach's throw catapulted the Cipher-Meister, Quirk's mastermind, toward the ceiling. Damn, that guy had an arm on him. The case flung open before hitting the stone. The plastic shattered on impact, exposing the platinum-coated electronics within.

She grabbed Zach's wrist, dragging him down to rug level as the air sucked upward, creating a wind that lifted her hair.

"What's happening?" Zach asked, but Ronnie couldn't answer him. Not with Lino about to clobber Francois.

"Shoot!"

"But you said—"

She didn't have time to explain that hydrogen was lighter than air. As the internal vortex strengthened, she simply pointed to Lino.

And even through his doubts, Zach raised his gun and fired, clipping Lino in the arm. The spark from the firing pin ignited a nearly invisible flame that climbed to the ceiling as the air drafted it up, catching the tent on fire. That white-hot hydrogen flame crackled along the edge of the fabric, sparking a yellow-orange fire. This conflagration stayed suspended midair caught by the updraft of the hydrogen flame.

Suddenly the wind shifted, pulling the flaming cloth toward the opposite wall. Lino must have exited, for he was nowhere to be seen. Francois was on the floor, but Ronnie couldn't tell if it was because he was following her orders or if he had collapsed there.

"We need to get out of here!" Zach yelled over the growing din of wind and fire.

"No!" she shouted back, tugging him to the carpet. "We've got to stay down!"

Even though it was becoming harder and harder to breathe, Ronnie calculated in her head exactly how much oxygen this rescue was going to consume. Would she save them from burning alive, only to kill them through suffocation?

Zach pulled her close, wrapping his arms around her as the fire danced and snapped above their heads. Even the plastic case hovered near the ceiling as sparks shot out of the electronics.

Come on, come on, come on.

Between the hydrogen displacing oxygen and the fire downright consuming it, they didn't have much air left to breathe.

"What is happening?" Zach asked.

"Nothing, damn it," Ronnie answered. "The platinum in the electronics should be acting as a catalyst to—"

Then an explosion rang out above, shattering the case. Anything that wasn't platinum fell to the floor, but all of those tiny platinum-coated parts? Those stayed suspended, helping hydrogen to bond with oxygen.

Mirroring the storm outside, thunder clapped overhead as water poured down.

"How?" Zach asked, trying to catch his breath as the oxygen level lowered even more.

"'H' two 'O,'" Ronnie commented. "Hydrogen just needed a little help to get together with oxygen, to create water."

"That's why it's harder to breathe?" Zach commented, gulping for air now.

Ronnie nodded, trying to conserve her own air. They just needed to ride out this phase until the combustible hydrogen was consumed then they could—

Without warning, Zach rose up, aiming his gun at the stained glass window. "Let's get some air in here."

"No!" Ronnie shouted, but it was too late.

Yes, Zach's shot blew out the window, and yes, the remaining hydrogen was sucked outside. Unfortunately, because of the built-up pressure, Zach too was pulled to the window. Ronnie grabbed hold of the heavy, gilded throne as the khan's body was lifted up and out of the broken pane.

Zach tried to scramble for purchase as he involuntarily headed for the window. She clutched the hem of his pants, but the wet fabric slipped through her fingers. Their eyes met as he gripped the broken edges of the window. If there were any way humanly possible, he would stay.

Unfortunately, physics dictated that he should go.

"Zach!" she cried as he vanished out the window in a final gush of air.

Tears streaming down her face, Ronnie held tight to the throne even as it was raised a few inches off the floor. Then with a *thud* it came back down. Rising to her feet, she rushed over to the window.

First Quirk. Now Zach.

CHAPTER 32

Cutler, Maine
5:01 p.m., EST

Zach felt raindrops hit his face, then splash off. The rain was cold—icy cold—yet Zach didn't seem to mind. Weird. All he knew was that not just every joint in his body ached, but every attachment to every joint seared with pain as well. And what in the hell had happened to his kidneys?

Something scratchy but soft lay underneath him. He probably should check what it was, but hey. He deserved a few moments, right? Zach let the raindrops fall and splash and fall and splash.

Then a voice, sounding distant yet urgent, called his name. "Zach!" A woman's voice. A determined voice.

Slowly, he opened his eyes and peered through a hole in the wooden roof to find a woman leaning over a stony ledge. He smiled. She burst into tears.

"Hang on!" she yelled. Why was she crying? Then she turned to the room behind her. "No! Francois! Don't leave without me."

The woman turned back to Zach. "I'll be right down."

"It's okay," he said even though he wasn't quite certain that was true. "Go after him."

"Are you sure?" she asked from the second-story window.

Even though it made his head spin, Zach sat up, at least partially. "I'm sure."

She gave him a radiant smile, despite the tears, and then bolted from view. He was sad to see her go and had a hard time remembering her face. He loved her. Of that there was no doubt, yet it felt as if he had only met her a few days ago.

Again. Weird.

Still, he could feel her lips against his. Wait. Could he remember that? They had kissed, right? With all of this passion built up inside, they had to have consummated it, didn't they?

That mystery could probably wait, though, since his priority might be to figure out exactly why he had fallen out of a castle window into an apparent hay shed. He might want to start there.

Rolling to his side, he stopped short. There lay a mummified corpse. A corpse with a crown.

Memories flooded back as Zach pushed away from the dead man.

Khan. Genghis's grandson if he wasn't mistaken. Who died from the plague. Urgency fueled Zach's muscles. Time to get the hell out of here. But another sparkle of gold caught his eye. A gilded dagger. How many innocents had died by that blade? Given the fact he'd lost all his weapons, Zach didn't have time to be choosy.

Taking the dagger off the corpse's belt, Zach rolled out of the hay and onto the slick paving stones. The rain now beat down, streaking down his face, dripping from his nose.

Things were still a little hazy, but he knew one thing for certain.

Ronnie needed his help.

* * *

Ronnie raced down the passage, trying to catch up with Francois. Forget bell or leash, the guy needed a freaking cattle prod. To make her leave Zach like that? Sprawled out, who knew how injured? But not even her feelings, her big time feelings for Zach, could matter now that they were so close.

Sprinting, she heard Francois going up another flight of stairs. Normally, she would ask why in the hell he was going up the stairs instead of down them toward the vaccine vault, but she already knew why. Lino.

The Hidden Hand's boy toy. The plan had been to draw him out, but not quite this far out, and certainly not up.

And why in the hell couldn't Francois trust her? She had a plan. Yes, it was dangerous, and yes, given every statistic and probability, it was going to fail spectacularly, but which of her plans didn't have those riders?

Francois's lust for revenge overshadowed their need to secure the vaccine.

Ronnie wished she could say she was running after him because of some warm connection. Like he had become her father figure or something, but the fact of the matter was, she feared he would take on Lino and succumb too quickly. They needed Lino distracted until they made their move.

Which had been explained to Francois like ten times. Clearly, Francois did not understand exactly how hard it was to break into one of the world's most safeguarded mainframes while running down a stone hallway.

Ronnie checked her lenses. Her hack was nearly complete. Well, it looked nearly complete. She'd never really gotten this far before to know where "complete" lived. She only needed a few more minutes to be sure.

Then a cry. Angry, pained, and aged, echoed off the walls.

Francois must have found Lino.

* * *

Lino stalked along the edge of the roof, eager to meet this betrayer hand to hand. So much preparation had been made for this day. None could spoil it. God's word would be uncontroversial. Who could challenge the Hidden Hand once it completed its stunning act of faith?

Francois, less sure-footed than before, stepped onto the roof of the castle. The area had originally been fortified as a helipad, but the men had taken to using the flat surface as a training ground. Given the lack of retaining wall and sheer drop, three stories down, the danger added some excitement to morning exercises.

Lino knew each and every crack in the stone underfoot. Each spur of rock that might trip one unawares. And what of his opponent?

While fury seemed to burn in the traitor's veins, exhaustion etched his features. Long, gray hair matted by rain framed a craggy visage. Wrinkled and old. Burnt out by a life dedicated to thwarting God's will. To think that this feeble, failing, faltering man had once occupied Lino's position. No wonder the Hidden Hand's success was only borne now.

Still, Francois strode toward him as the woman lingered in the doorway. Once he dispatched the old man, Lino had a delicious plan awaiting her. He might be able to be lenient with Francois. The burden of carrying God's will weighed heavily. Most could not bear it without cracking. For Brother Loubom, Lino would send him swiftly to his maker. The woman, though? The infidel? She would feel God's wrath… personally, and intimately.

But first, he must dispatch the old man.

Francois spoke over his shoulder to the woman. "May I use the steel end?"

"Go for it," the woman remarked as she typed against the stone wall.

The old man tossed the spear, catching it in midair, then tucking the shaft under his arm, preparing to strike. Lino would need no weapon other than his hands. He allowed Francois to lunge and commit to strike. Stepping to the side, Lino not only avoided the attack, he brought his elbow down at the bend of Francois's arm, knocking the spear to the side.

A perfect opening. Spinning, Lino brought his hand and base of the palm forward, slamming into Francois's solar plexus.

Only, instead of the old man dropping to the rain-soaked ground, it was Lino who had to stumble back.

* * *

Francois looked down at the vest Ronnie had provided. A perfect handprint was at the center, etched in gray metal. The fabric had become steel under Lino's thrust. A blow that should have shattered Francois's sternum nearly broke Lino's hand.

For perhaps the first time in his young life, Lino's face registered shock. His eyes dilated as he clutched his hand to his chest. So the whelp did feel pain. Francois pounced as Lino shook out the injury.

Francois stabbed forward with the spear, trying to gouge the wound from the stone knife. However, he missed Lino's midriff. Instead, he only tore his clothes. As Lino pivoted away, Francois yanked the spear back. The sharp edge was equally capable of cutting on the way back. This time the blade caught skin, tearing a thin line of red across Lino's side.

The boy's head snapped around, his glare piercing.

Not feeling quite so immortal?

The boy was nothing if not persistent, though. Lino twisted, bringing his leg around, slamming his foot into Francois's knee. The joint buckled, forcing Francois to use the spear as a crutch.

A backhanded slap from Lino split Francois's lip. Blood spewed across the slick stone. Francois brought the spear around low, trying to trip Lino, but the younger man jumped over the wooden handle then danced out of range.

Nearly panting, Francois let the cold rain soak into his skin. He had not come up here to this rooftop thinking he would ever leave the castle. All Lino had to do was outwit Francois's aged joints.

So with each swipe, Francois forced Lino closer and closer to the ledge.

To end one, the two must die.

* * *

Ronnie typed like a madwoman. Really, really mad. As rain streaked her glasses, adding a watercolor effect to the screens, Ronnie cracked the last firewall. She was in. She had the controls. Or at least, she thought she did. Once she rang this bell, there would be no un-ringing it. She would reveal to Lino and the Hidden Hand her entire plan.

If Quirk wasn't doing what he needed to do…If Zach wasn't in position…If she did this and it didn't work…

Well, the world would *end*. No, it was worse than that. The world would descend into the medieval hellish vision of the Hidden Hand. It was never good when you seriously considered that the dead could turn out to be the lucky ones.

So intent on her next course of action, Ronnie didn't hear the shift in the fighting.

"*Pendre!*" Francois called out.

Ronnie turned to find Lino leaping toward her. The rain and wind blew his linen jacket open. And she would have considered his graceful movements beautiful if he had not been leaping at her.

Ronnie tried to get out of the way, but slipped on the wet rock. It all felt like slow motion. Lino's look of pure hatred. Her frozen muscles. Even if she green-lit her plan right this second, it couldn't save her—or the world.

Then Francois was there, tackling the younger man. The two men hit the stone right in front of her. Ronnie scampered out of the way as Lino sprang up with Francois, rising more slowly.

"Run!" Ronnie yelled. Francois's part was over. Now it was up to her.

Either the older man did not hear, or chose to ignore her. He lunged at Lino, who easily avoided the strike, then brought his arm down, breaking the spear in half. Catching the blade in, Lino lashed out.

"*No!*" Ronnie yelled as the blade drove deep into Francois's stomach.

The old man clutched at the spear, almost seeming to want to keep it in his abdomen, but Lino jerked the blade out. The older man teetered, and then fell, landing facedown. The rocks around Francois pooled with bright red blood.

Lino did not even try to hide the savage pleasure he took from killing an old man. He stood in the downpour, spear tip pointed toward her.

"How does it feel to know that you are defeated?" Lino asked.

Ronnie tore her eyes away from Francois. She could do nothing for him but finish their shared goal. Get the vaccine. Save the world.

"Defeated?" Ronnie asked, typing again. "Um, awkward. We are on the cusp of victory."

Lino stepped toward her as she stepped away. "You will never get to the vaccine repository."

"Me? No. Zach? No," Ronnie said as she hit her earpiece. "Quirk?"

"Yes?" a rather annoyed voice said into her ear.

She'd never been so glad to hear her prickly assistant before.

* * *

Quirk shoved on the metal case, trying to get it through the hole he'd cut in the limestone. The damn thing was an inch wider than the stupid opening.

"Um, did you actually want something, Ronnie? Because I am a little busy here."

Leave it Ronnie to want to chat just when he was about to get the hell out of Dodge with the vaccines and antiserum. He looked back at the rows upon rows of refrigeration units that lay in the subterranean chamber. The Hidden Hand was ready to inoculate a whole bunch of new followers—that was for sure.

He was supposed to grab as many cases as he could, but the one thing they couldn't predict was how large the special carrying cases would be. They had assumed standard briefcase size. Instead, the Hidden Hand had, as always, gone jumbo. How the hell was he going to get the vials out?

Quirk peered through the opening he'd blasted. Not bad, although he probably shouldn't give up his day job. And he didn't have time to set more charges.

Stepping to the side, his wet suit squeaked as he tried once again to get the entire case through. It was futile, though. Sighing, and glad that Ronnie could hear his distress, Quirk opened the case and removed the smaller plastic cases.

"I expected a slightly warmer response to the fact that I was, in fact, still alive."

* * *

Ronnie was ecstatic Quirk wasn't just alive but as whiny as ever. The only problem with showing her assistant her full relief was the minor detail that Lino stalked her. She needed to keep him distracted for just a few moments longer.

Lino tossed the spearhead from hand to hand. "You think with your degrees and your science to be above God's will."

She kept pace with Lino, moving in a clockwise fashion. A slow dance that would have been sure to end in her rather quick death, if, you know, she wasn't *her*. Ronnie just needed to keep that blade away from her neck for a bit longer.

Data flowed down her glasses on the left and angelic script flowed down the right. Somehow science and the divine were going to have to get along for at least a few seconds.

"You realize your problem with this whole medieval part two thing, right?" she baited him. Hopefully, she was keeping him more interested in her words than in her jugular. "Each castle, like each firewall, has its back door. Its fatal flaw."

Lino's smile only grew. "And you think you've found mine?"

"Oh, yeah," Ronnie smiled right back. "We are walking off with your vaccine as we speak."

His eyes flickered across her features as a frown settled. "Never."

"The cavern?" Ronnie prompted. "The airtight, surrounded by rock, theoretically impenetrable, cavern?"

Lino gripped the spear shaft, his boastful twirling meeting its end. Rain beat down upon both of them. The wind threatened to blow them both off the side, yet each stood rooted in place.

"How," he hissed.

Ronnie shrugged, even though she impressed herself with the plan. "The sea caves." She looked out over the castle's wall to the raging sea beyond. The base of that sheer cliff was pocked with small alcoves created by millennia of battering waves. "It was only a matter of some properly positioned C4 to break through into the vault."

"All this was a ruse, then?" Lino asked, picking up the pace again. "You pretended to assault the upper layers of the castle to throw us off the scent of your man down below?"

Not wanting to look like she was gloating, she only nodded rather than rub his nose in it.

"So clever," Lino stated. "Yet ever so predictable."

It was Ronnie's turn to study Lino's features. What in the hell did he mean?

"Uh-oh," Quirk said into her ear.

"Uh-oh, what-o?" Ronnie asked, not really wanting to know the answer.

* * *

Quirk gulped as three gunmen entered the room. This was not part of Ronnie's plan. The men were dressed up all snazzy in their medieval attire. Kind of like being assaulted by people in a very mean Renaissance fair…in a mad scientist's lair. Clearly, they had orders not to attack so close to the precious vaccine vaults, but how long would that last?

"I guess we must have triggered some kind of alarm," Quirk said into his mic.

Ronnie didn't respond. She didn't have to. He knew her too well.

Either she pulled something out of the hat, like right now, or they were all dead.

At the least I got to meet the pilot, Quirk thought.

With a sigh, he waited for Ronnie's response. That woman had better live up to all the Robin Hood hacker hype. Otherwise, he was seriously going to haunt her in the next life and beyond. *Way* beyond.

* * *

Zach held the man in a chokehold, waiting until he fell unconscious. Taking advantage of the chaos in the courtyard, Zach backed another step into the stoop. Even with the disarray as the men roused from their Tasing, looking about as sure of themselves as Zach, it wouldn't take them long to spot the guy in the fatigues. Spot him, and then kill him.

Hence, the guy in a chokehold. Finally the man slumped, unconscious. Rapidly Zach stripped the man of his medieval-style uniform and donned it himself. Although from the plain tan color to lack of insignia, Zach had nabbed himself a page or squire. Not great.

How was he going to break into the security room as a lowly page?

Lowly or not, he needed to head across the courtyard and make his way into the upper turret. Zach wasn't exactly sure what he was supposed to do in the security room. That part of the plan was still a little vague. Actually, a lot was vague. The only thing that stood out in sharp relief in Zach's mind was the look of relief on Ronnie's face. That was going to just have to get him through everything else.

Stepping out from the stoop, Zach was met with a lot more activity than a few seconds ago. Men were regrouping into their squads or whatever knights called themselves. He'd better hightail it.

"You!" a shout called from behind.

Zach was loath to see who called him, but with dozens of armed men between him and the tower, he couldn't exactly make a run for it. Turning on the heel of his leather boot, Zach faced the man who had flagged him down. This one was dressed in full silver armor with a bright red cape flowing behind him. Okay, so that's what a knight was supposed to look like.

The guy didn't even give Zach the once-over. He handed him a thick parchment with a wax seal. Zach recognized the symbol as one of the angelic script. "Take this immediately to the war room."

Zach accepted the scroll.

"Make haste!" the knight barked.

"Yes, sir," Zach said, and then thought better of it. "My lord. I mean, my liege."

The guy must have thought Zach's awkwardness was still from the Tasing, for the knight grabbed him by both shoulders and gave them an urgent squeeze. "Godspeed to you."

As Zach set off, unnoticed by the growing throng of guards, he realized that maybe being a page wasn't such a bad thing, after all.

* * *

Lino slowed his pace, savoring the startled-doe look in the whore's eyes. Her soaked garments hung from her frame like ratty doll's clothing. Truly, she seemed just another cog in the wheel now. No arrogance or bravado.

He took a step closer, but she did not take one back. The distance they'd kept was melting beneath the downpour. Lino stepped forward again. Now he could see the details of her anguish. The lines that crept out from under the lenses, the deep furrow of her brow.

The spearhead felt good in his hand. The blade was stained with Brother Loubom's blood. Soon, another's blood would anoint the sharp edge. This average, broken spear would find a place in the Hidden Hand's new shrine. A legacy to Lino's contribution to a world ruled by God's mighty fist.

Was that a twitch of her lip? He glanced down to her hands. Those fingers, even though down at her side in apparent defeat, still flexed.

What was the heretic up to? Or did it matter? He would finish her before she could cast her digital magic.

"You will feel the heavens' wrath," Lino sneered as he took another step.

"Actually?" Ronnie said, not sounding cowed at all. "You'd best be the one to maybe watch your back."

Lino followed her gaze up the black tumbling clouds over them. From the bruised sky, a beam shot through, hitting the castle's edge, and then sweeping toward them. He retreated from the laser that cut the stone like butter.

"Guess Reagan got some things right."

* * *

Ronnie watched the blank expression on Lino's face. Guess the Hidden Hand wasn't big on US history. Lino truly looked at her as though she'd actually performed magic.

But she couldn't pay too much attention to the guy, since keeping that "Star Wars" laser turned on and *on-track* took some doing. No wonder they couldn't get the damned thing

CAROLYN MCCRAY

to work. It was like trying to herd a thousand feral cats, all burning at a thousand degrees Celsius.

Sending an X-ray laser generated from a satellite had been a brilliant, bold, and completely unrealistic endeavor in the seventies. Now, though? With her lines upon lines of containment code and algorithms upon algorithms to compensate for the variation in energy output? That strategic defense system was cranking out some serious joules.

And wasn't it fitting to use the laser-defense system against the world's greatest threat, the Hidden Hand?

* * *

Quirk clutched the vials to his chest as the chamber began to shake. Great. Now an earthquake. His luck just couldn't get much worse, could it?

But wait. They were in Maine, of all places—not Los Angeles.

His guards looked at one another, and then at the huge glass cases that flanked them. Yeah, Quirk wouldn't want to be them if those came tumbling down. Then the ceiling began to smoke as dust flew off the rock from a single pinpoint above the guards' heads.

Then the limestone turned a bright yellow, then orange, before a stark red beam punched through the ceiling. Once through the stone, it burned through the refrigeration units, vaporizing huge swaths of vaccine. Men scattered for cover as glass cracked and shattered.

If that wasn't an X-ray laser, Quirk had never seen one. Well, of course he had never actually seen one, since they weren't supposed to exist, but damn if it wasn't an X-ray laser.

If this wasn't a true miracle, what was? The Reagan Strategic Defense System worked. Quirk actually owed Ronnie an apology.

Then the laser arced to the back wall, cutting a perfect passage to the sea. The roar of the ocean filled the chamber as an unnatural lightning swept across the sky, angling back to the castle. Unfortunately, the guards noticed the escape route and raised their weapons. Hopping over to the exit, Quirk put his flippers back on. Someone really needed to put Velcro on those things.

Shots rang out as Quirk dove out of the hole. Sea spray filled his nostrils right before he hit the water. Bullets streaked all around him as he swam deeper and deeper, like a mermaid. They were all just very lucky that Quirk had a swimmer's body.

* * *

The laser swung back around, slicing through the stone, cutting a swatch between Ronnie and Lino. The man stumbled back as the crevice opened, loose rock crumbling underfoot.

The haughtiness returned to Lino's eyes. He clutched the spearhead in his hand, backing away several steps. Ronnie knew that he was not retreating. He was regrouping for a jump. Ronnie had no weapon. She couldn't swing the laser back around so quickly if she tried. And it had a far greater task at hand—making sure that no one followed Quirk and the vaccine.

Ronnie looked down at Francois, blinking away tears mixed with raindrops. He had been so brave at the end.

Would she be that brave when that knife was buried in her belly?

Ready or not, she was about to find out.

Lino crouched, preparing to make his dash, when a deafening *crack* resounded. The corner of the castle tilted as if it were nothing more than a foam toy. The section that Lino stood upon wavered, swaying back and forth. Lino delayed long enough that the laser made its way back in his direction.

No matter. The man gritted his teeth, snarling at Ronnie. But the gap became wider and wider. The laser got closer and closer. Lino's muscles bunched as he sprinted toward her.

Perhaps he thought that he could beat the laser. But Lino didn't realize that the colored core of the laser was only one quarter the diameter of the actual energy beam. The rest was invisible to the naked eye. Hence, the "X-ray" part of the laser's name.

Mid-leap, Lino was caught in the intense energy field of the beam, screaming as the skin was burnt from the entire right side of his body. As the corner of the building fell away, Lino tumbled with it.

Ronnie stood in the rain, trembling at the sudden silence.

CHAPTER 33

Plum Island, New York
4:07 p.m., EST

Amanda ran straight into a tray as she crashed into the infirmary. She had to choke back the smell. There were at least three dead and bloating corpses. No one to help her, and no help she could offer them.

She checked both cell phones again. Not only did they not have any bars, they didn't even have service. Amanda picked up the nearest landline. It, too, was dead. Henderson must have sabotaged all the communication channels.

Maybe she should have just stayed in the conference room and taken a bullet along with Devlin. Perhaps she would have been there when Jennifer was put out of her misery. Amanda squeezed her eyes shut against the guilt. She had fled for one singular purpose. Someone had to survive to explain the truth. Amanda couldn't let Henderson get away with it. Not if she could help it.

To think—the entire time he had been watching her like a snake might a mouse. Slithering in the background—waiting until the right moment to strike. Amanda pushed aside the thought and dug through the medicine cabinet. The thing was in disarray. How many Code Blues had the medical staff gone through until they realized it was a moot point?

Which didn't leave many supplies. Amanda checked one label, and then tossed the vial aside. She checked another, and another, until she found the one she was looking for. Stilling her trembling hands, she drew up the full vial into a syringe.

"I thought you'd come here," Henderson said as he walked through the swinging door of the infirmary. "Always the victim, aren't you, Amanda? Always taking on the weight of the world."

Yep. That was she. Except that she was done with the whole victim thing. Or at least, that's what she hoped.

"They got the vaccine," Amanda said, taking a step closer. "You know that, right?"

Henderson glared at her. "I cut off the cell phone tower."

"Before that," Amanda tried to sound confident as she took another step forward. "They texted me that they are on their way."

She held out Jennifer's phone with the old texts on it, hoping that Henderson's eyesight matched his age.

"You are lying."

"Why would I?" Amanda said as she inched closer. "I just want to die seeing the look on your face that you lost."

Henderson snatched for the phone, which she gladly gave him. It kept him distracted while she jammed the hypodermic needle into his gun arm. The phone clattered to the floor

436

as Henderson tried to bring the gun up, but his arm wouldn't obey. As a matter of fact, his hand contracted down.

"Epinephrine," she said as Henderson's eyes dilated to near-black saucers. "It's constricting your blood vessels as we speak." The director gasped. "And making your heart beat a hundred times harder and faster than it should."

He grabbed hold of a bed, trying to right himself as blood-tinged tears sprang to his eyes.

Amanda leaned in close, taking the gun from his spasming hand. "And you might be vaccinated, but that doesn't mean you don't have the plague."

Henderson looked down at his fingernails turning black.

"That's right—all of your antibodies are binding to the bacteria, clogging your capillaries, and now, with your blood pressure?" Amanda explained. "It is trashing those weakened blood vessels."

Doubling over, Henderson hacked and hacked, spitting out blood.

"Oh, yeah, and your lungs are a little fragile as well," Amanda said as she got out of range.

The man who thought he would be king of Plum Island gasped. His next breath sounded like scuba gear. His *last* breath sounded like a flood.

He fell onto a cot, his dead eyes staring blankly at the ceiling.

Amanda would have thought she would have felt a twinge of something. Sadness. Remorse. But all she felt was relief.

Grabbing as many drugs as she could, she stacked them on the crash cart and wheeled it toward the stairs. Since she had no idea if Ronnie had obtained the vaccine or if they were in fact on their way, she needed to stabilize Jennifer's condition for as long as she could.

Her own legs trembling, Amanda realized she might need to save some of the medication for herself.

* * *

Zach stopped his mad rush to the security hub as a brilliant beam of light streaked across the courtyard. Men yelled and scattered. Horses spooked and stampeded away. A section of the castle crashed down not a dozen yards from him.

Panic filled the air of the Hidden Hand's stronghold.

All this, Ronnie had done. Zach wasn't even sure how, but he knew it was her handiwork. But as much as he wished to stay and watch the guards lose their minds, he had his own work to accomplish.

Breaking into a run, Zach hauled ass to the turret. The guards lowered their spears as Zach waved the parchment with the angelic seal at them. Without question, they let him pass. Yep, it was great to be a page.

He took the stone steps two at a time, mainly because there was no way in hell he could take them three at a time. The staircase ended at a stout, wooden door. Two guards turned from the window, seeming startled that anyone approached. Zach again showed the parchment. One of the guards tried to take it from him.

"No," Zach said, pulling the scroll back. "I was told to deliver it directly to the…" Crap—what would the head of security have been called in medieval days? "Commander of the Watch." Yeah, that was it. Thank you, George R. R. Martin.

The guards opened the ancient door into a very modern room. Even Ronnie would have been impressed. Of course, she had already hacked her way into their mainframe. She had the keys to the kingdom with the exception of one very important function.

The auto-destruct. That one had to be done by hand, in person.

Now, if Zach could just remember how in the hell to do it.

* * *

It took the laser making its way back for Ronnie to snap out of her shock. She had done it. Well, maybe not done all of it, but if their luck held at all, Quirk should be securing the vaccine on the helicopter.

Now to rendezvous with Zach and get to that helicopter herself. Ronnie stumbled as she headed to the stairs. Francois's body lay so still on the cold, stone roof. One of them would not be heading anywhere ever again.

Ronnie dropped to her knees to check his pulse, even though it was way clear he was gone. Blood pooled so thickly around the body that even the storm couldn't wash it away fast enough. She had barely known him, and for the most part he had been a pain in her ass, but she couldn't help but feel her throat constrict as she closed his eyes.

Francois had spent the greater part of his life trying to prevent this tragedy. He had died to protect her. To protect the world. And who would know of it? Who would know that the name Francois Loubom should be ranked right up there with Abraham Lincoln and Winston Churchill? No, not up there with them. Above them.

That is, if they could actually get the vaccine the hell out of Maine and into the hands of the CDC.

With a silent promise to remember Francois always, Ronnie rose and ran for the stairs. Zach should be in position at any moment.

* * *

Zach was not in position. Not by a long shot. He couldn't remember much about the full plan. However, he did know that he was going to come in here guns blazing. Not decked out in a page's outfit with only the khan's short blade.

He should have already triggered the auto-destruct sequence and been hightailing it to the rendezvous point by now. Or, in his condition, figuring out where he rendezvous point was. Of course that meant he had to subdue the room.

Besides the commander, there were four other tech support officers in the room. Zach had only lasted this long in the room because he murmured something about waiting for a response to run back to the Captain of the Guard. Thank God they didn't ask him what the guy's name was. Zach's time was running out.

"Look!" one of the techies said pointing to a screen mainly filled with static. The only thing clear on the monitor was a bright red beam…heading straight for them. The loud cracking hum filled the air.

Which, on the one hand was great, as the men ran, fleeing the room. On the other hand, Zach was pretty damn sure the beam wasn't supposed to come anywhere near this room.

They needed the self-destruct to blow to make sure no one followed them to Plum Island.

Yes! That was where they were supposed to be heading. Plum Island. He couldn't head there if he didn't get the damned self-destruct online.

"Did you really think it would be that easy?" a voice said from the back of the room.

"Nothing's been easy, Grant."

Zach might be a little punch-drunk, but he could never forget the voice of the man who'd betrayed not just his partner or his agency, but his country as well.

Grant stepped from behind the bank of monitors, that shit-eating grin on his face. "What can I say? I land on my feet."

Sure, he did. Zach really shouldn't be surprised that Grant was here. "The Hidden Hand must have made a lucrative offer."

Grant shrugged. "Actually, it was I who propositioned them."

"Of course you did," Zach said as he inched the khan's blade from his belt.

"Right about when I tracked you to Graceland, I thought, *why*? I mean, why track you down when it was pretty clear who was going to win? Sometimes you've just got to pick a side."

"Actually," Zach said. "You kind of pick a side *ahead* of time, then stick with it."

Grant snorted. "That's your problem, Zach, always thinking so linearly." Zach loosened the knife, but the ex-FBI and ex-CIA agent brought up his gun. "Like I said. Linearly." Grant cocked his head to the side. "Did you know that after the Black Death, because of the smaller work force, wages actually rose? That the plague helped spur economic prosperity and helped solidify the middle class?"

Walking to the center of the room, Grant smiled. "The Hidden Hand has got some amazing room for career upward mobility. And, did I mention excellent health benefits?" Grant rubbed his upper arm. "A plague vaccine with each new hire. You really should read their pamphlet. It's pretty impressive."

"Thanks, but no thanks," Zach answered, praying that his ruse worked as the high- energy beam cut its way through the room. Smoke filled the air.

"Oh, well," Grant said as he leveled the gun. "I guess I won't be getting that 'refer a friend' bonus."

Zach menaced with his knife, but threw a sweeping low kick. Grant awkwardly avoided the kick, but that was all the distraction Zach needed. Rushing forward, he knocked Grant's gun arm to the side and sliced with the khan's knife. Grant screamed like the little girl he was, grabbing his side. He brought the gun around, as if that could help him.

All those hours Grant spent training in deception, he really should have spent some time in hand-to-hand combat. Zach elbowed Grant in the wound, forcing the man to drop his guard on the left side. Zach grabbed Grant's gun hand and forced it back around. Pulling the trigger again and again and again, Zach put three bullets in Grant's belly.

The man looked downright shocked as his knees gave out. Zach snatched the gun away as Grant slumped to the floor.

"How's that retirement plan working out?" Zach asked as he turned back to the task at hand.

Leaning over the control keyboard—now smeared with Grant's blood, Zach typed in his name. Ronnie was supposed to keep this specific, yet simple. The back door to the auto-detonation system opened. Then, of course, came the dreaded security question.

Who is the leader of the Ewok nation?

Seriously? A ray beam from outer space was about to fry his ass, and he had to remember something from *Star Wars*? Okay, so maybe there was some irony there, but still…

* * *

Ronnie rushed down the stairs still trying to get the laser under control. The damn stone castle dampened her signal, then the X-ray beam itself was ionizing the atmosphere enough to really fritz the connection.

No matter how hard she tried, the beam seemed to have a mind of its own. Basically the laser had gone rogue. Out the window, she watched the beam blink out for a moment only to appear two hundred feet to the left then back to the right. Right inside the security room. If the central mainframe was damaged, they could forget about any escape.

She stopped on the steps and used the stone wall to help increase her keystrokes' accuracy. It didn't make any difference. The beam danced along the wall, gouging it, then headed out into the fields, only to come back again.

Okay time for the beam to go beddy-bye. Ronnie typed in the override code only for the satellite to reject it. Um, not a great time for the beam to go all HAL 9000. She tried every trick in her very extensive list of tricks, but nothing worked. Then she realized why.

Sure, the satellite's job had been promoted as a way to knock nuclear missiles out of the sky; however, its higher purpose and function was to actually take out the missile silo itself. Specifically, the computer system running the silo.

Unfortunately, the only way she could hack into the satellite's controls so quickly was to convince the satellite that a castle in Cutler, Maine was actually a Russian missile silo in Siberia. At first, she could control the direction of the laser, but now that the satellite had locked on to the Hidden Hand's mainframe?

There was no keeping the satellite from the electronics hub.

* * *

The name of the Powerpuff Girls' creator?

Come on, Ronnie. It is *me* you built these questions for. Ask me the Kansas City Royals overall ERA or something. *That* he could answer.

He typed in Groucho Marx, knowing it was wrong but hoping the next question was one he could answer.

The screen flashed red, and then letters scrolled across. *Dude. Seriously, have you listened to nothing I've ever said?*

Clearly, no.

The walls vibrated as the laser chewed its way back through the castle's thick stone.

Okay. Last chance. What is the proper answer to this greeting…Hey, sexy.

Zach smiled. This one he could answer.

"Hey there, yourself," he typed.

The rest of the monitors went blank. The remaining screen bloomed a bright, happy green. A timer began ticking down as the laser broke through the door, aiming straight for him. There was nowhere to run and nowhere to hide as the air shimmered in advance of the blazing energy beam. Still, Zach wedged himself in the furthest corner.

Then the laser stalled, sputtering. It wove right, then left. As if it were a hunting dog who'd lost its scent. Still, the beam set fire to anything it touched. Zach covered his nose with his tunic. How to get around the laser without getting crispy-fried himself?

Inch by inch, the beam advanced on his position. Then the laser stopped, burning straight down. The floor melted away as the room thrummed with energy.

Zach turned his face away from the blistering heat. His last thoughts were of Ronnie.

Okay, maybe not last thoughts, as the beam suddenly lurched, buzzing away from him and the security room, making a beeline away from *here*. Not waiting for the laser to change its mind, Zach skirted around the now-gaping hole in the floor, Grant's body, and made for the stairs, only…well… there weren't any steps, at least not anymore.

* * *

Ronnie watched as the laser angled away from the turret and made for the southern fields. They were in luck that the Hidden Hand had planned for a lot of different attack scenarios, including a site-wide power outage. They had a generator and backup computer system in an underground bunker near the edge of the property.

All she had to do was boot that baby up, remotely. With the main computer system going down for the auto-destruct sequence, the satellite had latched on to the next most active electronic bay. And since that computer system was busy trying to figure out the last digit of pi and the Star Wars satellite was running out of fuel, they should be set.

That is, if they could get to the rendezvous point. Ronnie hurried down the rest of the stairs, jumping over a jagged gouge in the floor. All those hideous tapestries were now on fire, singeing down to their last thread. The only thing that kept the place from burning was the torrent of rain.

Ronnie kept to the center of the dining hall, and then made the first right. She hit the chapel doors at a run.

Streaks of light, from the lightning, the laser, or from those on high shone through the high, narrow stained glass windows. Windows decorated with angels of all types were each casting their own set of swirling angelic script on the floor.

Tentatively, Ronnie stepped inside the chapel. If the symbols had been captivating at the Metropolitan Museum of Art, this was...well, heavenly. She glanced up at the windows. Where were the symbols coming from? The stained glass, while beautiful in its own right, did not appear to have the pattern etched into the paint. How were the symbols appearing?

Then she noticed thin strips of glass within the glass. Though they appeared nearly indistinguishable from the other pieces, these clearly were picking up the ultraviolet waves from the laser, splashing the symbols on the chapel's floor.

It made absolutely no sense, though. How could the craftsmen of the stained glass windows know there would be ultraviolet light to reveal the symbols? For a devout non-believer, Ronnie's denial in the unknown was wavering a bit. Okay, maybe a lot.

Especially given the message of the symbols. It would take her several hours on the computer to read them all, but their meaning was clear.

Peace. Love. Hope.

Ronnie's eyes involuntarily filled with tears. Francois would have loved this place. A bastion of respite at the heart of such evil.

She took picture after picture of the symbols. They had to be recorded, but as the laser moved further and further away, sputtering more and more, the symbols faded.

A noise came from behind her.

"Zach?" she asked as she turned around, her voice still filled with wonder.

Only it wasn't Zach at the entrance. Instead, there stood a half-burned Lino. His right side was marred by heat and radiation. His face melded into a Picasso-like visage. Lino's skin, okay not really skin, but an oozing film glistened in the light.

The features untouched by the laser were equally contorted. Contorted by rage. The rage kept him moving despite his body's fatal injury.

Ronnie backed down the aisle toward the altar. She had no weapon and no defense as he stalked toward her.

"Bitch," he slurred as saliva dripped from the lipless side of his mouth.

"Look around you, Lino," Ronnie urged, pointing to the floor and the fading symbols. "Even the angels are begging you to let it go."

He closed his good eye against the sight, but the eye without lids must have seen what lay before him. Lino chose to ignore the message. "You will die," he spat out, sending chunks of tissue to the floor.

Ronnie gulped, keeping her eyes from the ground. Unfortunately, that meant looking at Lino's ruined body. But even in ruin, he seemed intent on revenge. And Ronnie was all out of toys. She'd even take the untested fibrillator, but it was back on the helicopter.

And where in the hell was Zach?

* * *

Zach's foot slipped. His fingers dug into the tiny cracks in the stone wall. His foot fished in thin air, then found a purchase. He hissed out a breath. Glancing beneath him, the ground was still too far down to jump and take his chances on a good roll.

Given the state of panic and disarray below in the courtyard, there wasn't going to be any help soon. Some were fleeing, while others stuck to their posts, trying to put out the myriad of fires that the laser had started, while others were combating flooding. He hated to tell them that in about two minutes, none of any of their efforts would matter. The entire complex would be blown sky-high.

Yeah, that kind of thinking wasn't going to get him off this turret any faster. Taking in another breath, Zach edged his way to a window ledge. He glanced in, but the room was blown out. No way down there. Nope, he had to make it down the sheer drop. Just another fifty of these holds on the way down, and he'd be good to go. Somehow, that did not make him feel any better.

After another slip, Zach righted himself.

"You!" a voice called.

Zach looked down to find the knight from before shouting at him.

"Page, to me!"

This was a bad idea. He wouldn't even try it, except for the fact that every other idea was actually worse.

Steeling himself for the impact, Zach pushed himself off the wall, twisting in midair. He hit the knight, knocking him from his saddle. The two crashed to the ground, but the knight's armor shielded them both from the brunt of the impact.

They sprang to their feet.

"That's a good man," the knight said, patting Zach's shoulder.

The guy was making it really hard for Zach to attack. After all, the knight had quite possibly just saved his life.

"I must be off," Zach said, pointing to the collapsing castle.

The knight nearly let him go, and then noticed something along Zach's neck. The tunic must have gotten torn in his fight with Grant, revealing the camouflage beneath. The knight went for his sword. Turned out that the guy was Hidden Hand through and through. The full set of armor probably should have clued Zach in to that fact.

Zach threw a punch, cracking into the man's nose, sending him reeling.

Scanning the area, Zach came up with no weapons. And that knight was regrouping pretty quickly, yelling for reinforcements. Then Zach saw it. A little black star embedded in a piece of wood. He snatched it from the railing praying that the Taser star still had juice. The only problem, the knight was encased in armor. How in the hell was Zach going to get it to the guy's skin?

Then the knight heaved back, raising his broadsword with both arms, exposing his midriff below his chest plate. Zach flung the star, nailing the guy in the belly. However, the star didn't fire immediately, and the knight swung the broadsword down, aiming for the crown of Zach's head.

Then the little Taser kicked in, knotting the knight's muscles, clenching his arms. The broadsword clattered to the ground as the guy fell on his side twitching and flailing.

Now, to get to Ronnie.

* * *

Ronnie tried to put the pew between her and Lino, but the man went berserk, smashing the wooden bench with a single downward blow.

The monster that had lurked beneath Lino's surface now fully out for the world to see. No more refinement. No more aloof arrogance. Lino was nothing more than raw, undiluted, fury.

She backed away until she could back up no longer. The edge of the altar poked into her spine.

Lino lunged forward. Ronnie gasped, clutching her fists so tightly that she popped beads from her gloves. Lino

ENCRYPTED

retreated seeming awfully pleased with himself. Now he was just toying with her.

"We will rise again," he sneered, pulling up his congealed lip.

This time he came at her, not toying at all. She tried to duck out from under the attack, but Lino caught her by the throat, slamming her against the altar. His burnt hand was moist against her neck. She could feel the actual muscles constrict around her windpipe. Lino's scorched finger dug into the flesh. Was he going to choke her, or tear her trachea from her throat?

Ronnie's hand groped behind her, trying to find something, anything, to use against him. One finger touched an object, only it was just out of reach. Her lungs screamed for oxygen as her sight constricted down.

With her other hand, she ripped at Lino's arm, gouging at his arm, shredding flesh under her fingernails. His grip wasn't *like* a vise. It *was* a vise. Only then did Ronnie realize that this might truly be the end. She would just be one more body they would find after the self-destruct did its job.

Closing her eyes, Ronnie tried to picture Zach, but her mind was past concentrating on anything else except getting air.

Then she heard the clattering of hooves against stone. She didn't think that was one of the "going to the light" events. Cracking open her eyes, she watched a white horse, a charger, really carrying her knight in shining armor. The armor glowed—or was it the loss of oxygen?

"Ronnie!" Zach shouted, but they all knew he would be too late.

Lino redoubled his efforts, forcing her back, clamping off her windpipe. Even in his state, he could sense victory. The only problem? Lino had forced her an inch closer to the cross on the altar. Using the tip of her fingernails, she coaxed the silver object to tip over into her hand.

With the last of her strength, Ronnie gripped the cross, pulling it from its stand, driving the end through the exposed muscles of Lino's abdomen. The silver sank in with a slurping sound. Lino's grip squeezed all the tighter and then let go.

"That is for Francois," Ronnie choked out as Lino fell to the ground, the cross sticking out from his belly like a flag.

Dizzy, Ronnie stumbled toward Zach as he dismounted.

As oxygen finally reached her lungs, Zach caught her before she hit the stone.

"Hey, sexy," he said brushing back her hair with his gloved hand.

Ronnie just smiled her answer, mainly because she couldn't use her throat yet. Catching her breath, Ronnie felt her chest rise and fall against the metal chest plate of Zach's armor. Granted, it was a little early in the relationship for dress-up, but still. *Damn.*

"Hey there, yourself," she responded.

Time to get off her butt. Ronnie pushed off the altar, although her muscles still shook.

"Take it slow," Zach said steadying her.

The only problem with that proclamation was the floor rumbling beneath them.

* * *

Zach grabbed Ronnie and tucked her under him as an explosion rocked the castle. He let the back of his armor take a pounding from the shattered glass, mortar, and rock. Finally, the debris stopped, only to have another explosion sound from across the courtyard.

"You did reset the auto-destruct timer for five minutes instead of three, right?" Ronnie asked.

Oh. Crap. He knew he'd forgotten something. A big something.

Ronnie must have read his response in his face, because she rose to her feet. "We have *got* to get out of here."

No kidding. The horse had turned tail after the first explosion and was long gone. Rubble and rock blocked the only entrance to the chapel.

"Come on," Ronnie said grabbing his hand as she climbed up onto the altar.

"What are you—?"

Despite a bruised neck and about a hundred little nicks and scratches, Ronnie beamed back at him as she pointed to the one remaining window. Above them soared the archangel. What exactly did that have to do with them, though?

She urged him upward until they stood on the altar, looking out the broken lower window to the raging sea below.

"Whoa," he said as explosion after explosion rang out and the very foundation of the castle shook.

As a fireball *whooshed* toward them, they ran down the altar and leapt though the window. The force of the blast caught them, hurling them out over the ocean. For a moment it felt like they were going to fly forever, then that nasty gravity kicked in and they plummeted down the cliff.

Somehow in it all, they never lost hold of each other's hands. That is, until they hit the frigid water. Zach gulped a breath before going under. Next to him, Ronnie plunged into the water, and then buoyed back up. Zach just kept sinking.

The armor. Trying to stay calm he tried to grope for the ties, but his fingers refused to loosen the leather ties. He kicked hard, trying to overcome the fifty pounds of added weight—to no avail. Zach could barely see Ronnie's shoes anymore as she broke the surface.

At least she was safe.

* * *

Ronnie gasped for breath, spitting out seawater. Explosions still rang out above them. The Hidden Hand apparently took their self-destruct mechanisms very seriously. So much the better.

Shivering, Ronnie spun around in the water looking for Zach. Where *was* he? And where in the hell was the helicopter? Quirk? The pilot? Then she felt something brush her shoe. Sucking in a deep breath, Ronnie dove into the chilly water.

The storm had churned up the sea, taking visibility down to almost nothing. With the exception of Zach's silver armor that glowed nearly as brightly as it had in the chapel. Very heavy armor. She swam down beside him as he kicked furiously, trying to get to the surface.

Grabbing the armor by the shoulder, she added her strength to the effort. Using every last bit of verve they had left, she got him to the surface. His face broke the water next to her, gasping and sputtering. Then he started sinking again.

No!

She blew out five times fast, then gulped a breath, and headed down.

Zach tugged on a strap, showing her what they needed to untie, but the leather knots had swelled in the water, making them nearly impossible to undo. Finally, as his face blotched, trying not to take a breath, Zach pushed her away.

Ronnie shook her head. He was *so* not giving up.

Zach stopped kicking, though. There was no way she could get him back to the surface without his help. His body sunk in the water. Damn him and his stupid idea of sacrificing himself.

Then her eye caught a glimmer of gold at his waist. Screw untying the leather. Ronnie grabbed the khan's blade and sliced at the ties. She only needed to get one side free. Bubbles tumbled from Zach's mouth. In another few seconds, he wasn't going to be able to stop himself from taking a breath.

Finally, the leather gave way, and the breastplate tilted, allowing Zach to duck under it. Side by side, they struck for the surface. Even with wind and rain lashing their faces, Ronnie had never been so glad to face a storm.

"Look," Zach sputtered, pointing up.

Above the conflagration that used to be the Hidden Hand's castle, a huge, glittering symbol rose. One like none she had seen before. Then, just as quickly, it dispersed along the wind.

"What?" Zach started, then spit out some seawater. "What did it say?"

"I have no idea," Ronnie replied, bobbing along with the waves. "No idea at all."

"Where is the chopper?" Zach asked as his teeth chattered.

That was pretty much the sixty-four thousand dollar question, wasn't it? Which of course, she did not have the answer to either.

So now that they didn't have to worry about getting crispy-fried, they had to be concerned with acute, fatal hypothermia.

Awesome.

* * *

Quirk pointed out the front windshield of the two-engine seaplane. "There! I think that's them."

The only response he got from the pilot was a grunt as the plane began banking starboard. Which was more than enough for Quirk. He hadn't even bothered to ask the pilot what happened to the helicopter, or where he'd gotten the seaplane. Quirk liked to keep the mystery alive in their relationship.

Making it look like there weren't nearly enough hurricane-strength winds, the pilot brought them down low over the waves, then landed softly on the ocean. Water sprayed out behind them as they slowed, pulling the plane right next to bobbing swimmers.

Quirk hopped out of the copilot's seat and opened the hatch door.

"Fancy meeting you here," he said, but then Ronnie frowned that frown.

Dog paddling in frigid ocean water was not her best look.

He helped her climb onto the pontoon and into the cab, suddenly regretting taking off the wet suit. Zach made it halfway up before nearly falling backward. Great. More sloppy wet hands all over his new sweater. Alas, fashion must, under only the direst of circumstances, take a backseat to function. Darn it.

Quirk surveyed the water. "Where's Francois?"

He turned to find Ronnie pulling a blanket over her shoulders. The way she *didn't* look at him told Quirk that Francois was lost. Even though he hadn't really liked the guy, seriously, black loafers with khaki pants, the Frenchman did smell of freshly baked sourdough bread.

Still, he didn't think Francois would want them moping around. Not with the Hidden Hand's castle afire and their precious vaccine in the hold. No, Francois would want them to haul ass out of here.

Which was exactly what Quirk had planned. Shutting the door, he gave the pilot the thumbs-up. Without hesitation, the seaplane skimmed out over the water. Quirk rushed to take his seat as the pilot lifted them off the ocean and directly into the storm's wake.

* * *

Zach peeled off his sopping-wet T-shirt. His chest and abdomen were a mottled black and blue—a harsh reminder of the last few days. Gingerly, he dried off with a towel. He glanced up to find Ronnie staring at his injuries. Zach had dreamed of her staring at his body like that, but not for this reason.

Donning the clothes that Quirk provided, Zach turned to Ronnie. "Your turn."

He held up a towel to provide her with some measure of privacy. It was almost hard to imagine that they had beaten the Hidden Hand. Well, they couldn't exactly declare "mission accomplished" yet. Not with Plum Island ignoring their hails. He wouldn't let himself consider the possibility that the Hidden Hand had taken over the facility.

Even under the best of circumstances, you know, those circumstances where everyone has succumbed to the plague rather than being hostilely taken over by a cult, the Hidden Hand needed to manufacture vaccine, lots and lots of vaccine. How could they do that if there was no one left alive with the skills necessary?

"We'll know soon enough," Ronnie said, touching his arm. He'd call her out on being a psychic, but they were all probably thinking the same thing.

"We couldn't come this far…"

He couldn't even finish the sentence. Instead, he lifted his arm, letting Ronnie tuck down against his chest. Heat mingled as their bodies tried to thaw out from their icy plunge.

As they flew, Zach thought of his mother and sister. Had they done as he told them? Stayed home? Avoided contact with anyone and everyone? Or would he go home to find a red "X" upon their door?

As Ronnie snuggled up against him, he put thoughts of his family aside. If there was one thing his grandmother had taught him, it was "no sense in worrying until the worry finds you."

Besides, he had the woman in his arms who just saved the freaking world. She deserved his undivided attention. He pulled another blanket over her back, and then on second thought, pulled another one over his.

"Thank you," she said, still with her cheek against his chest.

"For what?"

Ronnie tilted her chin up. "For riding to my emotional and *physical* rescue."

Zach leaned in, ready to taste her salty lips, but Ronnie laid her head back down on his shirt.

"Not here. Got it," he whispered as he kissed her forehead. The way her head rose and fell with his breath and how her arms wrapped around his waist, Zach wasn't going to complain.

* * *

Amanda huffed a breath as she inched the crash cart up the last stair. Winded, she leaned against the wall, trying desperately not to cough again. Her lungs hurt—physically hurt. She could feel where the bacterium had taken hold and burrowed in. She could feel her immune system trying to fight *Yersinia pestis*—to no avail.

She looked down the long, empty hallway. Amanda knew it was only a couple of yards, but it felt like five end-to-end football fields. Okay, it was time to admit that she, too, was in the last stages of the plague. Turning on the tank of the crash cart, Amanda put the mask to her face and inhaled. She stood there probably longer than she should have, replenishing her body's desperate need for oxygen.

But standing here sucking on the mask wasn't going to help Jennifer, if her friend could be helped at all. With one last inhale, Amanda turned off the tank and pushed the cart forward. The one wobbly wheel complained as they made their way down the hall.

After the gruesome scene in the infirmary, Amanda shouldn't have been shocked by all the blood pooling around

Devlin's head, but she was. No matter what a jerk he'd been, in the end, he'd saved her life—and paid the cost with his own.

Guiding the cart, she gave Devlin's body a wide berth as she made her way to Jennifer. The woman didn't rouse as Amanda turned her over onto her side. Pulling up more epinephrine, this time in a therapeutic dose, Amanda heard a groan. Dropping what she was doing, she rushed over to Devlin.

"Oh, man," he said weakly. "That hurt."

Amanda dropped to her knees, wiping away the clotted blood. Underneath it was a perfect line where the bullet had grazed the scalp. Okay, not just grazed it but dug into it, only bouncing off the skull bone.

"Is it going to scar?" Devlin asked as he sat upright, seeming stronger by the moment.

Given the fact that bone glistened back at her…oh, yeah.

"Here," she said, putting his hand against the gauze squares. "Put pressure on the wound."

He winced but obeyed. "And Henderson?"

"Let's just say that he got the sixty-second version of the plague."

Devlin cocked his head, but then seemed to think better of it. "As long as he's dead."

Yes, Henderson was definitely dead, but how much longer until Jennifer and Amanda joined him?

CHAPTER 34

Over the Atlantic Ocean
5:43 p.m., EST

Ronnie took aim. "Hold still!"

Quirk bobbed and weaved. How her assistant could avoid her in this cramped seaplane, Ronnie had no idea.

"No!" Quirk said, avoiding the hypodermic needle in her hand. "No needles."

Ugh! For such a hypochondriac, Quirk certainly did not like to take his medicine.

"It is the vaccine for the *plague*," Ronnie reminded Quirk as he tried to crawl under the plane's dash. She pulled him back into his seat. "Or, would you rather get the plague, and then have the antiserum injected into your belly?"

Quirk's eyes dilated. "No way. They have to put it in my abdomen?"

Of course they didn't, but Quirk didn't need to know that, so Ronnie solemnly nodded.

He gulped, then yelped, grabbing at his *other* arm. "Ouch!" Quirk yelled at Zach.

The ploy had worked perfectly. She'd spent the last five minutes convincing Quirk that she was the danger—only to have Zach come in from the other side with the vaccine at the last moment. Her syringe didn't even have any of the precious vaccine in it.

"Totally uncalled for," Quirk mumbled as he inspected the tiny pinprick. "Don't I get a bandage or something?"

"Better buckle up," the pilot said as he pointed to a lighthouse on the horizon. At least something on the island still worked, indicating the facilities still had power. Score one for the Plague Busters.

Ronnie strapped into her seat, watching the vague outline of the island came into view. The pilot banked as they flew over the narrow finger of the island. That wasn't where they were headed, though. It was to the broader stretch of the island, where the laboratories were positioned. As they descended, Ronnie noted the gray and blue buildings. Although, it was eerie. Not a person or animal moved. However, given the weather, she seriously doubted that anyone would be running around—with or without the plague.

Smoothly the pilot brought the seaplane around, landing on the surging waves, drawing them up alongside the small pier.

Zach cocked his gun.

Yeah. They still weren't done with those yet.

* * *

Zach urged the trio between the two main buildings. Protected from the rain, Quirk pulled out his palmtop.

"This is the entrance closest to the conference room," he reported.

Quirk shouldn't have known that. After 9/11, the island had come under Homeland Security jurisdiction. The plans to the laboratories were locked behind one of the highest security clearances you could get. This was Quirk, after all, so it came as no great surprise that the hacker was in the know.

Zach checked the door handle. The metal turned easily under his palm. Not good. Or at least not good for any hope of finding survivors. He looked at Ronnie as she frowned. What else could they do but investigate? Opening the door, they crept along the empty hallway. Blood smeared the walls and pooled on the tile.

"Aren't you glad we poked you?" Ronnie asked Quirk.

The young man simply checked his lymph nodes as they turned a corner. Several bloated bodies littered the floor. Quirk clutched Zach's arm. Under any other circumstances, Zach would have pushed him away, but seeing this? Zach was giving Quirk a pass.

They made it to the stairs. Just one floor up. Taking each step carefully, Zach led the way. Only the echo of their footsteps marked their passage. No other noise met them. Making sure the others were behind him, Zach jerked open the door to the second floor.

No bodies. Not even any blood. That gave him hope that maybe someone was still alive to help. If there wasn't? They didn't have enough fuel to make it to the CDC headquarters in Atlanta. And the rest of the level four laboratories simply didn't have the facilities to produce vaccine in the massive quantities they needed.

"It should be that one," Quirk whispered as he pointed to the conference room.

Hoping for the best but prepared for the worst, Zach made for the door.

* * *

Amanda held Jennifer's hand. It lay slack under her fingers. The woman still breathed, but that was about as much as they could ask of her. Despite all the medication pumped into her body, Jennifer was dying.

Coughing and spitting up blood, Amanda wasn't far behind. The glands in her throat had nearly cut off her breathing, and the pain in her joints? At least, Jennifer didn't feel the pain anymore.

Devlin sat in the opposite corner, still holding the gauze against his head wound.

How many hours had passed since Quirk's last communication? Was his team all dead, like Amanda's colleagues?

The CIA liaison's head jerked up. "What was that?"

She had no idea. Just then, the door burst open. A man with a gun rushed in. "Hands up!"

Only Devlin didn't comply. Instead, he pulled out his own weapon. "Who the hell are you?"

"The cavalry. Now, drop it."

Devlin's jaw tensed. "Not before you do."

The two men aimed at one another as a woman edged into the room.

"Guys, we are on the same side," she said surveying the scene. "Right?"

The men, however, did not lower their weapons. Another, skinnier, man burst in. "Or for goodness's sake! We have lives to save."

The skinny man strode right over to Amanda as Devlin pointed to the armed man.

"Dr. Rolph, I presume?"

"Quirk?" Amanda asked tentatively.

"Um," the man said, twirling around. "In the middle of the Black Death, a man *this* well dressed? Who else would it be than Quirk?"

For some reason, Amanda jumped up. Pustules and all, she hugged him.

"Let's watch the wool," Quirk said gently, moving her back. He handed her a small, plastic box holding dozens of small vials.

Amanda was afraid to let herself believe that it was true. Could the vaccine—and even more importantly, the antiserum—really be at her fingertips? She turned to ask Quirk if it really could be happening, but the slight man sat down hard next to Jennifer.

"Is she even…?"

Then Jennifer took in a rattled breath.

"Yes, but not for long," Amanda commented as she opened a syringe and pulled out an aliquot of the antisera. In theory, she should run multiple tests to check for the purity of the sample, its biochemical composition, and run several animal tests to be certain of the serum's efficacy. However, in this world ravaged by the Black Death, none of that mattered.

For Jennifer, for everyone, the Hidden Hand's immuno-logical concoction had better work.

"What are you doing?" Devlin asked from across the room. "You can't just—"

"Watch me," Amanda answered as she pushed the needle into Jennifer's vein and slowly injected the antisera.

"Wait. Don't you have to give it to her in her belly?" Quirk asked.

"No, but I do have to go slow. I can't risk an allergic reaction."

Quirk glanced over his shoulder, giving the other woman quite the glare. The woman just shrugged.

Amanda finished pushing the antisera. "Now, we are just going to have to wait and see."

* * *

Ronnie stepped between the two men. "See? Logical and reasonable behavior by the doctor. Let's take notes."

She really did not want to end up getting shot by some upstart agent of the CIA, HHS, DHS, or whatever branch of government he worked for. Zach moved to the side, keeping his gun aimed. He really wasn't exactly helping to defuse the tension in the room.

"Devlin," the doctor pleaded, "this is Special Agent Hunt and…"

"The Robin Hood hacker," Ronnie finished for Amanda.

The man's eyes flickered from Zach, to her, and then back again. "You are both wanted fugitives, then."

"Only because my ex-partner jumped over to the dark side," Zach growled.

"Yeah," Ronnie added. "He's still a little bitter about that, so Devlin, why don't you lower your weapon, so we can discuss how we are going to manufacture and distribute the cure to the weaponized Black Death."

Devlin scoffed, which seemed odd, given the fact that the guy was outnumbered three to one. Well, Quirk was a little preoccupied, so more like two to one. If only she had her magnetic disc.

"I don't know what world you and your *boyfriend* live in..." Ronnie knew that Devlin meant that as insult, but she kind of liked the ring to it. "But I'm not going to drop anything until I have proof."

"Her pulse is getting stronger," Amanda said from the sick woman's bedside. "The serum is stabilizing her."

"I said *proof*," Devlin emphasized, tightening his finger around the trigger. Then he swatted his neck. "What the—?" he said, and then listed sideways.

Ronnie turned to find Quirk holding a tiny blow dart.

* * *

"Ugh," Quirk sighed as Zach took the gun from Devlin and helped him to a chair. *Heteros.*"

"I'd totally forgotten about the micro-dart tube," Ronnie admitted.

"Yep," Quirk beamed. "Small enough to fit in your pocket, yet powerful enough to knock out an elephant, or a *douche*, whichever comes first."

The Fentanyl and Valium combination seemed to do the trick as Devlin swayed.

"She's opening her eyes," Amanda said.

Slipping the patent-pending blow dart into his pocket, Quirk sat next to Jennifer. Her eyelids were beyond puffy, and *forget* about dark circles. There were dark lakes under her eyes. But she was alive, proving that the Hidden Hand could get something right. The antidote.

"Slacker," he teased Jennifer. The tiniest grin answered him. "What, cat got your tongue? Or, you know, submandibular lymph nodes?"

"No," Amanda said next to him. "Don't you know?"

"Know what?" Quirk asked as Jennifer tried to bring her hand up.

"Jennifer's mute."

Quirk shook his head. "Um, darling, I have never seen a woman talk more."

"Text more," Amanda corrected. "If she has to communicate, she normally signs."

Weak, Jennifer brought her hand up and made a series of figures.

"What did she say?" Quirk asked.

Amanda chuckled. "Jennifer said, 'Leave it to the assistants to save the day.'"

"Um, yeah, duh," Quirk answered.

Okay, there was tangible proof the world would be right again.

* * *

Zach tucked Devlin's gun into the back of his belt. Even loopy, Zach didn't trust the guy. Turning, he found Ronnie watching Quirk, Jennifer, and Amanda. Tears glistened in her eyes.

"It's really working?" he asked.

Looking like she was trying to shrug off the moisture in her eyes, Ronnie nodded. "We should have enough to get as many of the scientists as possible healed to start wide-spread production."

"*You* did it, Ronnie," Zach took her hand. "You saved the world."

She swung her head to the side, kicking at the floor. "I think I preferred it when my contributions were anonymous."

"Really?" Zach questioned, pulling her closer. "You liked it better when we were just two voices on the line?"

"Okay, maybe *that* is an upside," she grinned that grin he had always imagined when they were on the phone. Now to see it? To experience it? Yes, all of the hell of the past few days became completely and utterly worth it.

He wrapped his arms around the lower part of her back. Zach searched her face looking for signs of whether Ronnie was ready. How long had they both waited for this moment? They had both risked everything for it. Zach leaned in, but she put a hand on his chest.

"I know," he said. "Not the right time."

* * *

"Oh, no," Ronnie said, grabbing his shirt, bringing them only inches apart. "I think it's the perfect time."

She closed her eyes as their lips met. Searing heat burned, warming her body through and through. Zach's kiss some-how managed to be gentle, and yet commanded her to give herself to him. And she did. Like no other man, Ronnie gave him every ounce of her love packed into this one kiss.

It was the most perfect moment in her life, until...

CAROLYN MCCRAY

She felt a cold, hard, metal handcuff snap onto her wrist.
Zach backed a step. "I am so sorry."

It truly looked like he meant it. Just like she did.

"No, I'm the one who is sorry," Ronnie said as she pulled out a little black box from her pocket and aimed it at the man she loved more than life itself.

The fibrillator did its job only too effectively. Zach dropped the other cuff and clutched his chest.

"Okay, that's our cue to leave," Quirk announced, rushing to her side and urging her to the door. "Exit stage left."

How could she leave Zach as he fell to the floor, twitching and gasping for air?

"Amanda, would you mind terribly defibrillating him for us?" Quirk requested. "It would be spectacular." Quirk was no longer content to just urge her to the door. He shoved her through it and into the hallway.

Ronnie balked, though. Could she go through with this?

Quirk jangled the metal bracelet on her arm. "You see this? This was Zach doing what he does best. What *he* thought was best. Now we've got to do *our* thing."

How come their thing was running—always running away?

"This is who we are," Quirk reminded her.

Ronnie heard the whine of the defibrillator paddles and then the loud *zap* of the discharge. Then the paddles whined again. What if they didn't work? What if she killed Zach?

"Don't be afraid to go to three hundred on that thing," Quirk yelled over his shoulder to Amanda as he pushed Ronnie down the hall. The paddles zapped again. "Move it!"

With a sad realization, Ronnie knew that Quirk was right. What was done was done. They were international fugitives. If they were caught, there would be no escape.

She had just saved the world; now it was time to save herself.

With a silent prayer to the angels who had been watching over them, Ronnie hauled ass for the exit.

EPILOGUE

Zach rubbed his sternum. His heart still hurt. Whether it was from the fibrillation or watching Ronnie run away, he wasn't sure.

He looked back at his desk—something else he was going to have to say good-bye to. It was weird to think that he'd been halfway around the world and back, hunting down the Hidden Hand's leadership, only to return to El Paso.

However, he wasn't staying for long. Just enough time to get his house packed up and then head to Quantico. Sure, they had scooped up some of the Hidden Hand's lieutenants in the field, but the real brains and financial backing of the cult? They were still at large. As it turned out, Lino had been nothing more than a page of sorts, running errands for the Hidden Hand. Until they tracked down the true power brokers, another bioweapon attack loomed on the horizon.

And no one was better suited to finding the bastards than Zach. He funneled every ounce of frustration into making the Hidden Hand pay for his loss.

Jamming the last of his personal belongings into a satchel, Zach took a look around the room. Too few desks were filled. Too many were left empty. Besides Ronnie, Zach had lost so many fellow agents. Either from Lino's savage attack or the plague, most of the men he worked with were lost forever.

Perhaps it was best that he was moving on. Way too many memories were here. Like Grant and his stupid smirk. That was one bastard he was not going to miss.

He headed to the exit when Danner came out of his office. "Hunt, can I have a word?"

Zach sighed as he followed Danner. He'd hoped to get out of there without any awkward good-byes. Zach had let the upper brass take care of his transfer. Nothing personal against Danner. It was just that the last time he saw his supervisor, he was holding a gun to his head.

Fortunately, Danner didn't ask Zach to sit down, nor did he seat himself. "On the behalf of all the men who survived that night, I just wanted to thank you."

"No worries," Zach answered, pointing his feet to the door. Most of what happened after that night was classified. Extremely classified.

"And..." Danner's lips pursed, and then relaxed. "I am sorry that I didn't trust you more."

Zach chuckled. "No, sir. You had every right to doubt me. I was carrying on an off-the-books relationship with a known felon."

"Still," his supervisor said, far more reflective than Zach had ever seen him, "I wish it could have turned out better for you."

Cheeks burning, Zach shook his head, the ache in his chest throbbing. "Nope. I pretty much got exactly what I *should* have expected."

"Well, then," Danner said awkwardly, "I guess I just wanted to say that you will be missed."

His supervisor put his hand out. Before Zach could take it, Warp burst into the office. "Sorry to interrupt, but are we taking our own cars or driving with the vans?"

"The moving company is taking care of everything, Warp." Zach replied. "We are flying to Virginia later tonight."

"Oh!" the techie said hitting his forehead. "Should have read the entire memo. Okay, we'll go pack our motherboards."

As they watched the techie's lanky frame rush from view, Danner chuckled. "Him or should I say, 'them'? Probably not gonna miss them."

Zach understood why. Warp had one of the most grating personalities in the world. However, Zach knew what they were up against in the Hidden Hand. He witnessed firsthand the extremely complex electronic security they employed. If he couldn't have Ronnie—and it still felt like a kick in the gut to admit that he couldn't have her—he was going to need the second best in the world, and unfortunately that came in a package bundled full of neuroses named Warp.

"I should get going," Zach said as he made his way to the door.

"Take care," Danner replied with a curt wave.

Taking care was about the last thing on Zach's mind as he got into the rental car. His own car was probably stripped down to the chassis somewhere in Mexico. So strange how something like that didn't bug him at all anymore. What a shift in priorities.

He gunned the engine and pulled out into a nearly deserted street. People were still leery about going outside and resuming their normal lives. A normal life? Zach seriously doubted any of them would get back to "normal" any time soon.

It took half the time to get to his house than it used to, and sure enough, the movers were already at work. Zach gave a nod as he made his way into the house. He really should be paying attention to what they were packing and what they weren't, but he was way too amped to care.

"This came for you," one of the men said, handing him a package marked with the seal of the FBI. The box originated from Quantico.

Zach ripped open the package to find a new tablet. They had been promising him one. He pressed the "On" button to find all of his files from the last two weeks already preloaded. Great. He could go down into the basement, get in one last workout before they flew back east, and get caught up on his reading.

Trying not to care that this might be the last time he went down those stairs, Zach made his way to the basement. The crew had pretty much packed up everything but the stationary bike. That was okay. That was all he wanted, anyway.

Zach propped the tablet up between the handlebars and started cycling. Maybe he could load his music from the cloud. Sure enough, it only took a few touches to the screen. He popped in his earbuds as Ratt began to play.

"Hey, sexy," a very familiar voice purred.

"Hey there, yourself," he answered with a broad smile.

* * *

Ronnie soaked in Zach's every feature. It had possibly been the longest two weeks of her life. She watched as his head bobbed from side to side as he cycled hard. But what in the hell did you say to the guy you *fibrillated*?

"You are certainly looking better than the last time I saw you."

On-screen, Zach's strong hand came up to his breast-bone. "Yeah, you could have warned me exactly how badly that was going to hurt."

"Or what?" Ronnie said starting off playful but getting doubtful toward the end. "You wouldn't have done it?"

He stopped cycling and stared straight into the camera. "I would do it again *right now* if I had to."

It was her heart's turn to flutter. Ronnie's cheeks blushed as she felt his stare. Even though he was half a world away, she could still remember the heat of his embrace. Damn the stupid United States Government! How long would it have taken them to figure out that Ronnie was on their side—well at least regarding the Hidden Hand?

They didn't have time to have Ronnie arrested or Zach investigated and up on charges. They needed to be chasing down the Hidden Hand—ASAP. So convincing the CIA, FBI, and probably NATO that Zach *was* going to arrest her was the only way that they could make sure he was in the position to head up the Hidden Hand task force.

And she, of course, had to play the part of the selfish hacker, only out for herself.

"So, what have you been up to?" Zach asked, getting serious about his cycling again.

"Oh, you know," Ronnie said, leaning back in her chair. "Running around the world, tracking down clues that you leave us in dead drops. Developing a truly untraceable point-to-point communication device capable of video conferencing."

Someone cleared his throat behind her. She turned to find Quirk's hand on his hip while the other hand held a paint can. "*You* developed an untraceable what?"

"Fine. *We* developed—" Quirk's glare made her correct herself again. "*Quirk* developed, with very minimal help from me, your tablet."

Her assistant was apparently satisfied that credit had been given where credit was due, and returned to painting the walls pure white. And somehow he had talked the pilot into helping. Ronnie left the two men in overalls to their task.

When she turned back to the screen, Zach was watching her intently. "Are you sure you didn't leave something out?"

Ronnie frowned. Did he know about the pesticide consortium she was going to hit next week?

"Nothing about a stash of plague vaccines finding their way to the front door of the World Health Organization?" Zach coaxed. "And a check for nearly three *billion* dollars to fund vaccinating underdeveloped countries? The Francois Foundation? Sound familiar?"

"Oh, yeah," Ronnie said biting her lip. "That."

"What happened to your island, Miss-I-Hate-People?"

It turned out that wanting to be left alone was only fun if it was your idea, not because the rest of the population had been wiped out.

"So I went on a little shopping spree for pharmaceuti-cals?" Ronnie joked. "A girl's gotta be true to herself."

But Zach didn't seem like he was buying her flippant attitude. He knew her that well. "Francois would be proud, Ronnie. I can't think of a better way to honor him."

Tears sprang to her eyes. This was not how this was supposed to go. And not just because it reminded her that she had spent nearly every last penny creating the fund. It reminded her of why she needed to forgo her island paradise.

Luckily, the music, if you could call it that, gave her a reason to change the subject. "Tell me that isn't Ratt playing?"

"What? What's wrong with 'Round and Round?' "

"Um, just about *everything*."

As Zach tried to defend his dubious musical taste, Ronnie moved the window of the streaming video to reveal her desk-top. The golden symbol from the Hidden Hand's castle glis-tened. She still had no idea what it meant. Which was why she put the gilded script where she could stare at it every day.

Alongside the screen, an IM box scrolled. No matter what she and Quirk tried, the script couldn't be stopped. They had changed monitors, video cards, and cabling, but each time they rebooted her computer, the symbols scrolled down the edge.

Whether Ronnie liked it or not, the angels were still talk-ing to her.

AFTERWORD

Thank you so much for reading *Encrypted*! I hope you loved reading it as much as I loved writing it.

If you enjoyed *Encrypted*, I would love to ask you a little favor. Please goo back to wherever you purchased this book (Amazon.com, etc.), and please leave an honest review.

Authors live and die by their reviews. The few extra seconds it takes you really helps us authors out!

Want more rollicking techno-thriller action? Check out the next section for other McCray thrillers!

OTHER WORKS BY CAROLYN MCCRAY

The Robin Hood Hacker Series – Carolyn's action packed techno-thriller series

Praise for the Robin Hook Hacker Series...

"The characters really jump off the screen, McCray makes them come alive with her crisp prose and clean development. Made me want to read the whole series and get to know these characters better. Recommended!"

Joe H. Dial

Amazon Reviewer

Having read Encrypted, couldn't resist the prequel. Answers a lot of questions about character relationships. Also, where did they get all those neat "gadgets?" Fast-paced, lots of action. Looking forward to more in this series. McCray at her best! The Book Goddess

Old Bartender

Amazon Reviewer

The prequel hooked me. Marvelous action, compelling characters, fun story. The novel itself did not live up to the short story.

Amazon Reviewer

David Bergsland

To purchase the Robin Hood Hacker Series on Amazon, click on the links below...

Hacked | *Encrypted* | *Binary* | *Cipher* (Preorder) | *Zeroes*(Available only in the *Robin Hood Hacker Collection)*

* * *

The Betrayed Series – Carolyn's controversial historical thriller series

Have you read the entire Betrayed series? From the prequel short story *Ambush* to *Mayhem*, the post-*Shiva* short story available exclusively in *The Omnibus Collection.*

Want them all in one place? Check out *The Omnibus Collection* - it is a $19.00 value for just $9.99!!!

Praise for the Betrayed series...

"Carolyn McCray's 30 PIECES OF SILVER proves that Dan Brown's crown is up for grabs. Part minefield and all roller-coaster ride, here is a story as controversial as it is thrilling. Hunker down for a long night, because once you start reading this book, you won't be putting it down."

NYT Top Ten Best Seller

James Rollins

Devil Colony

"With twists and turns galore the pace of Havoc never slows down, you are propelled along like an avalanche. Havoc is an accomplished thriller. I sort of hate to use the word "interesting" which sounds like a book report, but this novel IS interesting as well as being a great read."

P.B.Sharp

Amazon Reviewer

I am hooked on this series ...a great mix of religious history, action, and old fashion love. I know there is a sequel. I can nearly wait.

Niecy733

Amazon Reviewer

To purchase the Betrayed Series on Amazon, click on the links below...

The Omnibus Collection | *Ambush* | *Thirty Pieces of Silver* | *Targeted* | *Havoc* | *Covert* | *Shiva* | *Mayhem(Available exclusively in the Betrayed collection)*

* * *

MoonRush – Carolyn's pulse-pounding space thriller

It's 2049 and it's not gold the prospectors are looking for, it's "Star Diamonds." And these precious gems aren't in California but up on the moon!

Join Jarod and his team of treasure hunters, Rogues Incorporated, as they dodge a nefarious competitor, crazed moon-panning prospectors, and even their own government for the ultimate "motherlode."

Praise for _MoonRush_...

"Reading this book after taking finals at school was like taking a much needed vacation...to Outer Space! All the characters are so developed and unique and the plot twists and turns make this book rank so high on my list that I'm writing a review about it. Something that I don't normally do. So buy this book and get ready for some quality entertainment from some witty innovative writers! "

Lisa Thurman

Amazon Reviewer

"This was a fast-paced adventure with entertaining characters and an engrossing plot. Reading Moonrush was like watching a great blockbuster summer movie except that I could enjoy it while on the beach. Won't disappoint."

BookLover1960

Amazon Reviewer

"This book played out like an action packed adventure movie in my head. You know, an action packed adventure movie with a plot, and characters that you can really relate to, and care about. It's filled with everything from science fiction to teenage angst, and nerd humor. All of the elements of a great story are there, and that's what makes it so much fun."

DudeMcMan

Amazon Reviewer

To purchase _Moonrush_ on Amazon, click here.

* * *

Fated – #1 Historical Romance set in ancient Rome

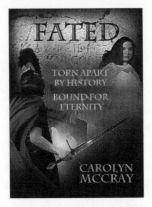

Torn Apart by History
Bound for Eternity

If you enjoyed the historical aspects of <u>30 Pieces of Silver</u>, I might suggest you try my latest historical paranormal romance, <u>Fated</u>. And yes, I know I just said historical paranormal romance and most of the guys out there cringed and went to scroll past. However, just like <u>30 Pieces of Silver</u>, <u>Fated</u> defies classification and has equally glowing reviews from men and women alike.

Set in ancient Rome, <u>Fated</u> is told from the perspective of Brutus in the months leading up to Caesar's assassination. <u>Fated</u> has the feel HBO's Rome—only with a unique McCray twist.

But don't believe me. Here are just a few of the early reviews for <u>Fated</u>...

"From Carolyn McCray comes a historical romance that will leave you hoping that for once, fate will be kind. You will be gripped from the first page to the last, caught in a love that spans eons and an ancient political intrigue whose consequence still reverberates

today. This is truly a masterpiece that stays with you long after you've turned the last page."

Emma Gilbertson
Reviewer
The Writer Bites Back

"I was enthralled by this book—enthralled by the time period, the romance, the characters, and the historical events unfolding... Kudos, Ms. McCray!"

Tessa Blue
@TessaBlue
Author of Children of the Lost Moon

"Fated is full of suspense. It does not let go... As usual, Ms. McCray's style and writing are brilliant."

M. Koleva

To purchase or sample *Fated* on Amazon, simply click <u>here</u>.

ABOUT THE AUTHOR

 I started out like most authors. I had a story in my head that would not shut up! LOL!

And since I love sitting around thinking up ways for my characters to have amazing adventures, the story for *Encrypted* bubbled to the surface. And if you know me at all, you know my love of all things tech. Add in my desire to blow things up (on paper, of course), and voilà! You have *Encrypted*.

If you would like to connect with me, check out my Contact Information section.

Made in the USA
Lexington, KY
29 December 2013